KILL THEM ALL

DJ SMITH

ISBN: 9781799002475

I am justly killed with mine own treachery.

CHAPTER

1

The last thing Melody Fox remembered was the song. Not the screams. Not the pleadings. Not the whimpers. Not the dead silence. Not the roaring inferno. Her mind had blocked out those sounds of hell.

The same damn tune had been playing over and over in her daughter's bedroom. It was Charity's current Emo favourite. Like all teens, Charity Fox swayed between nonchalance and passion. Melody liked Lana Del Rey and her *Video Games*. But she feigned indifference rather than spoil her daughter's enjoyment with the shock they shared something in common.

Totally uncool, mum was Charity's default attitude. Every parent goes through the same journey from hero to zero before they return on the other side. But her daughter would never return. She would never become the grown woman Melody would cherish with all her heart.

That was almost four years ago. The day Melody Fox's life also ended.

They came at night. Bad men eager to do bad things. A home invasion gone horribly wrong. That was the meme from outraged tabloids as they described the crime in every gory, bloody detail; from the gang they named the *Limehouse Monsters.*

Melody was working on her laptop in their home office. Her partner Paul was in the kitchen preparing a late supper. Charity was being dramatic in her bedroom; destroyed because her fascist mum had refused point blank to allow her thirteen-year-old to get a butterfly tattoo.

Their Limehouse riverside domain had been touted as one of the most secure homes in London. Ram proof gates. Security camera monitoring. On-site security. Unbeatable alarm system. Yet the men had breached their fortress.

The police told Melody that they apprehended the three villains within a mile of the crime. Given the traumatic memory loss, she had to be told almost everything that had happened to her. Back then, Melody was inclined to believe what she was told. She was a different person today.

Melody mistook the first yell for television noise. She was doing her job of developing psy-ops assignments for the Joint Threat Research Intelligence Group (JTRIG) based out of GCHQ. The disturbance startled her.

But the TV shouldn't be on.

Before her brain could process that thought, the second scream hit home. No mistake. That was her daughter. Without thinking, Melody was off the chair and out of the room. The scene unfolding was one of the few vivid horrors Melody could fully recall of that night. No matter how hard she tried to forget.

God, no.

Her exquisite daughter, her love, her life, Charity was

being dragged by her long hair across the living room floor. The brute was over six feet, and balaclava masked. To her left was Paul on his knees in the middle of the room; another brute pressing the barrel of a gun hard into the back of his head.

'Don't hurt my daughter. Don't hurt my daughter. God, don't hurt my daughter. Tell me what you want, please. Just tell—'

The man pulled his gun-hand back to lash Paul across the face with the barrel.

As Melody went to scream, she glimpsed the blur of a gloved fist steaming in from her side.

The brass knuckleduster smashed wickedly into her left cheek. The force sent her spinning down to the Italian mahogany flooring. There was no adrenalin rush to help. No movie heroics. And all the time that damned song was playing over and over.

She tried to rise from the savage blow that had already fractured her cheek bones. A steel-toed boot drove into her side. The kick broke three ribs and sent Melody skidding across the floor. Her skull slamming into the leg of the solid table.

Amanda Soresh – the head of neurosurgery who saved her life – assured Melody that this fracture alone could have killed her. She was lucky all it did was put her into a coma for seventeen months.

Lucky. Yeah, sure. Why not. Apart from the whole being attacked in your own home. Family murdered. What could be luckier than seventeen months in a coma?

Laying in a beaten heap on the floor, Melody tried to speak, shout, scream, but her mouth refused to move. Her body was already shutting down from the shock. More than anything, this would shame her forever. The bitter realization that she was incapable of protecting her family.

The most primal urge we have as a parent, and she failed that test. More than most, given her job, she knew that thought was supremely irrational.

There was nothing she could have done. But that knowledge didn't stop the never-ending guilt burning into her like acid on flesh.

Blood was seeping into her eyes as she lay where the kick landed her. She forced herself to open her eyelids. Swimming in and out of focus, she dimly saw Charity, about five feet away, on the other side of the coffee table. It would be the last time she ever saw her daughter's flawlessly beautiful face, in life or death. All that remained were digital images, random memories, and heartbreaking dreams of the woman-child. A lost girl preserved forever as a rebellious teen.

'Mummy.' As Charity dimly choked out the word, blood from her mouth dripped onto the floor.

'Shut it, cunt.' The monster who had dragged Charity to that spot, kicked her daughter in the belly.

Melody felt a giant sob well up. But there was no way out. It remained trapped inside; as they all were trapped in their luxury killing room.

The ghoul dressed in human skin. The beast who should be put down like a rabid dog. The inhuman grabbed Charity by the hair, yanking her up.

'On yer feet, bitch.'

'Mummy – mummy – No. No. No. Argghh. Argghh. You're hurting—'

Charity's raspy words were barely audible.

Melody tried to raise a hand. 'Don't. Please.'

Then her daughter was gone.

She was vaguely aware of drifting in and out of consciousness. How long that lasted she had no idea. She didn't hear the gunshot which killed Paul.

All the time, the song looped on and on. The song she hated as much as she loved.

It was her last memory about anything, until the very bright light shone painfully into her eyes.

'Hello, Melody. I'm Miss Soresh. I'm your doctor. Neurosurgeon, actually. Here, at St. Michael's hospital. If you can hear me, blink your left eye three times. I know, I know, it's confusing. Be brave once more, okay. You're safe.'

Melody took a second or two to think about those words. Why couldn't she speak out loud? She tried.

Her brain formed the words *I hear you. I'm not deaf.* But nothing came out.

Then she realized why this simple task was impossible – the tube down her throat.

Melody blinked. One. Two. Three.

'That's super, Melody. Well done. Well done indeed. Finally we meet. It's great to have you back.'

CHAPTER

2

Melody stepped out of the air-conditioned black cab into the dripping air of south-east London. The morning rain had given way to a sticky spring afternoon. As the taxi drove away, she fought the urge to yell after him. To scream for him to come back and take her home. But Melody no longer had a *home* – only shadowlands where she existed as a mere cipher of her former self.

Across the wide road, the imposing complex loomed up. The sign on the massive wall confirmed that she was in the right place—

Her Majesty's Prison RINGLAND, (Category A),
Eastern Way, Thamesside, London SE30 6LB.

Thirty yards away were the country's most dangerous men. Category A-holes: murderers, serial killers, terrorists, child abusers, rapists. Psychopaths and sociopaths to a man. The same *evil* Melody had the misfortune to meet four years ago. It was her second visit.

Melody closed her eyes for a second. She took a deep breath, cleared her mind, and crossed the road.

The instructions to book a visit and enter Britain's most secure jail were handily posted online. To get this far, Melody had been security-cleared in advance with her birth certificate, driving licence and passport. It would have been easier to meet the Queen.

After her personal possessions were stowed away, in an allocated visitors' locker, came the multiple searches. The female guard didn't merely pat her down, but rubbed her down. A metal detector wand was swept over her body. Melody was glad she wore jeans, even as they clung to her in the humidity. Another guard entered with a black Labrador. He was a friendly drug search dog who proceeded to sniff all around his new human chum.

Forty-five minutes after walking through the main gate, Melody was escorted by another guard down a harshly lit corridor. She had googled the prison layout; it was a variation on the classic design of a central hub with radiating spokes. Each *spoke* was another hub, with its own shorter spokes. The concept was designed to balkanize the large prison; reducing prisoner interactions, and preventing dangerous alliances forming.

She was escorted into the visitor area. It was surprisingly cheerful with high skylights offering plenty of natural light. There were thirty tables, half of which seated one man dressed in a dark blue boilersuit. Each prisoner had at least one visitor chatting animatedly. Except for the man in the corner.

He sat alone, ramrod straight, reading a book. Short cropped salt and pepper hair. A man of some consequence in Ringland. That much was obvious.

The guard tapped Melody's shoulder. 'Remember, Ms

Fox, the room is constantly monitored by cameras. You are free to interact with your subject. You will be reminded over the speaker when there are five minutes remaining. Off you go then. Don't keep Mr Fuchs waiting.'

He indicated in the direction of the man in the corner. Off she went. Mr Fuchs wasn't really reading the book. He had been slyly eyeing Melody – prison style – at all times. He rose from his seat as she approached.

'Alright, girl. Back again.'

His voice was low, throaty, abrasive. A lifetime of smoking no doubt contributing to the menacing growl underpinning his cockney accent. Melody held his gaze, determined not to show the slightest emotion. Not the slightest weakness. Stoic.

'Perceptive.'

'So – you in or you out? What the fuck's it gonna be then, girl?'

CHAPTER 3

The fire had been set as the men exited the Limehouse property. It had been a lucrative job. They had collected everything they came for, plus some added fun bonuses. They hurried to the transit van, parked at a meter on Narrow Street; anxious to be far, far away from the scene of their heinous villainy.

They were a tight crew who had rolled together since ganging up on their first incarcerations as teens. They found power and control was easier to exercise as a triumvirate of likeminded individuals. It didn't take them long to go from minor league bullying to running the institution; picking off the gazelles, employing the dimmer, and dominating the stronger.

Back in the world, it made sense to continue ganging together. The triumvirate had a feral loyalty making them far greater than the sum of their parts. They began with petty street muggings. It didn't take long to graduate to serious stuff. Not the drug trade though. That product line had a built-in routine which the cops would always suss. And they didn't want to tangle with serious criminal players, such as the Yardies.

They decided to specialize in one-off random jobs offering big pay-outs in cash and easily disposed of luxury items. High end jewellery, cars, and watches were particular favourites.

Tonight was definitely a step up. A real *take what you want* thrill ride. In the back of the van, two changed from their work overalls as Billy (the driver) cut right into Butch Row. Another right and they were soon heading east along the East India Dock Road. The plan was to take the M11 as far as the M25, then swing back home down to North London via Barnet.

Zipping through South Bromley, Billy could have easily slowed down and stopped like the good citizen he wasn't. He clocked the lights turn red two seconds prior, but Billy was on a thrill high.

Ah, fuck it.

He floored it. Even pulling away in first gear, the kinetic energy generated by a forty-eight tonne Tesco delivery truck is huge. Especially if it smashes straight into the side of your van.

The van's forward momentum was transferred instantly sideways. Spinning around twice, it double flipped on to its roof before skidding to a stop by slamming into a boarded-up Chinese restaurant: the *Golden Palace.*

The trio bounced violently and painfully around like a farmhouse in a Kansas tornado. If that wasn't bad enough, the police car following behind the truck sealed it.

Melody had been expected to die. But she was limpet-like in clinging on. The drama of the crime that destroyed her family played out while she lay unconcerned in the neurology ward of St. Michael's hospital. Oblivious as she was fed by a tube, and turned regularly.

The trial was a formality. All the evidence was in the crashed van with the perpetrators. Detective Superintendent Bill Hickman, from the Met's Homicide and Serious Crime Command, had done a stellar job in assembling the case and establishing the forensic trail that led back from Bromley to Limehouse.

It did not matter that the only eyewitness could not be called. The jury took two hours to find the three men guilty as charged. Judge Julian Young blathered for over an hour while letting the monsters smirk and mug to the gallery. Three women in the gallery screamed when he finally sent them down to serve a mandatory life sentence with a thirty-five year minimum tariff.

When Melody resurfaced, the medical staff had been deliberately vague about *events*. It had fallen on Ruth – Melody's sister – to go through the tear-choked agony of confirming that Charity and Paul were gone.

Detective Superintendent Hickman came to the hospital a week later. He had taken it upon himself to lead Dr Melody Fox officially through the painful events that had destroyed her life. He wanted to fudge over the exact details, to spare the poor woman. But she was relentless in demanding every last gruesome fact. He could hardly bear to say the words out loud of what wickedness had befallen her beautiful daughter.

Melody's voice was raspy and barely audible. During the three hours he'd been with her, she sipped regularly via the straw in the bottle of ice cold water.

'Appeals. What about appeals?'

'That's a reality. Par for the course, I'm afraid. I won't deny that. It could go all the way to Europe. But I, we – we have high, high confidence the convictions will hold.'

'Oh.'

'The, uh, physical evi – the forensics, are amongst the strongest I've gathered. All our skills were directed at bringing justice to these bastards.'

Her voice was straining badly as she struggled to pour out her pain. 'Thirty-five years? Bringing justice? Ah, right. But they're still alive. Still in their twenties. Out before they're sixty. What's it like in prison for monsters like them? Cushy I bet. They need to die. Don't you think? They deserve to die. Somebody should kill them. Kill them all. I'd pay.'

He let that slide. No doubt he would have thought the same in the same situation. He had a daughter for God's sake. He struggled for justification. 'Look, Melody, I know, I know, easy for me to pontificate, but please don't torture yourself any more than you already have. We have to believe in the system, because that's all we have. The rest is jungle.'

'Sure. Where are they?'

Thinking back, reflecting when it was all over, Melody realized that this was the precise moment where her actions were irrevocably set. Hickman had tried to steer her away from that reality, but she would easily find out.

'They're in Ringland prison. All of them.'

CHAPTER 4

'So – you in or you out? What the fuck's it gonna be then, girl?'

This was it. Ringland prison. Not quite the point of no return as that would come later. But it was *it*, nonetheless.

Melody stared at Aaron Fuchs, her recently discovered distant relative. Sixth cousins thrice removed, or something. That made him family, of sorts.

She glanced up at the cameras, paranoid that an operator was watching her right now. Zooming in on her alone, because this god-like watcher could sense she was thinking about bad things. About doing bad things.

'Yeah, don't you worry about them. No sound. Put yer hand over yer mouth, like this, case you was worried about lip-reading.'

Aaron scratched his nose with his index finger, then held the hand in place so his palm masked his lips.

Melody hadn't been worried until then. She complied and mirrored Aaron.

'Yes.'

'Sorry, girl. Didn't hear ya.'

Melody cleared her throat down to a whisper. 'Yes. I'll do it. I'm in, so to speak.'

'So to fucken speak? This ain't no fucken Home Counties game, girl. Kevin told me you was strong. That sounds fucken weak to me. Can't be doing wiv weak.'

Six weeks after Melody surfaced from her dreamless sleep, Miss Soresh allowed her to leave St. Michael's. One proviso: well, there were a few, but this was the biggie. Melody had to recuperate where she could cared for the foreseeable future. Her younger sister Ruth would not take *no* for an answer.

She had a large house in Totteridge, massive really. The immaculate garden was serene, and quiet, and perfect for Melody to recuperate. After nearly two years lying immobile in a hospital bed, muscles wither and shrink, while endurance collapses.

Ruth and Gerald's baby girl was on her way in few months to join little Freddy. And while Ruth understood this was going to be a painful reminder of her big sister's loss, nothing could be done about that.

The house was not far from Golders Green Jewish cemetery, where Ruth had the body of her niece interred in the Jewish tradition.

Paul McRae was Melody's fiancée and Charity's stepdad. His Catholic parents took Paul back to their home town in Northern Ireland.

The Fox girls' parents had been secularly and culturally Jewish. Not that religiously inclined, except for the traditional days. Melody had followed that path, but Ruth had rediscovered her faith in her late teens and was fully observant.

As her sister lay close to death in St. Michael's hospital, her niece lay in cold storage, seven floors below in Scotland Yard's post mortem complex. Gerald moved heaven and earth to enable the family to bury his niece as quickly as the police formalities allowed.

May her memory be a blessing.

Melody kept telling herself that every time she visited her lost girl. Daily for the first few weeks. But that couldn't go on forever. Nobody dared utter the words *moving on*, but her family were quietly concerned. Melody decided to cut down, visit Charity twice a week. She walked the two miles to the cemetery to build up her strength. It took a lot out of her, but she managed to reduce the walking time from two hours to an hour. She still had to get the bus back. Her next goal was to walk there and back again. Total Bilbo.

Melody had noticed the weird bloke a few times during the period of daily visits. He was standing in front of a headstone about thirty yards away from Charity. She caught him glancing her way more than once. Then she changed her visit pattern and he disappeared. Melody assumed their visits no longer coincided, and thought no more of him. Until—

Looking up from her daughter's headstone, the gangly stranger was striding towards her at pace.

'Bloody Nora. What's he want? Can't be doing with this.'

She contemplated turning tail and leaving, but that was ridiculous. It was a cemetery, not a bar. He waved. Too late now, he was at her side before she could move.

'Wotcha. Sorry love. Didn't mean to scare ya.'

'You didn't.'

'Okay then. Fantastico. Great. Kevin Fuchs. Eff. You. Sea. Haitch. Ess. Sounds like you know what, but pronounced Fooks. Kevin Fuchs, Esquire, of this parish, et cetera, et cetera, ad infinitum.'

Kevin stuck out his right hand. It was rough, grimy, calloused, like the hands she was used to shaking a lifetime ago in the military.

'Melody. Melody Fox. You know Fuchs is German for Fox, right?'

'Course I knows, darling. S'why I been keen to make your acquaintance.'

Melody sipped from the mug of strong black coffee as she carefully assessed Kevin Fuchs, Esquire, of this parish, et cetera, et cetera, ad infinitum. Her instant appraisal was Hitchhikers-esque: definitely oddball, mainly harmless.

They had walked steadily to *Nell's Kitchen*, a reimagined transport café on Golders Green High Street. Melody steeled herself for the usual *so sorry, terrible thing, what can I say, how are you coping* and all the other banalities well-meaning people said. But he didn't press beyond the initial platitudes.

As Melody sipped, Kevin munched into his free range bacon sandwich, slathered in organic tomato ketchup. Yes, that was its advertised name. She guessed Kevin – like herself – wasn't strictly kosher these days.

'Basically you don't know nothing about the black sheep side of the Fuchs family then? All the reprobates and ne'er-do-wells like meself.'

A memory (a fragment of Melody's past which had been stored deeply away) popped into her head.

'When I was a kid, about eight, we did this genealogy project at school. Dad digs out these huge photograph albums from a massive trunk, which I don't think he'd even looked at properly. Photos going back, what, must have been a hundred years. There was this one, very formal, severe – a couple and their six kids, two boys, four girls, from nineteen oh one I think—'

'Nineteen hundred and one. VR, Victoria Regina, like ER is Elizabeth Regina; and, God help us, Charles will be CR on the red post boxes, et cetera. Yeah, they was your great-great-grandparents David and Rebecca Fuchs. Mine too. David was a tailor, very good one by all accounts. Probably wearing one of his own suits in that photo. Anyways, they departs toots-de-sweets from some place called East Prussia, town called Königsberg. Very bad news for us Jews over there it was. Probably still is. Nasty fuckers, pardon my French.'

'I work – worked with the military. Feel free to fuck away till the cows come home.'

'Long story short, them two little boys you saw in the pic, Aaron and Isaac, well Isaac studies hard, becomes a doctor, real mensch, respectable like. David and Rebecca couldn't be happier. Your side of the family. Then there was the massive irrevocable split, like Moses parting the Red Sea.'

'Biblical.'

'Totally. Aaron, well see, he's just your natural born villain from the off in short pants. Brought shame on the family. Sociopath right? You's a head doctor, a shrink, clever like, you know this shit I bet.'

Melody smiled. She liked Kevin. 'Yes, I have the head doctor label to my name. Not really that sort of practicing psychiatrist. But yes, he could be classed as a sociopath.'

Kevin stuffed in another bite from his bacon sandwich. 'Knew it. By the mid-twenties, roaring twenties they called them, Aaron Fuchs, he's like this East End gang Kaiser. Thirty, forty guys on the payroll. Coppers on the take. Docks all covered. Goods in, good out, all gets sliced. Ins with the unions.'

'Sounds like a business.'

'Family business. Still is. Father to son to son. Like the bible says, Aaron begat Abraham who begat another Aaron, blah de begat de blah.'

'Where do you begat into this family tree, Kevin?'

'Very low hung fruit is me. That original Kaiser, Aaron who begat Abraham, Abe the Yid as he was not so affectionately known, after the second war, well, Abe also begat another nine others. One of them me granddad, Michael.'

'Good grief, how many Fuchs are there?'

'A lot love. A fuchs load. Ha-ha-ha. You should come meet.'

'Not such good company these days.'

'Don't have to be at Shabbat. My great-grandmother, let's see, she'll be like your great-aunt, Sharon. Great something anyway. Aged ninety-five. The Fuchs matriarch. Holds forth every Friday night.'

Kevin popped the final morsel into his mouth. As he chomped down, he caught Melody's knowing smile.

'If you ever do come, for crying out loud in your sleep, don't let me great-grandma know I ain't keeping kosher. Life won't be worth living even worse than now.'

CHAPTER

5

'So to fucken speak? Jesus. This ain't no fucken Home Counties game, girl. Kevin told me you was strong. That sounds fucken weak to me. Can't be doing wiv weak.'

Kevin had also told Melody many things in the two years since Charity's graveside introduction. The main one being: under no circumstances be indebted to Aaron Fuchs. Ever. He was not subtle on the subject.

'Bloke's family, right. But he's still a fucking psycho.'

Kevin could not begin to comprehend that this was the very attribute which made Aaron perfect. She hadn't *moved on*. She put on a moved on face to everyone. But she could never move on. Not while monsters in human form existed on this earth. When they were dead and buried, then maybe she could move on and rest. The key was Aaron.

'I'm not weak. Not any more. I was. I didn't know it. I bought *I am woman, I am strong*, type shit, as you do. You go, girl. But it was all a comfortable lie. I had no idea. Wasn't real. Till it was.'

'And you think this is? Real, like. Jesus girl, right corker aincha? Maybe this ain't for you after all. Maybe best you go back to your sad middle-class life as best ya can. What's left of it anyways.'

Primal anger blazed through Melody. Her right hand shot out and gripped Aaron's arm. Hard.

'Told you. I'm in. I'll hold up my end. You hold up yours. Three for three. That's the deal.'

Aaron perked up. 'We'll see. But I need to hear you say it, to me, out loud, right here right now. Don't need to be written in blood like, but I'm one a them word is my bond blokes. Very important to me. Only reason you're here. And for obvious reasons, this is the last time we meet. On the inside anyway. Too iffy that. For you too, by the by.'

Melody released his arm before swivelling around to make sure no one else was listening. Satisfied, she cupped both hands around her mouth to hide her lips and leaned across the table again.

'Okay. Have to admit, I was totally pissed off you wouldn't do as I asked. Assumed it would be a simple yes or no—'

Aaron leaned in, his lively grey-green eyes boring into her.

'And I was tempted. Yeah, why not. Girl's blood. Family. We Jews is big on family. All very old testamenty. Vengeance is mine sayeth the Lord. But do we listen to him? Do we fuck, ever since the fall and we went our own merry way. I'm up for that, right as rain, don't you worry. But then, I am a career criminal, as Judge McLean told me. Seven years into a twenty stretch. So couldn't help to start thinking, what's in it for me, specially as what I gotta do, ain't no fucken fruit cake walk. I mean, it's gonna be obvious to the powers what's occurring after two, maybe the first.'

'Okay, okay, now about that. I have conditions.'

'Be surprised if you don't.'

'Your three, they have to be – deserving. Not some petty gang vendetta.'

'If it were some *petty gang vendetta* as you put it, I wouldn't need you like, would I—'

'Kevin did mention you're still the bloke in charge on the outside as well.'

'Hang on, girl. When you's inside, ya hear shit all the time. What people do; what they've done; what they're in for; what they got away wiv. What they'll do on the outside. Why they're in isolation from other prisoners. Now I done shit. Bad shit, psycho shit even—'

'I have the internet.'

'But not against civilians. Right? See the diff? Think of me as the CEO of an international corporation, on extended leave like. I can't ask me employees to step outside their purview for some private concern of yours truly, no matter how pressing. All they wants is the moolah. The lifestyle. They ain't up for private retribution, even for me. Worse – they might get it into their noggins the old man's losing it. We don't need him or his irrelevant shit. Then you pops up, and I'm like what the fuck. This could work. So to answer your question, yeah, they all got it coming, and more.'

Aaron pulled out a small piece of paper from his prison overalls pocket. He pushed it halfway across the table, keeping it hidden under his hand.

'First off, you need to see this bloke. He'll fill you in on everything.'

Melody stiffened at the thought of a third party.

'Relax, doll. He's totally kosher. Trust me. As soon as the first, uh – assignment is delivered, I'll proceed to remove your problem. And so forth.'

Melody closed her eyes for a few seconds. She heard it again. The damn song. Over and over it played, bitter-sweet.

She placed her hand on top of Aaron's hand. Gently this time. This was it. She could still walk away. Nothing more to be said. He'd understand. They were blood, after all.

'Last condition. They suffer. Not quick, they have to suffer. And they have to know why they suffer. Beg for their lives. Beg for their mothers. But you show them no mercy. There is no mercy for these three. And you do it personally, not some hench-goon inside with you. Then you tell me about it after. In detail. Can you do that?'

Even though this was the sentiment Aaron was looking for, it still shocked him. He gently pulled his hand away.

'Agreed. Kill them all.'

Melody gripped the piece of paper tightly, before slipping it into her coat pocket. She took a couple of deep breaths, cupped both hands around her mouth again, and lowered her voice to the barest whisper.

'Kill them all.'

CHAPTER 6

Great-aunt Sharon hugged Melody like the return of the prodigal daughter.

'Welcome, Melody. Welcome to my home for this most wonderful Shabbat.'

'Thanks for inviting me, Mrs Fuchs.'

'Who is this old lady Mrs Fuchs you mention? Call me aunty.'

'Okay. Thanks. I will. Aunty.'

Sharon ran her bony, veined hands over Melody's face, like a blind person might do to *see.*

'You look exactly like my dear, dear sister Muriel, of blessed memory. Kevin, doesn't she look just like Muriel at the same age?'

'Never met Muriel. Remember, aunty? Died before I was even a twinkle. Nazis killed her. In the war? Doodlebug blew up her gaff in Limehouse.'

Melody could see the pain in her eyes, as they misted over for a second. Time had not diminished Sharon's sister.

Time would not diminish Melody's daughter, that she had vowed.

'Is this not the fate of the Jews for all time Melody? They chase us from country to country, and still they kill us in our own home.'

A silence descended as Sharon drifted off to distant tortured memories. Kevin smiled weakly before looking down at his shoes.

As quickly as she drifted, Sharon snapped back. 'Pah. Forgive an old lady her ramblings. Come, come, come to my table. It's almost time to bless the candles and celebrate the bounty of the creator.'

It was the sixth Shabbat since Kevin had semi-accosted her at Charity's graveside. He had been pestering her to attend ever since: Melody finally relented, making her way by bus from Totteridge to her great-aunt's semi-detached house in Edgware. She arrived a few minutes before sunset. The Jewish Sabbath beginning at sunset on the Friday and lasting until sunset Saturday. The men had already arrived back from the synagogue and assembled for the feast to follow.

Her sister Ruth also kept the traditional Shabbat and was always disappointed if her sister was missing. Melody hadn't mentioned the allegedly black sheep Fuchs half of the family. She wanted it for herself at the moment. A thing of her own, outside what had become her existence amongst her well-meaning family and friends. She told her sister that she was seeing Chloe and Ben Carrington.

The Carringtons were more than just friends, they were also business partners. Ben had been Paul's best mate since Cambridge University. Total opposites of course. Paul was all working-class Belfast and more cerebral than sporty. Ben was the posh son of privilege, real plummy Home Counties, following his dad into Eton, then Cambridge. Definitely more sporty than cerebral. Reserve for the rowing crew. Blues in rugger and boxing.

They had started their tech company *Peach* in dorms as a lark. Today it was valued at a billion pounds. Ruth knew the Carringtons were as devoted to Melody's recovery as her, thus understood completely.

Melody stood at the back of the dining room packed with about thirty adults and ten children. None of whom Melody knew existed seven weeks ago. Despite the wonderful spirit of her ninety-five-year old aunty, Melody was wishing she'd stayed home with the intimate ceremony of Ruth, Gerald and little Freddy.

As the woman of the house, Aunt Sharon set the huge table, which was ready to collapse under the weight of the food waiting for hungry mouths. Two candles, in their holders, stood proud amongst the delicacies. These represented the dual commandments to remember and observe the Shabbat. The two loaves of challah bread and glass of wine represented the manna from heaven provided for the Israelites in preparation for Shabbat in the desert.

Sharon reverently lit the candles. She then moved her hands above the burning wicks and the light, before covering her eyes with both hands, so as not to see the candles as she recited the blessings in Hebrew.

'Barukh atah Adonai, Eloheinu, melekh ha-olam. Asher kidishanu b'mitzvotav v'tzivanu. L'had'lik neir shel Shabbat. Amen.'

At the final Amen, Sharon opened her eyes to see burning blessed candles, thereby completing the ceremony.

The father of the house began the Shabbat meal. Sharon's husband was long since dead, so that task fell to her eldest son Daniel, a father of four. He poured wine into a glass from a large ceramic jug before reciting the blessing over it.

Challah bread is made from extra fine flour and eggs. Tasting sweeter than ordinary bread to symbolize that Shabbat is sweeter than any other day. Daniel recited another blessing over the challah before inviting everyone to share the first piece of bread, and start the meal.

Throughout the evening Kevin took it upon himself to introduce Melody to everyone. Most were aware of her troubles, but they were respectful in not delving further than heartfelt condolences as they broke bread and celebrated life with a newcomer, and each other.

Melody knew Kevin was *a bit of a rogue darlin'*. It was just about his pitch at *Nell's Kitchen* on that first day they met, along with all the other info on the history of the Fuchs. He had only recently returned from Spain (Basque country) where he had lived for twenty years. There he had cultivated a reputation for cultivating excellent marijuana in various illicit grow sites dotted around the nearby countryside.

He would start the plants from his own genetically modified seeds in hot-spaces secreted around his large rented farmhouse. Once transplanted outside, the bushes quickly grew to over eight feet tall; ripe for harvesting, then drying back at the farmhouse. Then selling.

'Problem was, darling, got too bleeding successful didn't I?'

'You can be *too* successful?'

'Like, yeah. Specially when you're basically in the drug biz. Where there's mucho moolah in the end there's mucho gangster. Turns out I got very green fingers. Both plants and pounds. I know, I know. Hard to believe innit. I was growing so much, got outta hand. Heavy hitters got to notice. And the fucking scousers. Always the fucking scousers. Pardonny me French. Had to leave everything behind: lock, stock and blunt. Bolted back. Staying over in

Crouch End so not too far from me Aunty Sharon's place. Looking after her. Sort of. Like I said, she is ninety-five.'

Kevin had mentioned the name Aaron Fuchs, but mainly in relation to the original East End gang Kaiser in the nineteen twenties. It was at this Sabbath that Melody took real notice of the name.

'Kevin, y'vicked boy. This is who?'

Melody turned to see a short, stocky man, staring at her with steel-trap eyes. He was quite unblinking, and unnerving.

'Crying out loud, Saul. Why you always sneaking up on people, scaring them half to life?'

'Alvays be avare who lurking behind, else—'

Saul ran the flat of his hand across his throat and grimaced dramatically.

'Yeah, okay I got it. I could be murdered at Shabbat. At Aunty Sharon's. By you. Melody Fox meet Uncle Saul. Saul Levin. Married my Aunt Gilda, my mum's sister.'

Saul clicked his heels together, bowed from the waist, took Melody's hand and lightly kissed it.

'Enchantez, mademoiselle.'

Melody smiled at the charm which had followed the unnerving stare in the blink of an eye.

'Enchantez yourself.'

'Gilda died. Israel. Two years ago.'

'Gosh, I'm so sorry.'

Saul shrugged. He was one of life's true stoics. 'Meh. Death visits all in the end. Be prepared to fight him like hell.'

Despite his cockney bluster, Arthur Daley act, and drug dealing bona fides, Melody had analysed Kevin as highly empathetic. The last thing he wanted was for Saul to start banging on and upsetting her.

'Okay, Saul, moving on. Hey, Melody. Never guess what

Saul does?'

'Vy guess vicked boy? I stand right here. I tell her. Save time.'

'No you don't understand. She's dead good. Melody's like this top psychiatrist, head shrink, right. Does all this personality shit for the army, right, Mel?'

Melody glowered Saul-like at Kevin. She hated people knowing what she did in her previous life. Most of which was top secret, covered under the Official Secrets Act for her lifetime. And beyond.

Kevin didn't have to be that empathetic to get the glare. 'What? Googled you. You're famous, girl. Go on. Sherlock Saul.'

Melody really didn't want to strop out as she was enjoying her mandated day of rest far more than anticipated. Though she would put Kevin straight on a few things later. She looked hard at Saul and immediately noticed a few markers.

'Right. First off, given your bearing, I'd guess you are, or probably were, in the military. Seem a bit old for active service.'

Saul wasn't that impressed. 'Yeah, vell, okay. But most Israelis serve in the IDF at some point. Not a leap.'

'True. But most are not in special forces, as you were.'

Saul reluctantly half smiled as Melody took hold of his hand.'

'May I?'

'Mais oui, mademoiselle.'

She lifted up his hand to get a better look.

'That ring, the other one, not your wedding ring, bears the crest of the Sayeret Matkal.'

Melody turned his hand around to examine the palm.

'Your hands are hard and fully calloused. Now, this is subjective, but I'm guessing you're not a manual labourer, digging ditches—'

'Not even gardening. Like this vicked boy.'

'Gee, thanks, Saul. Remember that next time you wanna chill out with a gratis ounce of primo. Locked in.'

Melody let go of his hand and moved in closer.

'You have a yellowy healing bruise on the side of your face, which, if I'm not mistaken – may I?'

Melody placed her left hand on Saul's shoulder.

'Beautiful voman lays lovely mitts on. Vy I fight that mitzvah?'

Melody undid the top three buttons of Saul's shirt, as he smiled with pleasure. She pulled back the material to reveal his tanned shoulder.

'A bruise which stretches down past your shoulder. And these other bruises in various degrees of repair. Which tells me that either you're the world's clumsiest man. Which I doubt. Or, you get into lots of fights.'

Kevin did an exaggerated fist pull of triumph.

'Booya. Told ya.'

'Given your background and the personality type required for special forces, you don't get into any fight you haven't initiated professionally. Or, one you intend to lose. And given Kevin said I'll never guess what you did, I have to conclude that you are not merely training, which your muscle mass suggests you continue almost daily. But that you are in fact the trainer. You teach some sort of martial arts.'

Saul stood shaking his head for a couple of seconds, before exploding into loud laughter.

'Very good, basm, Princess. Krav Maga. Vat else?'

'Told ya she was good, Saul. Head shrinker.'

'Not really *head shrinking*. That's just basic observation.'

'Vatever. You good. Good in the mind. I should teach you Krav Maga, Princess. My treat. Free gratis. Your money no good. Help you get vell.'

Melody bristled at the idea she was being head shrunk back by a stranger. 'I am well, thank you very much, Saul.'

'No, Princess. No. You not vell by long chalk.'

Saul gently put his huge hand around her bicep. You veak. I help. Come to Krav Maga for me. I teach you.'

'To do what?'

'Get fit. More. Defend yourself. Fight to death. Not your death. Other shmuck's death.'

'You mean – teach me to kill someone?'

'Ve don't say that. Ve say eliminate threat. By vatever you needs to do. Then you live. Other shmuck die. Simple. Vot you say, Princess?'

CHAPTER

7

Melody obsessively checked the creased scrap of paper Aaron had slid into her possession almost two weeks earlier. No mistake, this was the address scribbled in faded pencil.

Danny. 34 Snowdrop Street. Poplar. 8pm. Monday, 19.

Except it wasn't. Sure, there was a number thirty-two. There was a number thirty-six. But where 34 Snowdrop Street should be situated (on an overgrown, litter-strewn empty lot) there was a fenced off, burned-out shell of a house. A local estate agents sign had an additional *under offer* banner running diagonally across it.

Bollocks. What a waste of effing time.

It was eight-thirty. The street lights had flickered into life while Melody was silently fuming at Aaron. The street was quiet and suburban. A small car drove past. Not too fast. Not too slow. Not too suspicious.

As the Yaris continued on its way, she again clocked the Range Rover parked about fifty yards ahead. When the Yaris cleared it, the Range Rover's lights flashed once. They flashed again, twice. She was already half way towards it when they flashed three times.

The front passenger side door opened as Melody reached the vehicle. The windows were tinted so she had no idea who was flashing. She presumed and hoped it was the mysterious *Danny*.

Inside her canvas satchel, Melody gripped the ribbed handle of the Fairburn-Sykes Royal Marines fighting knife. The F-S was seven lethal inches of double-sided, scalpel-sharp blade: a modern copy of the classic killing tool designed back in the 1940s.

Saul's English dad was a Royal Marine in the 1950s before he took his family to Israel. Despite many fine Israeli alternatives, Saul swore by it as the most lethal close-quarter fighting knife ever devised. Even in relatively unskilled hands, it was the world's finest stabbing and slashing weapon; having been designed by the legendary RMC Colonel Fairbairn for maximum silent penetration. Saul had taught Melody a few tricks since that first Shabbat together.

'Ven push come to shove it in, ya gotta be vicked to ya bones. Then you live, Princess, and the meshugenah creep dies. Better that vay, right?'

Melody sidled around the door which stretched open over the pavement. She looked in. Sitting behind the wheel, a well-dressed black guy stared back at her. Melody warily assessed him for threats, as Saul had taught her. Yeah, this bloke looked like he handled himself well. About six feet two, sixteen stone, late-thirties, short dreads.

'Get in.'

'You Danny?'

'Don't be daft, love. There is no Danny.'

Melody mentally tensed, ready for flight or fight. The knife poised in case it was fight.

'Relax, doll. Name's Frankie Bishop. Mister Fuchs sent me. Just get in already.'

Melody got in already.

They had been driving in silence for about twenty minutes. Melody had started to ask a question, but Frankie put up his left hand to indicate *don't talk*. Instead, she gazed out of the passenger side window, her mind drifting as the unfamiliar London suburbs south of the Thames flashed by. Thoughts of how she got here, in the car, at this time. About to do something she wondered if she could ever go through with in the end – when push comes to shove it in.

THWACK—

The well-muscled man smashed the woman on the side of her head with his right fist. It was a brutal and vicious attack; and hardly a fair fight. She was toned: no shrinking violet at five feet ten. But he was over six feet.

Tumbling a few feet backwards, she fell on her backside, almost side-on to him. He grinned. She was helpless. He liked that. This was going better and faster than expected. Time to finish her off.

Moving in for the kill, he nonchalantly tossed the knife from hand to hand before rushing her. Blade thrust forward, aiming at her throat for a slash and gouge frenzy finish. Dead easy.

Or it would have been if, in a blink, the girl hadn't spun her floor-seated body one hundred and eighty degrees. As her right leg hooked around the man's calf, she pulled hard. His own undisciplined momentum catapulted him high in the air to clatter loud and hard in a vertebrae dislodging crash onto the fight mat.

Ouch.

The knife flew from his hand. But the girl didn't need to get it. Already up, in mid-air, she dropped from height, knee first into his groin.

Excruciating.

Ignoring his pitiful scream, she pulled back her arm so as to better rocket-thrust her balled fist into his windpipe. The kill shot.

'Enough.'

Saul's bellowed command ricocheted off the bare brick walls of the former factory in Neasden, North London. It stopped her dead in her tracks. The ground floor space had been converted into a training facility which Saul had named the *All Fight Club*. While he preferred Krav Maga, he respected all fighting forms; and all people willing to learn through dedication, discipline, and practice.

In the boxing ring, two young men were sparing under the watchful eye of Saul's friend, Errol Saunders. The former British and Commonwealth Featherweight Champ was spry for a man in his seventies.

Laid out in a grid pattern were six, twenty-feet square, cushioned fight mats. Saul prowled around his area of expertise keeping his eyes fixed on the various fight activities from the six trainees in today.

'Let him be, Melody. Y'vicked girl.'

'Wasn't going to follow through.'

Saul fixed her with his *he who must be obeyed* eyes. 'And don't pouty dem lips at me, missy, dis mensch's immune.'

First rule of *All Fight Club* was to obey Saul without thinking. Melody had learned that in two years of training in Krav Maga: the deadly street-fighting martial art developed by the Israeli Special Forces. Unlike the more formalized fighting techniques from Japan and China, the sole purpose of Krav Maga is to disable your opponent as fast as possible, using the deadliest of force. In the right hands it is killer lethal. Though now her friend, the former special forces colonel, and Krav Maga expert, was a man not to annoy.

The pout disappeared instantly and she withdrew from clobbering Patrick, still sprawled at her feet on one of the mats. He wasn't pouting either.

'How comes this durkshnit gets drop on you anyvays?'

Melody laughed. 'Durkshnit? No idea what that means, but it can't be good.'

The peeved Patrick, who had just been physically humiliated by a girl four stone lighter and seven years older, was even more peeved at the easy banter. 'Yeah thanks a bunch guys. Still here you know. Humiliated.'

'Answer the kvestion, Princess.'

'Last night was Kevin's fortieth, which you missed. There was drinking, eating, dancing and other human activities into the wee small hours of the morning.'

'Ah, you think vicked fuckers gonna ask ya nicely before they attack—'

Before Saul finished he was on Melody. In one sweep of his leg she was sprawled on her back, his hand gripping her throat. A human octopus wrapping all his limbs around her so she was unable to move, or even squirm.

His mouth was an inch from her ear as she tried frantically to turn her head. 'You finks some meshugenah creep's gonna give a shit about your party life. Ooo, don't be too rough, I vas out last night? Alvays anticipate vorld's full of vicked bastards, Princess. I tell her this all time. Vill she listen? No she vill not.'

As quickly as he had attacked, Saul was off Melody, extending his hand to pull her up. 'One final lesson before you abandon old Sau—'

CRACK—

The sound of Saul's head hitting the mat reverberated across the brick walls. The other Krav Maga students stopped their exercises and watched open-mouthed. She had grabbed his wrist hard, pulling him downwards savagely. Lifting her legs fast, she used Saul's own forward and downwards momentum to flip him over her head, crashing him behind her, hard and flat on his back.

Executing a physically demanding roll back flip, she was up and at him in a blink. She thrust the heel of her left foot down at Saul's fully exposed tracheae and windpipe, stopping the assault a half inch above the crush blow.

Despite the pain to his concrete hard head, Saul smiled like a father releasing his child to walk unaided for the first time.

'Gooder, Princess. Much gooder.'

CHAPTER

8

Frankie Bishop parked his Range Rover in the car park of the Tescos superstore in Lewisham. Melody still gripping the F-S handle in her canvas satchel.

He shifted his body towards her. 'I'm impressed by your caution. But you can release your death grip on that knife. Nothing's going to happen.'

'Yeah. I know nothing's going to happen, Frankie Bishop. But I am impressed by your observations.'

Frankie beamed and gave out a deep bass laugh.

'Touché, love. Mister Fuchs said you were all there.'

'Oh he did, did he?'

'Said to give you this.'

Frankie handed over an A5 envelope. She stuffed it into her satchel without taking her eyes off him.

'Thanks. What else did Mister Fuchs tell you about me.'

'Enough.'

'Not sure I like the sound of that.'

'Look, lady, I'm just the messenger here, not really my

place—'

'That's true, but humour me. Kind of important given the nature of the mutual transaction that's occurring, that I know who knows what. Wouldn't you agree?'

'Sure. That's not unreasonable. Mister Fuchs doesn't trust anyone, being paranoid, as I'm sure you've discerned. You got the qualifications to diagnose that I'm sure. But as far as anyone goes, I am his most trusted employee and only he and I know about this arrangement. A closed circle of he, me and thee.'

'And what does *me* think. About the arrangement?'

'Like I said, just the messenger—'

'Yeah, yeah, but you sort of are involved. Integral, as a conduit, right? You count.'

Frankie nodded at Melody's affirmation. 'Fair enough. Here's the thing. I get it. I truly do get it. Anyone so much as touched my, well, you know what I mean, I'd fucking do for them big time. Every last one. No doubt. But this is different? Isn't it? I mean, fuck, it's not face to face with the three cunts who done you wrong and deserve to die. That's hot blood no matter a lifetime has passed. I see that. Can probably see you doing that. Snuffing those lives. But this is cold. Total strangers. Just can't see someone like you has it in ya. Be honest.'

Melody could see his surface point. Even she wasn't totally sure yet, and she was the expert on conditioning soldiers to learn to kill and to live with the consequences. But Frankie was alluding to something even deeper than that.

Melody let go of her tightly gripped knife handle. She turned to face Frankie face on, look him straight in the eyes.

'The monsters that did this to my family and me? Total strangers too. But fair point. I get that. And you're thinking what if she fucks it up. Even worse, there are three fuck up chances. She could be killed herself. Or gets to the deed. Freezes. Can't do it. It's not her despite all the talk. But that's okay. Problem solved. No one's the wiser. But what if she's caught by the police. Confesses. Spills her guts. Mentions my name. Shit. This is going to blow back on me big time.'

Frankie half-smiled, nodded. She was good. 'Thought had crossed.'

Melody already knew this Frankie Bishop character was a deeds not words guy. Her professional opinion based on many years of expertise in body language, micro-expressions, verbalization, posture. She didn't even have to consciously assess people these days. She was like a supercomputer. The data came in, it was processed automatically within her, and the human equation answer popped, just like that.

Telling Frankie how he could trust her wouldn't cut it with his personality type. And she didn't want this dangerous bloke wondering about her constantly, musing on her expendability. She had to express that non-verbally. Right now. And irrevocably.

Melody pulled the knife from her satchel. It was Frankie's turn to be wary of this half-crazy with grief mother out for vengeance. She balanced the twelve inches of blade and handle on her left palm.

'This is the Fairbairn-Sykes commando knife—'

Half crazy or not, Frankie was still impressed she possessed such a lethal weapon

'My brother Eddie was a Royal Marine.'

'Then you know.'

'Sure do. Expert in close combat is Eddie. Taught it at Lympstone as an instructor for a bit, till he left the corps. Loves that beauty. Still has his original blade, far as I know.'

'Yeah, well I'm pretty good too. Taught by a real pro. And just to let you know—'

Melody lifted the handle from her left hand, and with one slow action sliced the razor sharp blade across her left palm. Frankie couldn't help but wince as the blood instantly oozed.

'Ouch.'

'There is no way this side of hell freezing over that I would ever screw over anyone, no matter what. If ship *me* goes down, there's only me on board. But it's not going down. Okay? We clear, Frankie Bishop?'

Frankie had to admit he was impressed, and appalled.

'Clearly you're nuts. But stand up nuts, not crumbly, flaky nuts. That's gonna hurt like a motherfucker in the morning. Could you try not to bleed onto the leather. Blood's a real fucker to get out.'

CHAPTER

9

Frankie left her at Brixton tube station. She guessed still not totally enthused, or on board, with his boss's game. But as a loyal lieutenant to Aaron Fuchs, he did not express that opinion out loud to the crazy lady.

Changing trains at Camden Town, she switched to the Northern Line's Edgware spur. The station was heaving with boisterous, in-your-face young people who had piled out of the pubs and clubs in the popular area for hooking up. Melody had been young and party-girlish once, and tried not to be too judgmental. But when the barely dressed girl (not that much older than Charity would now be) vomited all over her own ridiculously high heels, that was it.

Christ, Melody. Can't be doing with this anymore. You have to get back to some proper transport. Specially now.

The house was quiet; why wouldn't it be? Melody placed the envelope on the living room table and poured a glass of red wine. Ruth had been upset when her sister finally decided it was time to get her own place again. Her son

Freddy adored his aunt Mel, and the new toddler Calista thought she had two mums. But needs must. And what Melody needed couldn't be completed at her sister's home.

By any stretch, Melody was very rich. Paul had seen to that. Not the super-rich of being married, as they had planned that very autumn after five years living together. Then she would have inherited, by right, his share of the billion pound company he co-created with Ben Carrington. Instead, she had to settle for the provisions of his will in which she was a named beneficiary with no other legal standing. Of course, Melody didn't care. Money was the last thing on her mind, so she wasn't *settling* for anything. Her lawyer had explained the complexities of a last will and testament when the assets were wrapped up in a growing corporation such as *Peach*. Shares, stocks, voting rights, control, taxes, debts. The publicly traded company had to be protected just as much as loved ones.

Melody told the lawyer to give her the figure. The very thought she was benefiting from the death of Charity and Paul repulsed her.

It was a paper sum of at least forty million pounds. This included the value of the Limehouse property, various life insurance policies, cash in hand, and projected Peach stock values, which could only be sold after first offering them back to the company.

Even so, she chose to buy a modest two-bedroom terraced cottage in Golders Green, about a mile from her sister. (Modest in the sense size not price.) It was the least she could do to calm down Ruth.

Melody switched on the living room TV, muting the sound. She found the disk and inserted it into the player. As far as Charity was concerned, CDs belonged in an archaeological dig alongside other dinosaurs, such as 78s, 45s, albums, and mullet cuts. Her music was iTunes downloaded to her phone. And like everything else, they had all been consumed in the fire. But Melody had wanted something tangible, so she bought the CD of *Born To Die,* Lana Del Rey's 2012 debut album.

As Lana's soulful, melancholic pipes let rip, Melody took another gulp of wine before she picked up the envelope. She could feel the slight bulge of a flash drive.

TWANG—

Her mobile phone's personalized power chord made her jump as it vibrated across the highly polished table. The display flagged Chloe Carrington. The Who's *Won't Get Fooled Again* ripped into the opening answer me riff.

Chloe was a friend by assimilation as opposed to mutual choice. They inherited each other by virtue of the best friendship of their respective male partners. Luckily they clicked instantly in a sisterly way, being of similar education, background and tastes. Chloe had also been a rock alongside her bio-sister Ruth. Even so, this was bloody inconvenient.

Melody thought about hitting decline as she had an idea what the call was about. She paused Lana.

'Hey, Chloe.'

Melody knew that no matter where she was, even this late, even sitting in Cordingay House (her fabulous 17th century Oxfordshire manor) Chloe would be immaculate. No hair would dare be out of place on her perfectly coiffed head. Melody imagined her dressed like a supermodel on the catwalk of the latest Paris fashion show. Not that she was an airhead: Chloe had brains too, reading English Literature at Cambridge with her contemporaries Ben, and Paul. Now being loaded enough to run her own incredibly influential literary agency, named (naturally) *Carringtons.* Amongst her clients she boasted one Booker prizer, two Booker nominees, and three Crime Writers' Association

Dagger winners.

Chloe:	Hey, Mel. What you doing? Okay to talk?
Melody:	Just watching the telly, sipping a rather nice red.
Chloe:	Well, I've made my views clear many times. Honest to God, Mel. You shouldn't be brooding all alone in that pokey little place.
Melody:	Pokey? It cost nearly two million.
Chloe:	Exactly.
Melody:	Chloe!
Chloe:	Alright, alright, said my piece. I'll shut the fuck up right now dear heart. Sorry to be such a screechy bitch. You know why I called.

Yes indeed, Melody knew why her friend was pestering her. The Carringtons were super-rich. Not merely forty million rich on paper, like Melody, who truly didn't care. Add a couple of noughts to that when the next tranche of Peach stock was released on the New York Stock Exchange.

Naturally they had the patrician bug. Being altruistic makes rich people feel really good about themselves. Being super-rich makes them feel super-altruistic and super-good. Chloe's new project was a science foundation for inner-city kids, funded by her and Ben. Which was fine. Except her idea was to name it the *Paul McCrae Peach Foundation*, with Melody as its joint head. She was touched by the kind gesture – but her head was elsewhere.

Melody:	The foundation thingy?

Chloe: Yes. Look, I don't mean to be pushy.

Melody: Yes you do.

Chloe: True. You know me way too well, young Padowan. Have to live up to my Rodean nickname, Chlo-me-me-me. Kids can be little bastards.

Melody: Isn't that still your nickname, at the agency?

Chloe: Oooo, you little monster.

Melody: But now you're giving back.

Chloe: Exactly. With your help. You know Paul would have wanted this. Helping poor kids make something of themselves. Back in Belfast he didn't grow up comfortably middle class, like we three.

Melody knew this wasn't going away. Chloe was tenacious when she got an idea in her head. Melody simply needed to kick the time frame down the road.

Melody: Okay then, I'm in. But, one small, almost tiny proviso.

Chloe: Anything, dear heart.

Melody: Push the launch back six months.

Chloe: Really? Well, if that's what it takes to have you on board. Okay then. But I demand quid pro quo.

Melody: Of course you do. Crow away.

Chloe: Now you have time for a more hands on input. How about a monthly meeting of a newly constituted foundation board, of

	which you are joint head, with myself.
Melody:	That's rather reasonable. And thanks, Chloe, love. Appreciate the understanding.
Chloe:	No worries. But what on earth are you doing for the next six months that's more important?

Lana played through to the last track, and the house fell silent again. Born to die. Ain't that the truth?

Melody gulped the last of the wine. Suitably numbed and fortified, her hand still trembled as she picked up the envelope. This time the phone didn't ring as she retrieved the flash drive, and unfolded the single sheet of paper.

CHAPTER

10

Melody eyed Thomas Bentley as best she could from the other side of the bar. He was in his early-forties, tanned, full head of hair, sparkling teeth, and smartly dressed in a Hugo Boss charcoal grey suit. She was dressed-down in cheap, supermarket own brand jeans topped with a shapeless short-sleeved blouse.

In the days surveilling Bentley, she had experienced the pitfalls of being an attractive female sitting alone at various trendy bars around the City of London. Even aged thirty-nine, with all the traumas she had endured, Melody was back to the knockout that Paul had fallen for hard. The only difference being that her coal-black hair was long back then. Now it was short cropped and blonde, like Jean Seberg in *Breathless.* French New Wave cinema from the fifties and sixties being a particular favourite. She looked at least ten years younger than her birth certificate age. Bentley did not have the magnetic appeal of a young Jean-Paul Belmondo, though.

Nearly two weeks ago, she began her – *plan*, *adventure*, or whatever this was – dressed far more upmarket. But it soon gets boring and distracting rebuffing a never-ending stream of—

What you drinking, gorgeous? Let me buy you one. Or ten.

It was all depressingly uninspiring. Social media had done some good things. The improvement of the average chat-up line was not one of them. She had considered an actual off-putting disguise: leather-clad, lesbian biker chick with a few temporary tats on her arms and face. But that wouldn't have allowed her past the burly security deployed at these establishments. She settled for a theatrically dramatic red wig and Goth inspired purple make-up. It was startling. A different vibe from the usual expensive clientele, but not so off-putting to stop her at the entrance.

After eleven days of alleged surveillance she realized what she was doing. Psychologically, that is. *Procrastinating.* There were studies on personality types and procrastination. Links had been made with chronic procrastination and personality challenges, such as ADHD, extreme passive-aggression, obsessive-compulsive disorder, and revenge fantasies. Being a psychiatrist, Melody was prone to a higher level of self-analysis. Now she was asking if she was the one placing obstacles in her own way, to sabotage herself from executing the actions she consciously thought she desired above everything.

When it was all theory, and impressing Aaron with her resolve, it was easy to believe her own convictions. She was invested in that. Sure, she had insisted to Aaron that her (for want of a better word) *targets*, deserved their fate. He agreed. But then, he *was* a diagnosed sociopath. When she opened the envelope and read the name Thomas Bentley, she needed more than a sociopath's word that he was good to go to hell.

This much was true. Nine years ago, Thomas William Bentley was arrested for securities fraud, along with seven others working at Scimitar Capital Management in the City. Investors had lost hundreds of millions in what were alleged to be criminal activities, stock manipulations, insider trading. Melody vaguely recalled the scandal. It was the start of the massive media bloodlust that was to eventually roll over bankers and others in the financial institutions.

Bentley was remanded without bail as an extreme flight risk. He had access to private planes and boats. He owned properties abroad, including a cattle ranch in no-extradition Argentina. No doubt expecting a cushy open prison for the duration, he was surprisingly remanded to Ringland. The reason given for this supposedly non-violent offender was lack of space in suitable Category B or C prisons in the south east and London. The rumoured real reason was to scare the crap out of him to testify against someone higher.

He was scared all right. And not too clever for a bloke who was purportedly very bright. Bentley was incarcerated into a cell with your more traditional scumbag, in for armed robbery. This is where Aaron's knowledge kicked in. It was his second year in Ringland. As Aaron heard it later from said armed robber Sammy 'Shotgun' Simons, it went down like this:

Sammy knew the ropes and was keen to impress the influential Aaron Fuchs, now the big man inside Ringland. Sammy being a solo operator and Aaron being able to supply the essentials: protection, contraband, smokes, some chill out weed, access to a mobile phone to call the missus and his teenage daughter. All the gear to make Shotgun's holiday at her majesty's pleasure somewhat more tolerable for the next few years. First day out of two weeks' solitary, as they scoffed down the lunchtime slop in the prison canteen, Shotgun was eager to tell his tale as to why he had been in solitary in the first place.

'Anyways, Mister Fuchs, as I was saying like, the screws put this new geezer in wiv me. Bentley. Tom Bentley. Big bloke, should've been able to handle himself really. But right away I sussed him as some sort of ponce like. One a them posh accents like he had some guy's willy in his mouth when he spoke. Plus he looked terrified, you could tell he ain't never done bird before. But I ain't judgmental, mean takes all sorts right. So I says: "Top bunk's mine, you gotta problem with that? "No," says he.

'That's all fine and dandy like. So, we chin-wag, as you do. Naturally I asks him what you in for mate? "Securities fraud. Alleged. On remand," says he.

'Well when I finished laughing me arse off, I tell him, fuck mate, you ain't going to last five minutes in here. You know this gaff's full of real fucking criminals who'll lick their chops like a fucking lion does when he sees a gazelle. That would be lunch, by the by. And you're the gazelle in case you missed that. So I tells him he needs to rep up, make an impression that he ain't a bloke to be fucked with, because he done stuff on the outside.

'So, he sort of smirks like, he's relaxed a bit now, feeling looser y'know, bit more confident, me sort of taking him under me wing. And tells me "well actually" – yeah, he said "actually" like some Hooray Henry in Henley, he has done stuff on the outside, real deal stuff. Course now I'm really fucking intrigued as you would be. "Oh yeah, and what would that be sunshine. Do tell. Bit a shoplifting from Marks and Sparks. Lifted some bloke's wallet on the Tube? You a regular Charlie Bronson then?"

'Can tell he wants to brag something, but still a bit hesitant like. So, I reassures him, "Worse thing to be inside is a grass. Blokes like me, your professional criminal classes, can't abide that." If that's what he was worried about.

'Maybe he was, maybe he wasn't, but he's got the look now, I seen that before, yeah this fella's been a real bad boy and got away with it. So, to gee him up I continues, "Only thing worse than a grass is

fucking nonces and fucking rapists, them cunts got it coming big time."

'So this Bentley looks like he's turned fucking green, Mister Fuchs. Swear to God, fucking green. Then he shuts the fuck right up tighter than a nun's twat. Says nah he ain't done nothing on the outside he was just bullshitting trying to sound hard.

'Mind's churning over at this. Lying on the top bunk, and I'm thinking, fuck, what's this guy hiding like? So, I worked it out. He's smart but not street smart, even so, he can't be that fucking thick to think repping up to fucking molesting kids is a reputation enhancer. Right. Gotta be the rape. Guy's a fucking raper getting away with it on the outside. Then I'm thinking of my Tracy, she's sixteen next week Mister Fuchs. Sixfuckingteen. My little girl.

'Next thing I know I'm dragging the fucker from his bunk and kicking him in his smirking Hooray Henry ponce fucking gob. Red mist thing, y'know. Got him on the floor like, both knees pressed hard on his chest, choking the cunt, screaming like "Who d'ya rape. Who d'ya rape. Fucker. Fucker." Stuff like that.

'Anyways, Mister Fuchs, he's trying to answer, eyes popping, but I realize me hands is so tight he can't speak. So I stop and he spills it, fucking filthy pervert spews it all, yeah, picks them up in bars like, takes them back to his gaff, drugs them, then takes his time. Couple didn't never woke up. So he said. Next second the screws burst in, drags me offa him. Bang, two weeks solitary. Course never snitched. But thought you'd like to know cos I can't abide scum like that.'

That was the sole background on Bentley, provided on the flash drive. Was it true? Melody had no proof, except second and third-hand hearsay from convicted criminals. Hence, stalking Bentley for nearly two weeks. She had to be more than sure he was a multiple rapist. If he was the person as described in the so-called prison confession, there is no way he had stopped in the following near decade since. As a psychopath, his power-addiction would have progressed unchecked, added to the fact he had gotten away with it for so long. The feeling of omnipotence would be a strong trigger in him.

Except – she had nothing on Bentley so far, apart from him spending a lot of time winding down after work. His chosen field being expensive bars. As far as Melody could find, using the deductive powers of Google, the charges against Bentley and the others were quietly dropped when the whole case collapsed. He returned to Scimitar Capital Management. A year later he sued the Met for false arrest, false imprisonment, and severe physical trauma. The case was settled out of court for an undisclosed sum. Melody found a couple of obscure blogs which claimed Bentley received three million pounds in damages.

Bentley was one of the top people at Scimitar's London office based in the 737-feet high Leadenhall Building at 122 Leadenhall Street. It was about a mile from Melody's former home in Limehouse. She knew the area well. And the area knew her equally well, which was one reason she went for the radically changed cropped blonde cut, and the occasional wig.

He usually left work around six-thirty. Melody had been arriving by six, sitting outside the small pub opposite with a half of lager. He would always leave with a few of his young acolytes and walk to one of the local bars. Either that night's venue of *Memento Mori,* or one of three others: *Annatopia*, *The Bar*, and *Jungle.*

Melody would sit at a wall table, facing out, pretending to be working on her iPad. She would order a regular supply of expensive drinks, sipping slowly, but mainly discarding them. Cash payment, no credit card trails.

He would be surrounded by his acolytes and bottles of expensive champagne, chatting to any good looking woman who fell in the group's orbit. But that was it. No pick-ups. Maybe he was collecting phone numbers for later use, but she never saw it. He invariably drank and chatted for about an hour, sometimes two, before leaving his younger colleagues to drink on. Melody would be thirty seconds behind him.

She soon discovered the flaw in her attempted Sherlocking. Four days out of the eleven, Bentley strode off to grab a bite to eat at the famous *Prospect Of Whitby* pub situated on Wapping Wall. He liked to walk. Maybe that was his exercise regime, as it was a good twenty minutes hike on foot.

Like clockwork, Bentley sat in the Thames-facing pub garden and tucked into the delicious homemade Shepherd's Pie. That was fine. She could pad unseen behind him. Lurk in the bar area. Even tuck into her own pie. But no food that first time she laid malign eyes on her target, Thomas Bentley. Her stomach was in a raw knot all night. The realization it had become very real was an appetite suppressor. No longer the dark vengeance fantasy playing out in her head since she woke up in St. Michael's.

The norm had been for Bentley to depart the bar, flag down a black cab and presumably head back home. There was the flaw. Melody was necessarily walking. It wasn't like the movies when a string of cabs were also passing at the same time for the clichéd—

Follow that cab.

Melody had addressed her public transport problems via Kevin. One of his pals was a used car dealer, naturally. She wanted something that looked blandly nondescript and unthreatening on the outside; but souped up under the bonnet. Barry (the Barry of Barry Motors) found her a navy-blue 1999 Ford Mondeo that was originally an unmarked police car used in high speed chases. The 2015 restoration of new engine, gear box and suspension hadn't stretched to bodywork. He looked a little down at heel. Perfect.

Then there was the brand new Triumph 650 motorbike. The essential piece of kit for getting around London fast. Even more perfect.

Except they were perfectly useless tonight as once again Bentley walked straight out of *Memento Mori* into Armoury Lane. She exited and followed him towards Leadenhall Street. She could see his arm go up as he spotted a roaming cab. She reached the junction in time to hear him instruct the cabbie, 'Terra Turris, mate.'

As she watched the cab head to Canary Wharf, Melody finally admitted that she was going about this all wrong. She could vaguely follow Bentley till the Messiah came for the Jewish people. They had been waiting a long time, so it could be a while. And in the end, what was that going to accomplish? She was on the look out for future crimes to justify her taking action for past crimes. This was a losing enterprise. She had spent most of her time brooding at the vengeance she was going to unleash. The actual how was being made up on the fly.

She had to step this up. She had to get real. She had to somehow inveigle her way into Thomas Bentley's apartment in Terra Turris.

CHAPTER

11

'Wotcha, girl. Where you flipping been then? Missed ya. Blimey, what happened to your hand?'

Kevin ushered Melody into his terraced house in Crouch End. The pungent aroma of cannabis hit her before he opened the door.

Melody couldn't tell him where she had been, or what she had been up to, especially her bizarre, spur of the moment blood oath. She didn't want to involve Kevin at all, not even tangentially. But now she had another problem. It was probably a problem Frankie Bishop was qualified to advise upon; or at least know someone who could. But that was a non-starter. It was not that she actively distrusted him. She didn't want to widen her circle of people who led back to her.

'Chopping vegetables, bloody knife slipped and sliced. Razor sharp.'

'Should be more careful.'

'You should be more careful. I can smell this shit from

the street.'

Kevin steered her through the patio doors leading out to the overgrown jungle-like back garden.

'Crouch End, darling. Coppers never come down this street on the beat no more. Too busy over in Cricklewood.'

'Bit early to be toking, isn't it?'

'Nah, not doing this for fun. Been experimenting. Spliced together a few varieties and hot-room growing plants to check viability. You gotta self-test the product. I'm all about the quality control.'

'Thought you left that all behind in Spain.'

'Told ya, got green fingers. It's like a mania with yours truly.'

'Grow tomatoes like a normal person.'

'Where's the fun in that. Plus, London's bleeding expensive. Where've you been then?'

Melody lied, effortlessly. 'Sorry I haven't been in touch, been quite hectic actually—'

'Aunty was asking after you last Shabbat. She likes it when you come. Told her you'd be at your sisters.'

'Thanks. Yeah, I'll – I'll come over soon. Tell her, okay.'

'Will do. So, what's all this hecticness about then?'

'Remember my friend, Chloe? Chloe Carrington, married to Paul's partner—'

'Yeah. Never had the pleasure of meeting up, as such. She's perfect, right? As you tell it.'

'Thing is, Chloe's setting up this foundation for deprived kids, in Paul's name, and basically she's volunteered me to run it. Taking up a lot of time.'

'Sounds great, as a former deprived kid meself.'

'Oh sure. Anyway there's more. I mentioned Chloe runs her own literary agency, right?'

'Don't even know what that is.'

'They represent writers. Sell their books to publishers.'

'Oh, okay, like used car salesmen?'

Melody laughed at the thought of Chloe being compared to Arthur Daley.

'Yeah, something like that. Anyway, I told Chloe about my East End side of the family with its fair share of ne'er-do-wells and reprobates.'

'Thanks.'

'You know what I mean. Get this. Chloe tells me that one of her prestige authors, real literature type, Booker prize, reviews for the Times, Oxford Don—'

'But not a Don Corleone.'

'Ha. Funny. Anyway, he fancies trying his hand at writing a crime novel. Being a real stickler for research he's looking for verisimilitude in his work.'

'Very similar attitude? Sorry, what's that?'

'Means truthful, accurate, like life. Long story short, Chloe asked me whether I could help him out. Wants me to dig up a proper thief who would know stuff.'

'Stuff like what?'

'Oh, I don't know. Crim stuff. Like how to break into an apartment with state of the art security, guards, alarms, cameras. The whole shebang.'

'And you thought of good old, Kev?'

'Not you personally. Thought you might know someone, or someone who might know someone.'

'Ask Aaron. You been to see him, right.'

Melody was taken aback that Kevin knew about last month's visit. She hadn't considered that.

'Maybe.'

'Fucking hell, Mel. Did I not say keep away from him? He's bad news. What with him, the motorbike, that car, now this, what's really going on, love. Was born during the day, which is very fucken weird as I've always been ultrasensitive to sunlight, burn easier than a bagel in a toaster. But even so, it still weren't yesterday. Thought we was friends, let alone family.'

So much for Melody's subtle plan to get a contact from Kevin to help her; while keeping schtum on the real reason.

'We are friends, Kevin. And family – and there's nothing to worry about. Honest. Simply fascinated in Aaron from a clinical point of view. I wrote to him a while back, and he said come visit. So I did. That's all.'

'Alright, alright. You say so.'

'I do so. And you were the one who mentioned him in the first place. Remember?'

'Glad we cleared that up. And as it happens I do know someone who can help you with your—

Kevin raised both hands to provide the *I believe you* air quotes.

—"research." And what's more, you already know him. Know him real dead good, y'vicked girl.'

On the edge of Canary Wharf, Melody gazed up at the *Terra Turris* complex. Stretching to forty-three storeys, they were the tallest twin apartment towers in London. The latinized name was probably chosen to sound more exclusive than its more prosaic English translation of *Earth Tower*. The twin towers were linked by a *green* atrium-lobby containing the latest in fully serviced urban living for the mega-rich professional. Three restaurants, gymnasium, sauna, swimming pool, and a small cinema. It also boasted a security detail that would be the envy of a third world Banana Republic.

Bentley lived in apartment 2515 on the twenty-fifth floor. From there he could probably see London laid out before him, like one of those perfect miniature villages. The Thames winding its way west, past St Michael's Hospital where Melody had lain, life suspended for seventeen months. Then on past the lumbering giant wheel that looked ready to spin across the Thames into the Houses of Parliament opposite.

It's great to be very rich. When Melody remembered that she was, indeed, very rich, it all fell into place.

'Lehayim!'

Saul raised his shot glass to Melody. She reciprocated with her identical glass.

'To life.'

They knocked back the very expensive Belvedere unfiltered Polish vodka in one gulp. Saul barely blinked. Melody struggled to stop herself spluttering it straight back up The smooth lava-like liquid had burned its way down past her throat to her stomach lining. She wasn't a big fan of forty per cent proof liquor at the best of times. Four o'clock in the afternoon, in a Polish dive-bar in Vauxhall, was more like the worst of times for her. This was her fourth shot. No driving though. Uber day.

Saul had ordered the bottle for the table, and was way ahead on shots. Most of the other denizens were actual Poles speaking Polish. A few had greeted Saul when he rolled into the bar and filled their glasses for shots too.

'Vy you vant know this, Princess?'

'Research. I'm writing a book.'

'Okay, you say so. I should write book, no?'

'About what?'

'So much shit I do, Princess. You vouldn't believe. So much shit. Vengeance shit too.'

For a nanosecond, Melody caught the look of melancholy on the face of the normally ebullient Saul. That passed like a mere wisp as he poured himself another shot.

Melody held her hand over her glass.

'Vell, first principle, vy break into place, if you be invited? Art of vore takes many forms. Sometimes mensch is the varrior who charges enemy. Sometimes he stealthy cat, stalking prey, vaiting to pounce, tear throat out. Sometimes he spy in enemy camp. Unseen by big shots. Vanilla, like. You ever notice staff at hotel. Really say to yourself, that look like maid. No vey, Mo-che. She vear uniform, she maid. She blend. She go anywhere in that uniform. Peoples respect uniforms. Assume other peoples have right to uniform. Could be Oscar de la Renta. Could be Oscar za rat catcher. Don't kvestion uniform. See vot I mean.'

Melody did see vot he mean. 'You know Oscar de la Renta?'

'Meh – maybe.'

They talked a lot more about useful tools to aid ingress. Kevin was right. Saul could probably break into the Bank of England if he put his mind to it. But it was his first principle which cleared her mind.

CHAPTER

12

Melody breezed into the atrium lobby of the Terra Turris. It looked more like a five-star luxury hotel on the banks of the Amazon, except with far higher security. The soothing sound of cascading water washed over her. She half-expected to spot Indiana Jones behind the reception desk, cracking his whip. Or perhaps a dazzling parrot would swoop down from one of the rainforest trees and greet her in so-so English. Instead, it was the immaculate woman in her early forties who did the talking.

'Ah, Mrs Dalloway. Laura Finney, so glad to meet you.'

As they shook hands, Laura subtly took in Melody's uniform. A discreet £4000 outfit care of Stella McCartney, radiating class and money. The £2000 Bottega Veneta large intrecciato leather shoulder bag. The high priced, very high-heeled Jimmy Choo's. And the Ermenegildo Zegna honey-horn, couture sunglasses. They all completed the perfect power ensemble. Melody had passed the uniform test with something to spare.

'Hi, Laura. Oh my golly gosh, this is all so, so super-impressive.' Melody swept her hands and swished her body around as if she was taking in the Grand Canyon. Her shoulder length blonde wig swished with her.

'Isn't it just. And the security is to die for. Oh, that didn't sound right. Ha-ha. What I mean to say is the exclusive *residente* of Terra Turris value their privacy and their safety, both of which are covered by the annual service fee of one hundred thousand pounds per annum. I like to mention that up front, because frankly, my firm has vast experience handling this level of sales, and I've found it – self selects those for whom this service is an investment rather than a fee.'

Melody hadn't expected this hard sell on security, and felt physically sick. If only. Security. They had *the best* security in Limehouse. She fought back the aching anguish of never-ending guilt.

'That sounds perfectly reasonable, and I really do value that level of security.'

'Super excellent. Then shall we view l'appartment?'

Laura had her own electronic key for the Terra Turris viewings. Even so, she had arranged a visitor's key card for Mrs Dalloway. Once they were rising rapidly in the lift, Laura explained the super-duper security system to Melody.

'This is your visitor key card. You need that to access the lift. It's all very clever. And a bit creepy actually. The lift knows who boards it, and will not work if there's a stranger, even if they swipe a key card. Don't worry though. Once a property owner's facial recognition is in the system, they and their family don't need to do that. And you're already in the system now. Temporarily, of course, till you buy!'

'Great. Good to know, Laura.'

Not really. Not that Melody had any intention of buying the property she was viewing.

'What do you think? Super isn't it, Mrs Dalloway.'

'Oh please, call me Virginia.'

'Thanks, I will. Did I mention the owner was quite a famous author?'

'Beth Conway. You did. Once or twice.'

'She's virtually moved out, and I know there is interest from other parties. Time may be of the essence.'

Melody gave the impression she was mulling it hard.

'I understand, Laura. But I have a request. It may sound a little – eccentric.'

'Okay.'

'I'm a very spiritual person who picks up on the energies of places and people. It's very important to me, and—'

'Ah, like a feng shui type of thing.'

'Exactly. Something like that. But I do need to be alone to focus my chi, and access the vibrations.'

'The vibrations? Absolutely no problem at all. I quite understand.'

'You're sure, Laura? Don't want to put you out at all.'

Laura glanced at her watch.

'Absolutely, Virginia. I'll just pop back into the office, I have a couple of urgent phone calls I need to attend to anyway, and I'm just around the corner. An hour be okay to do your feng thingy?'

'Perfect.'

Melody gazed out of the window for a good five minutes before she made her first move. The grey dullness of the sky could not hide the sensational view of London stretching to the horizon. All those lives. She poked her head out of the door to apartment 4312. *Shit.* A young woman, about her age (dark black hair, tanned complexion, cleaning staff uniform) was busy hoovering the corridor carpet with an industrial sized machine.

Sod this. Melody owned the uniform. She owned the space. She had a right to be there, no fucking around. Melody strode confidently towards the lift. She smiled at the woman as she passed her. The smell of cigarette smoke radiated from her uniform.

'Good afternoon.'

The woman smiled back. She had a pleasant Spanish inflected accent:

'Good afternoon, Miss.'

Melody held her visitor key card over the lift scanner. It clicked to green instantly. She pushed the button for the twenty-fifth floor. The lift descended with no stops. Melody knew the complex was overwhelmed with cameras. The black-tinted Perspex dome, above her in the lift, probably had four angles to display. It all added up to there being far too many for each to be monitored continuously by human beings 24/7.

Use opponent's strength against him, sveetheart.

The trick in this instance, as Saul had told her, is normality. Belonging. Even so, she did take the precaution of changing her hair as well as her name. The shoulder length blonde wig did the trick.

Melody exited the lift and strode confidently to Bentley's door. Except for the number 2515, it looked identical to the one she had just departed. She resisted the temptation to *look around*, the way characters seem to do in movies while they try not to look suspicious.

She removed the surgeon's gloves from her shoulder bag and slipped them on. Next she lifted out the small black box electronic gizmo supplied by Saul. After he dragged out of her the likely scenario she was *researching*, the device arrived by motorbike messenger a day later. Saul also supplied printed instructions. If he had any other opinions about Melody's purpose, he kept them to himself. What a handy mensch.

On one side of the small electronic lock there was a 10-digit grey display window, and three small light diodes. The other side featured a one-inch protrusion about the width and depth of a credit card, or an electronic key.

Melody palmed the device, and inserted the key extrusion into the electronic key slot housed in the flat metal handle plate on the door. To prying eyes, it looked as if she had inserted the electronic key as usual. In fast succession, the gizmo's red diode lit, then the yellow, and finally the green. The lock to Bentley's flat clicked to disengage.

Melody was in.

Bentley was at work. She had followed him first thing and watched as he entered the Leadenhall Building. That was it for the day. He would not be returning home, based on past actions.

SILENCE—

Melody stood inside the hallway, heart pounding out of her chest. Part of Laura's sales spiel was the exceptional soundproofing at the Terra Turris. All she could hear was herself.

She took some deep breaths to calm down. Suitably calmed, gripping her trusty knife, Melody stealthily padded through all the rooms.

The bedroom threw her slightly. On the wall, above the bed, hung a life-sized metal framed photograph of the man himself. Bentley stood proudly on a podium, holding a gleaming gold scimitar. Behind him was a banner with the legend Scimitar Trader Of The Year 2017.

Well, there's absolutely nothing at all creepy about that, Melody. Not in the slightest.

She looked up to see the ceiling mirror above the bed.

Wasting no time, she investigated the two bedrooms, kitchen, bathroom, living room, dining room and study. Melody went through every drawer, wardrobe, and cupboard.

Nothing.

The apartment was expensively decorated in a minimalist style. It was cold, detached, and lacking any family touches. It also lacked any proof Thomas Bentley was any of the things Aaron swore he was. No locks of female hair. Assorted female underwear. Dead bodies.

Don't be so bloody daft, love. What sort of proof is likely to be lying around? He may be a monster, but he's not a moron.

Deflated, she slumped into the black leather sofa in the living room. This was the most comfortable item in the whole apartment. Even the bed had felt hard and uninviting as she lay looking up at herself.

She mulled it over in her fine mind. To her left, the ceiling to floor window didn't offer quite as grand a view of the London panorama as the forty-third floor. A couple of other tallish buildings partially obstructed that view.

She stared at the 100-inch TV bolted to the wall, imagining Bentley watching his favourite movies. And who doesn't like to relive the old classic or two every once in a while? The Godfather. Back To The Future. Star Wars. *My Favourite Sex Assault.*

Melody bounced off the sofa with renewed vigour. She checked the stopwatch on her phone. It was forty-six minutes since Laura left her alone. She couldn't risk staying any more than five minutes.

It hit her.

The ability to relive his greatest triumphs over and over again would fuel Bentley's omnipotence. That would have to be close to hand; ready to satiate himself, life-sized on the big screen in the privacy of his own home.

She checked the chrome and glass-shelved stand below the TV. A standard SkyQ box was on the top shelf. The middle shelf housed a Blu-ray player. On the bottom sat a smaller media player. She doubted Bentley would burn stuff onto a DVD or Blu-ray disc. There was too much of a risk that would fall into the wrong hands, from his perspective. Likewise with the media player. She immediately discounted anything on its hard drive for playback. The Cloud? Laptop? No. Too easy to fall into the wrong hands.

It had to be something easy to secrete away: memory cards, flash drives, or multiples of either. The twin vertical shelves housed his collection of Blu-ray movies. Again unlikely to be a hiding spot. Hide a memory card in one of the cases, and that's the very one opened by a friend.

Hey Tom, what's this in your Heat Blu-ray box. Bit a porn, let's have a look then. I'll just pop it into my iPhone.

She checked her phone. Three more minutes and she was out of here at speed, or else.

Think, Melody, think. Where? Where would he – the frame of the photo of himself.

She stood on the bed to remove the heavy frame from the wall. Laying it flat on bed, she lifted it up to check the back. Nothing there. Ran her fingers across the inch-deep bottom of the frame. Nothing. She did the same for both sides. Smooth and completely innocuous.

It's always the last place you look. Car keys. Remote. Evidence.

Bingo.

Melody ran her fingers across the top and felt the difference instantly. Instead of one smooth continuous surface, it had two faint lines running end to end. She pushed hard along the surface. The slat edged out to reveal a hidden compartment within the frame. Pushing all four feet of the slat out left revealed a row of plastic slots inside the tiny space. In each slot were memory cards.

She was stunned into passivity. Two minutes. She came back to life, picking out one of the cards at random. Hurrying back to the living room, she fished out the iPad from her bag. No time to watch now. She clicked the card into the card slot, and copied the entire contents straight to the iPad.

One minute. Melody stood back from the bed, checking the frame was perfectly aligned. Satisfied, she smoothed out the pillows and duvet.

'Hello, Virginia. Here I am. I'm back.'

Melody had clicked shut the door to 4312 about thirty seconds before her new best friend Laura opened it. Apart from a slight flush, Melody didn't have a fake hair out of place.

Laura was convinced she had closed the sale.

'Did the vibrations tell you anything?'

'Actually, Laura, you know what? They did. I think they told me all I need to know.'

CHAPTER

13

Memento Mori was housed in a substantial edifice built during the Great War for the Empire Bank of Rhodesia. It was one of the City's most stalwart, rock solid institutions. Times and tastes change. Today, the original marble and mahogany fittings echoed from noon till two a.m. to a different kind of money making.

Melody stood at the balcony rail, looking down at the new money relaxing after a hard day's work making more money. If the City was a church to worship manna, then this was its confessional: lubricated with the blood of Cristal, and every other bottle of alcohol under the sun. Had she been a Catholic, Melody too might have had something to confess after tonight.

She had seen the video. She could never unsee it. All she could do was make sure Bentley was never seen again. Forever and ever, Amen. She toyed with the morality of it all, while scanning below to see where Bentley and his hangers-on had positioned themselves. Had her coming actions moved from being a means to an end, to being an end in themselves. Had she given herself the self-justification of the greater good for her own sanctioned killing? A casus belli. Something that was still called murder in her part of the world. A sanction the state no longer deemed civilized for itself to perform on behalf of the baying vox populi.

Drugging a helpless woman into unconsciousness before violating her very being, her essence as a human, grotesquely, mercilessly; and filming it for your later satisfaction. If that irredeemable evil did not remove that violator's right to exist, to prevent the infection polluting the whole body, then nothing did.

Melody was not squeamish about blood and death. She was an MD, and that's the reality of the profession. In attempting to save life as part of one's oath, you can easily take life with your actions.

First, do no harm.

There was no harm in killing the infection that was killing the host organism. She could justify that greater good even if the powers-that-be no longer did. There was no stopping Bentley. The beating of a lifetime at Ringland had not stopped him. And what she had witnessed on the tape only demonstrated how careful he was.

It was logical that only death could stop him. That must be his punishment. Melody saw that clearly now. She only struggled with the method, and not the deed. At this moment, she was performing a necessary act of euthanasia for the general welfare of the community. As one might put down a rabid dog before it infected and eventually killed others in the greater society. Yet, why cause the beast more pain than necessary? And yes, okay, that was not her stance with the three monsters who slaughtered her daughter.

She had mused over and over about this one thing

during the past few months. All the while, the notion marinated within her. When it came to it, what would she do? Did she have it in her to coldly slit Bentley's throat? She knew how. Medical training supplemented by Saul training. If she could position herself with his compliance, all trusting, then the action would be over fast, and fairly painlessly. Her scalpel-sharp knife would see to that. And she was motivated fully. But Bentley was over six feet, and weighed around fifteen stone. A chubby weight, but it's impossible to deny biology and physiology. Most men are stronger and considerably more aggressive than most women. Even men not really in shape. Even against women who are trained, and know how to fight way down and dirty.

Melody did not want to engage Bentley as an obvious adversary at close quarters if she didn't have to. She was Krav Maga. She was Saul Levin. She would incapacitate him first with his own very drug of choice. Then quietly dispatch the dangerous, but docile threat. This monster would not feel the pain that perhaps he should. The agony which her daughter's killers will feel would be spared from him.

She scanned the willing flesh trading floor again. Where was he now she was dressed-up to kill. The blonde wig swished nicely. The Goth makeup was replaced with a more traditional allure. The outfit more Armani city-chic than the Stella McCartney of the day before. It still oozed class and money. But more power-practical. She kept the high Jimmy Choo's though.

Fuck. Has he gone already? Better get down th—

Melody span around and there was Bentley – large as life – right in front of her.

CHAPTER

14

Melody clamped her hand over her mouth as the downward draught of the helicopter's whirling blades churned up a mini sandstorm.

The army Chinook had deposited her in the heavily fortified compound of the British base in Basra, Iraq. That transport mission done, the pilot was up and back in the air before she had reached the small greeting party. A man in desert fatigues stepped forward with his hand extended.

'Doctor Fox? Major Bell.'

The major strong-armed Melody's hand. He was in his mid-thirties, tanned and anxious to get out of the baking 110-degree sun.

'Hello, Major Bell.'

This was a war zone. The Americans and the British were fighting a fierce battle to drive the Mahdi Army militia out of Basra. Yes, drive them out of their own land. She had strong opinions about us being the invaders in this asymmetrical war. Suicide bombers were everywhere. No one really knew who to trust. Behind the major, his personal security detail of two troopers constantly scanned around looking for trouble coming their way. While she was no expert on military arms, she had picked up enough knowledge in the past few months to know that their rifles were not standard issue SL-40s. These highly trained and kill-conditioned soldiers would have no problem killing the enemy. Unlike the four cases she was here to examine on the ground.

This had become very real for her. *A war zone? An actual fucking war zone.* People trying to kill you. While your precious three-year old daughter is oblivious, back in England with her grandparents for a week. It was all rather an adventure when Dennis Libby (her superior at the Ministry of Defence) asked if Melody would care to step in. He had some prior engagements to fulfil with their overall boss: Deputy Under-Secretary Menzies Asterion.

It was a big responsibility in her first year as a fully qualified psychiatrist, and this could be interesting. Now she was missing her cheeky, adorable little scamp Charity. Every day with her daughter was an exciting adventure in rediscovery of beauty in the world.

What the hell are you doing here, Melody? Don't even support this bloody illegal war. Bloody lies.

'This is Captain Hassan of the Iraqi National Guard. My liaison.'

Captain Hassan beamed before bowing slightly. 'As-salamu alaykum Doctor Fox. Welcome to my troubled country.'

She wanted to shalom him back. But maybe not such a good idea. 'Good to meet you, Captain Hassan. Glad to be here.'

The major gently gripped her elbow and steered her in the direction of billets. 'Let's get you settled into quarters first.'

As a lone female civilian, she was allocated her own small room with an en suite shower and toilet. Something of a luxury here. Melody didn't realize that until she saw how most of the other denizens lived in Camp Bold Strike. Camp Bog Trot to the squaddies.

Suitably showered, and on military time, she was soon sitting in Major Bell's office with the four case files in her hands.

'As you can see, Doctor Fox, we are waiting on your input before deciding on whether to proceed to full courts martial in all cases. Though if it were entirely up to me, well – esprit de corps and general morale are at stake here. We can't have our young chaps thinking they can't depend on their pal next to them to fire his fucking weapon at the enemy. Pardonez my French. It's turning into an issue.'

Melody didn't need any training to get where the major was coming from: Angryville. Not an official psychiatric term. On the Hercules transport from Brize Norton to Ramstein and then on to Baghdad, she read the files detailing the actions of the three privates and one corporal.

As a medical student, she developed an avid interest in how people can be conditioned to do things that seem to go against their natural inclinations. The interest first planted after seeing a movie about Patty Hearst. The heiress to the Hearst media fortune was kidnapped by equally middle-class, so-called revolutionaries. Five weeks later she was brainwashed into becoming a gun toting bank robber and all-round terrorist. From party girl student to ready-to-kill terrorist: how was this even remotely possible? That was fascinating to Melody on many levels. Her future path in medicine had become clearer.

From there she developed an interest in how people could be manipulated and made to do things. One of those things being to kill fellow human beings. The words of a guest lecture from medical school had stuck with her over the years. Former US marine Lt. Colonel Dave Mann quoted extensively from *Killing Machine: The Psychological Cost of Teaching To Kill in War* – his well regarded treatise.

'Contrary to misconceptions, at first most normal people demonstrate a strong resistance to killing. Even in combat. Even if their own lives and the lives of their comrades depend upon them firing a weapon. But virtually anyone can be conditioned to kill, certainly from a distance, with high powered weaponry. Military training is designed to remove constraints, give permissions, and make the act of killing automatic. It manufactures consent to murder.

'Of course, sociopaths and psychopaths do not have that normal constraint. Again, contrary to popular myth, the military do not want to recruit psychopaths. Nor do we want to transform citizens into psychopaths with no empathy for anyone, including their fighting comrades. It's a fine line. And it's one reason why normal men develop post traumatic stress disorder after combat. Killing a fellow human is intrinsically a traumatic event.'

PTSD was another area of Melody's expertise. She had to determine whether any of the four men were suffering from its effects from past deployments.

'I understand, Major Bell. You seem a bit angry.'

Bell stared at Melody for a few seconds, before laughing out loud. 'Very good, Doctor Fox. But you're not here to head-shrink me. Not today anyway. As far as I know. Now, you have complete licence to talk to Privates Morris, Smith, Polinski, and Corp—

KA-BOOOOOOOOOOOM—

The shockwave ripped through the office, slamming them both to the floor. As she fell, Melody gashed the side of her head on a metal filing cabinet. The blood oozed while her ears rang. She was too shocked to move, until she felt the major grab her arm, pulling her up from the debris strewn floor.

'Truck bomb. Outside the gate. My guess. Can you walk.'

Melody looked blankly as him. Her brain frozen into apathy.

He shook her a couple of times before slapping her cheek, hard. 'Doctor Fox. Doctor Fox. You need to move now.'

The sounds suddenly took form and comprehensible shape in her head; automatic gunfire over the screams and the shouts. That was why Bell drew his service weapon as he was pulling her to her feet.

The preternaturally calm major flipped over his desk, leaving the thick top surface facing the door. He gripped Melody by her shoulders. 'Listen to me. When I leave the office, you are to pull that filing cabinet across the door, then secure yourself behind the desk. Okay? You are to let no one in, until either I or another British officer knocks on that door and makes our presence known by name and rank. Do you understand Doctor Fox? Nod if you understand.'

She was nodding vigorously when the door opened. The major levelled his weapon at the entrance. He lowered it as quickly.

'Captain Hassan, thank the Lord you're okay man. Look, can you stay here, guard Doctor Fox while I assess our ground status and cas—'

BANG—BANG—BANG—

Hassan rapid fired his gun at Bell. Two shots hit the major dead centre in his Osprey body armour. The third caught him at the top of his shoulder, shattering the bone. The kinetic energy threw Bell backwards into Melody, the momentum then crashing them both to the ground again. Bell was pretty much lying across her on his back. She could see past him, up at Hassan as he stepped into the room, moving in closer for the kill. There was no clichéd look of crazed fanaticism in demented bulging eyes. Just the thousand yard stare of a man on his mission-path. Clearly he had no problems pulling the trigger.

Nothing flashed before Melody's eyes as Hassan raised his gun towards the major's head for the coup de grâce. She closed her eyes, seeing her little girl's face for the last time. Her smile. Her laugh. Her tears.

But it was Hassan's head which exploded, showering her and Major Bell with blood, bone and grey matter as she heard at least fifteen shots loaded in three automatic bursts into Hassan from behind.

She opened her eyes to see one of the major's security detail, standing combat stance over Hassan's ripped-open body. That extra-lethal looking machine gun still pointed at what was left of Hassan's head, while she almost vomited parts of the former ally which had sprayed into her mouth.

It was the corporal who had greeted her not long before. 'All clear, sir. Hassan's done. Let me help you up, miss.'

Melody's first tastes and smells of death in extremis, seared into her brain until something far worse came along to replace them. She never did examine the facts behind why these four highly trained young men had been unable to pull the trigger in combat.

Melody was choppered out of Camp Bog Trot the next day. Shaken, afraid, and suddenly very aware of her own vulnerability, and the vulnerability of her family. It was a fear that grew as her daughter grew. It never really went away over the years. She kept it well hidden and locked up. She was a psychiatrist after all.

But it was one reason why she had wanted her

Limehouse home to be so well protected from another *Hassan* opening the door. Murder in mind.

Lot of good it did her.

CHAPTER

15

Fuck. Has he gone already? Better get down th—

Melody turned around and there was Bentley. Large as a lifeboat, right in front of her, two glasses of champagne in hand, smiling affably.

She forced a smile back while scrutinizing him as one might examine a repulsive bug under a microscope.

'Hello there. I seem to have a spare glass of a rather nice vintage Krug 1993. Well, it should be rather nice at the bloody price. Care to join me?'

Melody's mind went into overdrive. The very bloke she was here to pick up, control and humanely dispatch had apparently sought her out. Why? One possible reason was obvious having seen the videoed evidence of two of Bentley's anonymous victims. Both had identical shoulder length straight blonde hair, and were of a similar build, age, height and facial type as Melody. She had assumed that would give her the advantage in controlling the inevitable encounter. But – Bentley had her on the defensive right away.

The glass of champagne being pushed in her face was uninviting. Melody had already reasoned that Bentley probably drugged his victims with *Flunitrazepam.* Also known as *Rohypnol.* Also known as a *roofie.* Also known as the date rape drug of choice for sociopaths worldwide.

As part of the Benzodiazepines family, Flunitrazepam is a powerful sedative. It gradually incapacitates, usually taking full effect between twenty-five to forty minutes after ingestion. It was this indeterminate time frame that made Melody also reason he would administer it in a drink away from primary contact with his victim.

Theory is one thing, until it's kicked in the teeth by reality. What if she was wrong? She had been known to be wrong. Those bubbles fizzing to the top of the glass might also fizzle through her brain, knocking down her synapses to slowly drag her under.

'Sorry, I said care to join me?'

'Don't mind if I do.'

Melody stepped forward and went to take the flute glass from Bentley as she half-stumbled on her high-heeled Jimmy Choo's. The glass slipped through her fingers and shattered onto the marble floor.

'Oh bugger. I am so, so sorry. God, I am so clumsy. Everyone says so.'

If Bentley was annoyed at a plan thwarted, his expression and reaction didn't reveal it. 'Forget it. Plenty more where that came from. Tom Bentley by the way. Have we met? You look familiar.'

He stuck out his hand. Melody grabbed it, exuding confidence. His grip was restrained, but firm and very clammy.

'Virginia Dalloway. Don't think we've met.'

He paused the required nanosecond before continuing:

'Who's afraid of Virginia Dalloway?'

She'd chosen the fake name as an insider joke to herself. Not expecting someone like Bentley to get it.

'Oh, well spotted. A well read man.'

'I try.'

'That's my mother's doing, I'm afraid. Big Virginia Woolf fan. Sometimes think that was the real reason she married my dad. To actually be Mrs Dalloway.'

Melody was impressed at how easy the spiel was flowing from her. It was all extemporaneous as she hadn't thought to back-story herself with a full character biography. She hadn't even thought she was playing a character tonight. That was a mistake she couldn't afford to make again.

'That's almost too perfect to be true.'

'I know. You can't make that stuff up.'

Bentley led Melody down the stairs, back to his small group standing at the long bar that gently curved off into the distance. It was a packed Friday night. He made the perfunctory intros to the group of eager young thrusters from his firm. Nobody was interested as they wound down after a huge week's trading. Once the nodded *hi, hi, hello, evening, g'day, hey,* and *yo* were completed they went back to themselves, ignoring her.

Bentley picked up a bottle of champagne from the bar and poured out a glass. He was amused. 'How about that drink? I'm going to place the glass on the bar, and you can pick it up yourself?'

That was better. And safer. Melody picked up the glass. Just the one drink would be fine.

'Lehayim.'

She regretted saying that as it left her mouth. That was stupid. Not dangerous, just careless. Pegged her immediately. Bentley didn't seem to pick up on her minor cultural slip.

'Cheers. So what do you do, Virginia Dalloway?'

Bentley spent the rest of the evening keeping her regularly lubricated. Or so he thought. She would pretend to sip until she could secretly dispose of the contents. It was the usual small talk people indulged in when they're out for the night, had a few and are trying to impress. Movies. Music. Sports. Some politics, but that can be dangerous if you vehemently disagree.

It was a surreal out-of-body experience. She was actually doing this. No doubt. She knew what came next, by her hand. In for a penny in for a pound of flesh. He blithely continued his own performance, oblivious as to how their roles had been reversed. The predator was now the prey. How many times had he stood in this very bar. The unsuspecting woman he targeted would be chatting away merrily, while he was looking right through her, smiling, charming, well-practised in his plotting. The thought revolted Melody as they swapped favourite movie scenes.

The best lies are those based on a patina of truth. On the fly Melody riffed on something she knew about: Carringtons. She told him she was a literary agent. It had a pleasing symmetry with the Mrs Dalloway shtick. He was a practised listener careful to keep the focus on her. He wasn't socially awkward around attractive women.

Eventually the members of his young crew drifted away as the evening raced on to its climax. Drunk or hooked up, or both. Melody was certainly pretending she'd had a few to drink. Not drunk. Just normal for a bar. She assumed Bentley was acting the same. It was about eleven when he made the move she was hoping for.

'So, Virginia. Look, first let me assure you my in tentions are honourable.'

'Oh, they are, are they?'

She deliberately placed a hand on his chest in a faux

intimate gesture. One thing she had learned was that the man was sort of charming. A little smarmy. But he had no trouble attracting women. Melody knew his pathology wasn't about that. While rape obviously led to a sexual climax for the rapist, it was an exercise in merciless power that these men craved. A misogynistic desire to subjugate, humiliate and hurt women. For whatever perverted justification they gave themselves, ultimately they wanted to destroy.

'If it's dishonourable to be interested in an attractive intelligent woman, guilty as charged, ma'am.'

'Oh. You are smooth, mister.'

'I am, am I not? But I'm also an old fashioned kinda chap. I was simply going to say if you want to come back to my place for a coffee or whatnot, I will not let you take advantage of me on a pre-first date, date. That means coffee is all you're getting. That and a cab ride home. Deal?'

This was it. Melody felt her throat close as a slight buzzing started in her ears. No, he hadn't roofied her. She knew a panic attack when she felt one. It passed.

'Deal.'

They exited the bar and walked along St. Mary's Axe chatting amiably. It looked ever so normal for a Friday night in London. But bad things happen to normal people doing normal things, all the time. She knew that intimately.

She placed her hand inside her canvas satchel. The *kit* was lying at the bottom ready for deployment. Her knife was safely sheathed, just in case. She also had a can of NYPD pepper spray, and an Israel military grade taser. As Saul had told her more than once—

Vy be unprepared, Princess? In for a penny good, in for massive overkill better.

As they reached the junction with Leadenhall Street, Bentley hailed a passing black cab. Melody climbed in as he gave the destination to the cabbie.

They headed down Leadenhall Street towards Canary Wharf. Terra Turris was about a mile away. About five minutes at this time of night. The whole thing was about to get very real.

They sat next to each other on the back bench seat of the taxi. They were not close. That was until the taxi suddenly lurched right as the cabbie executed a quick U-turn. The unexpected movement slid Melody across the seat into him. As she adjusted herself, they were heading back west along Leadenhall Street, away from Canary Wharf. She was thrown in more ways than one.

'Gosh, sorry about that—'

Bentley smirked out loud. 'No problem. Kind of liked it.'

'Where are we going then?'

'I did say my place. Remember? It's in Islington. Why? Where did you think it was?'

'Oh, I don't know. Nowhere really. Just assumed you lived around here in the City. Didn't you say that, in the bar?'

For crying out loud, Melody, shut the fuck up already. You're going to make him suspicious.

'No. I don't think I did. I mean, why would I?'

She took her own advice and shut the fuck up about it already. But it had rattled her. As always she had Saul buzzing in her ear—

Ver possible, you recce and choose fighting ground, and gets tactical advantage.

She had recced and chosen Bentley's place. Although technically *his ground*, it was ideal. At least, as ideal as she was going to get. The two main plusses being: he didn't know she was coming, and he assumed he was in control. And she knew the layout. No hidden surprises waiting. She had even planned how she would casually approach him from behind. hypodermic prepped for immediate incapacitation. He would be relaxed on the sofa drink in hand, while she supposedly freshened up in the bathroom. Now all that perp prep went up in smoke.

The cab pulled away from the three-storey Victorian terraced house on Rathbone Street, Islington. Bentley led her up the small set of steps to the post box red front door.

'My modest little gaff.'

'Very nice.'

While Bentley fished out a keyring from his briefcase and opened the door, Melody glanced around. The lighting threw off a warm friendly glow. Further up the street, a woman was bending down to scoop up the steaming deposit her golden retriever had dropped. Although quiet, the unending restless hum of London permeated. Distant beeping of car horns—

'Virginia. You coming in, or what?'

Melody snapped to. The front door was open and Bentley stood in his hallway. It was already lit up to reveal what looked like original Victorian tiling on the floor, stretching in about thirty feet. Now on autopilot Melody stepped into Bentley's *modest little gaff.* She closed the door behind her. There was no movie clanging shut of ominous finality. Merely a quiet clunk.

'Follow me.'

CLICK—CLICK—CLICK—

Melody's high heels echoed loudly on the floor tiles as Bentley led her down the hallway. Her right hand was already in her bag, gripping the handle of her blade. No way was she letting him manoeuvre behind her at any point. The autopilot had switched off. Melody noticed and heard something she hadn't clocked immediately. The hallway was dimly lit by three lamps, proportionately spaced along a wall covered in chintzy flower patterned wallpaper. The lamps looked to be copies of a traditional Victorian design. Naturally she had assumed they were electric lights. But she could hear the low hiss emanating from each. They were actual working gas lamps from the period. He ushered her through into—

'This is the living room.'

The only light available came from the hallway's gaslight fittings, until Bentley struck a match and turned the knob on one of the wall lights. The room was illuminated by a yellowy subdued glow. Bentley's ominous shadow was thrown onto the wall opposite.

'What d'you think?'

She couldn't say what she really thought. The room looked as if it had been time-transported from a novel by Dickens. It was the total opposite of his antiseptic Terra Turris apartment. Melody wasn't sure what to think about Bentley and his personality type now. She was unnerved though. Doubt was starting to rise in her, like bile from a bad kebab.

'It's – uh, it's different.'

'I know. It's not a replica. The house has been lovingly restored as it was circa eighteen sixty-nine. Just about everything is authentic to the era.'

Melody was slowly regaining her composure and her wits, if not her nerve. 'I'm impressed. And here I had you pegged as this ruthless kill or be killed hedge fund trader, when you're actually a Victoriana fanatic.'

Bentley was amused at his little deception. 'Okay, okay, confession time. Acquired the property as an investment about three years ago. The actual Victoriana guy that did it, he was this history professor at Oxford. Fanatic of course. Written a few books on the Victorian era. So he had this notion to do the restoration, but it cost him a fortune. Then his wife buggered off and left him. I had the cash. And it amused me. I actually like the Victorian times. People really knew their place. There was no ambiguity. You know what I mean?'

Oh, you mean like women? Yeah, I know what you mean.

Melody thought better of speaking that notion out loud.

'I suppose.'

Bentley smiled. 'Right, how about that coffee I promised? Not machine made of course. Hand ground coffee beans, Kenyan, with a real Victorian wall grinder, then on the gas stove in the Mokka. That's from Fortnum & Mason, I'm afraid.'

'Yeah, sounds good.'

Bentley walked over to the ornate, bulbous legged polished mahogany sideboard. The contraption resting on top had a *His Masters Voice* horn protruding out on one side; a hand crank on the other. He began to mess around with the device.

'Maybe a little period music. This is an actual Edison phonograph. The iPod of its day. The iPhono, if you will. Ha-ha. Just made that up.'

'iPhono. Very good. You're very witty.'

He had his back to her. Exposed. This was it. Melody's right hand went in her bag and gripped the knife handle. She had long thought she would be all steely-eyed resolve. Her fantasy. A relentless remorseless killing machine. But that was when she dreamed of personal vengeance against the guilty monsters. The cold reality was her hand starting to twitch slightly. As he started to crank the phonograph up to speed to play, Melody took a few steps forward to his exposed back. Her on the fly plan was to kick out his left calf, force him to his knees, while holding the knife blade point against his carotid artery, ready to plunge it straight in if he didn't comply. None of this inefficient attempting to slit his throat from ear to ear malarkey. Exactly as Saul had drilled her time after time, until she was able to subdue even him, in one smooth practised move.

Except her damn hand was now twitching even more. The more she tried to stop it, the worse it was getting. This was impossible. She had to let go of the knife before complete panic gripped her. The tinny Victorian music started up.

Bentley turned to face her. 'That's better. Well, better is relative of course. At the time, the idea of Puccini in your own living room was a sensation. One more triumph in the new enlightenment. They had no idea at how primitive they really were, right?'

Melody had removed her right hand from her bag. She gripped it with her left as she was convinced he would see it trembling away, even in this dim gaslight. Say something.

'Except in one hundred and fifty years our descendants will be able to see us in high definition. Millions of colours. Everything we ever did will be recorded, and look like it was made that very day. The good. The bad. The totally wicked. Maybe they'll also judge us as – lacking?'

Careful, Melody.

Bentley chuckled at the thought. 'Good point. And on that bombshell I'll be in the kitchen, which is at end of the hallway in case you wondered. Why don't you relax here while I brew up.'

Melody stood rooted in the middle of the room as she heard him clop his way down the hallway. She was anything but relaxed as the long dead soprano began her aria, from the bottom of a well, apparently.

The slight fluctuations in the flow of gas to the lights made the shadows cast on the walls flicker. None of us can escape our most basic primal fears which transform even the most prosaic effect into a creepy and hair-standing response. Melody's unease was growing exponentially. Whatever she was going to do, the time was now. Bentley was probably preparing to drug her coffee. As the fat lady sang on, Melody clearly heard the grinding sound of coffee beans vibrating thought the walls. That would keep him occupied for another minute.

She looked around at the room forensically for the first time. It was chock-full of authentic-looking period furniture, complemented by lots of bric-a-brac in the shape of vases, bowls, paintings, posed photographs, and figurines. Burgundy and mahogany were the dominant themes.

What's that I wonder?

One odd affectation. The deep-burgundy coloured velvet curtain. It was randomly hanging from a brass curtain rail in the far corner of the room's rear wall. She could still hear noises from the direction of the kitchen as she pulled back the curtain to reveal a door. She glanced behind to ensure Bentley hadn't ghosted back, coffee in hand.

The white-painted panel door had a Victorian cast iron handle assembly, with a key slot, although no key was in place. Melody turned the handle, and pulled on it.

CREAK—

Cringing as the door opened towards her, she looked around again. All clear. She pulled the door half open, then looked in. The air was cold, and it was pitch black. The inside of the door was covered from top to bottom with a 12-inch deep foam like material.

That's soundproofing, Melody, love.

She was fighting every last nerve telling her to go. Get out. Elvis the building. Right now.

Vengeance. It was a nice moral righteous fantasy while it lasted. Who did she think she was kidding? She didn't have it in her. The last five minutes had proved that. She was a trained healer who also knew how to kill. But she would never be a killer, no matter how much training Saul gave her. Turns out she was like those four squaddies at Camp Bold Strike. They all discovered they could not pull the trigger and kill another human being, even in hot-blood. Had their hands started shaking too?

Veak. Saul had her pegged the first time they met at Aunt Sharon's Shabbat. Maybe Aaron would understand her chickening out and still have the good grace to take care of her scumbags for her. Being family and all.

'You found my secret basement.'

She turned fast, but he was faster. His hand gripped her shoulder hard, then shoved her violently.

Melody tumbled backwards and helpless into the void.

CHAPTER

16

Tom Bentley had been demented all day. How exactly was he going to track down the young blonde woman who had spent fifty leisurely minutes in his apartment the day before. Even worse, she had discovered and taken something precious that could put him in the shitter for good. This was even more of a personal disaster than his beating at Ringland. That worked out alright in the end. Financially, at least. Today had not worked out, at all.

He had been so distracted he could barely breathe, let alone make strategic decisions that could cost his firm millions if he was wrong. Now there she was, a few feet away in *Memento Mori*, bold as fucking brass. He watched her walk up the winding staircase to the balcony. Great. This was his chance to get the fuck out of here. He wasn't ready for this. He had to prepare. That was his first panic thought. Then it hit him. Not necessarily.

The day before had been a good day until the end. He had arrived home at Terra Turris around ten-thirty, having indulged in his favourite meal at the Prospect. For exercise's sake, he walked off the carbs at a brisk pace for the mile and a half back home. After uncorking a chilled Aussie Chardonnay, he switched on the TV to watch an old favourite – *Game of Thrones.* He'd like to show that nice blonde Mother of Dragons a thing or two. She'd love it. Cersei Lannister? She was a bit too in your face aggressive for him, chop off his dick Reek-like, no doubt.

Bentley adored Terra Turris because of the security it provided. Fuck the green atrium. And the cinema. And the parrots, which he'd never even seen and doubted existed. Security was the main selling point that convinced him to shell out six million pounds to acquire the 99-year lease for a two-bedroomed flat in London. But that was external security. Given his predilections, Bentley was also paranoid about internal security.

The day after moving in, experts installed a sophisticated hidden camera, motion-activated surveillance system. It was controlled from the smart TV, with digital storage on the ostensible media centre. If anything activated a room sensor, the system recorded the movement. In his fours years' residence, he had never switched on the TV to receive a large red alert flashing on the TV—

INTRUDER ALERT

After the disbelief deflated from him, Bentley slumped back on the sofa. He watched for fifty minutes as this vaguely familiar youngish woman went through everything in the apartment.

Who the fuck is this? How'd she get in? What in the fuck's name is she doing. FUCK????

Was she a previous conquest? She fit his bill alright with the blonde hair, classic face in the Audrey Hepburn mould, and perky tits. She deserved to be put in her place no doubt. Taught who was boss. He had a good memory for faces, and she didn't seem to ring his bell.

Near the end of the violation of his personal being, he began to relax as much as he could. Worry about the rest later. Of course she had found nothing. There was nothing to find. All his activities were conducted off base.

Then she sat back at the sofa staring at the TV screen for two minutes solid. And he just knew she knew. She had his number.

Now he knew something this mysterious blonde didn't know. He was back in control. Insider trading. He knew she had been at his place. That gave him a major advantage. She was hunting him for some reason yet to be determined. But that was reversed. He had to do something, so it might as well be now. Prep or not.

Perfect. She was scanning the crowd below from the balcony. Time to sell her short. He was about to tap her on the shoulder – and maybe scare the shit out her – when the woman turned around. Was that some sort of sixth sense? Who was she?

'Hello there. I seem to have a spare glass of a rather nice vintage Krug 1993. Well, it should be rather nice at the bloody price. Care to join me?'

It gave him a real kick to play with her all night. Half teasing. He could see her mind working overtime. He thought he had lost her on the steps to his Rathbone Street time capsule. He'd accidentally left the gaslights on in the hallway from the previous weekend. He doubted if he would walk into that creepy atmosphere; and he could look after himself. She was tall even without those ridiculous heels, albeit a fit fighting weight. No match for him. When he glanced back at her, she was looking up and down the street: second thoughts?

The idea that she was there to kill him had flitted across his mind at various points throughout the evening. Was she so smart that she engineered their meeting, and only let him think it was his idea. He soon convinced himself that this was preposterous. She put up a good front, but whoever she was, and whatever she wanted, he was back in control. One way or another, he'd get it out of her in Islington. And she was his type; fun time all the way around.

CHAPTER 17

'You found my secret basement.'

Melody had dropped about seven feet before slamming into the basement floor. It could have killed her, except she landed on a mattress. That broke most of her fall, and at least one of her ribs. Her Krav Maga training did the rest as Melody automatically turned her body into a ball as she tumbled. Unfortunately, her momentum also carried her crashing forward uncontrollably.

Melody's luck ran out as her forehead smashed into the sink cabinet she couldn't see to avoid in the dark. It wasn't exactly lights out, as her brain exploded in a cascade of flashing lights that strobed in and out. She was vaguely aware of being dragged across the floor. Her disembodied leg was floating above her head. That one she couldn't work out. Maybe later.

She was semiconscious, but her brain couldn't process that in the moment. She guessed the lightning-show state had lasted about an hour before she regained compos mentis to fully comprehend the shit she was in.

At least she was still fully dressed in her Armani jacket and skirt. It appeared the basement was the only part of the house that had not been transformed into Victoriana. There was light now, courtesy of the single dim light bulb. It was dangling from the wire in the middle of the ceiling, which was covered with the same deep soundproofing material as the door.

Her ankle was padlocked tightly in a sturdy metal bracelet, attached to a robust chain. The other end of the chain linked to a heavy ring and plate drilled into the wall.

The mattress was in the middle of the room. She was lucky to have been shoved so hard that her trajectory carried her to that spot. Had he intended to kill her with the fall? Hard to say. Though she had to face the fact he intended to kill her now. She hadn't really left him any other option had she? It was her fault.

The room was kitted out as a bedsit. The crazy type of bedsit with a heavy-duty metal ring drilled into the wall; all the better to secure chained victims. And no stairs. Just a seven-feet drop. From the door above.

The chain was long enough to allow her to reach the contents of her new home. Everything looked new. The walls were cladded in the same soundproofing material as the door above. Melody did a quick inventory, looking for weapons. Her expensive shoulder bag, with the actual weapons, was gone.

There was a tiny kitchen table. The small fridge and freezer compartment was empty. A sink with a hot and cold tap. A comfy chair. A couple of kitchen wall cupboards, but not quite bare. Inside she found a two-pound bag of Tate & Lyle sugar; a small box of individual Nescafe sachets; a full roll of clingfilm; a packet of Tetley tea bags; a box of Coffee-mate; a plastic mug and a plastic teaspoon.

The floor was carpeted with a dark brown affair that felt comfortable under her bare feet. That was it. No knives, metal pans, or anything she could use as a weapon. She didn't feel like having a coffee, but she couldn't even if she had a sudden craving. No kettle.

It was almost funny. Painfully funny. She sat down on the comfy chair and thought about her situation. A situation entirely of her own making. The oldest cliché in the book. If you seek revenge, first dig two graves. She could have left when she had the chance. Now she was the one chained up in a basement.

Vell vell, Princess gonna feel sorry for yourself, cry like big baby yentle? You veak afteralls? Vorld don't owe you nothings. Gotta use vots around if ya vonts to live. Anythink's veapon in right hands.

Melody clanked back up. *Good.* At least there was no camera spying on her. She examined the table legs. They were hard moulded plastic and immovable without a saw to hack them off. Same with the moulded chairs. Even then, they had no inherent tensile strength to be transferred in a blow to Bentley's head. Maybe she could have sharpened them into a spear, but not with the plastic spoon.

The comfy chair was nothing doing either. The label on the back credited Ikea. She went back to the wall cupboards to check the contents again before grabbing the clingfilm. It took thirty seconds to unspool the reel, and deposit the material on the table. *Great.* The fifteen-inch long hollow cylindrical tube was made of a very thick, robust cardboard, as she hoped.

Ripping about five feet of the cling film from the main body, she wrapped it tightly around one end of the tube until satisfied it was watertight and robust.

Opening the packet of sugar, she poured the gleaming white granules into the open end of the tube. Filled to the brim, she tapped the covered end on the table. She repeated the process until it held as much content as the tube would take. Finally she took another long piece of cling film and wrapped it as tightly as possible around the open end. She gripped it in her right hand, made a couple of practice swings.

Melody had a weapon.

The famous scene in Die Hard popped into her head. When Bruce Willis killed one of the terrorists and sent him down in the lift with the handwritten sign for Alan Rickman. *Ho. Ho. Ho.* She wasn't announcing her news to Bentley. He would find that out soon enough.

Improvising was over. She cleared up the detritus from the table, stuffing the remaining unspoiled clingfilm under the mattress along with the flattened box. Where to secrete the improvised cosh?

Melody had been lying on the mattress for a couple of hours when she heard the door. Alternating between beating herself up at her own stupid unpreparedness, and Saul mentally screaming in her ear, exalting her to—

Take fucker down hard, Princess.

Saul was winning the mind games. Unfortunately for her, the chain length only allowed her to manoeuvre around the bedsit essentials. It didn't stretch as far as the wall, above which was the door leading to the living room. Not that there were any stairs for her to lurk under, jump him, take the fucker down.

Stay positive, Melody. The moment he enters your kill zone, blitz him with everything you have. Eyes, throat, balls.

She had thought to pretend she was still out cold. Lure him in. But she needed eyes-on to know his precise position. That meant standing tall, not cowering on the ground, probably the supine position of his innumerable helpless victims.

Hands on hips, legs and feet planted firmly, Melody stood defiant and poised as the door opened. An aluminium ladder lowered clatteringly to the ground. Bentley carefully swung himself onto it and descended into his pit.

The circular kill zone was marked in her mind. As it was for Bentley: he was careful to keep himself outside of the chain's circumference. She tried to hold his furious gaze – oh yes, Melody could feel his rage radiating like the sun – but her eyes kept being drawn to the gun he held.

He waited for her to say something first. Beg? Bargain? Plead? That figured with his malignant narcissist personality. He expected others to constantly address his needs first, without him even having to ask. He probably wanted her to apologize to him for some imagined grievance.

Melody forced herself to stop glancing down at the gun. She held his gaze. It felt as if time was running slowly, but she won the second round.

'Who the fuck are you lady? Fucking wicked looking knife. And a taser, which is illegal by the way. As is pepper spray. What the fuck? And don't give me that Mrs Dalloway bullshit. You dare invade my privacy. Steal something precious of mine. Gonna want that back, then maybe, just maybe we can go our separate ways, huh?'

'This has to be the worst first date ever, mate. Come on, let me out—'

'Oh, oh, you think this is a fucking joke. Saw the video of you violating my privacy. Where's my memory cards?'

Shit. This guy was even sneakier than she first imagined. Add *underestimation* to her lengthening list of fuck-ups.

'Somewhere safe. So long as I'm safe. You know – and alive.'

Bentley stared at her. This was a complication. Or was it? He was in a business of deception with head-fakes and bluffs used all the time to make money.

'Oh, this is one of those dead man's switch scenarios. You're holding the switch, in this case, video footage of me, which could be misinterpreted by the authorities, and said footage will automatically be released to said authorities if anything happens to you. That about right?'

Yes that was about right. He nailed it. Melody tried not to let the bluff show.

'Exactly right. It goes live on the Cloud if I—'

Bentley levelled the gun at Melody. 'Nah, nah, nah, see I don't believe you had time to do all that since yesterday. Makes no sense.'

'You ever used a gun, Tommy—'

'Don't call me Tommy. I hate that. It's Tom or Thomas. But in your case, Mister Bentley, sir, will suffice. And yes, I learned all about guns in the States. Enough to shoot you in, say the leg, then the elbow till you tell—'

'Was that a while ago, because you left the safety on.'

'No. I did not.'

Bentley angrily turned the gun in his hand to check. Melody was already five seconds ahead of him.

After improvising the weapon, she stripped off her bra, blouse and jacket. Stretching her bra horizontally on the mattress, she placed her IED (improvised enforcement device) at ninety degrees on top of it. Melody carefully positioned herself so the IED lay along her spine, the bottom end resting on her tail bone. Still on her back, and with the IED positioned correctly, Melody pulled both ends of the bra around to her stomach. She looped the bra ends tightly together before knotting them securely in place. After replacing her blouse and sleeveless jacket she lay for the next two hours, uncomfortably action-ready.

Simultaneously seething, beating herself up, and listening to Saul's constant chiding about not feeling sorry for herself.

While Bentley was prattling on, she casually dropped her right hand from her hip and edged it behind her back. She grabbed the IED and pulled it free.

'No. I did not.'

As Bentley stopped pointing the damn gun at her, Melody catapulted herself violently towards him, screeching like a banshee on crack.

At the same time her right arm arced back almost behind her head like a javelin thrower. Reaching the apsis, her body's own physics took over. Her arm flew forward at speed.

As her arm arced down towards the horizontal, she released the IED from her grip. An aerodynamic, nearly two-pound object, spinning forward at thirty miles per hour, delivering a kinetic energy of—

THWACK—SPLAT—

Bentley's nose exploded a Jackson Pollock red as the gun dropped from his hand. The IED bouncing back off his face and back in her direction, not even dented. After his initial stagger backwards, Bentley stumbled forwards in confusion and shock, grabbing at his nose, which was pouring blood at a high rate of knots.

By now Melody's launch had propelled her to the edge of the chain's leg reach. Though stunned, Bentley was still a good three feet away. Melody being five feet ten, it was more than enough to relaunch herself. Tumbling forward she death-gripped Bentley by his hair, and ears. Melody was now in supreme fight or flight mode, honed by Saul's relentless barking of orders at her. Melody's body was being pumped by a massive release of acetylcholine from pre-ganglionic sympathetic nerves which flooded her with epinephrine and norepinephrine from her adrenal glands.

Massive jolts of stimulants exploding her into instant physical reactions, triggering increases in heart rate and breathing, constricting some blood vessels, except where the body needed the overflow for action: muscles, brain, lungs, and heart.

Melody's superhuman survival grip would never be released this side of hell. Gravity did the rest, dragging Bentley down. His face hit the carpet, which smashed his nose again. Melody was back on her feet as he tried to bellow in pain like a wounded animal. His brain struggling to comprehend the past few seconds. That got harder, as—

BOOM—BOOM—BOOM—

Standing over him, she swung down her right arm three times into the side of his head. They could have been knuckle-crunching velocity, except it wasn't her fist. After making her first IED, Melody unstitched one of the arms to her Armani jacket. She poured the remainder of the sugar and the Coffee-mate into the plastic mug, then bound it snugly in place with more of the clingfilm Bentley had thoughtfully provided. After tying a knot at one end of the suit-arm, she slid the equivalent of a one-pound rock down to the bottom. She now had two IEDs. Ho. Ho. Ho.

The savage blows from the swinging object shattered Bentley's cheek bone, as the blows reverberated inside his terminally confused head.

What the fuck is happening?

Melody was still constrained by her chained ankle, but she had grasped instantly that Saul's drilled-in kill zone – her kill zone – was not the chain's radius. It was the chain's radius plus five-feet and ten inches. A mistake Bentley may have realized had he not been so full of himself. Especially about women. Women who didn't seem to know their damned place.

Melody had sufficient leverage to grip his head fully, still face down into the carpet. She dragged him effortlessly further into her bedsit lair by a combination of his hair and ears. Adrenalin: what a kicker. Her hands covered in blood from his still spouting nose, Melody dropped and straddled Bentley across his back. Something finally kicked in with him too as he started to struggle up.

He lifted his head, but that was exactly what Melody wanted for her choke hold. She slipped her left arm under his windpipe, and pulled up full weight, using her knees in his back for leverage. At the same time, her right forearm was depressing Bentley's carotid artery, effectively cutting off the blood supply to his brain.

Starve brain, kill body, Princess.

It was working as Bentley sagged down again. As night follows day, his brain, starved of two sources of oxygen, was automatically shutting down to help preserve its life. That was it. The fight was going out with his lights. Melody pressed harder. But even bad people have the fight or flight instinct programmed in.

In one supreme effort, Bentley dragged himself back from the beckoning blackness. Pushing up on to his knees, Melody was riding him like a bucking bronco as he swung himself violently around attempting to throw her off. He lashed back with his elbows and one caught her hard in the midriff. That winded her enough to loosen her grip slightly.

She realized that Bentley's brain was focussing. He had stopped lashing with his arms and was using them to push himself up back onto his feet with Melody still gripped, limpet like, to his back.

Fuck. Melody could see exactly what he was trying to achieve. Then he did it, stumbling back to safety.

There was nothing she could do as the chain uncoiled. Melody let go and hit the carpet side-on. As she tumble-rolled she could see Bentley standing away from her, bent double, hands on his knees, trying to force air into his oxygen deprived lungs. That wouldn't last long.

Melody slammed to a stop, flat on her back. The chain pulled hard on her ankle on full extension. Bentley was still sucking in air, holding his gushing nose. Won't be long. Then she saw it in the same sight line. The gun was lying two feet away from her. Melody's hand shot out to grab the Glock 19. She was familiar with the Glock series as Saul had insisted on giving her firearms training in his secret gun range.

Just in case, Princess.

But they all operate on the same basic principles. Still on her back, Melody pulled the stock to chamber a round. Bentley was almost on her as she levelled the Glock at him. He stopped dead, a yard away. While Melody remained expressionless, Bentley broke into a weird grin as he raised his arms, like he'd seen in so many movies. It's what you do, right?

'Okay, you got me. Whoever the fuck you are, what's nex—'

She squeezed the trigger.

CLICK—

Bentley jumped involuntarily before smirking. She was right after all, the safety was on.

In the dim light, Melody couldn't possibly see whether the safety was off. She just wanted him distracted for a few seconds. But unlike him, thanks to Saul she didn't need to look at the 9mm Glock 19 to flip the safety.

As Bentley took another step forward, she unhurriedly squeezed again.

BOOM—

The bullet ripped straight through his left shoulder and out the other side. The force span his body around so he was sideways on. He staggered slightly as he turned back to face Melody. The week had started so well for him too. It's hard to say who was more shocked. She would always remember his face at that moment. Bewilderment. Pain. Defeat. He would never remember Melody's equally shocked expression because—

BANG—BANG—BANG—

She shot him twice in the general area of his balls – how fitting was that? Though she honestly was only aiming for the biggest mass in front of her, lying flat on her back.

And then a head shot.

Bentley crumpled in front of her. Quite dead. Blood oozed from his body. Her adrenalin high suddenly kicked out as fast as it had kicked in. It was hard for Melody to distance herself from what she had done. Taking the blazing spark from another. The one thing which makes us all human. She felt something. It was quite an action to pursue with malice aforethought. Despite the feeling only a few hours ago that this wasn't her. She had made a mistake. The malice aforethought was being here in the first place.

Melody shrugged. Maybe she had it in her after all.

Mel, you moron. He better have that padlock key on him.

He didn't.

CHAPTER

18

'Jennings, where are you?'

'Down here, sir.'

Despite his position leading the Met's Homicide and Serious Crime Command, Detective Superintendent Bill Hickman liked to keep his hand in with the occasional hands-on detecting. These opportunities arose when a high profile case hit the fan. His overseeing of the infamous so-called *Kill Club* case had first brought his name to the front pages of the tabloids.

'Careful with the step ladder, sir. It's very rickety.'

Hickman followed the disembodied voice to the doorway. He wasn't a fan of the Victorian era in any way, shape, or ostentatious form. He had studied architecture at university. Mies Van der Rohe. Frank Lloyd Wright. Le Corbusier. Clean lines. Big spaces. They were more to his taste. This place was way too kitsch for him. Now this Sherlock Holmes-like vibe, right down to the authentic Victorian backdrop.

Detective Sergeant Leia Jennings rolled her eyes as the Forensic Unit continued about their work. The last thing she wanted was Hickman scrutinizing her every move. She had a detective inspector for that.

Hickman clattered down the ladder, dressed in the standard white forensics coveralls, hood and booties. Thirty years a copper made Hickman inured to the smell of death and the inevitable decay of all flesh. Which was just as well, because this basement reeked it into the walls.

'Detective Sergeant.'

'Sir.'

Hickman knew she was annoyed at him being there. He would have been too when he was a sergeant.

'Don't fret Leia, I won't be running the show. Given the previous history of the victim, and the huge payout he received for our fuck-ups, the Home Secretary is wetting himself. Wants to be in the loop on major developments.'

'They may want their millions back now, sir.'

Bentley had been taken to the Met's post mortem unit situated in the basement of St Michael's Hospital. Hickman wrapped his head around the bizarre scene that remained.

'What the hell is this place?'

'As best we can tell at the moment, Bentley had made himself a fully soundproofed basement cell. A *lair*, if you will. Which, as we know, is never good, sir.'

'He was suspected of facilitating massive financial fraud for crying out loud. Now this.'

'It's actually nicer than my first flat in Kentish Town. Except for the wall chain of course.'

'And the dead body. So what are we thinking. Somebody was attached to the chain, care of the late Thomas Bentley? Presumably a woman, unless we're thinking a Jeffrey Dahmer scenario. Got free? Shot him?'

Leia had been mulling over what had gone down here

since she arrived. The *victim* wasn't really the victim in one sense. From the scenario in her head, she had a sneaking admiration. She couldn't help it.

'Oh, it was a woman alright, sir. Shot him, and then shot herself free.'

Mel, you moron. He better have that padlock key on him.

Melody had searched Bentley's pockets. Three times. It wasn't there. She could try four, but the key was unlikely to materialize. Was this it? How it ends. Chained up in a soundproof basement no one else knows about. At her feet, a bloody corpse which would soon stink a hundred times worse than it did at the moment, which wasn't that great.

Mind you, it was a major improvement on her situation of a mere fifteen minutes ago. The answer was obvious. It was the only one. The one you saw in the movies a million times. Except in reality, Melody was not looking forward to firing a bullet (with supersonic velocity, delivering a kinetic force of forty-one thousand pounds per square inch) into a padlock on her leg and ankle.

Gun. Body. Padlock. Mulling the equation around for a minute or two – there had to be a solution. She could almost touch it. It just needed working out logically—

Yes, that might work. It has to work.

She struggled to drag Bentley's deadweight to the comfy chair. He was loose, rigor still at bay. After positioning him sitting up against the chair, she squeezed herself behind the body.

Ten minutes of careful twisting and manipulation later, she had the body exactly where she wanted it. Bending him forward from the waist, Melody stretched to her limit, stuffing the fingers and palm of his pudgy right hand in the gap between her leg and the ankle bracelet. That gave her a reasonable amount of someone else's flesh and bone for any bullet to accidentally penetrate before it hit her flesh and bone. She struggled to pull his right leg over and around her right leg. Again to offer some protection for her errant aim, or a ricochet from a direct hit on the padlock.

What a grotesque spectacle she must look with Bentley draped over and around her. Satisfied that this was as good as it was getting, she reached behind for the Glock. Twelve bullets left in the magazine: but only one right leg, and one head.

Melody aimed the gun at the padlock three feet in front of her, then repositioned her head as far behind Bentley's torso as she could. She took three deep breaths and squeezed the trigger—

BOOM—

The bullet slammed into the carpet six feet away.

You can do this, Mel. You can do this, slow it down, release the tension like Saul taught.

She moved her shoulders around, up and down trying to expel the tension. The same with her neck. Then her arms. Her muscles relaxed. Hand as steady as Everest as she took aim again.

The second slug slammed into the padlock, splintering its main body with one half flying into Bentley's hand before hitting knuckle.

Checked herself. No extra holes. Throwing off Bentley, she pulled the hot padlock from the bracelet.

Free at last.

Dawn's early light was waking up London as she recced the rest of the house. It was devoid of personal items except for a few clothes in the wardrobe; bathroom toiletries; basics in the kitchen; wine in the rack.

She reckoned about a quarter of the incidents recorded

on the memory cards were filmed here. Two were at Terra Turris, but the others? Melody guessed they were probably the victims' own homes. Maybe this was his evolution. The basement looked newly renovated. Maybe he was moving from rape, into something more all encompassing. There had been recent incidents of women imprisoned in monsters' basements for years, decades even. Perhaps he had been aroused at the thought of exercising such total power over one person, mental torture without end.

Melody shuddered at the thought, feeling more justified by the second in her actions. What she had done to save others, and offer some justice to Bentley's anonymous victims. She felt good removing and wiping away all traces of herself from the house using the bleach, surface cleaner, rubber gloves, cloths and bin liners from the kitchen. She did all this stripped naked, clad in ripped up bin liners tied around her feet, body, and hair.

The Dyson vacuum cleaner in the hall cupboard was fully charged, enabling her to obsessively hoover the basement carpet. She removed anything that had shed from her body. When the battery finally ran down, she wrapped the Dyson in a bin liner. She did the same with the rest of her cleaning rags.

It was a bright London mid-morning. Satisfied with her all-round handiwork, she scanned the area from a front bedroom window checking for cameras. They were everywhere in London: traffic, home security, businesses, cashpoint machines. No point going through all this to end up as a photo on Crimestoppers. As a *Place*, with a small park at one end, Rathbone was not busy with cars and looked monitor-free, at least until the junction with the busier road. Presumably, Bentley also had this sussed from his little rape-pad – or whatever he had in mind. He wouldn't want anyone on tape entering his lair. She wasn't sure about the park. That was possibly covered in cameras given the paranoia over child predators.

The Armani jacket was minus one arm. She ripped off the other, then went to his bedroom and picked up the white T-Shirt and a Chelsea FC cap she'd found earlier. In the hallway she removed the bin liners (except from her hands) and dressed herself. Underwear, skirt, T-Shirt, armless jacket, wig, baseball cap, sunglasses, and Jimmy Choo's.

She grabbed the four full bin liners, then Elvised the building into the gorgeous blue sky of a dazzling London day. There was no rest for the wicked, as she still had stuff to do and evidence to destroy at Terra Turris.

CHAPTER

19

Detective Sergeant Jennings finally had the next potential crime scene to herself. Hickman had returned to New Scotland Yard, leaving her to lead the team to what they now believed was Bentley's primary residence in Terra Turris.

The 999 phone call tipping the police to a body in Rathbone Place had been made from an untraceable mobile phone. She had listened to the recording archived by the emergency services call centre. The *sound boys* at the Yard would analyse the original thoroughly, but Leia doubted they would find anything. It was clearly made using one of those really annoying voice modulators that any Tom, Dick and Harriet can buy online these days.

Operator:	And what is the nature of your emergency?
Caller:	(*distorted*) Very dead body. Basement. Go to twenty-five Rathbone Place,

	Islington. You need to know—
Operator:	I'm sorry, did you say dead body—
Caller:	Don't interrupt. Only gonna say this once. The monster is not who he seems. He's a very, very bad man. The house is not his primary residence. That's in the Terra Turris apartments in Canary Wharf. Bye.

They all had the misfortune to have seen the three memory cards left at Rathbone Place. Jennings was in no doubt that Thomas Bentley was indeed a very, very bad man. Now she was looking at a huge, framed photograph of Bentley, laid face up on his bed at Terra Turris. Somebody had kindly left it there for them to see, alongside the series of memory cards stacked neatly inside the frame. Yet he was the murder victim here. A victim whose demise she was charged and duty bound to investigate, in order to bring that perpetrator to justice.

Melody lurked around the rear of Terra Turris for three hours. The servants' entrance. The downstairs to the upstairs. Plus ça change, plus, etc. The uniformed woman exited and immediately lit up a cigarette. Melody was back to her supermarket own brand jeans, and a cotton tracksuit top with attached hoody. Her own short cropped blonde hair was covered by the shoulder length straight, black wig facsimile of her own hair. Her skin was artificially tanned from a tube, to a healthy glowing brown. She could certainly pass for the woman's sister, even at third glance. At first glance, Melody hoped she could pass for her, at least for a few minutes.

In order to protect the residents from accidentally

mingling with the folks who kept their building pristine, staff used a discreetly placed service lift. It originated in the sub-basement; opening on every floor into a hidden service room. Melody stepped out of the lift into the service room on the twenty-fifth floor. She was in the smoke-reeking uniform of Maria-Inocente Pena. Maria was more than happy to rent it to Melody for an hour, along with her building key card, all for the princely sum of three thousand pounds cash. The not so innocent Maria drove a hard bargain from Melody's first offer of a thousand.

After navigating a public transport route to Golder's Green, her intent was to retrieve Bentley's footage that day. Melody still had her visitor's key card and was contemplating breezing into Terra Turris as if she owned the place. Then wait two days to ensure the Terra Turris security footage was deleted before reporting the body. Instead she collapsed into bed for eight hours solid sleep.

She was frozen in her current position, not able to do anything more until his apartment was secured. Which meant Bentley was bloating in the basement. Which meant Aaron was still waiting for her. She was in the game for real. All she could think of was the suffering others were about to feel. All her doubts were eliminated after Bentley. She was perfectly sanguine about was she was doing. It consumed her. She didn't care.

A cooler head prevailed when she woke up later that evening and recalled the young woman whose uniform reeked of cigarettes. It was still Saturday, and she had until Monday before Bentley was missed at work.

It went like a breeze. Melody was in and out of apartment 2515 in thirty minutes. Unplugging the Media Player slash security record/playback storage unit, she popped it into her rucksack. The four hidden wireless cameras were easy to locate.

In the bedroom she lifted down Bentley's picture from the wall. The incriminating evidence was still there. Apart from wrapping everything in a pink bow, there was nothing more she could do to help the police understand that Bentley was not the victim here. These anonymous women were.

She felt great skipping briskly to her Triumph 650, parked in an underground car park a mile away. After changing back into her bike gear, she rode to the North Circular. Then it was a short hop to Crouch End.

Kevin opened his front door and ushered Melody in.

'Blimey. Hell's bells biker chick. You's looking well. Glowing like. What you been up to? What's with the fake tan?'

'It looks fake?'

'No, not really. But I saw you like a week ago, and you was yer normal sorta non-tanned self. Now this, and the cool leather biker gear. I'd say I was worried and concerned, if not dazed and confused, but we already had that convo girl, and you like give me the old heave-ho. What more can a mensch do?'

Melody squeezed Kevin's shoulder. 'Heave-ho's a bit strong. I'd never do that, which you damn well know, right. So you can stop semi-sulking, okay?'

'Fuchs don't sulk.'

'Exactly – you've got them?'

Kevin walked over the living room bookcase. 'Not even going to ask. Yeah I got them. Both items. You owe me three hundred, by the ways.'

'Bargain.'

Kevin removed a mobile phone from the small shoe box on the bookshelf – handing it to her.

'Okay, this is what our American cousins call a burner phone. Part of a batch acquired six months ago. Maybe legally, maybe not. Who knows. Totally untraceable as to ownership. There is no way this can be traced back. Fifty quid's usage on the chip before top-up time via this card. Thames it when done and dusted.'

'Great. Will do.'

'And this little gizmo here's your randomizing voice modulator. Continuously distorts and changes pitch. You choose male or female. Can't be reverse engineered to an approximation of your real voice. Again pretty damned untraceable. Don't have to Thames that. Keep it.'

'How do I use it?'

'Easy-peasy, fast and breezy. Note how you clamp it around said mobile, over the usual speaking hole. Thusly. That done, then wire it to the mobile via your normal USB to mini-USB connector. Then speak in your normal posh lingo, and—'

'You think I'm posh?'

'Compared to yours truly, yeah. Anyways, comes out like a creepy horror movie voice. Seems a bit drastic to order pizza from Domino's, but you posh birds, y'know.'

Melody fished in her rucksack and pulled out a bundle of twenty pound notes.

'There's five, for your troubles.'

'For my troubles? Are you fucking kidding me, doll, fucking seriously? I said three—'

Melody was shocked into meek silence as Kevin angrily counted out two hundred pounds, and handed the notes back to her.

'How many times I gotta say we're family. I don't want paying, okay. I have no troubles concerning you. Ergo and forthwith and QED. You ask, and let it be done on earth as in heaven, et cetera.'

Melody's eyes brimmed. An emotional dam about to burst its banks after the past few days. 'Gosh, mate, I am so sorry. I know we're family. I feel that in my bones. In my blood. I am truly sorry I offended you. I really am. Forgive me. Please. Please.'

'Don't you fucking blubber on me, girl, else I'll be blubbing worse than a baba. I'm very emotional. Got it?'

Melody didn't blubber. 'Yes, I got it.'

'Good. Now we got that established, I was about to partake in a little testing of me latest hybrid cutting before I go for a full production run. Can to join me for a puff, or two?'

Melody hadn't smoked weed since Edinburgh Medical School. She had started smoking cigarettes when she was seventeen. Her first year training to be a doctor had put an end to that. Black lungs in specimen jars affected many that way. But she still enjoyed the occasional joint.

What the fuck. A relaxing chill-out joint or two could be just what the doctor ordered. Kevin was genuinely upset, which had upset her. She could put that important phone call off till tomorrow. The one that would initiate her righteous vengeance. Let Bentley rot away in his basement for another night, consumed by the maggots. Let his flesh blacken like his blackened heart. Let his lips stretch back over his teeth in that hideous death grin. *Fuck him.*

'Sounds great, Kevin. Let's do it.'

CHAPTER

20

'Let me top that up for you, Mel.'

Ben Carrington went to fill Melody's glass with the table's last bottle of Romancee-Conti: a Cote de Nuits Grand Cru, Pinot Noir. No doubt there was at least one more case where that came from. Melody's best friends did have a fully stocked wine cellar at Cordingay House, their 18th century Oxfordshire manor. One of their several properties dotted around the world in the UK, Ireland, Switzerland, and even more exotic locales. It's good to be mega-rich.

The dinner was completed and some guests were leaving the table, drifting away to various parts of the twelve-bedroomed house.

Melody quickly put her hand across her glass. 'Oh, better not, Ben. Driving, you know.'

'Oh, sorry. Thought Chloe said you were staying tonight as per usual. The Melody room is always prepared. And apart from that – have to ask. What's with that car? Ford

Mondeo. Twenty years old. You going for an EastEnders retro look?'

After the weed of two nights ago, Melody was wary about drinking anything alcohol related. She needed to be in total control at all times. In her giggling state at Kevin's place (it really was very good shit indeed) Melody almost blurted out her recent *kill them all* activities. That was stupid. Exceptionally dim. A moment of weakness with her fifth cousin twice removed, to the nth degree, or whatever.

She hadn't wanted to come to the Carrington's dinner party. But it was Chloe's birthday, and she had agreed months ago. Yes, the Carrington's diary was planned months in advance. They were like the Titanic. Once they got ocean-going there was no changing course on a whim. Damned inconvenient for Melody though.

'I know, I'm really sorry. But can't do it this time. Something came up last minute and I can't miss it.'

What had come up was Melody's obsessive need to follow every detail of the Tom Bentley case consuming the media since it broke. She was also waiting – knotted up – for the next domino to fall when Aaron fulfilled his end of their Faustian deal. She could hardly do that at her friend's party that had included a young royal; a cabinet minister; and – seated next to her – the Hollywood A-Lister who hit on Melody repeatedly. Erin was very attractive, but in the end Melody had to politely point out she wasn't even into men these days, let alone women.

They were in the huge drawing room overlooking the terrace and the sprawling Italianate garden. Chloe joined them from her seat at the other end of the thirty-person table.

'Or tell us about it apparently.'

'Oh, just something personal, Chloe, you know. No biggie. But it's early in the morning.'

'Now I'm totally intrigued. You have to tell us, Mel. Tell her she has to tell us, darling.'

Ben poured himself another glass, 'I would have cracked by now if Chloe was on my case. She's like the George Smiley of the publishing world. Well done, Melody.'

He had been his usually effortlessly witty, charming self tonight. She had always thought Paul and Ben had been the opposite attracts, odd couple mates. Chloe preferred the easy going steady chameleon who could fit in anywhere, and draw people to him like flies. Melody was drawn to the socially awkward, slightly unsure but actually brilliant Paul. Ben and Chloe had known Paul since college, and were devastated at his murder. The evil men do slices and scars the others left behind. They bore the pain of loss too.

Her friends weren't going to let this go. Melody lied. 'It's a Jewish thing. Religious, you know. At Temple. Then my Aunt Sharon's house. Remember? I've mentioned my aunt before. She's ninety-five. Such a sweetheart.'

Melody had discovered that polite, secular people tended to back off when religion came into the mix.

Chloe put a sympathetic hand on Melody's shoulder. 'I understand now. Why didn't you just say?'

The luminous clock in the dash showed 2.33 a.m. The M40 was dark and sparse with traffic as Melody gunned it back to London. It was the first time she'd pushed the pedal to see what the retro relic could do. As the speedometer climbed effortlessly past 115 mph, she backed off. Last thing she needed was a police helicopter recording her for future prosecution.

On the passenger seat, her mobile dinged to indicate a new text. Who texted someone at two thirty in the morning? She picked up the phone with her left hand. The sender was unknown and anonymous. She read the all caps text as the car dropped back to a reasonable eighty.

IT WAS THE WORST OF TIMES. IT WAS THE BEST OF TIMES.
TRIUMPH OF THE PACK

Talk about cryptic. What the hell did that all mean?

It had to be from Aaron, via Frankie. Obviously Aaron would have heard of Bentley's death like everyone else. She hadn't needed to send him cryptic messages to convey that. All she needed to do was wait, pretend all is normal; pick through a Michelin Star meal at her friend's mansion; remove another woman's hand from her knee. Three times. Twice from her thigh.

Normal life went on and other people assumed Melody was part of their normality. But she had stepped outside. She knew something they didn't. It felt like she was watching herself. Melody also knew if she heard a patient describe herself in those terms, she would be concerned and want to delve further.

If the wrong-way-around quote from the beginning of a *Tale of Two Cities* referred to Melody, she knew the *worst of times* could only mean one thing to do with her. That meant the *best of times* could also mean only one thing as well. Yet there had been nothing in the news about a death in Ringland. And she should know, obsessive-compulsively following the news on TV, the car radio, social media, twitter, her phone, and the internet.

In reality there was no reason why it would be huge news. The Bentley case was drowning out everything else. Plus – she had been stuck repelling under-the-table knee grabs since earlier this evening.

Keeping to the speed limit all the way, Melody was back

home an hour later. She reversed into the long single garage attached to the side of her house. Her Triumph 650 was parked side-on against the back wall. *Triumph of the pack*. She opened the side pannier nearest her. Empty. She leaned over the bike's seat and looked in the other side-pannier. Inside was a padded Jiffy bag. A pack, if you will.

The contents lay on the table in front of her. She had been staring at them for a few minutes. A hand written note. Business Card, black, embossed with the legend *Worldwide Boys Book Club* in gold letters. A stone aged Nokia mobile phone. The fourth item intrigued her. A memory card, exactly like the one Bentley used to record his deeds.

Melody picked up the note. She did not have to be a graphologist to see that the spidery, immature handwriting was scribed by a person who probably didn't do too well at school, or in exams.

Dear M.
I red what you done. Well done. Took guts. Proud of you. Don't you go fretting none becawse you know with what he done he had it coming big time. I was thinking about that deal you being family and all and what happened and everthing. Maybe I was not fare making you do something. It ocured to me therefores you needs to see and hear from thems what did you wrong. Maybe then you can feel peace with yourself plus your beloved daughter.
Yours faithfully
You know who
PS
Keep mobile supplied forthwith on you 3-4pm daily.
PPS
That biz card and the dark web is your next.

Melody pushed the memory card into the slot on her

iPad. The device popped up the media player, and the video started automatically.

The picture jerked around insanely. The audio was muffled and poor quality as the person holding what Melody presumed was a phone video camera, struggled to use it. The picture settled into a decent landscape display. The person holding the phone was pointing it at the back of the man in front. They were walking down a long corridor. It wasn't possible to tell who the man was, until—

'Is that fucker on?'

Melody immediately recognized the questioner as Aaron.

CHAPTER

21

Aaron Fuchs lay on his top bunk staring at the spider slowly consuming the small fly trapped helplessly in its web. It was just nature, red in tooth and claw. And he liked spiders. He once had a cell-mate who stamped on a giant daddy long-legs scuttling innocently across the prison dining hall floor. This was despite Aaron's explicit warning never to do any such thing. Fair warnings are not to be ignored. Fuck, even unfair warnings by him, or even fucking outrageous whims on his part, are not to be ignored. If word got around that they were, then, well, before long everything he demanded would also be ignored. His rot would set in. And that cannot be allowed to stand.

In return, Aaron publicly stomped spider-killer's face, on the floor, right there. If six screws hadn't pulled him off, and baton battered Aaron into submission, it would have been murder for sure. For a spider.

His loyal oppo Frankie texted him with the breaking news about Bentley. He was a bit surprised. He still wondered why he did it. Why make the devil's bargain and force Melody into her dangerous enterprise on the outside.

Fucken sociopath, mate. That's most likely why.

But she *was* family. And he had decided he was going to do something the moment he heard from Kevin Fuchs about Melody Fox. The scum had raped and killed a child. A child. A Jew by her mother. His blood. Not just his Jewish blood. His family blood, no matter how distant. That could not be allowed to stand. He no longer believed in God, if he ever did. All those times he dutifully attended synagogue as a kid in Bethnal Green. Where was God in Auschwitz when his kin went up in smoke? Never showed up there. Well, he was showing up – ready, willing and able. A vengeful god-replacement.

So yes, he was surprised Melody had it in her. And to be honest (or as honest as he could be) he would probably have done it for her anyway, now he knew the full details of the horror. His list was a bonus. It never crossed his mind that she would fail, or get caught, or die in the effort. He did have faith of a sort.

It also helped that he had people inside on his payroll. Screws who would smuggle in the latest mobile phone, for instance. Others who would clear paths if needed. Like today.

'Is that fucker on?'

They were walking along the service basement corridor which led from Ringland's B-wing where Aaron comfortably resided. They were headed to the stairs which led up to D-Wing. Prisoners supposedly had no access to this restricted area which housed the boiler room. Aaron had an all access pass. His able lieutenant Jimmy wasn't too bright, but he was six feet six, built like a death star, and ferociously loyal since Wham was a thing.

“Yeah, boss. Don’t you want me to pause it like, till we get there.’

Aaron was still astonished how the unsmart Jimmy had sussed how to turn on the phone, let alone pause it.

‘Leave it on now you got it going. Point it at the ground.’

‘You got it, boss.’

Jimmy lifted up the phone as he entered the cell currently home sweet home for Prisoner No. RL410884-A, one Errol Pettifer, serving life for shooting dead his best friend in a drug turf war dispute. Errol had had a little *accident* earlier in the gym, and was in the infirmary receiving stitches on the cut above his left eye.

This left Prisoner No. RL589374-A, William Terence Smith all alone, sprawled on his bunk, reading the comic exploits of the X-Men. Mystique’s blue form-fitting costume was one of his particular favourites.

‘What the fuck you want, mate?’

Billy hopped down from his bunk. All five feet six of him. He worked out. A lot. And he was an aggressive, lippy little fucker when mates had his back. But he was still only five-six.

He didn’t like this. He knew who this huge guy was. Aaron stepped into the cell from behind Jimmy.

‘Mister Fuchs, sir. Sorry didn’t see you there.’

The spider assessed the fly. ‘Have we met, Billy? Know this is a small community, but have our paths crossed, properly, before today?’

‘Yes. I mean no. I – uh, I mean like sort of. I just know how things inside is, Mister Fuchs. That you’re the man. Right?’

Aaron stood uncomfortably close to Billy. Close enough to see his Adam’s apple move up and down as Billy’s mouth dried up.

'I'm the man. Hear that, Jimmy?'

'Yeah, boss.'

Aaron smiled, then punched Billy in the throat with his brass-knuckled fist. Billy slumped down on one knee; one hand on the ground; the other holding his throat as he gasped for breath.

'Melody Fox sends her regards.'

Aaron had always wanted to crib that line, ever since he heard it in The Godfather. Or maybe it was Godfather 2? The occasion had never arisen until today.

Aaron pulled a strip of ripped bedsheet from his pocket, tying the shocked and terrified Billy's hands behind his back.

'What – why, what's – what's – Melody Fox?'

'Yeah, Melody Fox. Remember her? The woman you left for dead. Straight up murdered her child, Charity. Killed the wee mite in a way I cannot bring myself to speak of. Charity Fox, my blood, may her life be a blessing. You must remember her and what you did.'

'It weren't me. It weren't me. Honest it weren't fucking me. I didn't do nothing, except drive the van. Honest to God, Mister Fuchs I never did none of them things they said in the trial. That was the others. They went crazy. They done it. Not me. Made me sick to me stomach. Honest. You gotta believe me. It were them.'

Aaron tied Billy's legs together with another strip of sheet.

'But you did nothing to stop them.'

'Please, don't do this. I'm sorry. Help. Help.'

Billy began to babble and cry as Aaron put the bedsheet noose around his neck.

'You know who said all evil needs to triumph is for good men to do nothing?'

Billy shook his head as he tried to catch his breath.

'No.'

'Yeah, me neither. But it's like so true if you think about it. And I should know. Look at me. But then I never did nothing like what you lot done. I'm bad. Ain't hiding that. But fuck's sake, you lot. What the fuck is wrong wiv yas all?'

Aaron dragged Billy to his feet.

'You getting all this, Jimmy?'

'Crystal, boss.'

Aaron picked Billy up in a fireman's lift, head to feet, throwing him over his shoulder. Then he effortlessly tossed Billy upright, back onto his top bunk. He tied the other end of the sheet noose to the metal bedstead, knotting it tight.

'Whaddya doing. Why you tying that sheet like—'

Aaron slapped Billy hard on his cheek. 'Concentrate sunshine. Pay fucken attention. That's the problem with young people today. Attention deficit dis-fucken-order. Right, Jimmy?'

'Right, boss.'

'I just drove the van, that was my job see.'

'Just drove the van. Hear that, Jimmy. Young Billy here just drove the van.'

'Yeah, boss.'

'Honest to God, was shocked Mister Fuchs, sir, at what they done. Made me sick to me stomach and that's the God's honest truth.'

'He was shocked, Jimmy. God's honest truth. Fathom that?'

'No, boss. Can't fathom that.'

'I was always the driver. I let Millar do the brain stuff, planning and whatnot.'

'But you raped her, Billy. You must've heard. They found your johnnies in a plastic bag in the fucken van you crashed. She was thirteen, Billy. A baba.'

Billy shook his head vehemently. 'No, no, no. Medical expert said they was inconclusive. I swears on me dead mam's grave, I never did tha—'

Aaron pulled out a short blade and held it an inch away from the terrified Billy's eye. 'Admit it right now, son, that you did it. Come on, you'll feel better for it. Do that and there may still be a clean way out for you.'

Billy perked up at the thought of a way out. 'Alright, alright. You'll set me free then? Let me go?'

'Man of my word, son. Ask around. You can go.'

'Okay, I did it. I shagged her—'

Aaron grabbed Billy's nose hard and clamped his hand over his mouth. 'Raped her, Billy. You raped her. You have to admit that in your mind, Billy. Admit that you raped her or so help me—'

'Okay, okay, okay. I raped her. I fucking raped her. Alright. But Millar made me, I swear. Said I had to. And I never did nothing else. That was the others. Them lot. Like I said I was just the driver.'

Billy's shoulders slumped. It appeared to be an effort to tell the truth.

'See. Don't you feel better, son? That's it then. You spilled all, Billy?'

'That's everything, Mister Fuchs. I told you everything. We got a deal right? You let me go.'

'Sure, Billy. A deal's a deal. Arbeit macht frei.'

'What?'

'I'm setting you free, son. Letting you go.'

Aaron pulled hard on Billy's legs and yanked him from the top bunk. The knot in the bedsheet noose around his neck tightened. His legs dangled a foot off the ground as he thrashed helplessly for an agonizing minute, gradually subsiding as the life was choked out of him.

All the time Aaron looked Billy in the eyes as they bulged open in terror. He took the iPhone from Jimmy and zoomed in for Melody. He was positive she wanted to see the first of her daughter's killers die close up and personal. That was all she lived for.

Aaron felt immeasurably sad and truly heartbroken for the poor destroyed girl.

CHAPTER

22

'I'm setting you free. Letting you go.'

Melody was serene as the video ended with the monster's lifeless body hanging from his prison bunk. Aaron's henchgoon untied the binding on the man's arms and legs, while Aaron kept the video camera rolling. Then the screen went black with the time-counter reading 33mins 47secs.

She slumped back in her chair, released from the rigid tension-filled posture she had maintained for the entire – the entire what? The first thing that popped was *performance*. The entire *testament*. That was it.

There was a surge of relief at first. Even more than when she had engineered herself out of that basement. So many things had been put into motion to achieve the outcome she had witnessed being played out for her benefit. And it actually happened. She had made that happen. Her. Melody Fox.

She thought back to meeting Hickman for the first time.

Nice bloke for sure. Caring. Probably fantastic at his job. Right there, in the hospital, barely able to speak through her raspy throat, she told him straight up:

Bringing justice? Ah, right. But they're still alive. Still in their twenties right – out before they're sixty. What's it like in prison for monsters like them? Cushy I bet.

His reply enraged her, even then, laying helpless and weak, as he loomed over her, the carrier of the righteous sword of British justice. 'We have to believe in the system, because that's all we have. The rest is jungle.'

She wasn't that Melody any more. Not now she had the justice most others were denied since the abolition of capital punishment. Except – he hadn't suffered. Smith's justified execution was quick, almost humane. Aaron had promised he would suffer, like Charity and Paul had suffered, in agony and screaming.

The temporary beatific high died and was immediately replaced by an inchoate anger. She would have to get a message to Frankie who could pass it on to Aaron. The other two had to suffer.

Dawn was breaking as the grandfather clock in the hallway chimed out five times. Exhaustion hit her face on. She had to get some sleep. The next target could wait. A small pile of incriminating evidence was piling up on her living room table. In particular the memory card still inserted in her iPad.

Did she want to keep that? Snuff film porn? What was she going to do? Become a *Bentley*, keep foul deeds secreted away nearby for future reference? To be played over and over for her own ghoulish satisfaction?

Too tired to play out that moral maze in her mind, she took the items upstairs. For want of a better alternative, she tucked them under the mattress.

Melody slept and dreamt. Not of Charity and Paul. She

dreamt of her and Aaron in that cell. Only this time she pulled out Smith's legs, laughing as he swung and kicked and died.

Resurfacing twelve hours later, Melody was refreshed, renewed, and with total recall of her dreams. She understood perfectly that she was on some unsustainable roller coaster high. She was trained to understand that her body was producing its own chemicals to facilitate this drug-like euphoria. She didn't care why. It was still the best Melody had felt since she was last whole, almost four years ago.

Sky News was blaring in the kitchen. The female newscaster was making a big deal about Sky not showing some grisly video of hostages being decapitated. They had all watched it of course. The woman boasted it was their job as journalists. What made them the final arbiters of what the public could view?

Not a word on William Terence Smith. The coffee was brewing in the machine when the front door bell rang. Her sister wasn't expected. Melody muted the TV and weighed whether she wanted to answer it. No way was it Chloe. Maybe Kevin was reciprocating the visits she had been making to him.

Please no weed, Kev.

Creeping into the hallway, she peered through the security viewer in the front door. *Bollocks.* A fish-eyed Hickman stood on the front steps. This wasn't what she wanted right now. She was way too raw. Too blonde. Too different. Maybe Hickman might notice.

Yeah, also too paranoid, Mel.

Scooting upstairs to her collection of wigs, she found her original Melody – long, black, luxuriant. It transformed her back from the real short spiky blonde no one else knew about.

'Mister Hickman. What a surprise.'

'Evening, Ms Fox – Melody. Sorry about dropping in unannounced. Hope I'm not disturbing you?'

'Not at all.'

'Thing is, I've something you will probably want to hear first hand from me. May I come in?'

He was alone. Surely he wasn't here to further his enquiries? He couldn't have linked Melody to Bentley. Could he? Did he suspect? Fishing expedition?

Regaining her composure Melody led Hickman through to the living room. She indicated the sofa but he remained standing.

This is insane. Get a grip, Mel.

'Just made a pot of coffee if you'd like?'

'That be great. Black no sugar.'

Melody shuffled off to the kitchen. Hickman followed. There was nothing she could do but let this play out. Picking up a couple of mugs Melody poured out their coffees.

'So – Melody. You moved out from your sister's house.'

'Yes. Time to move on. Oh, you didn't go to Ruth's first did you?'

'Actually, yes.'

'Sorry.'

Well, it's all looking great. You're looking well.'

Hickman kept glancing past her at Sky News on the TV. After waking up so refreshed, she was back to tense and edgy.

'What's this all about then Mister Hickman?'

He cleared his throat as if he was about to address the United Nations. He would never forgot the day he had to inform this poor woman about what had happened to her, and her family. Nor had he forgotten her bitter reaction. Sure, he would probably like to have seen the perps dead too. But he was not allowed to opine those sentiments officially. Not if he wanted to keep his job. This felt like good news to him.

He splurted it out unemotionally. 'William Terence Smith, as you know, one of the criminals responsible for the deaths of Charity and Paul – he's been found hanged in his cell at Ringland prison.'

Melody had been preparing her shocked reaction since Hickman followed her into the kitchen. Panic over as she realized it was a courtesy call. Hickman had been kind and caring to her about the case. He had gone way beyond what a policeman at his rank would be expected to do. Of course he would feel obliged to deliver this news himself. She had decided on muted controlled surprise. She wasn't a good enough actor to fake emotion or tears.

'Oh. That's – uh, that's, well I'm not going to lie. That's good news for me.'

'I couldn't possibly comment. In an official capacity. Let's just say I will not mourn his passing, and leave it at that.'

Melody leaned across the table and squeezed his hand. Her eyes had welled up. She wasn't faking.

'Thank you, Mister Hickman. I appreciate what you did, taking time out to come and tell me personally. I know you have, like, a million others who you could've fobbed off that task to. Or not even bothered at all. Let me hear it on the news.'

'Victims are too easily forgotten in the justice system, Melody. We all need to do more.'

'Did he leave a note?'

Shit, Melody. You're asking details. Was that a mistake? Would an innocent person ask details?

'Oh, you mean like a suicide note?'

'Yes. Sorry, I assumed it was a suicide? From what you just told me.'

Melody. Love. Just shut the fuck up. Never speculate in front of a policeman about death.

Hickman took a gulp from his mug. 'Oh, that's nice coffee – cause of death has to be determined at the inquest. Thamesside Coroner's Court. All suspicious deaths have to be determined at an inquest.'

'Suspicious?'

'That's just police speak, sorry. Any death in a prison is by its nature treated as *suspicious*, given the scumbags incarcerated inside. That's the law.'

'Yes, of course. I actually know that. Mind's a bit slow. What with the news and all.'

'It's a lot to take in. Mixed emotions I'm sure. Off the record, my officers tell me it looks an open and shut suicide. Smith shared a cell with another lifer who said in his statement Smith had been depressed. His girlfriend and child had moved on, as they say. No longer visited. New boyfriend. The reality of the next thirty odd years is a sobering thought even for the most hardened. He had an opportunity to cheat that. Looks like he took it. Quod Erat Demonstrandum.'

Hickman stayed for a respectable period, took a second coffee, and departed soon after. Duty done. She resisted the temptation to ask him about Bentley; the case consuming the news until the next atrocity took over. She had to admit it gave her a charge to know something he didn't. That knowing enigmatic smile with the locked secret. The *Melody Lisa.*

She needed to do something. Saul closed the factory at nine so it was too late for a Krav Maga session and the opportunity to beat the crap out of someone. Kevin would want to chillax on the dope, now that he had finally roped her in to share a joint. Might as well strike while the irony was hot.

The embossed black business card, courtesy of Frankie via Aaron. She stared at the name.

'Angus Sebastian Malcolm Ainsworth. Who are you, and what naughties have you been up to?'

CHAPTER

23

'Mrs Dalloway, the headmaster will see you now. Go straight in.'

Melody had been sitting uncomfortably outside the headmaster's study for forty-five minutes. Her gaze drawn to the oak door, as solid and imposing as a medieval castle gatehouse. It was the last day before half-term, and she picked up the heightened excitement in the distant chatter of the schoolboys echoing down ancient stone corridors.

She imagined the generations who had waited to pass through that imposing barrier into the inner sanctum. Past the ominous brass letters spelling *Headmaster*, below the school crest of St. George slaying his dragon. All encompassed by the proud Latin motto: *Honor. Officium. Victoria.*

The noises and smells transported Melody right back to her own schooldays spent at the Harrowdeene Preparatory School for Girls. The tweed-clad headmistress, Miss Comfort, assuring her own fretting mother: 'Here at

Harrowdeene, we are immensely proud of our long tradition in welcoming all into our hallowed halls, including those of the Jewish faith. Rest assured Mrs Fox, young Melody is in excellent hands, with Harrowdeene.'

Even after so many years, it's hard not to morph instantly into the persona of a powerless errant schoolchild. The prolonged agony of waiting to face the fierce wrath of headmistress, after some school infraction – huge then, but below petty in the heartbeats of life.

Melody smiled politely at the school secretary and walked into the headmaster's study.

The old Nokia phone rang. It was the day after Hickman's visit, and she had followed Aaron's instruction to keep it on her person between 3p.m. and 4 p.m. Melody recognized Frankie's not so dulcet, more Dulwich, tones.

'Tower Bridge tow path, Rendez-View café, eight-thirty tonight.'

'No problems, I look for—'

The line went dead. So much for formalities. She packed her canvas satchel with a few essentials, including: Johnson's wet wipes, Smashbox make-up purse, Fairburn-Sykes Royal Marines fighting knife. That wasn't for Frankie. That was well sorted. But a girl had to be prepared. There was no way she was going anywhere weapons-free and unplugged these days. Packing the satchel into the Triumph's pannier took her all of a minute. It was 4.06 p.m. Two hours to kill before she headed out into London traffic. Probably taking the bloody awful North Circular as far as Epping Forest, before heading south down the A104 to the Bloody Tower. Plenty of time for more research on one Angus Sebastian Malcolm Ainsworth.

A famous quote popped for her. It sounded apocryphal,

but it wasn't. It was uttered by Willie Sutton, a legendary bank robber in America. When he was finally captured in 1934 by the FBI an agent – clearly a proto-profiler – asked him—

'Why do you rob banks, Willie?'

Willie's answer was elegant: 'Because that's where the money is.'

Melody understood that you can never beat the simple logic of the criminal mind. She hadn't thought this way prior to her current experiences. It was a tangential leap in basic understanding. Her job had involved psychological operations (psy-ops) and many other forms of military conditioning. Thinking out strategies to get people to take actions for a desired outcome. Surrender their position as enemy combatants. Reveal vital information under interrogation, not under torture. Kill fellow human beings who their direct superiors had deemed worthy of death. Getting people to do things that most of us feel are unnatural.

But criminals? They are unconcerned as to the *why,* in the sense of the motivation. They don't sit around analysing *why* am I doing this heinous act. They are already, to various degrees, sociopaths by definition. You have to detach to do horrible deeds to others. If criminals are concerned about the *why* at all, it's only the *why* in the sense of the ultimate satisfaction it will bring.

Why do you rob banks? Money dummy. Why do you teach children? Because that's where the children are.

Obvious is it not? Once you make that leap it's a horrible epiphany. Melody was only just discovering this entity called the *dark web.* The internet for bad shit and even worse people who are into criminal activity. It's not available to be googled or binged. It even has its own digital currency known as crypto. A supposedly untraceable method of payment for said criminal activities.

Legend has it you can hire hitmen on the dark web. One thing you can most certainly do is trade drugs. She had just learned of the Silk Road. Small deals and cartel quantities, both sellers and buyers are hooked up on the dark web. A smorgasbord of delights: cocaine, LSD, MDMA, ecstasy, speed, heroin, and cannabis. Which is why former cannabis producer and small shipper Kevin was her dark web master. Once again, he wasn't happy about it. Once again, he helped out with minimal questions asked.

She double chained the Triumph at a traffic meter slot on Royal Mint Street. Both wheels, then both chains to the meter's metal pole. She sauntered down Tower Bridge's north-side steps to the towpath below. The sun had all but disappeared and the towpath's bulbous glass lamps had clicked on. The floodlights surrounding the Tower lit it up dramatically for the many tourists still crowded in the area. Frankie was sitting at a table outside the *Rendez-View* restaurant.

'Hello.'

'Take a seat, love.'

Melody would have preferred Frankie's seat, with the restaurant's wall protecting his back, and the panoramic view of everything in front of him. Not a coincidence Melody was sure.

'Got you a cold one. Non-alco, assume you're riding that beautiful silver machine.'

'How did you get into the garage. That's a good lock, hard to pick. Didn't notice any marks when I checked it.'

Frankie smiled. 'Watch the movies at all?'

'Not for a while.'

'I love me a bit of escapism. You probably missed them Mission Impossibles then. Set in London. Part anyway. Cruise is awesome, as usual. But there's a big scene in this very restaurant. I watched them shoot it. Took four nights. Lasts two minutes. Anyways if you do get it on DVD, freeze it about ten seconds before they move off, I'm in it. For about two seconds, in the crowd.'

'Fascinating, Frankie.'

'Not being facetious, doll. Trying to say I assumed it was mission impossible, yet you did it. And I was there, briefly I suppose. Has it helped? Feel anything?'

She felt like not being interrogated by Frankie Bishop. 'Appreciate the vote of confidence. Aaron got my voicemail I take it.'

'That he did. He understands your concern. He promised a certain level of merciless retribution would be meted out. That is true, but you have to understand—'

'Understand this. How I feel is cheated. That was painless. No hurt there.'

'Whoa, lady, calm the fuck down, and keep your voice down. Jesus.'

Melody calmed the fuck down. That was daft. Frankie was merely the messenger.

He leaned in, lowering his voice to a hissed whisper. 'You have to understand the method was the first, uh – down payment, so to speak. In order for this to continue, without spooking anyone, in particular the filth, the first example was always going to have to be easily explained. Accident, illness, suicide. Thought you'd have guessed that. You seem bright.'

She recognized her rage had gotten the better of her. That was worrying. Of course, deep down, she understood Aaron was right. It had to be that way.

'Fair enough. I'm sorry.'

'That said, Mister Fuchs is delighted at the outcome and looks forward to his next successful, for want of a better word, mission.'

'Okay. Fine. So do I. Mission is good too.'

'Great.'

They chatted like a normal couple for a few minutes, which Melody found unexpectedly enjoyable. Frankie was a surprisingly interesting chap. It was only 9 p.m. when he left her to finish the non-alco drink. She had only been up for four hours. Her internal clock was skewed and the night was young. There was plenty to do. She phoned Kevin.

'Sure you wanna to do this, Mel? It's full of skin-crawling shit.'

When he was producing and dealing in Spain, Kevin sold to a selective clientele in the UK using the Tor Network. It was an essential tool to access the mysterious *dark web*. He would only deal with new customers introduced by someone whom he trusted, and who vouched for them personally. He used a general forum known as *Weed Whackers*. The name wasn't chosen for its subtlety. He had his double-key protected site inside the forum, where his customers could shop and order their dope for shipping small quantities in sniff proof packaging.

'I am a medical doctor, and a psychiatrist. I can cope.'

'Yeah, keep forgetting that salient fact, mainly because I ain't never seen you do no doctoring. Or psychiatring.'

'I'm in session with you right now. It's not looking good.'

'Oh very funny, Doctor Strangelove.'

'One of my fave flicks.'

Kevin again offered Melody the joint he had been toking on.

'Now this variety is very mellow, with a smooth trajectory high, sure you won't take a hit? Do you good.'

'Better not on the bike. And do assume I know bugger

all.'

'Only thing worth knowing, the internet, the world wide wot-have-ya, is the greatest human invention since fire, right? That's bleeding obvious. But, and we love big buts, its greatest attribute is its biggest problem. For some that is—'

'Let me guess. Anonymity and the lack thereof?'

'Correctomundo. Basically that's it. Some people want the benefit of the internet's scope and want it all on the quiet for their own deviant purposes. And I ain't talking about the ridiculous fact this perfectly harmless cannabis indica used for recreational porpoises gets you banged up.'

'Yeah, okay, Bob Marley. How do I get into the damned thing?'

'That's the thing, love. Dark web is like this cool term, but all they is, is a load of websites. Publicly visible, like Amazon. Now, like you live at an address, and someone can post you a letter, it'll arrive at the address right? Every website has an address, called a IP or its URL.

Melody was getting impatient.

'Even I know that.'

'Then you got it. Amazon wants their IP address to be found by everyone, right, obviously. But them other nefarious websites hide the IP addresses of the servers what run them. They can be visited by any web user, but it's dead hard to work out who's behind the sites. And you can't find them sites using search engines.'

'So how do I find something I'm looking for then?'

'What are you looking for, Mel? Last week it were burner phones and voice modulators. For research. For that dead famous author, who has asked you to help him and whatnot, right? Now this. Anyone else I'd say this sounds like trouble. Except it's all for this book. Better be a best seller.'

She couldn't tell him the truth. That she was setting out on a hunt, based on a man's name, and his job title, written in pencil on the reverse side of a business card, for a cryptic organization called *Worldwide Boys Book Club*. Sounded nuts when you said it out loud like that.

'Okay then. Can we please get on with it, Kev?'

Kevin took another deep drag. 'Like I said, many dark web sites use something called the Tor encryption tool to hide their identity, easy-peasy. But there are others. On the other end, you use said Tor browser to hide your identity, and spoof your location. When a website is run through Tor it has much the same effect.'

'So, both ends are hiding in plain sight?'

'Exactly – matter of factly. Multiplies the secrecy effect. To visit a dark web site that's using Tor encryption, you have to use Tor as well. Your IP is bounced through several layers of encryption. Ergo and ipso facto, looks like it's another IP address on the Tor network. So's the IP of the website. Bit like the old doubling the grains of sand on a chess board trick.'

She understood the apocryphal grain of rice multiplier reference. An exponential increase in secrecy above the already secret act of using Tor to visit a website on the open internet – at both ends. It made sense.

'Yeah, but—'

'Yeah but what you want to know is how the hell do I find it? This mythical site for research porpoises only?'

Melody smiled. 'Yeah. That would be useful.'

'Ah, well. That's the hard bit. You need the exact same encryption tool as the site. Plus, crucially, need to know the URL to get to it. Then more than likely, an encryption key with a password to even enter the site. Maybe even a key generator with a challenge code on top of that.'

Melody groaned inside. 'Is that all?'

'Well, there's also the added worry that somehow you yourself are being spied on by the worldwide internet filth. Remember, love. Paranoia is your best friend.'

CHAPTER

24

'Mrs Dalloway, the headmaster will see you now. Go straight in.'

Bourton School had been entrusted with the education of the sons of professional men for over two hundred years. Lawyers, doctors, entrepreneurs, captains of industry, everyone who's anyone. All flocked from the shires and the burgeoning industrial cities to the green rolling Oxfordshire hills. Bourton produced the men who would rule the empire. Men like Angus Sebastian Malcolm Ainsworth.

As Melody sashayed into the study, Ainsworth stood up from behind his imposing solid oak desk. He was smoking a pipe, for which he made no apology – nor attempted to extinguish.

'Mrs Dalloway, good to meet you. Please, take a seat.'

Melody had complemented her shoulder-length auburn wig with a tweedy no-nonsense country get-up, topped by a green, waxed Barbour. That last detail wasn't a prop bought for this purpose. She owned it from her former real life as an almost wife and mother. She also wore a pair of tortoiseshell spectacles, with plain, non-prescription glass. The effect was very Home Counties.

Bourton School nestled proudly outside the small village of Bourton-on-the-Water – about twenty miles west of Chloe and Ben's manor house. Melody parked her Mondeo at Ye Olde Royal Oak pub in the village, and walked the mile to the school.

A stocky man – a shade under six feet tall – Ainsworth shook Melody's hand, careful not to grip too hard. On his desk Melody clocked the framed photographs. A family shot of him, his wife and two young boys. The boys looked identical. Then separate head shots of both boys aged about ten; confirming they were identical twins.

The walls were festooned with framed photographs of the school and school activities. Sporting events, chess club, theatre, plus a yard-long panoramic shot of the entire school, masters and boys. He was a sporty chap all round. The most prominent sport featured was rugby union. And the most prominent person in the rugby shots was Ainsworth in kit. But there were also photographs of him in cricket gear, playing tennis, and skeet shooting with a large-looking shotgun.

Melody sat in the lower chair on the other side of the study desk. Ainsworth poured tea from a sterling silver tea pot into a bone china tea cup resting on its matching saucer.

'Milk and sugar, Mrs Dalloway?'

'Two sugars please. And call me Virginia, please, Mister Ainsworth.'

'Actually, Mrs Dalloway, we much prefer formality over familiarity here at Bourton. It's one of the charms our parents so desire in a rapidly devolving world. Hence, my correct title at all times, from staff and pupils alike, is

“Headmaster,” Mrs Dalloway.’

Oooo, get you. Your wife and kids have to call you headmaster as well?

‘Forgive me – headmaster.’

Ainsworth stirred Melody’s tea before handing the cup and saucer to her.

He sat down and picked up a sheet of paper from his desk. ‘Already forgotten. Now tell me something about little Archie.’

Melody sipped. It was a refreshing, high-quality Darjeeling. ‘Archie’s eleven next birthday. And, well – my husband Jeremy thinks he needs toughening up, but he is a very sensitive boy. Other children can be cruel, can’t they. Archie doesn’t complain but I think he’s being bullied at his primary school.’

‘Let me assure you, Mrs Dalloway, we do not tolerate bullying here at Bourton. We build character through discipline, hard work, academic excellence, and sporting prowess.’

‘That’s good to know. Because our children are so precious don’t you think? So easily damaged in the wrong hands. Like the lilies of the field, children can bend with the wind of life’s challenges. But they can’t survive being stamped down by heartless brutes.’

Melody made sure to meet Ainsworth’s eye as she pontificated. Was there was any flicker? Any hint that she was addressing him, his inner soul, directly on a higher plane?

‘I like that analogy, Mrs Dalloway. That’s very good.’

It didn’t register at all. It was the last thing she needed to know before returning to her new lair.

‘Okay, it all here. Six months rent in advance. Five per cent discount for good cash. Here, receipt for nine thousand pound. Here keys.'

Melody grabbed the keys from the shifty looking Ukrainian who claimed he owned the large *Maida Vale* house. He wrote Maida Vale, in capital letters, in the ad, but it was more south Kilburn. The house was divided into nine flats. Her newly rented abode was No.9, and the top flat.

'The landline phone is still active right?'

'Yeah, last scumbag did runner last week. You want take over pay, see them bills stacked on living room table. Phone tell thems, save me problems. Got Sky satellite on roof also, if want.'

One tip she took from Kevin was to exercise paranoid caution on the dark web. The authorities are not stupid. The NSA (in the United States) and GCHQ (in the UK) devoted fair chunks of their time to trawling the internet (including the dark web) with massive supercomputer arrays. They crunched teraflops of data analysing and investigating. While a great deal of those resources were devoted to international terrorism, Scotland Yard and the FBI directed these agencies to other high-profile domestic crimes, such as child-sex rings, and child pornography.

Though Melody knew she was on the side of the angels, she needed to pretend she was in league with the devil to confirm her target as supplied by Aaron. Once her brief lecture from Kevin had sunk in, there was no way she was polluting her own house with what she was expecting to find. Paranoia did indeed rule. Despite the alleged anonymity, she had evolved beyond her gung-ho, laissez faire approach to Bentley. A blonde wig, fake tan, and skulking around expensive bars wasn't going to cut it with this one.

We're all creatures of habit. Melody lived in Maida Vale

for a year after medical school. When she decided that her action plan needed a temporary location from which to operate, she gravitated straight there. It was also well placed to bike it from Golders Green and Crouch End, and Saul's place.

A quick trawl around the local newsagents soon yielded the right ad in the window. Cash did the rest. The available landline was a bonus. She needed that to trawl the dark web. Now she was also dark and anonymous and untraceable.

Creepy Volodymyr was keen to hang around this dark-haired English beauty who had handed him nine grand in crisp fifty-pound notes. Keen to get started she bum rushed him out.

But she couldn't start yet. The phone's junction box had a BT logo. Dialling 100 she eventually got through to Gavin on the BT Fibre Optics Sales Team. Gavin was as helpful as could be. But even at his most helpful best, he couldn't get her hooked up in less than two working days.

Then came the matter of payment. It had to be direct debit from a UK bank account. Aaron had done very little materially to assist Melody. It was better for all parties to keep all contact to a minimum, and via an intermediary. One thing he did offer was a bank account she could use for clandestine purposes.

He slipped the details to her at Ringland after she confirmed she was in. 'Totally kosher, girl. Barclays Bank. Account name is I. MacFarlane. PO box number. A few thousand in the account. Use it if you need to do something anonymous and urgent.'

Gavin inputted the account into his computer. After a short delay, he was back, and very upbeat.

'Okay, Ms MacFarlane. Looks like the direct debit has gone through A-okay. The order's placed. You could receive your new fibre optic router by tomorrow, depending on the post. As it's already a BT line, there's no need to involve an engineer. Just follow the simple instructions in the box, and you should be flying online anytime after twelve noon the day after tomorrow. Is there anything else I can help you with today?'

There wasn't. There also wasn't anything else Melody could do until she was flying under the radar the day after tomorrow. Time for a severe work-out session with Saul. A bit of knife-work wouldn't go amiss either. Maybe some rock-face climbing, which Saul reckoned was the best all-over muscle exercise.

CHAPTER 25

'How's it going, sergeant?'

Leia was gazing absentmindedly at the Bentley murder board on her office wall at New Scotland Yard. Had the investigation been going anywhere, she may have been pleased to see her Detective Superintendent.

'Nothing but dead ends, sir. On the Bentley murder, that is. All a bit frustrating. We have ninety-three women who've come forward to claim Bentley raped them, going back almost twenty years. It's a very delicate situation. We've taken head shots of the victims from his video record, and clothing shots. Now we're trying to match them with any women coming forward to report Bentley assaulting them at some point.'

Hickman felt the disgust rise in him. 'Jesus. My daughter's his target age.'

'We ran the victims head shots for missing persons. We got one hit. Poppy Andrews was reported missing by her parents on July 7th 2001. She appears comatose on a video recording with a date stamp of 4/07/2001. We're assuming she died, and Bentley disposed of the body. The parents have been informed. Well, Poppy's dad has, her mother suffers senile dementia. It's unlikely the Andrews will ever get to bury their daughter.'

'What a nightmare.'

'Tell me about it. We have rape survivor teams working with the victims. About half seem credible and within his hunting grounds. They frequented known haunts of Bentley, or worked with him at some point, or knew him via a third party. Every last one wants to hang a medal around the neck of whoever topped Bentley. Which under normal circumstances tends to make them a suspect.'

'Understandable. But our job is to hang a conviction on that person no matter what we think. It's up to the courts to decide sentence.'

Hickman moved close to the murder board. He hadn't brought his reading glasses so had to squint. Taped to the board was a large monochrome photograph of Bentley exiting *Memento Mori*. Next to him was the woman with shoulder length blonde hair. The picture was not of the highest quality. It was impossible to make out the face above the fact that she was a well dressed, blonde-haired, female, most likely aged between twenty and forty years. Which narrowed down the list of suspects to a million Londoners.

'The mystery blonde is still the last person he was seen with alive? As far as we know.'

'That's her. Can't make out her face, but sure as hell's a popping those shoes are Jimmy Choo's. Eight hundred pounds.'

'Take your word, sergeant. How come there isn't security video from inside the bar?'

'Oh there is, sir. And she's in it. Only problem being it's

her back, her side, or any other flaming angle where she doesn't' show her face.'

'She's smart then?'

'Oh yes, sir. Very. And cunning. Knew what she was doing alright. Had to have had all camera angles sussed. No way it's an accident the only shot of her face is from a distant street camera she hadn't clocked. Total premeditation.'

'You think she stalked him. Targeted him?'

Hickman noted that Leia puffed up with something approaching pride. 'Oh no doubt, sir. That girl knew what this geezer was up to alright. Maybe – past victim? Hard to think Bentley wouldn't recognize her thought. She deliberately placed herself to be picked up, let him make the move, and then take her back to his place. That took guts, if she knew what he was.'

This was the day-to-day part Hickman missed about being a detective. Seeing the scenarios unfold, getting into the mind of the killer. Yes, much of that was a romanticized version of the tedious legwork needed to catch and convict crims. But even that beat spending most of his days getting into the minds of the bureaucrats he served, above the public.

Hickman was happy to muse in front of his sergeant. 'Then something went wrong for her though, presumably back at his, oh what shall we call it – his lair. He sussed her out, got the upper hand, chained her to the wall like a dog.'

'Then the bitch bit back. Ripped out his throat. Metaphorically speaking. She shot out his balls, actually, sir. If you've seen the post mortem report.'

'You know Leia, if I used the B-word in public, even about a killer lady, I'd probably lose my job.'

'Balls, sir?'

Hickman smiled. Jennings had a quick, ready wit, and

knew when to deploy it with superiors. He liked that. She would go far. 'What about his primary residence? The Terra place? We know she went there for some reason other than to just lay out the evidence on a platter for us.'

'Not a thing, sir. It's very well covered for real-time security. But they only record footage on a one-day loop. Then it's digitally recorded over.

'Eh? Why?'

'Turns out the residents don't want a permanent record of themselves, or whomsoever, entering or leaving the building, sir. Would you?'

'So, we have no forensics, no fingerprints, no video, no photographs, and no idea of who did this, except a blonde female between twenty and forty. And to top it all, every woman in the country is applauding whoever killed him.'

'Yeah. Piece of cake, eh? Sir.'

CHAPTER

26

Reflected in the laptop screen, Melody could see her painful black eye. That was courtesy of Saul from last night, training at his *All Fight Club.*

He did it on purpose. She knew that. She knew why. To teach her a lesson. Everything he did was to teach her a lesson. It really pissed her off at times. What was she? Five?

'You think you big girl now, eh, Princess? Learn all Saul got?'

She was dressed in street clothes: jeans, T-shirt, and her biker boots with steel toe-caps. Saul didn't hold with fancy judo or karate type uniform durkshnit for Krav Maga. It was street fighting. That meant training in the clothes you wore when cornered on the street with no choice but to fight for your life.

He was fighting barefooted, bare-chested, in just a pair of shorts. That was it, except for the stupid Guy Fawkes mask. It was the first time Melody had seen the scars covering his chest and back. She knew better than to ask.

She asked about the mask instead, trying not to laugh at the ridiculous sight he cut.

'Dumb fuckers. Imagine dumb fucker vot vant to beat shit out you. Like this. Naked see. Nothing to grab him by. No jackets, pants.'

'Yeah, but, Saul, when exactly is a naked guy in a mask going to—'

SMASH—

Melody crashed onto her back on the training mat. Saul had dropped to his haunches, swivelled around on his left leg while his right had swept both her legs from under her. He was upright again, as she lay stunned for a second. Saul went to stamp on her chest. It wouldn't have been anywhere like full force, he didn't want to kill her. Melody didn't hang around to find out. She rolled sideways, and scrambled up to spin around and face him.

'So, Princess, you miss Shabbat vonce again. And Kevin says vot he says. You know vot he says.'

She had a good idea. 'I'm going to dispose of Kevin one of these days. Bury him in his bloody garden. Great compost for his weed.'

They were circling each other now. This is how Saul wanted to play it? Bring it on, old man.

'I bets you vould. But vy? I make him talk. I haff powers. You should be coming to Saul for needs. Like phones, voice modulators. I got better suppliers.'

She knew that. But unlike Kevin, Saul would eventually drag out of her what she was doing. Going to him for the door electronic gizmo was a mistake. He hadn't questioned her beyond the book cover story. Yet.

He feinted to go left. Melody anticipated the feint and positioned herself to counter his right attack. She knew he was smiling under the mask. He always did, as she had gradually learned, bit by painful bit, how to defend herself from him over the past two years. The mask was distracting, deliberately to draw her eyes up and away from his hands and feet.

'None of your business, Saul.'

Saul stopped circling her and pulled off Guy. He looked serious. But then, even when he was laughing, Saul managed to look serious.

'I make good guess vot you doing. My intelligence unit, ve do lots a shit, like put two and two together. Aaron Fuchs? That Smith shtik drek?'

Saul spat on the ground at the mention of the late William Terence Smith.

Melody was shocked. One reason she hadn't confided in him was the thought he would try to talk her out of it. She was his princess now. And kings do not let their princesses traipse into danger. She was daft to think Saul would not piece it all together when a piece was taken off the board in close proximity to Aaron Fuchs. He hadn't mentioned Bentley. That name would be a leap, even for him.

'You think I can't do this thing you think that I'm doing? You're wrong, Saul. I am doing it. If you're thinking of heart to hearting me into not doing this thing that you obviously think that I'm doing—'

Saul tapped his head. 'Whoa, whoa, Princess. All this thinking things makes head hurt. You vonts dark veb for some reasons. I know, I don't know. I knows real pros. Not amateur like our beloved Kevin. Okays. That's alls.'

'*Amateur*. I'll tell him that.'

Saul smiled. 'Here.'

He flicked the mask towards Melody. As she stretched to catch it—

THWACK—

Saul pirouetted on his left leg, swinging his right leg head height at Melody. He caught her on the left side of her face. It was a controlled kick. As Melody knew, he merely wanted to teach her a lesson. Not damage her.

'No distractions, Princess. Never follow shiny objects. How many times vots I gotta tells ya.'

She felt around the eye. It would be probably be tender and swollen for a few more days. Lesson learned. Melody and her laptop were waiting high up in the Court Café overlooking the Great Court at the British Museum. She felt in need of a caffeine hit and had just knocked back a quad-shot espresso.

It was a new laptop bought specifically for her latest assignment. *Assignment* was the word she'd settled on. She did searches for Bentley. It had been five days since anything new had appeared.

A young man plopped down opposite her. He looked like the type of person with whom Saul would hook her up for this assignment. Short cropped receding black hair, long bushy beard, and lots of tats showing on his bare arms. He was lugging a rucksack.

'Hey, you a friend of a friend?'

He spoke excellent English, though Melody picked up a hint of a German accent.

'You mean our stocky Israeli friend?'

He looked flustered for a second, as if Melody had broken some rule of secret meetings. 'You're supposed to say, "a friend in need is a friend indeed".'

'Sorry, Gunter.'

'Scheisse. He told you my real name?'

'No, he said I'd be speaking to *Gunter*. You just told me it was your real name. Well done.'

He went a shade of pale below his already very white skin. Maybe he didn't get out from his basement much because interpersonal subterfuge didn't seem to be Gunter's thing.

'Double fuck.'

'Relax. Everything's cool.'

Sorry, yes. No worries. So – our mutual friend indeed says you have a need to hack into a nasty site that's rather difficult to crack?'

'For me, impossible.'

'That's why they call me Mission Possible.'

'They do?'

'Nah, just made that up on the spot. I quite like it.'

Gunter pulled a metal and rubber laptop case from his rucksack. It looked butch enough to survive a direct nuclear blast. He placed his laptop on the table and began typing away furiously.

'I'm in your machine. Nothing installed except the O.S. Great, that's very good. Let's get this done.'

Melody looked at her laptop. Gunter had closed her browser.

'How did you do that? Control my laptop?'

'You're kidding right? Public network. No security. Just think if you'd had your bank's electronic login and password saved on it.'

Gunter connected a cable from his laptop to Melody's machine. A couple of windows opened on her laptop screen.

'Now what?'

'Given enough time it's feasible to work out every possible password combination. But that time, in say a 512-bit encryption cipher, could be something, oh I dunno, approaching the age of the universe, or something, if you don't have a super-massive mega-computer. And even then, it's a really, really long time. Humans would've gone extinct. Freaky huh?'

'My mind is blown, Turing.'

Gunter's fingers were typing away like crazy. Things were popping open all over Melody's laptop.

'Turing. That's good. Thing is, the dark places our – uh, mutual friends says you need to go are populated by paranoid freaks. They don't tend to pick their pet's name, or their birthday, or *password* as their password.'

'Remind me to change *Melody* as my bank password.'

'You scoff. But people do that. Anyway, we assume that these other people don't, them being of the nefarious persuasion. And we can't know what we don't know. What we do know is they use the front door, which as I mentioned could take a very long time to crack.'

Melody reasoned. 'But why use the impregnable front door when a back door may be wide open eh? Mission Possible?'

Gunter smiled. 'Sites and systems are designed by fallible human-beings. They write code. They make mistakes. I mean, you use Windows. It's full of stupid mistakes which the uber smart exploit to gain access to the servers, upon which every website, chat room, forum, or whatever, has to reside. Now, you'll note these three new icons on your desktop.'

Melody looked back at her screen – there they were.

'Okay, now here's what they will do to help.'

Back at her Maida Vale (but really south Kilburn) flat, Melody stared at the screen. It was past ten, and if she had anymore coffee she wouldn't be able to sleep tonight. She went to brew another pot.

Gunter was a big help. At least, Melody assumed he would be, once she found something on Angus Sebastian Malcolm Ainsworth. She wouldn't take Aaron's word that he fit her criteria. She chuckled at the thought she now had criteria. From Hickman's first meeting at her hospital bed, to Bentley in the basement, she had been filled with a burning, unquenchable rage. A rage she had to hide from family and friends. The emotional strain of hiding the new Melody Fox was enormous. Some days she felt she would spontaneously combust in the fruit and vegetables section of her local Waitrose. Doctor Melody would certainly proscribe therapy for patient Melody.

Her original stalking of Bentley were the actions of an absolute beginner. Only one thing mattered then – the relief her action would inevitably bring. The rage controlled her. Like an addict who knows that their addiction is killing them. Yet, their knowledge makes no difference.

When the enormity of her intent overwhelmed her, almost at the point of no return, she panicked with the thought that she couldn't commit to the job. It just was not her. Even though she had the absolute proof of Bentley's monstrous deeds. If he hadn't damn near killed her, she was about to walk away.

But he did. And she did too. So no, Melody would not take a business card, and Aaron's word. It was too tenuous. And what were her new criteria for retribution? She boiled them down to three principles.

There must be incontrovertible proof that the target is involved in activities which are heinous, and depraved, and truly harm others.

The target is (or would be) a recidivist who could never stop their behaviour.

The target has killed and gotten away with it repeatedly. If her assignment hit two out of three, she was good to go.

Googling *Ainsworth* on the ordinary web revealed he was the headmaster of one of the UK's top rated public schools. The organization's name on the card had given her an idea of Ainsworth's extra-curricular activities. Worldwide Boys Book Club. Aaron's written *PPS* stating 'dark web' had written the script in her mind.

It was all she could do to keep her coffee down. The thought of kids being hurt. Charity. It was too much.

She checked Worldwide Boys Book Club and WBBC, not expecting links to a website. She wasn't disappointed. At the moment, it was a name embossed on a business card. There were millions of links containing one of more of those four words. That was hopeless. She tried variations of the four words with the addition of Ainsworth's name, to see if anything popped. Not a thing. No associations from the usual search engines which had crawled and catalogued the internet with their vast farm arrays of computers.

She had needed the help of outside expertise on the dark web. She had that now. But it was all pointless if there was still nothing to direct that knowledge on. It was like trying to hold water in a bucket with a hole in the bottom.

Following this Ainsworth character around, as she did Bentley, didn't seem the correct approach.

Correct approach? See, Mel, already you're thinking like a pro.

She browsed the Bourton School website again. It opened with the imposing school crest and Latin motto: *Honor. Officium. Victoria.* Honour. Duty. Victory. The headmaster's page had a photograph of Ainsworth in his cap and gown. The brief biography revealed he had graduated from Cambridge with a first class honours degree in Classics; and MA in Roman history from Harvard. He also had his own Wikipedia entry. She clicked the hyperlink that took her to an expanded biography.

He was quite the Latin scholar, having published dozens of articles and several books. One interested her: *Give Me The Boy And I Will Give You The Man: How The Romans Raised*

Their Children. The long title was shorter in Latin. Melody clicked on the book's hyperlink and the page on Amazon popped up. She enlarged the book cover. No reason really, merely idle curiosity. She was thinking of buying the Kindle version for £9.99 when—

The book's front cover had the first part of the title in Latin only. *Da mihi puero et tibi dabo virum.* Things always seem obvious when you have the answer.

She typed *register.com* into her browser. Gunter told her it was the best place to check the availability of domains for purchase, and those already registered.

It took her a while to type every word order variation in Latin of *worldwide, boys, book, and club.* They were all available to purchase for the bargain rate of $39 per year, $70 for two years and so forth. No one had ever registered these dot com Latin-themed sites. Nor had they bothered with co.uk, .ru, .fr, or any of the country suffixes.

Bollocks. She metaphorically banged her head against a brick laptop. It was very frustrating. She was going to have to steel herself and try to infiltrate dark web chat rooms in an invented paedophile persona. This could take a while.

Give me the boy and I will give you the man. The notion bubbled rapidly to the surface – *da mihi puero et tibi dabo virum.*

She entered the Latin phrase verbatim, no spaces. *Groan.* Yes, that was available. Another thought. She tried again with the Latin for the more direct 'Give me the boy.' *Bugger.* No luck again. Maybe just not obscure enough for Ainsworth. Okay, how about trying it backwards?

It had been a long day. Her face was still throbbing from the Saul kick. She had bruises on her arms and hip from the heavy landing. After Gunter had completed his stuff and departed the café, she had taken the opportunity to wander around the British Museum, mainly in the Egyptian Rooms.

So one last go, then call it a night. Puero mihi da.

Sorry, this domain name is not available. Would you like to see who owns this domain name?

Damn right Melody wanted to see.

CHAPTER

27

Oh, I'm sorry, headmaster, but unfortunately I have decided little Archie will not be joining the Bourton School next term, or any other term, in fact, for as long as you are on the planet.

Melody told herself to stop talking to herself as she sounded nuts. Two days after her interview with Ainsworth, she poured another black coffee from the almost empty vacuum flask. It held three pints when she started.

She was in the Ford Mondeo, parked in Hangman's Lane, about a quarter mile from Ainsworth's picturesque Cotswold country cottage. The car was tucked into a natural lay-by, flanked by the iron gate and fencing to a field where recently sheared sheep grazed. It was a warm and breezy Saturday morning.

It was half-term at Bourton School. The few remaining boarders were cared for by a skeleton staff that did not include the headmaster. Ainsworth was booked into a three-day UN-sponsored symposium on *Education in The*

Global Economy being held at Somerset House in London.

Melody knew his itinerary precisely. Yet she still wanted to make sure he was on the move. No *Bentley* hit and miss adventure this time. Not if she could help it by meticulous planning. She left her flat at 5 a.m. packed, prepped and ready. Then it was straight on to the M25, before cruising up to the M40. She pulled under the tree at 6.37, poured her first mug of coffee, and waited.

His Audi A4 edged into Hangman's Lane at twenty to eight. After waiting for two minutes, Melody set off after him. She caught up on the M40, and kept three cars behind for twenty miles as he set the 65 mph pace to London. Once they passed the Stokenchurch exit at junction 6, she zipped past his Audi.

After finding a parking meter on Adam Street (off the Strand) she strolled the short distance to Somerset House. The air was hot and sticky, with none of the cool breezes of Oxfordshire. Every half hour the array of water jets in the expansive granite-paved courtyard splashed into life; spouting up from the cobbles to perform a refreshing syncopated dance. She started to fret slightly after the second spurt and no Ainsworth. He should be here by now, half an hour behind Melody at the most. She checked her watch for the tenth time in ten minutes.

Sigh of relief.

Ainsworth rushed across the courtyard, a man in a hurry trying to catch up to his tight schedule. She followed him into the main entrance of Somerset House. There was no way he would recognize Melody as the tweedy Barbour-clad Home Counties mother of little Archie. Her persona was now the Bentley-blonde, shoulder length wig, expensive jeans, T-shirt, and the £800 sunglasses.

He followed the signs up the stairs for the *Education in The Global Economy* symposium while she waited near the entrance. Sure enough, having signed himself in, Ainsworth bounced down the stairs with an extra skip in his step. He wasn't planning on spending Saturday, Sunday and Monday doing good. He was going to be doing bad. Very bad. That was his plan.

Melody's plan was somewhat different.

Sorry, this domain name is not available. Would you like to see who owns this domain name?

Damn right Melody wanted to see. But the information didn't help. The domain name was registered by an unpronounceable name, at an unpronounceable address in Azerbaijan. Basically untraceable. Not that she ever expected to see Ainsworth as the proud owner.

Time to bite that nasty bullet she had been avoiding. Was she ready for that repulsive act? Fortified by a few big sips from her generously filled glass of whisky, she clicked the Tor browser icon installed by Gunter. It opened like any other browser. Nothing sinister there. She typed in the domain *Puero mihi da* and pressed the enter key on her keyboard. The tiny *please wait wheel* whirled around and around as if the laptop was reluctant to enter this dark sinister place.

The site opened to little fanfare. A simple black page with red lettering. At the top was *Give Me The Boy*, and below that the *Da mihi puero*. In the middle of the screen were two white boxes. The top box was *Entry Key*. The one below was *Challenge Code*. Kevin and Gunter had both mentioned these as likely obstacles. Gunter was the only one who said his solutions could possibly (he emphasized *possibly* numerous times) crack the entry guardians by bypassing them, using exploits to the site's written code.

Melody minimized the Tor browser. She clicked the

desktop icon named *exploit one.* Gunter explained that the software would analyse the site's basic structure, looking for known vulnerabilities that it can exploit to bypass the security. It could take a minute, or it could take an hour. If it was taking two hours, Gunter implied it was never going to happen. Under those circumstances, his fees were quite reasonable for some real brute force approaches. There was only so much he could offer gratis for friends of Saul and their own laptops at home.

It took about twenty minutes for a pop up to tell Melody: run *exploit 3.* She did as instructed. Things happened – a lot faster. The whirlymajig whirled around for about thirty seconds. Hey presto, the site opened.

It didn't look sinister. Worse than that, it looked like a wrongly advised child adoption agency with its 1990s clunky look. Plastered all over the homepage were headshots of young children: mainly boys, but there were a few girls. The children covered all races. Melody was already feeling nauseous, and violated as a human being. That was about to get worse. Far worse.

The logo at the top displayed as Worldwide Boys Book Club. Below that, a horizontal menu gave four options: *Videos/Buy. Videos/Share. Forums. Join.* She took another gulp of scotch before clicking *Videos/Share.*

The page opened. Once again there were no great design techniques. Rather like the basic Drudge Report website layout, simple text as a hyperlink, the page scrolled down seemingly forever with links. The text entries were all along the lines and variations of the very first entry: *Little Danny's First Time.* Melody looked at that text for over thirty seconds until her eyes couldn't focus anymore because of the tears.

She went to the bathroom, splashed her eyes in warm water for a good half minute. When she returned the same page stared back at her.

You have to do it. No getting away from that. You have to see, if only for a second.

Another gulp of Scotch. Clicked onto the first video link. The video opened on the face of a little boy, no more than six or seven years old. The camera pulled back to show him playing with a small action figure, superhero or something. Off screen a man shouted in a foreign language. The little boy was in a child's bedroom. The door opened and two men entered.

She forced herself to watch the images for two minutes before overwhelming nausea hit her. Rushing to the bathroom, she reached the toilet just in time to retch into the bowl. She slumped onto the floor for a few minutes. Despite the rage she was feeling, Melody could not face delving more into the site that night.

Next morning, Melody woke to a throbbing head. She needed to refuel before another misadventure in depravity land. A couple of codeine tabs, plus a leisurely visit to a nearby transport café settled her stomach. Aunt Sharon would have been horrified that she wasn't keeping kosher.

As refreshed as she was getting, Melody returned to the laptop, still logged into the website. No need to watch anymore of the hideous home videos. Time to check out the forums to see if she could locate Ainsworth and confirm his role in all this.

Most schools of psychiatric thought placed paedophilia in the range of mental illness. Some even claimed it can be treated successfully. Melody was no longer of either school. To her, the forums showed an army of malignant narcissists caring solely about their own perverted gratification. They preened with self-justification because deep down they knew that their behaviour was evil. Most were well-educated and exhibited good grammar. There were no real names displayed, of course. Each forum had its own moderator. Though why they needed moderating beat Melody; what could the members say that could be any more depraved?

The leading moderator went under the moniker *Emperor Tiberius*. Who else? He moderated several forums, and enjoyed displaying his academic superiority, including an inability to stop using Latin phrases. Melody assumed this was Ainsworth.

She diligently scanned every foul forum on the list. The final one was headlined as *Future Events*. It was moderated by the ubiquitous Tiberius. Even though the site was secure (as far as the members knew) posters were circumspect in what they said. Euphemisms and code words were clearly a way of life with these people. The habit was so ingrained, they maintained the façade even in their own company. The big chatter on future events was billed as a members' special. Emperor Tiberius had first mentioned it six weeks earlier on the forum time line with a post—

> *MAJOR ANNOUNCEMENT*
> *Dear Members, I am pleased to announce a truly special event to whet the appetite of the most jaded of palates!! In the words of the Roman Emperor Caligula, "I have existed from the morning of the world and I shall exist until the last star falls from the night. Although I have taken the form of Gaius Caligula, I am all men as I am no man and therefore I am a God."*
> *The last time we offered a similar taste of bountiful bacchanalia was three years ago in the lush, sloping hills of Tuscany. All who attended will attest to it being one of their lifetime highlights that will never be forgotten.*
> *As you might expect, the planning for such memorable gatherings is long, complex, and expensive!*

Given the prestige nature of the proceedings, we understand that this will not be within the wherewithal of all members. The golden ticket buy-in is set at €50,000 in the usual Bitcoin, and there are a limited number of 12 invitations available on a first come, first served basis. This itself should tell you the truly exceptional and guaranteed nature of the pristine goods on offer by auction. The auction reserve for each item will be €8000.
Members unable to meet the exclusive cost need not fear that they will miss out completely. The entire two days of feasting and fun, will be professionally videotaped at the highest quality, with all identities pixelated, and will be available to download for all to delight-in for your satisfaction at a small cost.
In order to attend, the full cost of the ticket must be paid up front. There will be no refund if you are subsequently unable to attend. Comprehensive details will be forwarded to you privately once the fee has been deposited and cleared. I can inform all that the luxurious venue will be hosted in Belgium, and the date is 27 May – 29 May.
Please indicate your initial interest in the forum and I will contact you with fee arrangements, or to answer any question on the quality of the merchandise.
Thank you members.
Libertas inaestimabilis res est
Tiberius

'Libertas inaestimabilis res est.' Freedom is a thing beyond price. There were twenty replies to the announcement. They clearly had put a price on taking some poor child's freedom to be a child. There could be a dozen of these monsters gathering in one place. In eight days time. She looked at the screen for a long time, mulling it over. Eight days? She better get cracking.

CHAPTER

28

After observing Ainsworth stride jauntily from Somerset House, Melody hurried back to her car. No need to follow, not yet anyway. She knew precisely where he was headed for the next couple of hours.

Crossing Waterloo Bridge onto the A2, London's outer suburbs raced by, morphing into the garden of England. Melody was too wrapped up in thoughts to notice Kent's simple beauty. She had ugliness on her mind.

Engine idling, she lurked in the Mondeo, outside the DFDS ferry terminal in Dover. Ainsworth's Audi turned up thirty minutes later. She spotted him approaching and slipped into the queue for the ferry. He joined ten cars behind her. Time to see if Saul had come through as he promised.

'There ya go, Princess. Top paper.'

Saul handed Melody an Israeli passport with her face

looking out. She was – for the next few days – Elsa Cohen, born 9 July 1989 in Tel Aviv.

She had bypassed Kevin as instructed by Saul. He didn't ask why she needed the passport, and she didn't volunteer.

'That young? Flattered. How good is it?'

'How good she asks? Is the Chief Rabbi Jewish?'

'Okay, sheesh. I only asked as I'll be the one handing it to some passport control bloke, trying not to look guilty.'

'Feh. Thinks I lets you use drek like some pisher. This real. Not forgery. Don't ask, but Saul still has friends. Vitch mean you have friends, alvays, Princess.'

Melody leaned in and hugged Saul. 'Thanks you old grump, appreciate it.'

Saul hugged back harder, then handed her a standard set of front and rear number plates, plus a driving licence. 'Less of old. Elsa is permanent Brit resident, passed driving test, and drives Ford with these kosher plates.'

'Wow, that's great. I didn't even ask about those items.'

'Vey is mir. I know. Lucky Saul knows this shtick. No point fake passport, real car.'

'Yeah, I did think of that, just wasn't sure what to do.'

'Vot you do. Find other same type car, maybe in scrap yard, maybe you have source at DVLA, who knows, ve all have secrets. Anyvays enough this megillah. Elsa Cohen also registered owner of a Ford Mondeo, just like you. Funny old vorld huh?'

The mill-pond crossing from Dover to Dunkirk was spot on the ninety minutes promised by DFDS when she booked a few days earlier. Passport and car cleared the official controls nicely, as promised by Saul, also a few days earlier. She kept Ainsworth discreetly under observation as he sat in the ferry's lounge for most of the sailing. He drank bottled water, nothing alcoholic. A few minutes before the ferry slipped into Dunkirk harbour, he popped out onto the open top deck to smoke his pipe.

Melody exited the Dunkirk terminal ahead of him. This was the tricky part. It would be getting dark soon and she needed to keep him in sight, driving on the wrong side of the road to God knows where. She had scoured the site, but was unable to discover the precise location in Belgium.

So far so good. The E40 was reasonably busy heading in the direction of all the major Belgian cities. It was still light when they drove almost in tandem the six miles from Dunkirk across the Belgian border. The horizon was endlessly flat, with no rolling hills to break the view. There was ample traffic to keep three cars between her and the Audi A4. It was headlights on as she passed a road sign declaring 20 km to Ghent. Maintaining the three car distance, the moon was high above the horizon. High scattered clouds regularly drifted across.

The Audi's right indicator flashed at the sign for Ursie. They exited the E40 as a trio. Ainsworth's Audi, a Volkswagen Beetle, and Melody. Really tricky now. Given Ainsworth's predilections, maybe he was hardwired to check if he was being followed?

This narrower road was Roman straight. They had travelled about seven miles in convoy, when the VW turned right, leaving her a quarter mile behind the rear lights of the Audi. Ainsworth had maintained a steady fifty mph since they left the motorway, and she matched him. She passed a sign showing Ursie 5 km, when Ainsworth indicated left and started to slow down.

Fuck. The Ursie road was deserted in both directions. It was going to be obvious to him that the car behind was turning with him. Maybe too obvious, given his paranoia. As he turned into a narrow lane, Melody kept going for a further hundred yards. She slammed on the brakes, and performed her fastest U-turn ever. She zipped back to the turn – now about a minute behind Ainsworth.

The lane was full of sharp bends, but the countryside was ironing board flat. Melody could easily track the headlights of Ainsworth's car a half mile ahead. They swept across the wide fields which had few trees and no hedges to block her view. Every so often there would be a few lights from a cluster of houses, or a distant farmhouse. Presumably if he looked in his rear-view mirror, he might also spot her car lighting up the Belgian countryside.

Think positive, Mel. He has no idea you've been stalking him since he departed the Cotswolds. Belgian roads are not deserted.

Keeping pace, Ainsworth's headlights abruptly vanished from her sight. A momentary panic gripped her. She had come too far to lose him now. A few seconds later she reached the thickly wooded area where the road sliced through trees on either side. A couple of hundred yards into the woods, another lane came up on her left. Melody slowed down to stop a few yards before the turning. The tree canopy blocked out the moon, but her headlights lit up the rough wooden sign pointing to *Martens Haus.*

She turned off her headlights, but that was no good. Way too dark to navigate safely. She compromised, switched to side-lights and slowly edged down a rough track at a measured 10 mph. The canopy of trees either side again blocked any moonlight. If she was wrong, Ainsworth would be long gone and untraceable, buried deep somewhere in the heart of darkness. Then it was back home and back to the stalking board.

The track took a sharp hairpin right, and then quickly veered left. The pervading gloom was broken by light leaking out in the distance. Ahead, the woods looked to peter out into open land. Beyond that was a well lit large house.

She stopped the car again to assess her next move. She couldn't leave it here. In fact, now she gave it some strategic thought, it was a bit daft to drive half-cock down this narrow path. Anyone could come up behind her, at any second. Melody switched off the sidelights and exited the car. As she did, a bank of clouds suddenly cleared their passage across the moon, and revealed some detail. The large trees were spread further apart than they looked whilst driving. Walking a few yards ahead, she could make out a gap of about twelve-feet between the next pair of trees standing guard over the track.

Yeah, that can work.

Melody carefully drove the Mondeo off track, between the two beech trees, before switching the headlights onto high-beam. Now she could see without being seen, she carefully navigated the car between the natural layout of the trees. At about fifty yards in, and hidden from the track, she turned off the ignition and the lights. It would be a real bugger to reverse out, but needs must and she'd worry about that later.

She sat silent in the darkness, clearing her mind. Melody had always been drawn to the mysterious woods – and their duality in our collective consciousness. Dark and light with a tranquil beauty abundant with nature – and a home for all our childhood terrors.

As a child, she would scour her local libraries for anything featuring these magical places: fairy tales, folktales, Famous Five books, nursery rhymes, and poetry. A snippet of her absolute favourite poem had been playing on her mind for quite a while—

'The woods are lovely, dark and deep, but I have promises to keep.'

Promises to keep. As she pulled the boot up, headlights

scythed through the trees. Another vehicle coming down the winding path. Melody instinctively dropped to the ground. The outline of a car passed the spot she had stopped at five minutes earlier.

That was a close one. Melody pulled out the small suitcase, and lifted up the grey carpet which lined the boot. She unwound the bolts securing the spare wheel to the chassis, and lifted it out. Feeling around the surface, Melody located and peeled off the two-inch strip of black duct tape to reveal the deep slice running across the tyre. Peeling back the tyre from the rim, she removed the hidden goodies: taser, telescopic baton, and pepper spray. They joined the large rubber torch, military grade binoculars, and a length of strong nylon rope already packed in her rucksack.

Suitably armed, Melody climbed into the back of the car and removed her long blonde wig. Ahh, that felt cool and good as she rubbed her head, still in its unnatural cropped blonde state. She stripped off her travel clothes and changed into black jeans, black T-shirt, short black-leather bomber jacket, and black bobble cap. Over her knees and elbows, she strapped on mil-spec protectors. The final sartorial touch were her black biker boots with the steel toe-caps for added kick-the-shit-out-of-someone power.

Lastly – she secured the F-S knife to her thigh, ensconced in the thick leather sheath Saul had constructed. Satisfied that she was good to go, Melody grabbed the rucksack, and went.

Miles to go.

CHAPTER 29

Melody crept stealthily through the trees towards the light radiating from a large house. Beyond the foliage she could make out features. The steep red tile roof perched atop the five storey home. Towering above the roof were five white-painted chimney stacks. From her approach, the treeline ended about fifty yards from the property. It was as if the house had been plonked down in the middle of the woods with trees encircling it.

She lay flat on her stomach, in long grass, to the left of the front drive and courtyard. There it was. Ainsworth's Audi, together with a surfeit of top of the range vehicles. Easy to see because the house was lit up like London Eye on New Year's Eve. The courtyard's extra-bright, intruder-deterring lights illuminated the Range Rovers, Bentley, BMWs, Ferraris, and Porsches. The eclectic mix of plates showed maybe a dozen people had arrived from Europe and beyond. Switzerland, Belgium, Holland, France, Germany, Spain, Italy, and the UK.

Maybe this wasn't such a great idea, you moron. Too many people. What would Saul advise?

She knew the answer to that before she asked herself.

'If in doubt, get da fuck out, Princess.'

She was in the process of getting the fuck out – wriggling backwards on her stomach towards the trees – when a deep rumble boomed through the air. Backing up to the nearest tree, she took cover, poking out her head to see a truck hauling a shipping container.

As the truck stopped in the driveway, a man exited the house. He looked to be in his fifties, balding, pot-bellied, casually but expensively dressed. Exiting behind him was Ainsworth. Melody gripped the binoculars tighter at the sight.

The driver climbed down from the cab. He exchanged words with (let's call him *Martens,* for want of his real name) and Ainsworth, before they all skipped to the back of the truck. The driver unlocked the large padlock securing the container's retainer bar and pulled open the twin doors. Ainsworth stared into the container before turning to the driver and giving him a thumbs up. The driver pulled on a handle on the base of the truck to extract a metal plank, about ten-feet long. He dropped the free end on the ground and shouted instructions into the container. A few seconds later the first dark-haired head of a child appeared. The little boy shuffled hesitantly down the plank. Melody's hi-mag binoculars made it easy to spot the tracksuit top and long pants worn by the boy. On his feet were a pair of new trainers. But that wasn't what caught Melody's eye about his feet. No – the only thing she saw was the metal bracelet around his ankle, attached to the chain running back into the container.

As the little boy continued shuffling down, Ainsworth ruffled his hair, in a mockery of a paternalistic gesture. The frightened child shrank back at this grotesque touch. The next boy appeared six feet later, attached to his tiny companion by the same chain. Melody clamped her hand over her mouth to stifle her cry of despair at the pitiful sight. The procession continued until twenty young boys were assembled in the courtyard, bound together as you might imagine slaves in a chain gang.

Most were of a brownish complexion with dark hair. Perhaps of Arabic descent, given the current migrant chaos gripping the continent. A couple of fair-haired and fair-skinned lads made up the merchandise. She remembered the news reports (a few years back) of the Yazidis being slaughtered en masse by Islamic State terrorists. A substantial proportion of their people had northern European features of blonde hair and blue eyes. That made Yazidi women and children prized sex slaves for the depraved barbarians. Having escaped that hell, these unfortunate children had run straight into another set of monsters.

It had been twenty minutes since the children were chain-shuffled into the house. There was no getting the fuck out for Melody now. No way this side of hell. Saul would approve. What exactly she was going to do was a work in progress. Ainsworth had to take a backseat. To be dealt with at a later date if necessary. She had gone to great lengths to ensure no one knew she was in Belgium. Mobile phones are easy to pinpoint for locations, so she had deliberately left her devices back in London. Besides she was on a job (she had to laugh at the idea of *a job)* and assumed there would be no one worth contacting until completion. Can't have Chloe ringing about the foundation while she had Ainsworth in her sights.

Once the kids vanished into the belly of the beast she circumnavigated the trees surrounding the property. There was the house, which was more of a mansion like the Carrington's pile. Away from the property she reconnoitred a traditional wood built barn which had been converted into the ultimate home movie theatre.

The large stone garage had been converted from stables, and it comfortably housed the ten classic vehicles inside. They included a Jaguar E-Type which Melody recognized instantly, her dad having owned one when she was a child. Her eyes lit up at the sight of the large Ford pick-up, a classic F-100 from the 1960s. The owner had thoughtfully provided wall plaques noting the provenance of each classic vehicle in his collection.

With a plan forming, she scooted back to the tree cover at the rear of the main house. Martens wandered out from the conservatory holding a bottle of champagne. The impressive swimming pool featured unimpressive, disgusting looking men splashing around. Gold jewellery, tight Speedos, hanging bellies. As if these people could be any more repulsive. She would have liked to march right over, slit their throats, watching as the pool ran red while their worthless lives drained away.

Calm down, Mel. That's impractical.

Scanning through the binoculars she spotted a potential ingress point. Around the left-hand side of the property, a few feet up from the rear, a set of stone steps led down to a basement door. Melody repositioned herself a few feet past the rear of the old barn.

A white ceramic sign, with *Serviteurs* printed in Delft-blue, was screwed to the basement door. Doubtful there were any servants on the property tonight. There was a small window to the left of the door. This was most likely a relic of the semi-feudal past, but who knows? Perhaps she could use this as a base of operations inside?

This side of the house was not lit up like the front

courtyard, or the rear with the pool. There were fewer overlooking bedroom windows and none showed light in the rooms. She waited until the moon was indisposed in cloud cover, before dashing unseen across the well-kept lawn.

Melody gripped telescopic baton's stippled rubber handle. Flicking her wrist in a well practiced move, the baton shot out to twenty one inches of aircraft grade aluminium. She was about the crack the window glass, then thought to try the heavy door handle.

CREAK—

The door swung open. It was dark. She felt around for a light switch. Hanging from the wooden-beamed ceiling was a single lightbulb. It revealed the original kitchen for this grand house. Obviously the room had been the central hub of the servants' lives. A real life Belgian Downton Abbey.

There were two exits out of the old kitchen. She opened one door to see a short corridor leading to a spiral, wooden staircase at the end. Melody clicked the torch and pointed it up. The steps spiralled all the way to the top of the house, to what she guessed were those attic windows protruding from the red roof tiles. She started to climb. The wood creaked and groaned slightly on each step up. Clearly the design was for servants to glide around the house unseen on the main staircase; precisely as in the Terra Turris. Plus ça change, and so forth. She stopped at the small landing on the ground floor. Distinct and clear voices emanated from behind the door frame where the original door had been replaced and sealed in by plasterboard. She clicked the torch off, ensuring no light leaked to the other side.

The man was speaking decent English with a guttural Flemish or Dutch accent. 'Gold for sure old chap. That would be my top tip. I myself have ten million Euros in gold coins stashed away. Been the currency franca for five millennia. For sure, it's almost liquid franca. Ha ha. Good start when everything turns to shit and paper or plastic is Weimar worthless. Okay, okay, I see your face and my hobby horse bores you. Okay, we should start the auction soon, for sure Angus.'

'Yes, tempus certainly fugits doesn't it. Lovely home you have by the way. That old barn is perfect for our little soirée. Oh, and the bedrooms are to die for. Our guests will get their fifty thousand Euros-worth and more.'

It took all of Melody's self-control not to burst through the wall like a Ninja avenging angel, gutting them both on the spot. Now she knew the sequence and location of events. She didn't have much time. If the worst came to the worst what else she could do? Her priority was to save the children from the monsters.

Crap, Melody. You don't even know the emergency number for Belgian police. Is it 999?

Worst case scenario unfolded in front of her. Hoofing it back like a maniac to her car. Reversing through the woods – at night. Taking off, finding the nearest police station open, maybe at that Ursie place? Which might be a tiny village for all she knew. Then convincing said coppers that she was not a crazy Englishwoman who, in any case, was also pretending to be an Israeli. In a kosher car but fake number plates.

The floor landings were identical to the ground floor with the door frames plastered over. The fourth had a working door in place. Melody examined it for cracks between it and the frame. The room on the other side was in darkness. She turned the doorknob and pushed gently. It refused to budge. Pushed again, harder. Some resistance, but the door moved a few inches. Flashing the torch through the crack, she saw that the object was a waist-height dressing table. Applying more pressure with her shoulder, the dressing table slid across the varnished wooden floor. She was in.

She switched on the light to see a Louis Vuitton suitcase open on the bed, contents strewn besides it. On a small bedside table was an ancient rotary phone.

Brrrrrrrrrrrrrrrrr – *Good.* A dial tone if she needed to make a call.

The sound of voices wafted up from somewhere. *Outside.* She clicked off the bedroom light, hurried to the window. A large group of men were ambling from the house towards the old barn she had scoped out earlier. Angus was correct, it was perfect for their depraved soirée. The wooden structure had been completely renovated, whilst retaining its original rustic features as a working barn: thick wooden beams, slatted exterior panels, and stone floor. The interior had been fitted out as a home movie theatre, completely soundproofed, with thirty plush seats facing the large screen.

Angus led the group. That was good. But where were the children? Unless they had been moved in the few minutes since she entered, they could still be inside being prepped for God knows what. She knew what, but what happened after? She shuddered. Again.

The bedroom door opened into a well-lit corridor. All was quiet. Flicking out her baton again to its lethal 21-inch length, she was going to have to blitz it. The end of the corridor led to the main staircase. Sounded clear. There was a light switch next to her. Pressed it. The stair lights went off all the way down. *Bonus.*

Down the carpeted stairs Melody crept. Reaching the first floor, the higher-pitched sound of children's chatter wafted up from below. Still no resistance, all the way to the bottom of the stairs and a corridor. This wasn't the main staircase. That would have led to the impressive reception hallway spied through her binoculars.

At the end of the corridor there was only a right turn. Turning right she padded along the L-shape to the single door. This was the children's location alright. There was no door lock. But there were three sturdy bolts positioned at the top, bottom, and across the middle of the door. As quietly as possible, she tugged them free from their tight insertion into the door frame. The whispered sounds inside subsided. Gripping the baton tightly, she turned the door knob.

Melody pushed open the door, ready for anything. Anything except the sea of small frightened faces facing her as she stepped into the spacious and oh-so-civilized reception room. The fine marble floor complemented the expensive period furniture. The walls were adorned with paintings in the style of Dutch old masters. The main door to the room was closed, presumably locked. Not that Melody was going out that way. Most importantly, the curtains were drawn.

Both parties stared mutely at the other for a good few seconds. Thankfully they were alone, their captors otherwise engaged. Their chains had been removed. Their track-suited attire was intact.

Stepping towards them, the children herded together, shying away from her. She realized what a frightening figure she must look, dressed in black, holding a baton. Dropping down on her haunches to their height, she pulled off the bobble hat to show them she was a woman. A mother.

One of the fair-skinned boys whispered something. It sounded Arabic, but she had no idea.

Melody pointed at herself. 'English. English.' She scanned the sea of tiny frightened faces. 'Anyone speak English? Anyone?'

The boys stared back at her, completely unresponsive.

She tapped her chest a few times. 'Melody. Mel-o-dee. Mel-o-dee.'

The fair-skinned boy caught on quickly, pointing at her. 'Mel-o-dee.'

'Yes, yes, Mel-o-dee.'

He tapped himself on his tiny chest, 'Sabrin,' then bowed slightly.

'Sabrin. Hello, Sabrin.'

She had to get the boys out right now. But they had no idea she was trying to rescue them. As far as they were concerned she might have been a bad lady to add to the list of bad men they had encountered. Melody was still calculating her next move when—

CLICK—

A key was inserted into the door lock. The children heard it. A look of panic spread across their faces. The herd automatically shuffled towards her, maybe the presence of a mother-figure had triggered something in them. She stood upright, holding a finger to her lips.

'Shhhhhhhhhhhh.'

Melody walked to the door as the key was being turned. The children parted like the Red Sea to let her by. As the door opened, she positioned herself against the wall ensuring it opened towards her. The already traumatized children were naturally looking towards her: the weird blonde lady who had appeared from nowhere. Melody smiled, once again holding a finger against her lips. Sabrin whispered something to the other boys. Most of them stopped staring at her and shifted their gaze to look at the person entering. Smart boy.

Smarter than her apparently. It was the driver. What she'd failed to notice was the mirror on the wall behind her when she first entered from the other door. She saw it as he slammed the door shut. The same time as he saw Melody behind him.

The rotund driver lumbered around. Six-feet tall and overweight. Not in the best shape, but you're not in this vile business by being an office wimp.

Melody leapt forward swinging her baton down hard, intent on breaking his knee, then his shin. Gravity would drop him to the ground. It was great strategy, if he had not managed to block her vicious baton swing down with his fleshy right forearm—

CRUNCH—

His humerus splintered with the force of the blow.

'Agggghhh.' The driver's scream flowed effortlessly into a volley of expletives in a language Melody took as Flemish, maybe Dutch. But he was still standing. And dangerous.

Just von rule on vicked kadokhes, Princess. Put on ground, put in ground.

As she had lost the tactical surprise for a close-in blow, she changed tack instantly. Saul had managed to hardwire her with a newly evolved ability to think on her feet.

Pivoting on her left foot, Melody swivelled with a head-height, steel toe-capped boot to the driver's face. She connected, but not fully. The driver swayed back just as her boot scraped along his cheek and chin.

Now off balance, she couldn't stop herself tumbling forward to within his deadly orbit. Like a wounded beast he lashed at her with his good left arm, smashing her in the stomach, violently spinning Melody sideways, crashing her through the ornate glass coffee table.

She was on her back, winded. He was on her before she could recover – straddling Melody across her chest. She tried to roll him off, but sixteen stone was too much. A super-weight advantage nullifying her superior skill. As he put his large left hand around Melody's throat, trying to squeeze the life out of her, she could see past him to the terrified boys, clustered across the room.

Squeeze – squeeze – squeeze.

She had left his right arm dangling broken, but it was her windpipe being crushed hard. Again he was babbling at her in foreign. She could guess his sentiments.

'Who the fuck are you lady? What are you doing here. Better tell me else I'm gonna rape the fuck out of you then throw pieces of you bit by bit into—'

Her knife thrust up into the driver's body just below his ribs on his left side. At the same time she sliced it left, right and left, then up. Then twisted it mercilessly further and further with each stroke – ruthlessly following Saul's orders to the letter. The relentless shredding of his internal organs meant there was no coming back for him. Or her. This was brutal. A personal and up-close execution of someone who had seen her face without make-up, fake glasses, multiple wigs. It was inevitable.

He didn't scream. That was the shock, and his body shutting down. The hand around her throat went limp. She pulled her knife out, finally initiated in blood other than her own. He slumped sideways, landing on his back, his last breaths wheezing out.

Scrambling to her knees, Melody gasped for breath. In, out. In, out. She pumped air into her lungs. The little hands began tentatively as the children flowed around her. Patting, touching, feeling her back first, then her head, and her arms. The smallest boy, who looked about five, hugged her arm tightly. Melody ruffled his hair. It was the right thing to do. Sabrin tugged at her sleeve as he pointed at the door where she made her entrance.

She nodded at him and pointed. 'Yes, yes.'

He didn't understand her words, so she tried to keep her voice modulated and calm; or as calm as she could be given recent events. 'Yes, yes, Sabrin that's right, that's right.

We're going, sweetheart. Don't you worry about that. In a second, munchkin, okay.'

She scrambled to her feet, knife still in hand, dripping. The boys looked up at her pleadingly waiting to be told what to do. Ushering them towards the far door, they moved as one, constantly looking back at her for reassurance. She made gestures to indicate to wait for her. They understood.

The boys were untroubled that the driver was groaning quietly while his life ebbed across the marble. Presumably they had seen far worse in their brief lives. She returned to the monster. Rifling through his pockets, wiping the blade across his chest, back and forth, smiling as she looked into his rapidly failing eyes. She stuffed his wallet and truck keys in her bomber jacket pocket, then relocked the main door. As an afterthought, she dragged the chaise longue across it.

Arse into gear, Melody.

She rushed back to the boys still waiting patiently.

'Okay kids, follow me.'

CHAPTER

30

It was a good plan at the time. The best of a bad lot.

Melody raced across the lawn towards the barn. After marching the children down the servants' stairs, she reluctantly left them in the dark in the creepy kitchen. It wasn't good, almost as if she was abandoning them, which is what many thought. Sabrin was a natural leader, despite being no more than eight years old. She concentrated on him. He quickly grasped her pidgin-attempts to visually communicate her intent. Which he whisperingly relayed to the others, calming them down a notch.

Her plan was get them out of the house and use the stone garage as a staging post. But first—

She reached the side of the barn housing a fair proportion of the platinum members of the Worldwide Boys Book Club. Removing the nylon rope from her rucksack, she glanced around the corner. The original eight-feet wide barn door had been replaced by a substantial modern facsimile, reclad in original wood panels. One of the double doors was closed, while the other was half open. Not perfect, but needs must.

Deep breaths, Mel.

She pulled down the front of the bobble hat to reveal it was more a ski mask with eyes and mouth apertures. Stepping out – *shit.* Ainsworth and Martens hurried out of the barn, striding across the lawn towards the conservatory entrance to the house, forcing her to shuffle back to the side of the building.

'What in fuck's name is holding him up? You told him to assemble the merchandise right, Angus?'

'Of course.'

Melody waited until they passed the swimming pool before she raced to the barn entrance. As the monsters disappeared into the conservatory, Melody calculated two minutes before they twigged something was up, and smashed their way into the reception room.

She closed the open door and prepared the rope. Melody had been skilled in tying sailor's knots since a young girl. One of her first memories was her avid yachtsman father teaching her to tie a basic slip knot. She promptly tried it out on her toddler sister Ruth. Their mum was not pleased.

She tied the rope in a bowline knot, slipping it over the 12-inch long horizontal handle, pulling it tight. Looping more rope around the handle, she was – what, what was she going to do? Reality struck. This wasn't going to work. No way in hell was this rope keeping anyone in this barn, no matter how many times she looped the handles together. Even her notion of utilizing the hoist beam (jutting out about twelve-feet above the ground) was impractical.

It was a good plan all of five minutes ago. Should have stuck with her first thought, but had balked at the obvious flaws. Now she had no choice.

Seconds later she raced through the side door into the stone garage. On her earlier torch-lit recce inside, she noted the ignition keys to the vehicles dangling from hooks screwed into the wooden panelling. Weird how Martens and his ilk could be so careful and paranoid on one level, yet trusting on another. She rolled up the garage door opposite the Ford F-100 pick-up truck and leapt in the driver's seat.

It revved up first time. Noisily. Easily heard from a distance. Turning right outside the garage, Melody edged the pick-up across the gravel onto the lawn, down the side of the house to the barn. She scraped the passenger side of the pick-up across the barn door leaving no gap between it and the exit. The door was the only entrance and exit to the barn. They were trapped inside alright.

Get out of that, fuckers.

Stepping down from the pick-up, Melody hustled to the edge of the barn and hurled the truck's keys towards the woods. She rushed back to the vehicle, and grabbed her rucksack. *Shit.* Martens was running towards her from the conservatory. More like half-jogging, as he didn't look in the best of shape.

Grabbing the baton from the rucksack she flicked it to fighting length. Ainsworth must be still inside. *Good.* Deal with him later. From a large group down to two. Melody liked these odds over those of thirty minutes ago. He started shouting at her in foreign as he jogged closer.

'Hey you. Hey, what are you doing? You have no right to be here. Move that truck now. This is private property. You have no right.'

Melody doubted *she* would be shouting at a totally black-clad figure holding a 21-inch metal baton, while rushing towards them. But each to his own. Martens must have realized this too when he got within a few feet. He stopped dead in his tracks. And stopped shouting, turned and tried to run back.

My turn. Melody tripped one of his flailing legs. As Martens tumbled face forwards into the turf, she baton-clobbered the side of his head.

'Halt, halt—' He struggled onto one knee. One hand up defensively as if to protect his face further, whilst babbling in foreign. No avail. Melody right-cross smashed him in his fat face. A deep cut oozed open over his eyebrow as he fell backwards onto his substantial arse. The returning backhand smash split open his right ear. He probably couldn't hear his own scream in stereo.

To be sure, she stomped down with all her weight onto his right ankle. Now he was down with no Lazarus revival, she pulled the taser from the rucksack. Pressing 50,000 volts into his chest, the thought flickered that maybe it would stop his heart. But he had no heart. Marten's body convulsed, and went rigid before he flopped into limp unconsciousness.

No time to dead-weight move him far. Had to get the kids out before Ainsworth reappeared. Melody dragged Marten's unconscious body the few yards back to the pick-up. She sliced off a length of the nylon rope, enough to expertly hogtie his hands and feet together, leaving him flat on his belly. She dragged him under the pick-up, leaving him hogtied face up. It looked incredibly uncomfortable. *Bonus.*

THUMP—THUMP—THUMP—

The men inside must have heard something was up. The banging was accompanied by confused shouts. Melody rushed to check on the door. There was no way out with the heavy pick-up blocking it. *Good.* Let's see how these bastards liked being jailed inside with no escape. She smirked at the irony: now to get those kids to saf—

BANG—

The slug whistled past her ear, shattering the driver's side window. Glass shards flew everywhere.

Melody reflexively jumped a foot sideways from the audio shock and glass eruption. She span around to see Ainsworth halfway across the lawn, walking purposefully in her direction. He must have witnessed what she did to Martens. His hand slid back as he ratcheted another shell into the pump action shotgun.

BANG—

She was already throwing herself to the ground as he let fly with the second pull, still walking forward. The shotgun slug, hurtling at 1400 feet per second, slammed into the middle of the pick-up, inches above her head.

Crap, this isn't part of the plan.

With her face still in the grass, she heard the second ratchet, a good few yards closer now, chambering a third shell.

CLICK—

Nothing happened. Maybe it misfired? Who knows. Melody was up and sprinting along the front of the barn to escape around the back, and regroup. She'd just made it when—

KABOOM—

The Ford pick-up truck's petrol tank exploded in a fireball as the intense heat from the slug penetrated its fuelled-to-the-brim eighteen gallons. Melody had just made it to safety to the side of the blast radius.

Pressure from the shockwave barrelled into Ainsworth, slamming him hard into the soft ground. The shotgun skidded across the grass. Melody saw her chance.

She was on him as he struggled to his knees. Straight kicking, with no leg swing, the sole and heel of her heavy boot rammed into Ainsworth's face, from forehead to chin.

The force knocked him back onto the grass. Down for the moment, but maybe not out.

She glanced back at the truck to see if anyone was racing to jump her and assist Ainsworth. The explosion had not destroyed the pickup. And unlike the movies, it had not cartwheeled away uncontrollably, thirty-feet in the air. It was exactly where she deliberately left it, resolutely blocking the exit. Only now, petrol-fuelled flames engulfed the vehicle. Everything combustible was burning out of control, raging against a wooden building, with Martens underneath, bellowing incoherently. The grass was ablaze. There was nothing to be done for him even if she'd been inclined.

The fire had jumped to the door, which was well alight. Beyond that, the flames were spreading up and across the barn's wooden panels in both directions. What began as indignant shouts from inside were merging into panicked inchoate screams. The trapped realizing the sudden, extreme peril of their hell-like situation as killer heat and smoke penetrated.

No time to worry about them, Mel. They made their burning bed. Let them die in it.

She turned back to Ainsworth. The rugby-built coward had decided not to re-tangle with her, instead he was legging it back towards the Martens Haus. The desire to chase the bastard down and end it now was almost irresistible. She resisted. Half a minute later, Melody was back in the semi-dark basement kitchen, gathering up the bewildered children.

The Pied Piper of Golders Green led them up the basement steps onto the lawn. The flaming orange glow was impossible to miss. The boys' eyes were drawn irresistibly to the fire, as the entire structure was ablaze in the wood-fuelled conflagration. Flames and smoke danced high into the air, a good twenty-feet above the roof. Had she felt an ounce of pity for the trapped men, their agonizing screams for help might have sounded pitiful. That emotion was reserved entirely for their victims. She hadn't set the fire. That was another act down to Ainsworth.

A small burning aperture, a few feet above the hoist beam, shot open. A figure engulfed in flames, screeching like a dying Banshee, catapulted from the gap, crashing into the burning pick-up. There was no more movement, or sounds. It was terrible for the kids to see. Melody was momentarily shocked and horrified by the gruesome image too. She clicked back into gear—

'Sabrin – Sabrin. Come on, come on, follow me. Let's get out of here.'

On Melody's command, Sabrin turned from hypnotically watching the fire rage and the man burn. His saviour was edging up the side of the house towards the front courtyard, waving her arms to get them to follow. He caught on immediately and began to rouse his small charges into action. They dutifully trotted after her, along the side of the house, past the stone garage, and into the courtyard.

Most of the intense security lights had been switched off at some point. It wasn't pitch dark, but it was dim. The truck and its container were still parked where she had watched the driver unloaded his human cargo less than an hour ago. She scanned the front of the house to see if Ainsworth was in sight. *No, thank God.* Then she saw why. All the cars were there, except the Audi A4. Looked like Ainsworth had cut his losses and bolted, leaving his precious platinum members to their fates, which he must have computed as grisly. Maybe she would catch up with him on the ferry and pitch him over the side? Sabrin and the children were staring anxiously at her. They were not going to like this part of the escape, but it was the best of a bad set of options.

Ushering them together, she herded the kids towards the container truck as a distant wail of sirens interrupted. They all stopped and listened. The familiar sounds of help and rescue were definitely heading their way. Maybe neighbours saw the orange glow in the night sky and called it in. That changed everything. She had to go. Right now. Leave the boys for the authorities to take care of. No choice.

Melody went down on her knees and indicated that the boys huddle around her. Sabrin was the first to hug her tightly, quickly followed by the rest of them. As her eyes welled up, she thought of her daughter; her forever little girl who she hadn't saved.

They gripped her hard. And it was harder to abandon them like that. It felt wrong, but she had no choice.

The headlights of the fire engines were beginning to slice through the lines of trees as Melody disappeared back into the dark woods – deep and lovely. She watched, safely hidden, as they pulled up in the courtyard. The firemen poured out to the confusing sight of a dozen young boys still looking to the woods.

She could do no more to help them.

CHAPTER

31

'Good, you're awake.'

He was awake. Just about. He was also bound by his neck, chest, arms, and legs to a beech tree, about fifty yards further into the woods than her car. Oh – and Ainsworth was naked.

'What – what the – what, who are you, what's – Jesus where's my bloody clothes? Let me go.'

Melody had reached her car as a fourth fire engine trundled its way to the Martens Haus. Followed by three ambulances, and five police cars at regular intervals over the past hour. That was the last of them. But as the Mondeo wasn't visible to anyone passing, it was prudent to wait. It would take her a minute to reverse out without headlights. Then another couple to edge out of the treelined path, in an area currently lined with the authorities.

It had been a long week since yesterday, parked near Ainsworth's Cotswold cottage. She was creeping back to her car after taking a nature toilet break—

CRACK—

The unmistakable sound of a branch breaking underfoot. Melody stopped, dead still, peering off to her left. In between the layers of trees was a faint red glow. As distinctive as Satan's eyes himself.

She approached him from behind as he leaned back against a tree still sucking on his pipe. Obvious now. The first fire engine had been making its way up the winding path to Martens Haus as Ainsworth was heading away in his Audi. Only one choice: pull into the trees before they spotted him. She reckoned he had grabbed all his belongings that tied him to his crimes while she was getting the kids out. He was so close to making it too. Libertas inaestimabilis res est.

He must have sensed something, turning as Melody pressed the taser into the side of his neck. 50,000 volts crackled into his face and chin. Rigid for a couple of seconds, then lights out.

Melody stood a few feet in front of him, beaming the torch in his eyes. He squinted, attempting to focus. 'What – what the – what, who are you, what's – Jesus where's my bloody clothes. Let me go.'

She edged closer, the beam making him squint harder in attempting to see his interlocutor.

'What's wrong, Angus? Don't like to get naked in front of a grown woman?'

'Do I know you?'

'Little boys. That's what turns you on, right?'

'No, no, no, no. You've got this all wrong. Those boys – young men, we were giving them a better life. They wanted to be here—'

'Are you fucking kidding me?'

Ainsworth's tongue flicked out and over his parched lips; reptilian, calculating. 'You don't understand, we're all born sexual beings, as children. It's our nature. It's natural. It can't be suppressed. It should be celebrated. It's society that's enforcing unnatural laws. The Romans, the Greeks, the Egyptians all understood this perfectly. Thousands of years ago. You think there isn't a reason why these natural desires are expressed over and over throughout our history? No matter how much the morality police tell us what sexual orientation they are prepared to tolerate at any point in time.'

A seething Melody stepped forward, within spittle distance. He could see this crazy woman was holding some sort of blade in her right hand.

'Is that right, headmaster? Our children are so precious, don't you think? So easily damaged in the wrong hands. Like the lilies of the field, our children can bend with the wind of life's challenges, but they can't survive being stamped down by heartless brutes. Right, Tiberius?'

'Jesus – Mrs Dalloway?' He stared at her, confused struggling against his confinement. Her knots held him firmly in place, the nylon rope digging harder into him, chafing and bloodying his skin.

'Not really.'

'What do you want from me?'

She hadn't thought to question him, but it was a good opportunity – perhaps a name to pass on to Interpol.

'That driver, who does – sorry, who did he work for?'

'If I tell you, will you promise to let me go. They're all dead right? They have to be the way that place was burning. That's like twelve blokes. What difference does one more make to you?'

She considered his offer. 'Sure. I'll let you go. But you

killed them, when you shot the truck. And it blew up. Remember? That's not down to me.'

'The driver worked for some sort of Turkish mafia gang out of Cologne. They handled all the logistics. Everything. Procurement. Transport. Delivery. It's a pipeline of people smuggling. No one cares, especially about the kids.'

'Okay. Any names?'

'The uh, gang, are known as the Red Wolves. They're like the Visigoths. Their leader is Mehemet Ozal, that's the chap I dealt with.'

'That's fantastic, headmaster. I'll pass that along to the authorities.'

'You can let me go now, like we agreed right? We had a deal remember. Why are you even doing this? What's it to you? I mean, what the hell are you doing here anyway?'

It was a reasonable question given his position of being tied naked to a tree. 'You like quoting the Greeks and the Romans. "Wrath is necessary and cannot be denied. One cannot win anything without wrath. If it doesn't fill the soul, if it doesn't warm the heart: wrath must then be used to serve us, not as our master, but as a soldier." Right?'

'Aristotle. Well done, you know some of your classics, but what's that got to do wi—'

Melody's hand moved with lightning speed. She was not trained as a surgeon, but as a first year resident she had been in the operating theatre. Properly maintained, the Royal Marines' Fairburn-Sykes is operating theatre sharp on both edges. Unlike a short scalpel, its blade is 7-inches of lethal slice and dice power.

His balls and penis were hanging in the first slice, clean off in the second pass. He saw her hand move back and forth, and felt something, but not much for a couple of seconds. His brain sort of knew what she had done.

He tried to scream, but Melody's hand was already

clamped hard over his mouth. She thought of an answer as the blood poured from him into the earth, and before his eyes had totally dimmed.

'I'm here for the children, *headmaster.* Maybe God sent me in his place, because he sure as hell ain't around much these days.'

CHAPTER

32

'This inquest is now concluded with the verdict of death by suicide. I would like to thank the jury members for their service. You are now dismissed.'

As the gavel banged, Hickman hurried across to catch Dr Patel – the crown coroner for the London Borough of Thamesside.

'Raj, hello.'

'Bill, as I live and breathe. Slumming in my humble coroner's court. Not exactly your esteemed haunt of the Bailey. How's Vivian?'

Hickman and Raj Patel had been pals since the good doctor's days as a duty police surgeon for the Met in the late 1990s. They had been in the trenches together on many a gruesome crime scene. And Raj's mother made the best damn curries west of the Ganges.

'Great. You must have us over for curry. Been too long.'

'No problemo, Hickster. I'll deploy the maternal unit to fire up the pots. Uma has finally conceded total defeat and lets my mum cater, with almost zero moaning and nookie bans. How's a week this Saturday sound?'

'Sounds good to me.'

'Now that's decided, what's up?'

'Don't take this the wrong way, but you are absolutely happy with the verdict? Suicide?'

Raj's eyes narrowed. He was very protective about *his* court. 'Shouldn't I be?'

Hickman scrunched up his nose, silent fart in a lift like. 'That's the problem, I'm not sure. I was sure when it first dropped on my desk. I sort of had a personal interest via the one living victim of the crimes he was convicted of. Pleased in a way to give her some good news. Not that there is any good news here really. But you know those little itches I get when something seems a bit off. This started to really itch last night.'

'Weeks later? Why?'

'I dunno. It's – uh, well, hard to put a finger on it. You know irritating old me.'

'I do indeed. But aside from actual video recording of the fellow doing the deed, all we ever have is the evidence as presented at the scene. The physical, forensic and witness evidence is all well beyond reasonable doubt. Hence the verdict.'

'It's just he didn't seem the type.'

'Really, Bill? Not the type?'

'Yeah, yeah, I know, Raj. Any beat copper talking like this, I'd have bounced to desk duty. Heartless scrotebag Smith was, yes. But he was in a tight little crew. His family for all intents. And three of them were banged up together. Support structure inside, see. He wasn't isolated and lonely and stricken by remorse.'

'I see your itch, but I will raise you the evidence. Again. Besides aren't there more than enough real victims out there to be concerned about.'

'Yeah you're right. Seen the papers about this Belgium thing?'

'Detective Sergeant.'

Leia Jennings stood to greet Hickman as he entered her office.

'Afternoon, sir. Everything alright?'

'Did you hear the William Smith coroner's verdict came back as suicide?'

'I did not, sir. No surprise there.'

'No. Open and shut really.'

Since the Bentley murder, Detective Sergeant Jennings had written eight more active murder investigations on her board. Hickman was particularly interested in that one case. Unfortunately for her, almost two months later, this was the coldest case still active. And it was slipping inexorably down the list of solvability-probability. The key was identifying the mystery woman with the shoulder-length blonde hair leaving *Memento Mori* with Bentley. So far, not so good. If only these criminals would leave clues like they did on TV.

'Just to update you on the Bentley case, sir. Another two female victims have been positively identified from the tapes. That's twenty-three so far. There's probably more who realize they're victims but can't face the trauma of even talking to us about it.'

'So it's dead-end time until something new turns up.'

Leia was glad he said that. That was the reality, and she was getting tired of having to say the same thing every time her Detective Superintendent *popped in as he was passing*.

'You nailed it, sir. Unfortunately.'

'Spoke to Harry Linedon, Chief Constable of

Oxfordshire last night—'

'Oh, okay.'

'Wanted to fill me in on that Belgian thing.'

'Belgian thing?'

'Over the weekend?'

'Away hiking, sir. Brecon Beacons, long weekend.'

'Ah. Dozen paedos burned to death. Child sex ring. It's all a bit nebulous. Bloody horrendous though, from what I gather. Plus there's a British connection. Oxfordshire. And London. In passing.'

'Be honest, sir, try not to tune into the news these days on downtime.'

'There's a lot being held back. The Belgians don't have our tabloids biting at them, so it's easier for them to withhold information from the great unwashed.'

'What's the connection here.'

'Angus Sebastian Malcolm Ainsworth. Headmaster at some posher private school in Oxfordshire. And probably the main paedo ringleader, turns out. The dozy Belgians only found his body yesterday, twenty-four hours later. Not roasted, like the others. In the woods nearby, tied to a tree with his, uh – privates chopped off.'

Leia grimaced involuntarily. 'Ouch. And blimey.'

'Blimey indeed.'

'So – the official thinking is what exactly, sir?'

Hickman was still digesting the whole complex incident as relayed to him by the Chief Constable. He hated getting criminal information second hand, let alone third hand.

'Okay. The Belgians think the sequence of events runs like this. This Ainsworth character runs some international paedo ring. He sets up an auction of young boys in Belgium. Rich bastards from all over Europe are invited. The kids are transported from Turkey chained up in a shipping container. Some third party intervenes. The transporter driver was found literally gutted in the drawing room. The poor children are rescued. Ainsworth's Belgian partner and twelve others are burned alive when a pick-up truck explodes, after the petrol tank was lit up by a shotgun slug, probably fired by Ainsworth himself. Who then escapes, avoiding the police and the fire brigade, called by a neighbour. Ainsworth is then hunted down and Jack the Rippered in the woods by our mysterious friend.'

Leia was stunned. She resisted *wow* as a suitable response. 'There's no doubt Ainsworth wasn't just in the wrong place at the wrong time.'

'None. His home was searched late last night, conclusive incriminating stuff on his laptop, and other evidence. The wife thought he was still away, seminar at Somerset House. Well, that's her story.'

Ever the detective, Leia automatically started to see patterns and similarities and connections. Her mind lit up. The obvious one leapt out. Despite popular fiction and the movies, vigilante type incidents were incredibly rare. You wait years for one, then two coming along within the space of two months?

'Not our case is it, sir? We have no jurisdiction or interest in this whatsoever.'

Hickman shrugged. 'Absolutely. There's no stepping on anyone's toes from us. Especially the Belgians who have enough on their plate with those terrorist nutters running amok.'

'And yet, sir, there's more?'

Hickman smiled at the woman whom he was starting to think of as a protégé. 'Actually there is one more salient point involving our, well I did use the Ripper word. The person the Belgians would like to help them with their inquiries.'

'They have a description of him?'

'Yes. Indeed. Except it's not a him but a her. According to the little boys who spent some time with their rescuer, she spoke to them in English, and had blonde hair.'

'A blonde-haired her?' Detective Leia Jennings looked suitably gobsmacked as her mind whirled into gear and started to make connections. Crazy connections.

'Not that this is Scotland Yard's case, or that you have any time to officially follow up tenuous connections about mysterious blondes in unrelated cases from different jurisdictions.'

'Of course not, sir. Nor would I ever dream of it.'

CHAPTER

33

'Darling, forgive me, but you look dreadful. I was going to say fucking dreadful but Ben has been chiding me for excessive use of expletives.'

'Oh thanks, Chloe. You're such a yenta.'

'Well it has to be said. What on earth have you been doing to yourself?'

You wouldn't believe it if I told you, Chlo-me-me-me.

It was two in the afternoon. Ten hours since Melody had parked the Mondeo in her new lock-up garage in south Kilburn. Not wishing to take any more risks, she replaced the fake number plates with the real ones before collapsing into her bed.

The plan had been to catch up with as much sleep as possible. That turned out to be five hours. Chloe had helpfully woken her at eleven o'clock with five insistent separate calls, till Melody was forced to answer. The urgency was to remind her of the first meeting of the newly inaugurated board for the *Paul McRae Peach Foundation.* And yes, she had forgotten, having been rather busy in Belgium.

Chloe was, of course, immaculate. Melody looked perfectly fine, not at all dreadful, apart from a little tiredness showing around her eyes. She had thrown on her leather biker gear to Triumph it across London to the Peach corporate HQ in Canary Wharf. Biosphere One (fancy name for the purpose built facility housing the few hundred Peach employees) was located on the outskirts of Milton Keynes. A half-hour drive from the Carrington's sumptuous Cordingay House.

Melody had been gazing out of the huge window in the Peach corporate boardroom. From her perch on the 40th floor of the Prime Building, the sweeping bend in the Thames obscured a direct view of her former Limehouse home. She was just another blip on a river that flowed back to the Romans, back further still, beyond human settlement. The old river would be here long after we are all forgotten blips in history.

After Chloe's pestering – and her late start – Melody had been first to arrive for the inaugural meeting of the foundation's newly constituted board. She had no idea what she was supposed to do.

Chloe guided her and it went well. Minutes were taken, decisions made, budgets set, fund raising discussed, action plans agreed. The great and the good in their natural habitat.

The board comprised seven, including herself. Ben and Chloe. Professor Julian Adner, the famed geneticist from Cambridge. Mary Mackintosh, founder and president of Main Capital. Neel Modi, Emeritus Professor of Mathematics at Oxford University. And finally – at Melody's insistence – Amanda Soresh, the neurosurgeon who had saved her life at St. Michael's Hospital.

Three hours later and she was out of there. It would

have been two hours, except Amanda insisted on a little personal chit-chat; which stretched to a semi-interrogation on her recovery so far. Melody was praying this was not going to be a recurring theme every time they met. She had finally managed to draw Amanda to a conclusion, when Ben collared her as well—

'Okay, proxy girl. Got a second for the money grubbing world, as well?'

Although she rarely thought about it, Melody was an important voting shareholder in the company. Before the Limehouse incident, Peach had two classes of stock: 'A' shares, and 'B' shares. Both classes had voting rights, but while the 'A' shares had one vote per share, the 'B' shares represented a super vote of ten votes per shares.

'B' shares were owned by a select few key insiders: namely the founders who put in their talent; original key investors who put in millions of pounds; and big investors who joined the boom later. Unlike 'A' shares, 'B' shares didn't trade on the public markets. Not just any Tom, Dick or Harriet could buy them. They were controlled by complex rules directing how and when, and to whom they could be sold. 'B' shares were in possession of Ben and Chloe, plus four other director/investors, in varying percentages. The seventh person being herself with 8.7% of the total of super voting 'B' shares. A small but possibly crucial swing vote amongst the other big hitters.

Following Paul's death, the watertight *Key Man Agreement* between Ben and Paul, ensured the majority of the 'B' shares in his estate reverted back to Ben. Paul's estate receiving a monetary value based on a complex equation. Ben to pay that sum to the estate's beneficiaries in full within five years. It was all kosher. Both partners were happy to agree to it as legally binding when it became clear their little university venture was going to take off. The young think they will never die. But in his will, Paul had subsequently bequeathed, to an outside party, the maximum he was allowed to bequest in 'B' shares. That being 8.7% of the absolute total of those shares. That party being Melody.

While Melody was in her long dreamless sleep, the corporate world orbited on. The fact that a stock holder is unable to vote at any particular time is irrelevant. Clinging to life in St. Michael's ensured Melody couldn't exercise her 8.7% voting when Peach split its ordinary 'A' shares creating 'A' and 'C' classes of shares.

As the original 'A' share holder's shares doubled, the price dropped in half. While the 'A' shares remained with one vote, one share; the newly created 'C' shares had no voting entitlement. At the same time the 'B' shares voting bloc rose from ten votes per share, to twenty votes per share. While the ordinary shares doubled for outside investors, their voting power was diminished. The manoeuvre was a blatant and successful attempt for Ben and the select few to retain as much control over the company as legally possible. Investors are there to make money, that's all the control they care about. As of issue day, the voting 'A' shares were trading at £174.78 per share, while the non-voting 'C' shares traded at £157.48. Melody knew this because of the large ticker display in the boardroom which relayed share price changes as they happened. She did like that figure, as she still held 57,000 'of the 'A' shares she also inherited in Paul's will.

As to the rest? That was the environment for which Melody had no real interest. And that was before she had embarked on her current path, allowing her even less time or inclination. Her cut-throat tendencies had moved on elsewhere. She had given Ben her continuing proxy two years ago, as she trusted him implicitly to act in her best financial interests. She was fully entitled to attend every regular 'B' shareholders meeting in this very boardroom. Her own virtually unused Peach-allocated laptop was docked on her nice Nevada desk, in her own Peach office, just along the corridor on the 40th floor. It filled daily with cc'd highly confidential information. Ergo, Melody saw the proxy as a win-win. No effort, and continuing reward.

'Okay, okay, not too sure to be honest, out of the blue. Can I think about that one and get back to you, Ben?'

Ben liked the Silicon Valley casual look for himself and all Peach employees. He came to the meeting from Peach's gym still in shorts and T-shirt. For an hour daily he religiously maintained the middleweight Cambridge Boxing Blue physique of his youth.

'Yeah sure, love. There's absolutely no hurry. At all. Just a thought.'

'Okay. But you know you have my proxy anyway. You know how I feel. I don't think about it, but now that I think about it, I do feel connected to Paul with that connection. Does that sound cat lady nuts?'

'Sounds all too human. Though with the *Paul McCrae Peach Foundation,* you might see that connection there as well. But it's just a thought.'

Ben looked at his massively expensive watch. Melody had no idea what it was, but if he was wearing it, it was massively expensive.

'Yes, I have to fly too, Ben.'

Ben laughed at being caught. 'Yeah, getting the chopper from the roof to the Biosphere in ten. No doubt you haven't read any of the multiple emails about Project Red Dancer? It's beta testing today, need to pop in to see the troops.'

Melody shuddered involuntarily as she watched the helicopter lift off from the roof of the Prime building. Even after so many years, the sound of the whirling helo blades brought back the horror of Camp Bog Trot. She was a different person from the frightened young mother who thought Major Hassan was about to shoot her in the face. Before his head exploded all over her face instead.

As the Carrington's personal transporter headed straight to the Thames before turning upstream, Melody strode back to her allocated parking spot below the Prime Building. Another big benefit of 'B' shares.

Frankie Bishop stepped out from behind a pillar as she was about to pull on her Bell helmet.

'Wotcha, love.'

The old Melody would have jumped a foot in the air. Krav Maga Melody. Fairburn-Sykes Melody. Sanguine Melody. They were all in control.

'Bloody Nora, Frankie. Don't sneak up on a girl like that.'

Frankie indicated that she should come to him. 'Behind the pillar. Camera blind spot.'

'How did you know I was here?' She thought about her own question for a second. Looked back at her bike. Remembered the Ainsworth package which Aaron left in her garage. Didn't wait for a reply. 'You desecrated Helen and planted a stinking tracking device on her, didn't you?'

He smiled. 'You named your motorbike Helen?'

'Helen of Troyumph. So?'

Frankie laughed. 'Very girly power empowering.'

'Now am I going to have to rip her apart? Find the tracker bug.'

'Okay Steve McQueen, let's take a step back. Yes, I admit Mister Fuchs requested a little GPS insurance policy for your own protection—'

'My protection?'

'But what's the downside? Really? Think about it. What if something untoward had occurred in Belgium.'

'You knew I was in Belgium? Car tagged as well then.'

'If we didn't know then, we do now. You certainly made the news. Mister Fuchs is well pleased you're safe and well, and back home.'

Frankie reached into his jacket pocket and retrieved a small, black velvet-clad jewellery box. He handed it to Melody.

'Mister Fuchs wanted me to give this to you. Personally like, so I can explain the significance.'

Melody opened the box lid. Inside was a gold Star of David attached to a gold chain.

'It's beautiful.'

'Solid gold. It belonged to Mister's Fuchs' daughter Sophia.'

'Didn't know he had a daughter. Knew he had a son.'

'Two sons. One living daughter, lives in California with her family. Has for years. He never sees her. Plus Sophia. She died, when she was six. Meningitis. He was banged up at the time. Happened so fast they never got him to the hospital in time. He wanted you to have it, if you promise to wear it.'

Melody welled-up at the thought of another parent losing their young daughter. She slipped the chain around her neck. Pressed the dangling Star of David into her skin. Closed her eyes for a second.

'Of course I will. Honoured to. I'm just so, so sorry about his daughter.'

'Yeah, well he ain't no emotional man is Mister Fuchs, that's for sure. Calculating like, as I'm sure you know by now. And it was way before my time, course. But when he lost his youngest son Samuel, couple of years ago—'

'Oh, that's awful.'

'I ain't never seen him so low.'

'Kevin only ever mentioned Adam, and even then he

wouldn't really talk about him because of – well you know what. Him being, uh – running the biz in his dad's enforced absence.'

'Running it, eh?' Frankie laughed. 'Yeah, well Sam was Mister Fuchs pride and joy see. Clever kid like, went to university and all that shit. Supposed to make something of himself, not involved in all this malarkey. Then Mister Fuchs heard about your troubles around the same time. Though he never knew you personally then, but he knowed all about your side of the family.'

Melody was stunned. 'Aaron was already aware of me, his distant cousin six times removed?'

Frankie winced, realizing maybe he shouldn't have mentioned that. His boss surely would have told Melody had he wanted her to know. Time to change the subject.

'Be that as it may, apart from the treasured object around your neck, Mister Fuchs has two more items for you, as per your agreement.'

Melody took the flash drive from him.

'You should make these like Mission Impossible. This message will self-destruct in five seconds.'

'Yeah – that's a good—'

BANG—

They stopped mid-chat. The car door slam echoed from the other side of the underground car park. A car engine fired up a couple of seconds later.

'Yes. Okay, now this is info on your next – person of interest.'

'Oh don't be so coy, Frankie. He's my next target. I am now a woman who has targets. Believe that?'

'Yeah, and if I was you I'd be very careful about this one. He ain't no lone wolf scumbag type like the other two. They was easy, in relatively speaking terms. Both anonymous, thinking they was untouchable. Never saw you coming that's for sure. Don't get me wrong I was impressed, but—'

Melody had been observing Frankie's body language change. 'You disapprove of this one don't you?'

He thought about it. 'Let's just say, this vengeance drug you've mainlined, is it really helping you? Do you feel better? How long can you keep this high running? Think Charity would want her mum to maybe die, becau—'

Melody exploded at Frankie's liberties. 'Don't fucking lecture me on my dead daughter, mate, okay? And don't you worry about me because I can handle myself. Ask those paedos in Belgium if you don't fucking believe me.'

Frankie half backed away, hands up in a pacific gesture. 'Okay, okay. Jesus. Sorry I said anything. Just be careful with this one, all I'm saying. Honest, love.'

Melody took a few deep breaths to calm the rapid spike in her heart rate and blood pressure.

Calm the fuck down, Melody.

'Fine. I'm sorry. I know you think you're helping.'

Frankie handed her a second flash drive. 'Compliments of Mister Fuchs. His next instalment payment of his latest debt. Here's the deal. When you get home, pop this flash drive into your laptop. It will automatically execute and install a programme called Remote Viewer—'

'Okay.'

'Now the timeframe is still to be determined. If you want satisfaction, make sure you have Remote Viewer running from noon onwards tomorrow, and be ready to spend the rest of the day waiting. And watching.'

CHAPTER

34

Melody had been staring at the laptop for over an hour in her south Kilburn digs. She didn't want her viewing pleasure disturbed with unexpected door-knocks from Hickman, her sister, Kevin, or Jehovah's Witnesses. It made sense to do all her work here and keep Golders Green clean.

Frankie did say watch all day. Grabbing the laptop, she hurried to the kitchen to prepare another pot of coffee. The brew was dripping through the filter when *Remote Viewer* flicked into life.

Frankie had explained the mechanics of an encrypted live stream from Ringland. One of Aaron's protected minions – inside for cyber fraud – had set up the tech. The live stream was being uploaded to the Cloud and then downloaded to Melody's laptop. There was about a five second delay. Now she was the one accessing the dark web for nefarious purposes.

The quality of the picture was amazing, though there

was some camera shake in the wide-angle shot. The sound was equally impressive. She could see a dozen or so inmates exercising on equipment that wouldn't be out of place in a high-end West End gym. Three prison guards were visible, oblivious to being caught on camera too.

The camera swung around 180 degrees to selfie Aaron holding the Go-Pro in his outstretched right hand. The wide-angle lens showed him flanked by his large oppo Jimmy, and another prisoner. Dressed in gym shorts and T-Shirts, they were sweating after exercise.

'Alright, girl.'

It was the first time she had heard directly from Aaron since her visit to Ringland over three months ago.

'Hi, Aaron.' She felt a bit daft at her automatic greeting in reply. The solo cast was strictly one way. He couldn't hear or see her. Her hand absentmindedly gripped the Star of David.

'Got your message last time, love. Came through loud and clear. Jimmy you know. This is Ian.'

Ian raised his hand and smiled embarrassedly for the camera.

'Here we go then, girl.'

Aaron swung the Go-Pro back in the direction of the prisoners, and let his arm drop to mid-thigh level. Ian ambled off towards the centre of the gym. Melody couldn't recall the faces of the monsters who attacked her family at Limehouse. She only knew them from mugshots shown Hickman as she recovered in hospital. Then later, from the internet research which she forced herself to undertake.

The man on the treadmill she recognized instantly. Glenn Borthwick. He looked thinner than in his chubby smug shot; and the numerous photographs printed in the newspapers. Hickman confirmed he was the brute who had smashed her in the face.

Aaron stopped by an exercise bike, careful to focus on Ian as he ambled past Borthwick to the rear of the treadmill. Borthwick was jogging at a clip. When Ian surreptitiously caught the back of his heel, Borthwick's momentum sent him crashing head first into the machine front. He bounced off and skidded to a halt, blood streaming from his broken nose. Ian carried on walking, all innocent like. But Borthwick's scrambled brain was able to figure out what occurred. Two other prisoners were bellowing with laughter. Borthwick leapt up like a mad man, running and screaming at Ian.

'You're fucking dead. Fucking dead you cunt. Fucking dead.'

Borthwick got in a couple of wild swings against the back of Ian's head, before grappling him to the ground. By then two of the guards were on Borthwick. They dragged him off. The third guard grabbed one of Borthwick's arms, yanking it backwards. In a few seconds they had him on the deck, one kneeling across the back of his legs, while the other two applied arm restraints.

'You're fucking dead, Jass.'

While the picture was brilliantly clear for Melody, the intent wasn't. Aaron swung the Go-Pro to selfie himself again.

'Phase one complete. Stand by for phase two.'

The screen cut to black. Melody had no other option but to stand by again.

She stood by for an hour before the screen flicked into life. This time the Go-Pro was strapped to Aaron's chest. The point of view was the same as that in the first person shooter mode Melody remembered from Charity's video games. The arms and hands of the protagonist – you the hero – are visible as if they're your own arms cocking guns, chambering rounds, or wielding swords.

Aaron didn't appear to be wielding anything as he approached the prison infirmary. He turned to check on Jimmy bringing up the rear. As Aaron reached the door, it was being held open by a nervous looking guard.

'Alright, Mister Fuchs.'

The infirmary was the equivalent of a small A&E ward. There were four full-sized trolley beds curtained off from each other. They were identical to their A&E hospital cousins in all respects, except one: the built-in leg, foot, arm and hand restraints.

'Everything set, Mister Palmer?'

'Yes, sir Mister Fuchs. Totally. Duty nurse went off shift five minutes ago. Overnight nurse don't come on for an hour. Budget cuts. Walter went for his break same time, be gone twenty minutes, minimum.'

'Frankie delivered the package to your missus?'

'That he did, Mister Fuchs. Most grateful. Very handy that, cost a living and all. Uh – will it hurt?'

'Gotta be convincing, son.'

Mister Palmer winced at the thought of convincing.

'Cheer up, Mister Palmer, you're already in the fucking infirmary. Where better?'

Melody's fingers were locked tight, pressing the Star of David so hard into her palm it left an imprint. She wished it was her instead of Aaron about to leave a permanent imprint on Borthwick. She no longer had one scintilla of doubt upon the righteousness of her cause; or to her witnessing that righteous justice. Some people deserved to die for their heinous acts. Nuremburg showed that. That was vengeance if ever there was. It was a truth universally understood since the dawn of man. Alternative views were the aberration on thousands of years of precedent. They were the outlier now in control. In the absence of society making that hard choice, others had the right to step in and administer natural law. It was in the Talmud, the Old Testament, direct from God. If you believed those books.

Aaron pulled open the curtain surrounding Ian's bed.

'Okay, Mister Fuchs?'

'You done great Ian lad.'

Palmer selected a key from his large key ring and undid Ian's restraints. As Palmer went to pull back, Ian grabbed his uniform jacket lapels then head-butted him viciously in the face.

Staggering backwards as his nose exploded in blood, Jimmy stepped in to mule kick Palmer in the balls. Down he went groaning and bleeding in equal measure. Aaron picked up the key ring and handed it to Ian.

'Be a good lad, Ian. Strap Mister Palmer to the bed. Gentle like. Then get the supplies.'

From behind one of the other curtains Borthwick heard the commotion. 'Hey what the fuck's happening out there. I need some more fucking painkillers. In fucking agony here. It's me human rights, fuckers.'

Aaron pulled back curtain number two.

'What the fu – Mister Fuchs?'

'Glenn Borthwick? Right? We ain't never been properly introduced. Aaron Fuchs, denizen of this ever so humble manor.'

'I knows who you are, Mister Fuchs. Or was, leastways.'

'He knows who I am Jimmy. My reputation precedes me. You's in for, oh what was the thing wot you done.'

'Bit of B and E.'

'Ah, the old breaking and entering. Takes me back to my youth. But not quite in your case sunshine. You done quite a bit more than that, right?'

Borthwick smirked, as if he thought Aaron would be the hard man impressed with his exploits.

'Dog eat cat world ain't it, Mister Fuchs. Be honoured if

I was in your pack inside. Respect.'

'Speak German, Glenn? No course not. Thing is me old sauerkraut, did you know Fuchs is German for Fox?'

A furrow of doubt appeared on Borthwick's forehead. Before he could answer, Ian reappeared with the various supplies from the medical cupboards. Aaron took the roll of 4-inch wide elasticated bandage and a big ball of cotton wool.

Borthwick struggled against his restraints as the sight of the unrestrained Ian. Something was definitely up. 'What the fuck? What's that fucker doing loose?'

'Don't worry about him son. Jimmy, please.'

SLAM—

Jimmy punched Borthwick in his six-pack gut. Deflating faster than a punctured beach ball, Borthwick gasped, trying to shout; but nothing came out as Aaron stuffed the ball of cotton wool into his mouth. Then he wrapped the bandage tight Borthwick's head covering his nose and mouth.

'Probably wondering, "what the fuck is happening to me. This ain't right." Nah, nah, nah, this is dead right sunshine. This is your punishment for what you done to my family. Because that's what families do, they looks after one another. They helps one another. They does each others favours.'

Ian handed a plastic container to Aaron.

'Probably wondering what's that he's holding.'

Borthwick got his second wind, thrashing around helplessly.

'Oh no, what's that I hear you say. You can't cos you're bandaged up like Christopher Lee's Mummy.'

Aaron unscrewed the container top.

'Well, in me hand, Glenn-boy, is four pints of medical grade alcohol.'

As Aaron cascaded the liquid into the bandage, all over

his head and mouth, Borthwick coughed and spluttered, like a terrorist being water boarded.

'Which they uses for all sorts of stuff. Like sterilizing and purifying.'

Aaron poured half into the head bandage, then doused the rest over Borthwick's torso and legs.

'Fire being mother nature's purifier, Glenn. Sure, fire destroys. Then there's hell fire, if you believe in all that malarkey. Us Jews don't believe in hell, matter a fact, if I recalls me Talmud. But fire also cleanses and refreshes, and allows for the renewal of life.'

Aaron handed the empty container to Ian, who wiped off Aaron's prints. That done, he handed a disposable cigarette lighter to Aaron. The liquid had stopped pouring down Borthwick's nose, and he was breathing easier, rather than slowly drowning.

'And as I don't believe in hell, you're gonna have to burn here on earth for what you did to Melody Fox and her beloved daughter Charity. May her life be a blessing.'

Aaron flicked on the lighter flame, and threw it on Borthwick's legs. The ignited alcohol raced up Borthwick's body, setting his head alight. The pillows and bedding erupted in flames as he thrashed around with no escape. The fluid down his throat was last to ignite as the inferno was taking hold. Breathing became an agonized horror before it became impossible. The bed was now a raging inferno as Borthwick writhed his last. Finally, the smoke alarms kicked in.

Melody was in a trance-like state watching him burn: the monster who almost killed her. It was surreal. But not like a movie. That's what people always say when they are caught up in something violent that they've only ever seen in a movie. It's their only reference. Melody had that reference play out in Basra. That was her movie moment when Arnie, or Bruce or Wolverine kills the bad man as he's about to kill the girl. This was surreal because Melody had dreamed of it for so long. And it was happening in one of the ways she had imagined it, not because it was happening.

BEEP—BEEP—BEEP—

The smoke alarm fifteen miles south of Melody pierced into south Kilburn. The trance was broken. The water sprinklers sprayed on as Borthwick burned on. Now totally inert, and quite dead. He had suffered all right. And yes, Charity did not magically appear at her side. But she had long since rejected the false dichotomy which people always brought up. It was an absurd presumption by those who had not suffered unimaginable loss.

CHAPTER

35

'My client fully understands his rights and is quite prepared to make a statement, Detective Sergeant.'

The interview room was harshly lit, to make its denizens feel uneasy and more compliant. As if being held at New Scotland Yard was not unsettling enough for most people. Ian sat on an uncomfortable plastic chair, next to his lawyer, at a metal table bolted to the floor. The four corners of the room had a camera fixed at the nexus between wall and ceiling. Extending up from the table, pointing at Ian's face, were three ultra high definition cameras. There was no escape the all-seeing eyes. No cheesy inefficient two-way mirrors here.

Leia couldn't hide her surprise. Hardened criminals such as Ian Byrnes were rarely keen to cop to their crimes. Not many of them had an expensive lawyer of the calibre of Sarah Olongo-Hitchens, as they confessed to heinous murder. Waste of money really.

Hickman was watching the proceedings at the *FFACE*

unit in the basement complex at the Yard. The new Forensic Facial Analysis & Capture Equipment was proving a useful tool. The three ultra high definition cameras capture the smallest micro-expressions indicating the veracity of a suspect's answers. But even these cameras loved Sarah Olongo-Hitchens. Her delectable skin shimmered like the smoothest, most expensive dark chocolate the Swiss have to offer. Her short Afro emphasized her beautiful, classical African face.

'Well that's certainly not what I expected, Ms Olongo-Hitchens, given the severity of the charges—'

'Life is full of surprises, sergeant.'

'True. But before we get to the written statement, I just need to ask Mister Byrnes, Ian, to run through the sequence of events again, as he claims they happened. If that's okay.'

Sarah looked at her client who nodded that it was indeed okay.

'Ask away, sergeant. My client wants to fully cooperate with your enquiries.'

'When exactly did Mister Byrnes become your client? You are rather expensive and he has been inside for fifteen years for arson and murder, has he not?'

Sarah bristled. 'I said you could question my client, not me, DS Jennings.'

Leia smiled sweetly. She enjoyed using passive-aggressive techniques to get under the skins of rich defence lawyers.

'No offence intended. So, Ian, do you have anything to add or amend regarding the sequence of events? I find it hard to believe you would do what you did based on an everyday contretemps in the gym. You burned a man alive. Seems a little drastic? Even for Ian 'Burns It' Byrnes.'

Ian sighed as if the whole thing was now boring him. He wasn't tense or worried. Why would he be? There was nothing they could do to him now. And he knew his story by heart. Aaron Fuchs had made him recite it out loud, in his cell, every day for the last month. He was a cunning bastard was that Mister Fuchs. Ian had no idea why he wanted Borthwick dead though. Never asked. Fuchs kept that close to the vest. Nor did he know when his part in the deed would be done. Just be ready for the nod and his missus got the other half of the half million. She'd stuck with him all these years he'd been banged up. Never ditched him for a new bloke. She could have. She was a looker. Even now. Never missed a visit with the kids. Bloody saint really. That sort of loyalty needed rewarding, especially as all hope was now abandoned that he would ever get out again to provide for her.

'– and that was it. He was gone. I did it. Story. End of.'

Leia stared at Ian for the whole ten minutes it took him to repeat what he told her on the ride from Ringland to the interview room. He was as relaxed now as he was then. The visual evidence didn't contradict a word he said. Thing was, Byrnes, the arsonist for hire, had an exemplary prison record. So why? Was it really out of character? He had been inside for murder, despite seventeen years of non-murdering. Maybe he just snapped? It happened with criminals who already suffer from lower impulse control.

'I most strongly advised my client to exercise his right of silence, but as you have just witnessed he was determined to make a clean breast of it. That being the case, should we get started with the written statement?'

Leia shrugged her shoulders in admitting there was little else she could do. She pushed the yellow statement pad and black biro across the table to Ian.

'Okay, Ian, if you could please write down what you have just told me, we can wrap up this interview. And get you back to prison for the rest of your life.'

Hickman leaned back in his chair and rubbed his eyes. The bright monitors hurt after an hour of continuous focussing. The *FFACE* technician had assured him the micro-readings indicated that Byrnes was genuine in his responses. No telltale ticks to indicate deception. Hickman realized the absurdity of trying to use indication of guilt to prove innocence. But he couldn't kick the notion that had bubbled up to his ever suspicious brain. Within two months, there had been two very explainable deaths in one prison. Fair enough. But that both involved the guilty parties in one case. One utterly heinous case. Seriously?

He did wonder whether his personal investment in Melody Fox was interfering in any way? Would he have even noticed a seemingly unrelated prison suicide, and a prison murder, had it not been for her ties to that one case?

CHAPTER

36

The life was slowly being squeezed out of Melody. Two large hands around your throat will do that. A knee pressing into your chest as the same time, giving the crusher maximum leverage to apply lethal pressure, being an added bonus.

Prying off the crusher-hands was not an option. They were twice a big as her mitts, giving crusher the advantage in pure strength. Black spots were racing across her eyes as her brain was fast being starved of oxygen.

The day (Melody's officially sanctioned catch-up day) had started out so well. She had her next target. But the demise of the late Borthwick left her more emotionally drained than she envisaged. His silent scream played around her head, forcing her to get out of bed early. It was not guilt. The image was horrific on a human level. She constantly fought any feeling of empathy. She had to. Ergo – she had erected an impenetrable barrier to keep feelings from breaching her defences.

After spinning on the hamster wheel for months she needed to step off, if only for a day. No planning, plotting, scheming, or even gloating. Plus she had at least one bone to pick with Kevin.

You're not getting off totally, Melody.

Kevin appeared in the Ploughman's beer garden at noon as Melody sipped a half of bitter shandy. She phoned him at 8 a.m. expecting to wake him up, but he was on his way out of the door. He was very mysterious as to his plans, but reluctantly agreed to meet at this small village pub in deepest Hertfordshire. It was a moderately warm day and she had enjoyed the forty mile blast up the A10 on Helen.

The mystery continued as she followed his old Land Rover from the village, then down a one-car-wide country lane for a few miles. Compared to her recent Belgian sojourn, she could certainly appreciate this pleasant trip to the country. The land here was more undulating and pleasing to the eye, with gentle hills breaking the horizon.

Kevin turned from the narrow lane onto a rough grass-covered *off-the-beaten* track. Vegetation was a dense mixture of shrubbery, brambles, hedgerow and gorse on either side. It all looked much the same to her un-green eye, which was more attuned to the urban jungle. Kevin pulled over into a slight indentation in the side of the path. Looked like someone parked here regularly, the grass being driven down flat from repeated use.

Melody followed as they climbed a steep, rocky trail through dense brambles and other uninviting scratching bushes. It was not the sort of route others would stumble on by accident, there being no discernible route to follow. Kevin's higgledy-piggledy path lurched left, right and up. The climb made worse by Melody having to lug a five-gallon plastic container full of water on her back. Kevin carried two identical containers.

A hacked-out plateau appeared amongst the vegetation. The hill continuing up for another few hundred feet. There was a large plastic water barrel to one side, a few garden implements scattered around, and—

'That's a cannabis plant? Bloody enormous.'

They stood besides a seven-feet tall bush wider than both of them combined. Kevin gave her a detailed lecture on his horticultural venture as he pottered about, watering and feeding nutrients to his giant baby. It didn't quite go in one ear and out the other, but Melody was mulling whether to spoil the day with a bit of interrogation. She had to know.

'Cousin dear, remember the first time we met? "Kevin Fuchs. Eff. You. Sea. Haitch. Ess. Spelt like you know what, but pronounced Fooks of this parish, et cetera et cetera, ad infinitum," if I recall precisely.'

'Cor blimey O'Riley. Sounds precisely like me. Guilty as charged.'

'Did Aaron tell you to make my acquaintance.'

Kevin's usual smile froze into place as his mind worked overtime. 'No. Don't be silly, darling. Course not – not exactly.'

'Fucking hell, Kevin. Not exactly?'

'Well, might have mentioned to him, casual like, that I was visiting mum and spotted you. Blow me over like a dead donkey there's that woman from the papers. Told Aaron in passing. Y'know he's like obsessed with all that genie-wotsit family tree shit. Already knew about the Foxes.'

'He made out you told him about me after we met.'

'Told you, Mel. He's family and all, and I love him, but Aaron is a control freak psycho. Believe me, what he's inside for? Tip of the Titanic. You wouldn't believe what the old geezer is capable of—'

She laughed, couldn't help it. 'I can actually. I'll be alright.'

'You keep saying that, girl.'

'What happened to his son. Not Adam. The youngest one, Samuel?'

Kevin's face darkened. 'His father happened. Like I said, control freak. He decided Samuel was going to be the good son, no family business for him. Well, Sam was a right clever clogs anyways, so why not. Posh private school in Oxford or some such. And nothing like Adam. I mean, I'm basking over in Basque country, so I only gets this guff second hand. Irony is, well, ironic. So there's no way I'm asking Aaron any of this—'

Sometimes his continuous verbal runs annoyed her to the point of yelling: 'Kevin!'

'Okay, okay. Long story short, Sammy trots off to the London School of Economics, falls in with the wrong crowd, gets hooked on the wrong shit, smack, eventually crack, I hears, not like this chillaxing medicinal herb.'

'Junkie?'

'Total. Dealing too. Kills him in the end. Found with a needle still in his fucken arm. A week later. Rats and such like. You don't wanna know. Believe that? The good son.'

'Bloody hell. What about Aaron? Does he—'

'No way. Never been into shifting pharmaceuticals. Can't abide them on any level, and that was before Samuel.'

The life was slowly being squeezed out of Melody. Her chest was pinned down by the weight of the assailant's knee. He had come out of nowhere swinging a tyre iron at her head. Yeah, she wasn't expecting it. It was her bloody day off for crying out loud.

She responded using a classic Krav Maga move with her

left forearm, using the thug's own momentum to redirect his arm away and down. At the same time she right-punched him in the Adam's apple with her balled fist, staggering the creep in his tracks. The swivel-kick to the head in her steel-toed biker boots would have been perfect to finish him off, but the throat chop wasn't enough to slow him.

He grabbed her swinging foot at his head height, throwing her backwards to hit the deck.

THUD—

No time to recover. He was on top of her, throttling away. Black spots were racing across her eyes as her brain was fast being starved of oxygen. This had to end now.

Melody's stiff-armed her right palm and slammed it under his chin. His head snapped back as blood and stuff flew from his mouth. The shock forced his hands to release their death grip from around her throat.

Before he could react, she straight-punched him in his balls twice, before rolling him off her chest. Scrambling to her feet, Melody was about to stomp him in the face several times when he beat his arm on the ground.

'Submit Princess, you von. Submit. Enough.'

Melody grinned. This was the first time she made Saul submit. She had lived for this day since he first decked her. The first day of training at his *All Fight Club.*

'Bollocks, Saul. You could've killed me with that iron bar.'

'You? Princess? It rubber bar. And vot, about old mensch me? Straight palm ram under chin? Lethal veapon. Brokens two teeth minimum at back.'

Melody extended down her hand to help him up. 'Quit whining old man. Could see you were wearing a gum shield. No teeth broke.'

Saul gripped her hand and hauled himself up. They

faced each other. Grinning manically with his bloody gum shield still in place, Saul looked like a crazy toothless man begging on the street. He grabbed her in a huge bear hug.

'So you humiliate old man, try to kill. Make submit first time. Finally, make me proud, Princess.'

He was crushing her more than when he had his hands around her throat. 'Hope you're not going to cry, you old sod.'

Saul released his grip. His eyes were definitely moist. 'Cry? Meh, vicked girl vorse than deadly Delilah. You fertummelt, Princess. Made eyes water with sneak punch to baby makers. That all.'

'Funny bloke, Saul.'

Saul half limped to a trestle table on the back wall. He grabbed a plastic bottle of spring water, glugging down a few mouthfuls down before dousing his head with half the bottle.

'So, vos little incident in Belgium. Some evil schlumps had bad end. Vot a Vorld.'

'Yes. I read that too.'

'Shalom to righteous who protect the little children. For they vill know his love. Amen.'

Saul and Melody stood silently for a good half minute. It was the first time he had treated her as a true equal, and not as a child to be cajoled, trained, taught, directed, pummelled. All with love, and all for her own good, of course. But still, it was the firm love you would show a child. This was the closest she had seen Saul come to being quietly impressed.

'So—'

'So, Princess. Your journey continues.'

That was a bit enigmatic.

'Look, I was wondering—'

'Good, basm. You vant for Saul for something on

dangerous road? MAC-10, sound suppressor, very excellent thirty mag, easy conceal, case maybe this time, vankers come strapped. Maybe Heckler & Koch MP-7. Take out platoon one mag. Mil-spec surveillance shit. Body armour? Vish Saul, and poof, like Aladdin magic lamp it appear.'

'Well, I was wondering—'

'Name it.'

'Could I have a bottle of that water too. It's really thirsty work kicking your arse, not-so-old man.'

Saul looked dramatically to the heavens. 'Vey is mir. Vy you punish me so viv this von.'

CHAPTER

37

'The next item is a particularly fine example of the muscular realism of the American artist George Bellows – entitled *Fight Night At The Roxy*. The oil on canvas was completed in 1909. Bellows was from both the Ashcan School; and the school of hard knocks. Both movements rooted in the brutal realism of working-class life in early twentieth century America. The bidding to start at three hundred thousand pounds. Do I hear three hundred thousand pounds?'

He did not. Melody glanced across the rows of faces in the auction room at Sotheby's. The auctioneer was not hearing anything yet, so Melody indicated the opening bid with her hand.

'Three hundred thousand pounds to my left. The bid is three hundred thousand. Do I hear three ten?'

From behind her, the next bid came in.

'Three hundred and ten thousand from the gentleman at the back, do I hear three twenty?'

In short order the stakes rose to five serious bidders scattered through the room; plus Melody. An auctioneer's dream as he was soon able to drive the bids up to one million six hundred thousand, now in increments of fifty thousand pounds. The bids were already past the world record for a Bellows. The rarefied atmosphere slowly dropped the four other serious bidders. As an unserious bidder, Melody could afford to be in until almost the end. Unfortunately, the last man standing, who she had been matching bid for bid for the past half-million, had blinked on her last bid.

Fuck a duck. Do they take Visa?

'The bid is one million, six hundred thousand pounds to the lady on my left.' He paused for dramatic effect and glanced at her pugilist opponent. 'The bid is to you, sir, one million six hundred thousand pounds for *Fight Night At The Roxy* by George Bellows, going once—'

Melody liked the painting. She had developed a new appreciation of the pugilistic arts.

'Going twice—'

Even so, she didn't want to walk away with it tonight at over a million and a half pounds. She could, but it complicated her liquid finances – and she had enough on her canvas as it was.

'That's *Fight Night At The Roxy*, for the last—'

'Two million.'

Life imitates art completely. There was the clichéd gasp from the crowd as her opponent delivered what he assumed was the knock out punch to the blonde bombshell.

The auctioneer looked directly at her, as did all eyes in the room. She didn't like that scrutiny. 'I have two million pounds from the gentlemen. Do I hear two million one hundred thousand?'

Melody tried to look as pained at losing as possible, while shaking her head in a dejected but dignified *no.*

'That's two million pounds going once – going twice—' He banged the gavel hard. 'Sold to the gentleman.'

There was an enthused ripple of applause. All eyes left her and turned to the winning gentleman. He looked fit and in his mid-forties; close cropped hair; scar down one cheek; dressed impeccably in an expensive suit. As she hoped, the man acknowledged her by nodding, smiling, and winking. He was smug and satisfied. And ripe for plucking.

He was waiting as she sauntered out of the auction room towards the exit onto Bond Street. Melody was all Armani business suited, carrying a sleek, black, metal briefcase.

'Cracking fight, but you know what they say: a good big-un always beats a good little-un. Boom. Boom. Boom.'

The man had a controlled Liverpool accent. Close up, Melody noted his dazzling white teeth. They looked very expensive. He also had two large goons standing a few feet away, eyes lasering into her. Equally expensive. They had rip-out-your-throat teeth.

'And I suppose I'm the good little one in this fight?'

'You were knocked out by a vicious uppercut to the wallet.'

Melody put on her best flirty laugh. 'True. And to whom do I owe that dubious pleasure?'

'Mark Higgins. At your service.'

Saul had throttled her neck too hard. Melody could still see his hand prints in her skin the day after. To hide the evidence, she covered up with a Hermes scarf. That was the least of her problems.

Hickman's unexpected visit after the Smith *suicide* had spooked her. What if she had been careless and left incriminating *stuff* (also called evidence) out for him to see. It was the dark web shenanigans which had spurred her into action; but it made sense to move everything that pertained to her extra-curricular activities from Golders Green to here. The almost Maida Vale flat being Melody's permanent base for this part of her life.

Melody had inserted Frankie's third and final flash drive into her laptop. In the right circles, ex-boxer Mark Higgins was known to be the country's biggest drug Czar. The nearest that Britain had to the boss of a Columbian cartel. Those circles being law enforcement. He had never been convicted of drug related offence. Not even simple possession of marijuana. Yet, the police were convinced he was the kingpin of an empire stretching across the globe. A kingdom supplying every recreational drug in the UK: cocaine, heroin, ecstasy, speed, and methamphetamine. If people could snort, ingest, inject, or smoke it, then Mark Higgins was the force behind it. He was personally responsible for untold deaths and misery.

She wondered how Aaron had these police files so helpfully provided on the flash drive. They detailed Higgins' life since he was forced to retire from a promising professional boxing career at the age of twenty-three. Washed up in Liverpool, he drifted into petty crime; and then into selling drugs for a local dealer in Kirkdale, Liverpool. It wasn't long before his hardman prowess as a boxer promoted him to enforcer for said dealer, Terrence McCready. It was at that point Higgins must have realized why enforce for the dealer, when he could be the dealer and enforce for himself.

The unsolved disappearance of Terrence McCready was believed to be his first murder. Unsolved in the legal sense, and in there being no corpus delicti sense. Liverpool police had a fair idea of who disappeared *Big Mac*, as he was known. Clicking the folder named Murders, it opened dozens of subfolders listed and named in date order. She clicked the folder: Terrence McCready_25-6-1993. Multiple files popped up, including a document named Witness 'A' Verbal Statement. Transcript_19-9-93.

CASE: Disappearance of Terrence McCready/14/5/93
WITNESS NAME: Derek Michael Jones aka Witness 'A'
INTERVIEWED: Tuebrook Police Station, Liverpool 13.
DATE: 19/9/93

WITNESS STATEMENT
My name is Derek Michael Jones but mates call me Degsy. Currently of no fixed abode. I admit I worked for Terrence McCready in supplying cocaine and ecstasy to punters around Kirkdale, Liverpool 5, usually on Stanley Road and Scotland Road. I also had regulars at the Beats Up club in Matthew Street, Liverpool 1, during the weekends, though some of the bouncers would sometimes stop me entering if they spotted me.
On the fourteenth of May 1993, I was told by Steven Scott to get back to McCready's base which is an old oil and chemicals drum reconditioning factory, off Commercial Road in Kirkdale, for a word. This worried me because McCready is a nasty bastard and is known to do all sorts of evil stuff to other sellers if they was short of any money owed to him.
Upon arrival, I noticed present was three other sellers like myself, Drew Parsons, Mickey Thompson and Dave Kendall, plus Mark Higgins who I knew from when he sold stuff like me and the others but was now working as a minder. McCready said that someone was being very naughty and stealing from him, and that they must be made an example of.
I was shitting myself because sometimes I did skim a little of the product and sell it separate to make some extra cash. Anyway

McCready picks up this axe and says that thieves should have their hands chopped off, which is just mental. Anyways I thought for sure he meant me, when he turns to Higgins and says "Ain't that right Mark".
The next second he sort of swings the axe at Mark Higgins, but Mark was very fast. He punched McCready in the face and grabs the axe off of him. Then Higgins swings it right at McCready and sticks it right in his chest. It was horrible. Blood was spurting everywhere and I thought I was going to pass spark out. Anyway, McCready sort of falls to his knees with the axe sticking out of his chest. So Mark Higgins pulls it out. Then swings it right down at McCready's head. Kills him stone dead. Well he gurgled for a bit, then twitched. Higgins then told us to stick McCready in one of the oil drums that was lying around from when it was a working factory. I never saw what Higgins did with it afterwards because it was still there when we left, and that's the God's honest truth.
After that we was working for Higgins full time. And to be honest it's been way better since. Got paid more, got paid straight away. And Higgins is dead clever. A right clever bastard don't you worry. I mean I assumed he was this punchy boxer, but he started taking security measures against you lads. Said McCready was a scouser thicko who Darwin had removed. I had no idea what he meant then Dave Kendall explained it to me. Made sense.

The follow-up action memo reported that two days after giving the statement, Jones also disappeared. There was speculation that he fled the city to go down south and start a new life. Some speculated he had caught the ferry from Holyhead to Ireland, where he had family on his mum's side. The police were convinced he had been murdered by Mark Higgins to silence him. That would be two murders in the space of five months.

None of the three, named by Jones as being fellow

witnesses to the murder of McCready, would cooperate on the investigation. Who could blame them? The Merseyside police realized that they had a new serious player in the region's drug trade. They started their official dossier of Mark Higgins' alleged activities.

The thousands of police documents on the flash drive painted a timeline as the ruthless Higgins progressed onwards and upwards. By the early 2000s, he had established supply pipelines in South and Central America, in Thailand, the Philippines, the Netherlands, Pakistan and Afghanistan. The bodies continued to mount. Low level dealers found dead. Car bombings in Columbia. The drip-drip of young people dying from overdoses, or bad batches of a particular product he was pushing.

In 2005, ecstasy pills, believed to have been manufactured by Higgins, led directly to the deaths of three young people at one rave. Six more were hospitalized with kidney damage, one had permanent brain damage. Their lives changed for the worse, forever.

All the while Higgins prospered. By 2010, police forensic accountants at the Fraud Squad estimated his net worth to be above five hundred million pounds. Naturally, he had diversified into multiple industries, with hundreds of companies to launder his cash, mainly abroad. Melody agreed with the presumed late Derek Michael Jones that Mark Higgins was a right clever bastard. He was obsessed with his own personal security. Even more paranoid than Bentley.

She opened the Higgins_2018 folder to reveal three subfolders.

UK Residence_2018: Higgins lived in a virtual fortress in East Sussex named *Montesquieu Keep*. A 15th century turreted castle, in fifty acres of robustly fenced land, with total security camera coverage. And an actual moat. She couldn't believe it. Another *turris.*

The police had failed to penetrate the interior and there were no current photographs. However they had secured the original estate agent details from 2010 when Higgins bought the listed property for £30 million. In 2011, he submitted detailed plans for interior renovations. Melody committed the layout to memory, just in case.

There was also the flock of two hundred rare breed sheep grazing the land. Sheep are a great security device against anyone walking across open land at night. They bleat like crazy when worried by strangers.

You learn something new every day, Mel.

Personal Security_2018: Higgins never went anywhere without a team of four security men. He tended to employ ex-military types, mercenaries who had no qualms about protecting a major drug kingpin. They were slightly more trustworthy than criminals, being content to be well paid; and not constantly plotting on stealing from their employer. Each man had a legal shotgun licence, but Melody guessed they were well-armed, when back at Castle Higgins. Apart from these four, the grounds were covered by eight other guards. No one was burying an axe in Higgins' head while he slept.

Personal Habits_2018: The cops may have consistently struck out in proving anything on Higgins, but they were persistent. They kept an up to date book on his leisure and love life. Higgins now had the money for the very best. He was unmarried and liked to keep a rotating bevy of beauties as female companionship. There was always a slot open for someone worthy.

He was often seen at Christies or Sotheby's, bidding on works of art. Money and taste do not necessarily live in the same room. In Higgins case they shared a house, at least. There was a list of the works of art he had publicly purchased. Higgins had a soft spot for the Impressionists. He did have one affectation which obviously related to his former life. Apparently Higgins had moved from the art of boxing, to an obsession with boxing as art. He recently sold a Jean-Michel Basquiat painting of Joe Louis that fetched £8.7 million at Christies. The police suspected he used his art dealings as another method of money laundering.

She went straight to the Christies website to check for upcoming auctions. There were a few sports themed works of art coming up for sale, but they were all horse racing. Bingo. There it was. An artist called George Bellows was being sold in three days. She had no idea whether Higgins would be there, but it was the only plan she had to get near him. Like every con man in the world will tell you, in the very best cons, the mark comes to you and initiates contact. The mark doesn't see the con because he thinks he is in control from the very beginning. This con works even better with a more intelligent mark who has control freak issues.

Melody had three days to work out how to make this Mark come to her – entirely of his own volition and with the impression it was all his idea.

CHAPTER

38

'Mark Higgins. At your service.'

'Congratulations Mister Higgins I wish you well with your purchase. It's a beautiful Bellows, and a well fought match.'

'Mark, please. And you are?'

Higgins stuck out his hand. Melody reciprocated, making sure she sublimated her desire for a strong Krav Maga grip, opting for the fake, girly response instead.

'Virginia Dalloway.'

Higgins had a type. Not exclusive, but the police surveillance photos of his current and previous female companions demonstrated a bias for straight haired auburn beauties, with green or blue eyes. Given the ubiquitous public surveillance cameras his preferred female was good for Melody too. A welcome change from the blonde-look in her two previous outings.

'Are you into boxing as an art form, or is this just a paid gig for you, Virginia?'

'You got me. Working on behalf of a client who wishes to extend his sporting portfolio. Sounds bloodless I know. Just investments. But I've had a thing for boxing as depicted in the arts ever since I went to the Met in New York as a kid. Saw the stunning Hellenic period *Boxer At Rest* bronze—'

'You're joking girl. I have *Boxer At Rest* back at my place.'

'Sorry?'

'Ha – what I mean is I have a brilliant copy, should be brill as it cost me a fortune. Copy sounds unbelievably naff I know. Like a cover band. It's a work of art in its own right.'

'Impressive. My great-granddad was a boxer. My uncle still owns a gym over in Harlesden—'

'Wow, and I took you for a total posh bird. Mea culpa. Have I got egg on my face.'

The man had a certain oleaginous charm. But Melody remembered the axe as Jones described it being buried in McCready's head.

'And here we are, both in Sotheby's, bidding in the millions.'

'Yep. Ain't life grand.'

'Lar-dee-dar.'

She felt the stare of one of the security men to her side; forcing herself not to engage him in a stare down. The other bloke was constantly scanning back and forth looking out for threats. These guys were professionally serious and not to be taken lightly. She had steered him to make contact on neutral territory, so far so good. Maybe she needed a rethink and a re-evaluation. Maybe not push it?

'Hey, here's an idea, and shoot me down in flames, but maybe you'd like to see my *Boxer At Rest*? Pop over to my place. Think about handling my portfolio while you're there? Think you'll find it impressive and rewarding to get your hands on. Got my limo waiting.'

Bloody Nora, Mel. Is that a massive double entendre or what?

If skin could actually crawl, Melody's skin would have been making its escape half way down Bond Street. Yet this was the plan to breach his security. To use her sexuality to arouse his interest. Now she felt uneasy. Was it too easy? She didn't want to sound too eager, though his ego could probably assume it was all down to his irresistible mannish charm. Maybe jumping into his limo to go to his impregnable home wasn't such a great idea. That had been one of her contingencies. Even though Frankie warned her this target was not like the others in degree of difficulty. Not by a long shot. No general's war plans survive the first skirmish with the enemy. Who said that? Napoleon? Patton? Montgomery? No matter. It was true. Seeing those two minders close-up and personal was her first skirmish.

'I'm not so sure about that, Mark. We have only just met after all.'

Higgins pivoted on the head of a needle. 'Oh, oh, you think – no, no. That came out all wrong. I'm having a select supper party at my place tomorrow night, to celebrate the Bellows acquisition, and I'd love you to come. Bring a date if you like.'

Bring a date. Was that a conman's move. To put her at ease and feel in control. Was she now the mark? There's no way he could know her true intent. Was there? No matter how paranoid he was.

'You already arranged the victory party even though you hadn't yet bought the piece?'

'Virginia, there was no way on God's little green earth I was walking out of here without that piece. When I set my mind on something nothing stops me. Just the nature of the beast.'

He touched her arm. Apparently she was his next piece. Time to get the queen roaming the chess board to topple the king.

She smiled sweetly, as if totally charmed by this rough diamond who had clearly made something of himself. 'Then I'd love to see your Boxer tomorrow. As to handling your portfolio, let's see how that goes before either of us commit fully to a hands-on relationship.'

CHAPTER

39

Leia Jennings had always loved solving mysteries. She was the little girl who solved the mystery of the sudden disappearance of Marley, her faithful mutt. He had been around since before she was born; until she returned from infants' school one day to find him gone. Her dad told her Marley had left home to retire to a farm in Wales. Her dad was almost crying. Dads don't cry. That was the iron rule of dads. And he loved Marley as much as Leia loved Marley. He was easy. He soon cracked under her relentless questioning.

Leia didn't buy her dad's story then. She didn't buy coincidences either. The coincidence of two members of a vicious gang both dying in prison within two months was too convenient. Not convenient for them of course. Damned inconvenient to be burned alive, bandaged like a Mummy in a Hammer Horror film. Damned inconvenient to slowly strangle as you dangle from your own bedsheet. Yet both deaths held no official mystery in themselves for

Leia. They were *solved*, in the broadest sense. One suicide. One murder. It was the link that was the mystery.

Something else was bugging Leia. The coincidence of two hidden serial abusers: one of women and one of children. They too had gruesome deaths within two months of each other, thereby piquing the interest of Hickman. He thought he saw a link. And he all but told Leia that she should investigate if there was an actual link of the mystery blonde woman in both cases. Not officially though. He made that clear. The Belgian affair was not the Met's case except tangentially because the victim passed through London as an alibi.

He hadn't articulated to her any worries about the prison deaths, either officially or unofficially. As a copper, you can't afford to be invested in the pain of the victims and their families. You are generically sympathetic, but that's it. Leia was a Detective Constable in Humberside when the Limehouse Monsters case was raging down south. Only yesterday – when checking the case files – did she discover how hands-on Hickman had been in the case. Going above and beyond in comforting Melody Fox after her miraculous recovery. He was invested in her well-being as a *victim*. Maybe that was why his infamous itch had not alerted him to this other amazing coincidence.

Leia glanced up from her laptop. She had to tidy this bloody room in her New Barnet terraced house. Two walls in her girl's den had bookcases stretching from floor to ceiling. Stacked with at least a thousand books from her favourite reading genre: crime. Conan Doyle, Connelly, Crais, Christie, Child, she loved them all, not just the 'Cs'. A pity they weren't in alphabetical order. Don't get her started on the DVD movies and TV series collections.

First principle. Cui bono – who benefits? Apart from society as a whole who benefits from the deaths of two men guilty of heinous murder. Assuming that there is a link, then someone went to lengths to hide it. That indicated conspiracy, and a conspiracy by definition needs more than one. Depending on the views of the victim's nearest and dearest, the obvious beneficiary would be the person who wants vengeance. That didn't leave room for a big list in the Limehouse Monsters case. One name at present.

Except – Melody Fox was hardly in a position to exact vengeance, was she? According to Hickman, she was a damaged woman who could not return to her profession as a psychiatrist. It was preposterous on its face. Yet the only person who directly benefited from the death of these two, as a pair, was Fox. That one fact was irrefutable. On its face.

Leia returned to her laptop, still connected to her official login for the Homicide and Serious Crime Command system. Her request to Ringland for its visitor records had taken a day to be acted upon. Their system was down for maintenance, or some such excuse for tardiness. It wasn't like it was a murder enquiry or anything. Once the digitized records arrived by email, she soon found the name along with the time and dates of two visits a month apart. She was neither surprised nor sanguine. Her hunch about ultimate motivation had paid off. She then had to request the video footage of the time periods.

Leia watched the second visit again for its glorious twenty minute entirety. On the face of it Melody Fox was quite normal. The other face was the infamous Aaron Fuchs. A relative, though somewhat removed. She was disappointed to see Melody had long, thick, black hair. There was also nothing inherently suspicious about a woman visiting her relative in prison.

No audio. Human right to privacy. It was suspicious how they cupped their hands over their mouths to prevent the possibility of lip-reading. Didn't prove anything to anyone in an evidentiary or legal sense. But – come on. It proved something to Leia in a *what are you hiding* sense.

Before becoming a copper, Leia did a term at university studying law. The fundamental principle of English Common Law on contracts being *consideration.* Without this consideration there is no contract. Each party to a contract must be both a promisor and a promisee. Each party must receive a benefit and each suffer a detriment. This benefit or detriment is referred to as consideration, which must be something of value in the eyes of the law.

What if Aaron Fuchs was, in fact, agreeing to supply the vengeance that Melody Fox could not supply herself? Fair question. To which the corollary would have to be: what consideration was she offering to complete their mutual contract?

It was obvious to her. And if Leia's evolving musings were correct, then the third and final Limehouse Monster (the ringleader, Anthony Gary Millar) was indubitably, my dear Watson, next for the chop.

It was way out there. Very Patricia Highsmith. She could see why Melody Fox would want these monsters dead. It was all too human. But wishing death in the darkest recesses of your soul isn't a crime. Unless you believed God saw the lust for vengeance as a crime in itself. Leia had an ambivalent feeling about Bentley, and she wasn't even related to the victims. But why would Aaron Fuchs care about Bentley at all? Did they have any connection? Then there was Ainsworth. Why him? Neither of them had done Aaron any wrong in the past. Sure, they were lowlife scumbags and all-round monsters. The world is full of men like that; so why them?

Also, Fox was a respected psychiatrist living with a de facto billionaire before her life was ruined. She spent seventeen months in a coma. According to Hickman her muscles were so withered she could barely walk for two months. We're not talking Lara Croft here. That's where Leia's bubbling-up theory crash landed before it even took off.

On the face of it.

CHAPTER

40

Melody opened the sleek case she had taken with her to Sotheby's. Her nebulous idea of making contact, and taking it from there was being adjusted on the fly. Having accepted Higgins invitation to his little soirée tomorrow, there was no way she was getting trapped in a medieval fortress-like prison, with actual guards and mercenaries patrolling the grounds. What the hell had she been thinking? Rather – not thinking.

Twenty minutes since she had rebuffed Higgins' invite to hop into his limo. That was not the only reason she had wormed her way close to him. She had asked Saul what he knew about tracking devices, and planting them on people.

'No vey.'

Instead he supplied her with one of the hi-tech gizmos to which he had endless access.

Okay, Princess, here's vot you do. Device picks up all phones in twenty metres circle. Boom. No vorries. No good. Need selection. Set target range for very close, and get device in close and personal. All techy mumbos-jumbos. But bottoms line, device clones other phones GPS. Heyo presto, you gots perfect tracking device using other schlump's own phone. Undetectable.

She lifted the GPS tracker from her case. Thanks to her little performance, she had managed to place it within two feet of Higgins, so fingers crossed.

Melody touched the screen and it exited sleep mode. The *Captured Devices* icon on the screen was flashing. She tapped it and a list popped up. Two numbers. Her own, which she had tested it on with Saul. And an unknown mobile phone number. She hit that number. A menu popped up with multiple options. She tapped GPS location and a satnav style map displayed instantly. The flashing red dot was hovering on Piccadilly. It moved slightly in the direction of Knightsbridge. Brilliant. She should have done this with Ainsworth instead of all the malarkey trailing that miserable schlump's car.

Pulling out of the parking meter bay on New Bond Street she headed towards Piccadilly. The red dot turned left towards Vauxhall Bridge Road, then over Vauxhall Bridge. Looked like Higgins was taking his recently acquired booty back to his East Sussex Keep. Should she follow him all the way?

The drive-by was to scope out exactly what his secluded Keep looked like. The only approach by car was via a small B-road with a substantial treeline either side. They petered out to reveal a fifteen-feet red-brick wall, topped by razor wire. Melody drove at a steady thirty past a gatehouse manned by a guard who controlled the substantial iron gate. She drove on for a hundred yards following the line of the wall until she passed the 90-degree turn, and the trees picked up again.

Her decision not to enter the Higgins domain without any real exit strategy was looking better by the second. Driving down the B-road for another mile she came to a village sign for *Major Wharton.* It also implored 'Please Drive Carefully'. She would if she could find a bloody loo, having been on the road since Sotheby's. It was a three pub village, and all three were in the village square. She hustled into the Cat & Fiddle carrying her mission *go bag* and the sleek case.

A rad-chick Melody emerged from Armani into black Levi 501s, biker boots, black T-shirt and black denim jacket. Having pulled off the auburn wig in London, Melody was back to her Jean Seberg cropped blonde. The two young guys playing darts in the saloon, stopped to stare. One hundred and eighty.

The barmaid brought out the tuna-salad half-baguette while she sipped her ice cold coke on the small patio at the back of the pub. The tracking iPad was showing the red dot as stationary in the centre of the Keep.

What now, Melody?

A re-re-evaluation. Maybe she should keep her dinner date in the *Keep* tomorrow? She had gone to all that trouble to make Higgins notice her, waylay her, and invite her. Melody balanced the risks.

Pros – walk in through the front door; other people around; opportunity to poison the bastard's food or drink; no risky physical confrontations. *Cons* – trapped inside; other people around; lots of security who were undoubtedly very good at physical confrontations.

Perhaps Diazepam? An excellent muscle paralytic that kept the victim immobile, but conscious. It dissolves very well in alcohol: tasteless and odourless.

Lorazepam? 10 milligrams would flood Higgins' central nervous system receptors, delivering a knockout dose for at least an hour.

Maybe Suxamethonium – the instant paralytic being the go to incapacitation drug for mental health professionals. Perfect for subduing distressed patients; a solution she had used on a number of her military charges.

They were all great. Not fatal in themselves, more the prelude that allowed the fatality to be further administered. She would have to deliver the fatal blow as Higgins lay incapacitated. In that case, there was always the reliable Doctor Shipman method. He injected his helpless victims with a morphine overdose which stopped their hearts within minutes. The verdict being heart attack. Sounded a plan.

She was still mulling the drugging options when the red dot edged its way across the tracking map. Higgins was on the move.

Drug-mulling would have to wait. The dot was headed onto the lane leading to Major Wharton. Was he popping out for a pint in his local? Unlikely.

She was concerned enough to hurry to the pub front. From her vantage point she watched as a black Range Rover with tinted windows drove past.

Returning to her table – passing the leering glances of the local boys – she had a big decision to make. Higgins was heading fast towards the south coast: a good twenty minutes ahead as Melody finished her tasty baguette and drained the coke.

Ah, bugger it.

The little red dot had been stationary for a while when Melody almost caught up. She parked Monty the Mondeo two miles away on the outskirts of the small Dorset coastal village of Seaclift. (She had finally named her car.) It was a prudent distance to continue on foot. The sun was dropping below the sea horizon as she checked through her rucksack: taser, baton, knife, pepper spray, torch, mil-spec binoculars. The comfort of kit made her ship shape and ready to go. She pulled on her bobble hat and hiked towards the red dot.

Seaclift's naturally sheltered harbour had been home to dozens of small fishing boats up to the 1970s. The traditional way of life for centuries. All gone now. Sunk almost without trace as if they had never existed. Their only record being the granite monument at the new marina's entrance informing all of their sad fate. She clocked the new berths with their expensive yachts bobbing gently in the controlled swell.

The sun had finally dropped below the horizon, leaving a shimmering orange-pink line of its remnants faintly visible out to sea. The stars shone here with far greater vibrancy and crystal clarity than she got to enjoy through London's semi-permanent haze.

According to the tracker's map, Higgins (or his mobile phone) was located a mile further on, outside the village but still near the sea front. Past the marina, Seaclift petered out into a stone beach backing up thirty yards to an almost vertical cliff, peaking at what? Eighty feet? Maybe a hundred?

The lights of the marina disappeared from view with the path following the curve of the beach. A bright moon was rising, illuminating her quiet-as-possible crunch across the stones. She could hear herself but reasoned the swell of the tide would mask the noise. She checked the tracker, the red dot distance indicating 800 yards ahead. The cliff's height was gradually declining from its peak as she continued on. After hiking for another minute, the faint glow of lights beckoned ahead.

She reached a small secluded cove with a wooden jetty stretching out thirty yards into the sea. Bobbing in the water was a sleek speed boat. The type that reared up menacingly as it sliced through the water at tremendous pace; powered by two huge motors at the back. The perfect drug-smuggler craft.

Laying belly down in the shingle, she spied two men exiting the speed boat, each gripping a large plastic barrel. At this distance they were mere silhouettes, no way to make out if one was Higgins. They made their way along the jetty to the stone steps carved into the cliff, lugging the barrels to the top.

Melody paused and waited, undecided. There was only one path to the top of those cliffs. It would take her at least ten seconds to get to the steps, another ten to leg it up them. Then what?

Point proved. The men returned almost immediately. They made the same trip back and forth with each lugging another barrel. Six trips after that for a total of sixteen barrels, no doubt packed with street drugs worth millions. Melody was surprised Higgins was so hands on. Her default assumption was all the dangerous, clandestine importation of product would be delegated down to minions and disposables. He gets caught with this and he's going down forever. Maybe there was more going on? Or maybe, like a good sociopath, Higgins was also a massive control freak who trusted no one. He had never been close to being arrested, so it worked for him.

What had Saul said to her—

Du farkirtst mir di yorn, Princess. Vorld class control freaker. Let me help, I got skills and contacts.

It had been ten minutes since the last barrel run. This was it. Melody strapped the knife sheath to her thigh before gripping the baton. Ready to roll.

She bounded up the steps two at a time, baton fully extended to battering length. If anyone appeared at the top, she would rush them instantly with a head, nose, throat, knee, and ankle smash in that order. Then she would push them off the steps to hit stone, maybe thirty feet down, no mercy. These were bad people exploiting others for money. No compunction about that.

All clear.

She scoped the scene. Thirty yards ahead was a large semi-derelict building. Light leaked from shuttered windows on the ground floor. A small van and a Range Rover were parked on the left side of the building. Melody scooted right, to the other side where she had spotted a smaller, corrugated iron shack. It was the only vantage point offering good cover. Passing closer to the main building, the weather-distressed sign was readable in the moonlight. It stretched across the front, below the top floor window, with the legend: 'Jones Bros. Boat Supplies.'

Half the roof was missing from the shack, but at least she was out of sight. It reeked from a century of dead fish. On the right side of the main building a winch and pulley jutted out from a large opening on the first floor. A linked metal chain dangled from the top of the winch to six-feet above the ground.

It was tempting. And there was no light or movement emanating from the first floor. Part of Saul's training was strenuous climbing wall sessions using ropes. This culminated with two weeks in the Dolomites. Weights were great, but nothing beat hauling yourself up ropes using only your arms and upper-body strength. That was useful muscle work the body remembers, and works to improve the efficiency of oxygen flow to those working muscles. The effort nearly wiped her out at the time.

Stretching up, she grabbed the rusted chain with both

hands, pulling down hard a few times. It held firm. Using the hand over hand technique, she hauled herself up until she could grip her legs and feet around the chain for additional support. That was better, just a few feet more, then—

Instant freeze. Fifteen feet in mid-air, almost at the top of the chain, ready to grab the winch and swing herself through the opening. The voices were outside, but from the opposite side of the building. She dangled and swayed slightly as her own physical exertions were transferred into chain movement. The indistinct voices stayed in place. Was that Dutch? Like her Belgium tryst? She couldn't make it out. But they were not coming any closer.

Great.

A few seconds later she slid silently through the opening onto the floor above where Higgins was presumably conducting illicit drug business. She lowered herself gently to the deck and stood stock still. The thought popped *why had she done that*? Sure, she gained some sort of tactical advantage, in one sense. Higher ground. Element of surprise. Those sort of Sun Tzu things. But how did it help in her actual mission? This wasn't remotely her original plan.

She pulled the torch from the rucksack and pressed it on. Large empty crates were scattered across the wooden floorboards of the storage area. *Shit.* Planks. She placed one foot forward slowly to test for any telltale creakiness. There was the slightest movement – but tolerable.

The storage area door opened into another room, only this one was leaking in light. To her left, a set of stairs led down to what used to be the work area below. The interior window, directly opposite, looked out over the work area. Well, not really a window, as the glass had long gone. Maybe this was the central hub of an office, where the eponymous Jones kept an eye on his workers.

Melody crept her way over to the former glass window – again careful to avoid the giveaway creak factor. She dropped to her knees and shuffled the last few feet to the gap frame. The light below came courtesy of six large gas lamps. They hissed quietly in the background illuminating the men.

It was a five man meet – including Higgins, no longer in his expensive suit. His garb was utilitarian black overalls, black gloves and a red Liverpool Football Club baseball cap. Melody had no interest in footy, but she recognized the Liver Bird crest because Charity loved to play that *FIFA* video game, and she was only ever one of two teams. Liverpool or Juventus.

Twelve of the barrels were stacked in twos on the floor, next to the large white plastic picnic table. The remaining four were on the table. Their lids had been removed and some of the contents were piled in front of their respective containers. The heavy duty, transparent plastic bags were about 18-inches square; each packed tight with thousands of small, purple-coloured pills.

A man was removing the bags one-by-one from the fourth barrel, placing them in front of said barrel. Higgins watched him relentlessly like a Liver Hawk. As did the man standing next to him. He was the thug in the police files named as Higgins' only trusted partner. Paul O'Grady, a fellow scouser, and violent felon who had served time for GBH.

The man doing the counting spoke good English with a strong Dutch accent. He dropped each bag in the pile as he counted it off.

'Fifty-seven, fifty-eight, fifty-nine, and, finally, Mark, we have the sixty in container four. I trust you are for sure satisfied with your sample count?'

'Sound as a pound lar. Quantity wise. You happy, Oggi?'

Higgins accent was a more pronounced Liverpudlian than when he was oozing his artsy charm at her twelve hours ago.

'Looks the biz, boss. Need that quality test though.'

'After four years you think I'd try to fuck you, Mark? That's a hundred million Euros street sale right there. Fresh from our manufacturing facility in the Ukraine. Delivered to Amsterdam two days ago. To my platinum customer. There's no fucking going on here.'

'Let's hope not, Claes. Get the gear, Oggi.'

O'Grady picked up the bag at his feet and took out the equipment for chemical analysis.

Melody assessed the three men who had smuggled in the massive drug shipment by fast speed boat. Nothing special, just your average criminal types. There was no indication of a superior physical threat. Not as individuals maybe, but certainly as a group. Not that she had any intent of tackling Higgins now. This was clearly a massive error. Best get the hell out, through the back and down the chain. Despite the fake bonhomie of partners in crime, the under-the-surface tension was palpable. At least from Higgins and his oppo. Though this was her first major drugs sale. Maybe that's normal when one party is supplying Class-A drugs and expects several million Euros from the other.

'Yeah, looks good, boss. Primo MDMA. Top quality.'

Doctor Melody was fully cognizant of the chemical methylenedioxy-methamphetamine. Better known to users in its abbreviated form of MDMA; street name ecstasy, molly, and many others. She had dealt with its unfortunate side effects as a junior doctor in A&E.

Claes was anxious to conclude his business. He muttered a few words in Dutch to his three comrades before beaming a reassuring smile. 'We good Mark?'

'Oh sure, Claes. Never doubted the quality of your merchandise.'

'Excellent. Then, the twenty million and we'll be on our way.'

'Though I do have one question, Claes. Who the fuck is this guy?'

Higgins pointed to one of Claes's men. Standard jeans and T-shirt. A few tats on his forearms. The bloke was surprised to be the centre of attention.

'Why?'

'Why not?'

'Okay. As you ask nice. This is Bruno.'

Melody concentrated on Bruno. His left hand started tap-tap-tapping against his left thigh. That was a coping method for a stress response if ever she saw one. The body has to find a way of dissipating stress and it will find any outlet available, like water and electricity.

'Bruno? Oh really? And who the fuck is Bruno when he's at fucking home. I ain't never seen no fucking Bruno before. How long's he been with you?'

Bruno stepped forward as if to speak, but Claes put his hand on his arm. His voice rose an octave. Also stress. And annoyance. 'About two years. And you have seen him. Last year in Thailand. He's a good boy. Done his time in prison.'

'Dutch prison? You been banged up in a Dutch prison ain't ya, Oggi? What they like?'

'Like Disneyworld, boss. Mickey Mouse. Piece a piss.'

'Not impressed with Club Med, Claes.'

Claes stiffened. 'Mark, what's the real problem here?'

'The problem here is your man Bruno. Really.'

Melody could see Bruno's hand still tapping his thigh, non-stop now. This did not look or sound good. Her hand automatically gripped the handle of the F-S as she ran through options.

'My man is not your problem, my friend. There is no problem. But even if there was a problem, it would still only be my problem. With the greatest respect.'

'Beg to differ, Claes, old pal.'

In a blink, Higgins pulled a handgun from his overalls, levelling it in the general direction of the Dutch. Melody couldn't clock the type and manufacturer of the weapon, beyond it looked like a 9mm semi-automatic, probably with a minimum fifteen round magazine.

'Whoa, whoa, Mark. What the fuck you doing, mate?'

Bruno had stopped tapping his hand. His tension had been released. Whatever he'd been stressed about had passed.

Oh crap, Mel, time to go.

Before she could shuffle backwards from the window opening, O'Grady fished a sawn-off shotgun from his bag, pointing it directly at Claes.

The Dutch blokes were caught on their heels. All they offered were worried looks and their hands flapping around ineffectively.

'Thing is, Claes, I pays out a ton of dosh on security, because I'm paranoid like. Not just the heavy muscle, but intelligence. Think of me as a mini state. The United States of oh, Marka, if you will—'

'Fucks sake Mark, where's this going?'

BOOM—BOOM—

Two shots hit Bruno full in the chest. He groaned in shocked disbelief as he fell backwards, landing on his backside, sitting up, blood rapidly staining out across his T-shirt. Nobody noticed Melody's involuntarily leap and gasp. They were too busy watching as Higgins calmly walked around the table.

BOOM—

He finished off Bruno with a shot in the forehead.

Bruno jerked and slumped to one side. There was a shocked silence as the two remaining Dutchmen were transfixed by the rapidly pooling blood flowing from their former colleague.

Melody held her position. It was unlikely they would be lugging the unfortunate Bruno upstairs.

Claes finally reacted. His voice on the edge of complete meltdown. 'Fuck, Mark. What the fuck, Mark. You just capped my friend Bruno.'

'Relax, Claes. He was an undercover cop from Dutchland. Real name Raymond Van Niesel. Married, two kids.'

'How? I don't understand. How did—'

Higgins and O'Grady kept their weapons pointed at the group.

'Like I said, I pay a fuck load for information. A mega fuck load, matter of fact. Have to. The filth's been after me for years. It's like a fucking vendetta, them being really bad losers as they've never laid a glove on yours truly. Ever. So when one of me sources in the Met gets wind of his excited Dutch colleagues, well naturally this has to be addressed.'

'Yes, okay, I understand now. You couldn't tell me because if I had a mole, it may have tipped off the fact that he had been discovered? This is good, ja. Right?'

'That's right, Claes. It is good. For me.'

Melody detected the menace in Higgins' tone directed towards Claes. The man got that too. The fact his long-time partner and his pet goon were still pointing their weapons at him, probably reinforced it.

'Me also.'

'Yeah, that's the thing, pal. I'm their real target, not you. You are just a means to that end. No offence. And the dearly departed Bruno here's been on your arse for the entire two years you vouched for him. Seems they got you dead to rights, mate. Video. Audio recordings. Phone calls. Fucking Bruno, eh? Sorry.'

'Fuck. Double fuck.'

The penny had dropped for Melody before Claes. Then it finally dropped for him. She guessed old Claes wasn't that fast on the uptake. After all, he did have a mole in his ranks for two years.

'Be that as it may, Mark, I'm solid. They'll get nothing from me, especially about you. You know that. We go back too far.'

'Yeah. That's true. We do go back too far, lar. Bruno here knew all about you. Problem solved. You know all about me. As soon as Bruno doesn't report in, they'll roll you up faster than a Turkish carpet.'

Melody could hear the desperation pouring out of Claes. 'Yeah, but I'm solid, mate. Totally solid. You know me Mark.'

Higgins laughed. 'Nah, no you ain't. Solid as mad woman's shit. They'll offer you a deal for me, short sentence in Dutch Jail Med, and you'll fuck me like a Thai ladyboy. In the arse. It's what I'd do to you. To anyone.'

'No way Mark, no fuck—'

BOOM—

No leap this time as Melody had seen that one coming from orbit. Higgins shot his good pal in the face. As his dead weight dropped, the last Dutchman standing turned to run. He'd reached the door as O'Grady raised his shotgun to head height and fired, catching the man high on his left shoulder. The man's momentum span him around as he crashed through the door to make it outside.

Melody's ears were ringing from the extra loud blast generated by a sawn-off. Higgins looked at O'Grady who was moving his jaw around and rubbing his right ear.

'Don't just fucking stand there, finish the fucker.'

O'Grady bellowed he understood before legging it from the building to hunt down the injured Dutchman.

The noisy madness of the past few minutes was replaced by a deceptive quiet. Bruno was a cop. One of the good guys. Higgins had just slaughtered a good guy in cold blood. In front of her. She had done nothing to stop it. Again.

She gazed down on the oblivious Higgins. He was alone. The first time. If only for a few minutes. Still armed with a 9mm, and more than enough bullets to put two in her head. This wasn't a suicide mission.

Time to admit discretion was the better part of valour. Higgins lived to fight another day. Which meant that the final monster, the inhuman, the one who had raped her daughter and shot Paul in the head, he too lived an extra day, or three, of his miserable existence.

Melody began edging backwards on her knees.

CREAK—

CHAPTER

41

That was too loud for a rat or a cat. That was a person sized noise. Higgins vaulted the stairs three at a time, gun in one hand, lamp in the other. The old gaffer's eyrie was empty; but the door leading to the loading area was swinging shut. He rushed through to see the black-clad figure disappear out of the opening to the old winch. Higgins dropped the lamp and followed.

The intruder had shimmied down the chain and was on the ground as Higgins reached the top chain. He considered shooting there and then, but decided it would be better to chase him down. Then have a leisurely chat before putting a bullet in his head.

Higgins dropped the final few feet from the end of the chain to the ground.

CRACK—

A vicious blow smashed into his right elbow, fracturing it instantly, and forcing him to drop the 9mm. The next savage hit shattered his right knee. Unable to sustain his weight, Higgins' right leg gave way and he fell backwards. In the space of a few seconds he had been disarmed, disabled and rendered helpless to stop the third blow smashing into his jaw, taking out his two front, incredibly expensive, teeth implants.

Higgins' left arm was raised in a defensive posture as the fourth blow was arcing down to the top of his head when –

BOOM—

The shotgun shell blasted the relentless attacker full-on in the chest, throwing him backwards onto the ground. Higgins lowered his good arm and looked up.

'Fucking hell, Oggi. What took you so long.'

'Other flying Dutchman. He's kaput by the way. Thanks for asking. Who the fuck's this?'

Higgins forced himself to his feet and limped over to the inert body lying face down in the grass. He wiped the blood from around his mouth and lips as he felt for his missing teeth.

'No idea, but he was well trained. Think me elbow's broke. Knee ain't too healthy.'

'Jesus boss, your teeth's smashed in.'

'No shit? Thanks for the update. Roll him over, fuckwit.'

O'Grady leaned down and manhandled the body over.

'Fuck I got blood on me hands now – Christ it's a girl, boss. She's deffo gone.'

As O'Grady wiped his bloodied hands on the grass, Higgins looked down at the body. The blast had caught her dead centre, right over the heart. Oggi was always good with the sawn-off. He was right about the blood. Her entire torso was oozing sticky red with it, soaking through her denim jacket. The air reeked of gunpowder and iron. Pity he couldn't get to ask her who the fuck she was.

Higgins gazed at the blonde-haired female. She looked

familiar, but he couldn't quite place her. No matter. One more body to dispose of efficiently.

CHAPTER

42

The dull throb of the twin, 1500-horsepower engines reverberated through Higgins' body. He was aching madly from the humiliating beating that tall blondie gave him. Even so, he had to get one of these crafts for himself. It was a doddle to drive on the open sea. The plaque on the cockpit dashboard told him it was a *Hustler 41 Razor Power Boat*. This one would be having an unfortunate accident after tonight. That was of little consequence as he could afford a fleet if he felt so inclined.

He was slicing through the water at a leisurely 70 mph away from Seaclift. The dial indicated a top speed of 130 mph; he didn't fancy pushing it to that limit until he had more experience. It was cooler than on land, and the sea spray was refreshing as it hit the open cockpit. A good forty miles out into the Atlantic should suffice. At this rate they would be there in twenty minutes. This was always going to happen, the extra body was unexpected, but it didn't change anything. He would have liked to unearth who she was. But she had to go the same way tonight. No bodies left behind was his credo since McCready.

Sitting in the twin seat next to Higgins, O'Grady was looking a little green. He hadn't liked boats since his first ride on the Mersey ferry as a kid. The sway and the bounce on the water was making him ready to puke.

'Oggi, go strip the bodies. Everything. Then lug them up. Gonna have to slice open their bellies and chop off their hands before we dump them overboard. You up for that. You don't look well.'

'Don't feel too fucking good, boss.'

Higgins laughed manically. 'But better than them lot, right mate? Smash in their teeth as well. For dental records in case they wash up.'

O'Grady swung his legs over the fold-down centre seat, which was also the step into the standing-up midsection pod, leading down to the cabin below.

He had fireman-lugged all the bodies by himself from the building, down the cliff steps and along the jetty. Higgins told him he was fucked with his arm and knee. Who was he to argue?

He ducked down into the cabin. At six-one, there was still a clearance of two inches to the ceiling. He had roughly dropped the bodies in one by one; the girl last. They had shifted with all the bouncing. Mark must think he's the Lewis Hamilton of the sea the speed he was going.

Great – now he was picking up deadweight in a confined space. He bent over the girl to pull off her jeans first. She was lying face-up, horizontally across two of the blokes. The blood had congealed now and was merely dampish and not dripping. He was concentrating hard trying to unbutton the annoyingly stubborn top button of her Levi's. The perfect position for Melody's F-S knife to shoot up, stabbing him straight through his chin, past his tongue, and into the roof of his mouth.

Unbutton that, fucker.

'Good, basm. You vant for Saul for something on dangerous road? MAC-10, sound suppressor, very excellent thirty mag, easy conceal, case maybe this time vankers come strapped. Maybe Heckler & Koch MP-7. Take out platoon one mag. Mil-spec surveillance shit. Body armour? Vish Saul, and poof, like Aladdin magic lamp it appear.'

She glugged down her bottled water, after making Saul submit for the first time. Saul was correct, she had to get real about protecting herself. Sure, she had survived; but with almost reckless disregard so far. Higgins was different. A professionally scary man with pro protection.

Two days later she was back at the *All Fight Club* for a personal fitting of the new acquisition. She tightened the Velcro straps of the sleek black body armour vest until it felt firmly comfortable. It was over her T-shirt but the vest was designed for undercover operatives.

'Okay, Princess. Lightveight, vear under clothes. Easy-peasy. Right. Looks standard issue Kevlar, polyethylene body armour. Right?'

'Well, yeah, as far as I know. Which is what I've seen in the movies.'

'Vell you in for tops treat. Thank Saul. Okay. No von see anything like this yet. Top secret next-gen undercover from Mossad—'

'Oh yeah.'

'Vot's problem vith vork undercover? You undercover, so how comes you vearing armour if supposed to be civilian? So if shot, you bleed. You vant baddie see you bleed think he kill you. Not come in for head shot. Give small tactical advantage. Alvays look for tactical advantage, basm.'

'Er, yes. I suppose so. And how exactly does this—'

Saul pulled a .22 pistol from his waistband behind his back and shot Melody dead centre of her chest.

Even the force of a relatively small .22 slug kicked like a mule and staggered her backwards, then down on one hand. That would bruise up nicely.

'Fuck, Saul. You shot me. Fuck's sake.'

She automatically put her hand to her chest and could feel the sticky liquid oozing from the body armour vest.

'Good shot for old man, eh?'

'That's not me bleeding then? Tell me this hasn't got actual blood bags inside it, because that would be gross and horrible.'

'Smart girl. Massive heat generated by bullet or shotgun impact creates chemical reaction on ballistic layer of vest. Manny explain, but vay too techie for this schlub. Basically added chemical to smell like real blood. Clever clogs, huh?'

'"That's great, Saul. But this is shot now. Literally shot. And I'm covered in uh – smells like blood. Haven't you got a normal one that doesn't bleed?'

'Meh, sometimes you totally alter cocker, Princess. No. I insist. You'll see.'

Melody's F-S knife shot up, stabbing through O'Grady's chin, carrying past his tongue, and into the roof of his mouth.

Unbutton that, fucker.

O'Grady's eyes bugged-out in shocked disbelief. Hands to his throat as he tried to scream. Hard to scream with a knife pinning your tongue to the roof of your mouth that's rapidly filling with your own blood.

She pulled the knife down and out, before lunging

forward, knocking him on his back. In a flash straddling his chest. Clamped her left hand tight over his mouth. Blood oozing through her fingers. His whole body screamed at him to cough and splutter out the blood seeping down his throat. Still stunned and shocked into inactivity. Any second now, things would kick in and O'Grady was going to start thrashing like a cornered wild animal in its death throes.

He had a few stone on her. There was no time to faff around trying to slice into his carotid artery, and hit herself with an arterial spray. Melody nonchalantly flipped the grip on the F-S, from push up to plunge down.

O'Grady went from ineffectual flapping to clawing at her hand, still clamped hard over his mouth.

She let go. But it was too late for him.

With all the force she could muster, Melody plunged down into the top of his skull with 7-inches of double-sided razor steel. The blade sliced effortlessly through bone and embedded deep into the grey matter. O'Grady spasmed uncontrollably for a few seconds, then stopped.

She yanked out the knife. Pulled herself up. Looked into his eyes. He was still there. That spooked her. Though you had to admire the tenacity and the will to live. There was a blood-caked splutter as he attempted to speak. He raised his hand but nothing except blood left his mouth. His light clicked off. The breath leaked from his body, like air from a punctured tyre. O'Grady deflated into dead weight.

Melody also slumped back. A wave of exhaustion washed over her. It had been a long day. It wasn't over yet. The whine of the engine changed. The boat was slowing down. Did a speed boat have brakes? Not long after, the craft spluttered to a becalmed stop. The sudden silence was a relief as the dull throb of those engines matched the throb in her head.

Higgins turned off the ignition and pocketed the key. 'Fuck, Oggi, that girl. Un-fucken-believable. I just put it together. You're not going to believe this. I know who she is—'

He ducked down into the cabin.

'What the fuck you been doing down here, Oggi? Bit of necro—'

ZZZZZZZZZZZZZZZZZZZZZ—

Melody had finally caught a break in a day of near-fatal missteps. When they *killed* her, and she was playing dead on the grass, Higgins rifled through her pockets and her rucksack. He was looking for something to ID the bitch: driving licence, credit cards, mobile phone. All he found were her miscellaneous mission equipment. He had already met the business end of her baton. On any other day he would have been obsessively crazy to find out the identity of this kitted-out female. Right now he didn't have the time to enquire – what with several bodies to dump. O'Grady threw in her rucksack with the rest of the bodies.

When Higgins finally saw what Oggi had been doing (getting himself dead) it was too late. Melody stepped from her other ambush spot(in the luxury shower) pressing 50,000 volts into the back of his neck.

Boats are a treasure trove of strong, useful ropes. Which is just as well as she had neglected to replace the one deployed to good effect in Belgium. She dragged the zapped-out Higgins into the shower unit, propping him up against the rear wall. His hands and feet lashed tight together behind his back with unbreakable, self-tightening bowline knots. Slipping a separate noose tightly around his neck, she looped it around the brass safety rail at the top of the shower cubicle. Satisfied he was secure and primed,

Melody turned on the shower and doused him in cold water.

Higgins spluttered then roared back into life. Pissed off too. The tasering, the broken elbow, the fact he couldn't move his arms or legs, now this soaking.

'Turn that fucking water off, bitch.'

Melody obliged. As the drenching subsided, Higgins finally focused on the person who had him stitched up nicely like a kipper.

'Jesus fucking Christ. You was dead. Fucking blood and everything. How the fu—'

Melody tapped on her chest. She wanted info from him so she played along, maybe quid pro quo would work. 'Body armour.'

'But the blood.'

'Long story. Not relevant.'

'It is you right? That fit bird from Sotheby's? Look different but I appreciate fine cheek bones. Dalloway right. Nicole Kidman red hair was a nice touch. Clever.'

She granted him a smile. 'I thought so.'

'Told you, darling. Could have seen *Boxer At Rest* at my place, gratis. Don't need to fucking string me up. Who the fuck are you?'

'If I told you I'd have to kill you.'

Higgins eyes wandered behind her to focus on the bloodied corpse of his loyal mate for over twenty years. Melody could see his mind working overtime on how to get out of this and murder her. As horribly as possible.

She pulled on the rope leading to the noose around his neck. It tightened, painfully ripping into his flesh. No choice but to struggle to his feet as the noose half pulled him up. She stopped pulling when he was on tiptoes, one inch from being slowly strangled. Keeping the tension, Melody looped it around the brass grip rail.

As a further humiliating incentive, Melody levelled his own 9mm at him. It was a Glock 19 with a fifteen-capacity magazine. Minus the four shots he had fired. To show she meant business, Melody pulled back the slide to check if there was one in the chamber.

'Okay, darling. You made your point.'

'Was that Dutch guy you shot really a policeman?'

'Fuck, this what this is about?'

Melody pointed the Glock at his head.

'Alright, alright. Yeah, fucking rat fuck was. Happy?'

'Just wondered that's all. I'm not that interested in you. I want information on someone called Aaron Fuchs. Believe he's in your line of business.'

Higgins laughed as best he could from his precarious position. 'That old kike Fuchs? Not really, doll.'

Melody saw a rapport opening, and took it. 'Yeah, fucking Jews. Who do they think they are?'

'Correct blondie.'

'He screwed you over too?'

'Yeah, you could say so, the selfish prick. Matter of fact me and him have got previous from way back. But I got the fucker back dead good.'

Melody beamed at him. 'Oh really. Do tell.'

'Yeah, you'll like this. When I was, uh – expanding my little enterprise from up north, late nineties, I got introduced and hooked up with Fuchs. He had this distribution network all set up, ships, lorries, contacts in South America. So we talked business blah de blah. You know how it is.'

The more Higgins struggled to loosen the knots behind his back, and he was struggling mightily, the tighter they would get, burning into his wrists and forearms. The pain in his elbow couldn't be helping either.

'Don't stop, Mark.'

'Deals were set, monies outlaid. You get the picture?'

'Ah. I do now.'

'Then fuck him but Fuchs pulls out. Really fucked me over big time. Lost money, time, effort, you know. But what could I do? Back then I'm just this skanky-arsed scouser. He's the big kike, Aaron Fuchs.'

'Tell me about it.'

'Yeah, well time passes, and what-have-you. I've sort of let it go, gone onto bigger and better. And he's doing time. But blow me down if something don't come to my attention. A name like. Sam Fuchs. Posh lad over at the London School of Economics, and he's dealing my product small time to his student pals. Way down the line to me of course. But I like to keep an eye on everyone who's linked to me. How I stay ten steps ahead.'

Her head was spinning at this news. She calmed it down. 'Sounds perfect. Get your own back via the son. That's got to be a painful blow to any parent. Some revenge huh?'

'You get it right. You should let me go, we can still do business. Whatever that business is, I haven't a fucken clue at the mo.'

Melody reached over and pulled down on the noose rope. It dug deeper into his windpipe.

'Continue.'

'Fuck, yeah okay. Jesus. Right. So, anyway, this is too delicious. Old man Fuchs is inside, and I got his kid dangling. See, he's using his own products as well as dealing said product. Hooked up to the fucken eyeballs. Only one way that goes in the end.'

'There a point to this story?'

'Okay, long story short. I pulls the degenerate fucker inside for a while, let him think he's working for us. And I'm thinking this is going to kill Fuchs. His kid the straight one. Then I thought, fuck this. What will really kill fucker

Fuchs is his kid croaking with a needle in his arm. Likely happen anyway on its own, or maybe not, or who knows when. Besides I was bored with keeping him dangling. So I arrange that. Shot him up with a hot-dose and dumped him in a crack den in Cricklewood. Neat. Right? Fuchs doesn't even know. No one does. Police had it down as just a regular overdose.'

Melody seethe-smiled. Not only at the smirking casual confession to killing Aaron's son. Angry because she now understood how *she* had been manipulated. Yeah right, as if Aaron wouldn't find out Fuchs had his son killed. It was supposed to be Melody doing the manipulating. Kevin did warn her.

She didn't warn Higgins.

BOOM—

The 9mm slug ripped into his right knee. He screamed as his leg gave way pulling his body down. The noose tightened insanely under his own weight, strangling his scream at birth. He tried to stand but his foot slipped on the blood streaming down his leg to the shower base.'

'That's for the policeman.'

Melody knew he would be dead within three minutes. Strangled by his own inability to stand. There was nothing he could do. A just punishment.

BOOM—BOOM—

She decided not to wait. Two in the chest near the heart. It was faster than he deserved. He had killed someone she was related to. She never knew Samuel. She didn't even know he existed until recently. But he was family. They shared blood.

'That's for my family.'

It felt good. Higgins was finished. Which meant she had fulfilled her side of the bargain. Only one more piece to be removed from the board, and that was out of her hands.

But that good was instantly negated. Aaron's conniving fell into place. This was not good.

CHAPTER

43

'And you're one hundred per cent sure about this?'

Leia nodded enthusiastically at Hickman. The nearest person she had to a mentor. She had run through her observations with him. It was late. From Hickman's office window – behind his desk – she could see the brilliant moon hanging over London. Her spiel had been going for twenty minutes. He was still listening.

'I know. Sounds crazy. And there's no actual evidence here. But it's the sequence that's super-important, sir—'

'Sequence?'

'Scumbag dies outside. Another scumbag dies inside a few days later. Twice. And, you know the old Sherlock Holmes cliché slash dictum, when you eliminate, blah – what is left has to be, et cetera et cetera.'

Hickman was still churning it around. If she was correct, it answered many questions on two high profile, unsolved murder cases. How often were victims also the perpetrators of heinous crimes. On the other hand? The suspect?

Seriously? It was unfathomable to him. How could that be possible? Yet, Leia was correct. It made sense logically. It made sense emotionally. When logic and emotion combine, it's an unstoppable force. Ask Churchill.

Hickman would never forgot the two hours he had spent with Fox in St. Michael's hospital, explaining the last painful seventeen months of her life. Her raspy, barely audible voice; a body hewn down to skin and bone; held together with atrophied muscles. She could barely lift open her eyes. Despite that, her fierce will to live dazzled like a distant supernova. He had turned off his copper's antenna and dismissed what he took to be natural, normal human rhetoric.

'They need to die. Don't you think? They deserve to die. Somebody should kill them. I'd pay. Kill them all.'

From Melody Fox's mouth to three years later. Two down. One to go. And his smart, thorough, tenacious underling had connected some not-so-random dots.

There were other possibilities. There had to be. Could she really be the perp? Shoot the rapist Bentley multiple times, possibly in self defence. Castrate the child-sex-slaver Ainsworth in cold blood? Not to mention the burning alive of a dozen others. Though he had heard from the Belgians that the likely sequence of events put Ainsworth as firing the shotgun which ignited the truck's fuel tank.

Perhaps she was merely a conduit from Aaron Fuchs to somebody on the outside. The apocryphal hitman. That made sense. It also made Melody Fox an accessory to murder. If she was the one who hired somebody to do the foul deeds, it was still murder. But then – that blew Leia's working thesis of a quid pro quo murder pact. And what about the woman in the photographs?

'There's a film about this sort of thing isn't there, Detective Sergeant—'

'*Strangers On A Train*, sir. Novel first, actually. Patricia Highsmith. Then a Hitchcock flick. But it's not really the same. Two people meet on a train, at random, and get talking. Plus it was a one-for-one murder. And the second one never happened. And he didn't get away with it, the one actual murderer that is—'

Leia clocked Hickman glazing over at her mutant-like knowledge of the crime genre.

'My point is, the fictional, fantastical aspect of the whole theory. Nothing happened, Leia. Except in some very imaginative writer's head. As we know, true crime is not like fiction, being most times banally unimaginative. Serial killers don't taunt the police. They don't fixate on a particular detective. They just like killing. Even the Ripper note has been proved a fake—'

'Which one, sir? Rippers that is?'

'Both, wasn't it? Then there's rarely a list of equally weighted suspects, with clues scattered about to make a satisfying whodunit mystery, *Murder On The Orient Express*, and suchlike. My point is, despite the obvious unlikely elements, I have to admit, you may be on to something—'

'Thank you, sir.'

'Or, at least sounded an alarm bell to make sure, on the off chance this is a related and linked series of deaths, that the potential number three is removed from immediate danger.'

'That's prudent, sir. Though as far as I know, we haven't had the concomitant murder outside of prison to trigger the consideration of the contract.'

'That we know about.'

'Should I make the arrangements regarding Millar's safety?'

'Straight away.'

'And what about Ms Fox, sir? Maybe time to call her in

for a little chat? Unless you want to see her first? Unofficially that it. Get a feel for her present state of mind?'

Hickman leaned back into his office chair, sinking deeper into the sumptuous leather. If it was anyone else, would he hesitate? Leia must have read the Limehouse files by now, and know all about his emotional involvement in the case. He couldn't be seen to be playing favourites.

'Ask her in. Purely voluntarily. Turn up on her door step. See if she bites.'

Leia smiled her set of perfect choppers at the prospect. She could bite better than most. Certainly better than Melody Fox. Of that she was sure.

CHAPTER

44

Melody closed her eyes for a second. She must have dropped off instantly, being startled awake by Roger Daltrey exclaiming how he *won't get fooled again.*

She grabbed her phone from the passenger seat in the Mondeo, still two miles outside Seaclift, ready to bat the hell out of Dorset. It was Chloe. They hadn't talked since the first board meeting of the trust at Peach's corporate HQ in Canary Wharf. Melody let it play until there was *fighting in the streets.* Might as well get it over with.

Melody: Hey, girlfriend. How's it going?

Chloe: Some friend! Thought you'd died. This is like, the tenth time I've called this week.

Melody: Oh, stop being so bloody dramatic Dame Judy.

Chloe: Feel more like Dame Edna, traitor. What on earth have you been up to

	that's more important than Chlo-me-me-me. Ha-ha.
Melody:	Chloe, love. If I told you, I'd have to kill you.
Chloe:	Oh very funny. Like you could harm a fly, let alone me.
Melody:	Anyway, I'm actually about to hit the sack so, phone you tomorrow for—
Chloe:	Lunch tomorrow at The Ivy. Catch up and whatnot. I've booked the table for twelve thirty, so you have to come.

Lunch tomorrow was the last thing on Melody's mind. But she felt guilty about neglecting her best friend over the past few months. They used to talk three or four times a week. Then the whole Aaron thing started. Her part of the contract was over. She could sleep the sleep of the wicked when Millar was gone too.

Melody:	Yes, love to.
Chloe:	Oh, and Ben said could I ask you if you'd thought anymore about the shares? Whatever that means. You know I hate all the grubby talk of money and commerce, darling. Ha. Ha.

In truth, Melody hadn't given it a second thought since Ben broached the subject of relinquishing her 'B' shares back to him. It would give her a lot of liquidity. But it would also sever her last real link to Paul's other baby. She would still have the 57,000 ordinary 'A' shares, but they would simply make her – *ordinary*. And Melody felt anything but ordinary.

Melody was bobbing up and down gently in the small, inflatable rubber dinghy floating off the starboard bow of the *Sunseeker*. The name of the craft was now clearly visible in the half moonlight.

She had finally caught a break on this mission. After knotting together fifty feet of separate ropes, she soaked the entire length in engine fuel. The craft was fitted with high-performance engines running on a highly explosive petrol mixture to outrun any boat the authorities had. Diesel fuel engines would have been useless for what she planned. She knew this because of the battle-hardened squaddie in Iraq cheerfully instructing her on fire bombing a car. *Has to be petrol. Diesel don't punch it. Like a limp dick at an orgy. Pardonez-moi my French, ma'am.* The only thing out of Iraq which Melody admired was the cynical squaddie humour.

The six containers of spare fuel (25-litres each) were stowed away at the back. Half of one container soaked the rope sodden, while the rest she liberally poured throughout the boat, including the bodies.

She was gutted about the Dutch undercover cop – he deserved far better. As did his wife and two kids. But needs must, and this pressing need was what must be done. She couldn't lug Raymond back to shore in the small vessel, with its tiny outboard motor. And she couldn't power the *Sunseeker* back any further than she had already brought it. Ten miles out was pushing it anyway. What if she ran into a coast guard vessel?

After knotting one end of the rope into the fuel inlet pipe, she played out the length and dangled the other end just over the side. She fired up the dinghy's motor before igniting the rope with the matches she found on board. Zipping out about fifty feet, Melody stood up and fired the flare gun directly at the *Sunseeker's* cockpit. The petrol whooshed into orange flames, quickly enveloping the entire exterior.

Not hanging around, she grabbed the dinghy's tiller and turned the outboard up to full revs. About a hundred yards away, the makeshift ignition cord finally burned its way to the fuel tank.

KA-BOOOOOOOOOOOOM—

Unlike the movies, she gleefully looked back as the *Sunseeker* exploded in a massive fireball, lighting up the night sky behind her.

CHAPTER

45

'Sorry I'm late.'

Chloe was on her second glass of Montrachet when Melody plopped herself down.

'It's okay, darling. Not like I have an international literary agency to run.'

'Fashionably late. Hey, did I just walk past, is that – you know who?'

'Hugh Jackman? Yes. Gorgeous isn't he? Shooting some movie at Pinewood. You're glowing by the way. Even in that leather bike gear. What are you up to, being so – glowie? I need some of that.'

Melody shrugged. 'Getting out and about a lot more these days. Keeping busy, you know.'

'Yeah, well, I don't know. That's the point. But keep doing it, because it suits you, whatever the hell *it* is—'

'I will, Cho-Cho.'

A waiter appeared carrying two stemmed glass bowls filled with crushed ice and whole langoustines.

'Took the liberty of ordering. All your favourites.'

As they caught up over the huge mutant shrimps, then the grilled seabass, Melody drifted away to the events of the past twenty-four hours; and the rather large bone she had to pick with Aaron. What had he done for crying out loud? She had a good idea thanks to Higgins' revelations about Samuel Fuchs.

As soon as Melody woke up at nine thirty, she googled a few phrases, such as *Sunseeker* and *boat explosion,* Nothing popped. She was ten miles out when the boat went up. Too far to see from land. Unless a passing ship saw the orange glow (and assuming it didn't sink) the *Sunseeker* could be floating off the south coast for a while before being spotted.

If they found the wreck of the *Sunseeker*, Higgins death surely would be a direct link back to Aaron. The assumption being that the cops were aware Samuel Fuchs was a midlevel dealer in the Higgins' organization. That put them on the path of putting E and MC squared together in looking for motives. Samuel died. Higgins died. Then it was a short leap to her. QED.

Before she left, Melody texted Frankie to demand a direct talk with Aaron. Having livestreamed the execution of Glenn Borthwick, he clearly had no problems communicating to the outside.

'—then I jumped off the Peach roof, and landed on all fours, like a cat—'

Melody half caught that last bit. 'Like a cat? Sorry, what?'

'Just checking you're still with me here?'

Melody seamlessly lied to her best friend. 'I'm sorry. I am distracted, you're right. It's my cousin Kevin. You've not met. I'm worried about him. We're quite close these days, ever since, well, you know. He's – keep this to yourself – well he, you know, sort of grows stuff. The stuff you can smoke.'

'Oh, so sorry, darling. Family is everything. I understand. But if you have a supply of great weed then drop some off. Introduce me to your cousin. Sounds deliciously outré and black sheepy. Ben and I still indulge occasionally. It's very relaxing, as you know, I'm sure.'

That was a surprise. She wished her lie had been about someone else now. 'Oh. Okay.'

Chloe checked her watch: gone two. 'I have to fly anyway, got a neurotic writer to calm and soothe in half an hour. Donald's brilliant and talented. But has to be told that. Constantly. It's all very wearing. Bloody writers.'

'Then thanks for the distracting lunch. Hope I wasn't too wearing.'

'You? Never. Oh, and I hate to be the nagging borehole, but the shares? Please call Ben and let him know what you want to do. He says it's a bit pressing with some potential Chinese investors. This high finance goes way over my head.'

'Will do.'

Melody sped Helen of Troyumph down the Strand towards Tower Bridge. Frankie texted while she was finishing her refreshing peach sorbet. Instructions to meet outside the Tate Modern. Frankie liked his Thames haunts for meets. She double chained Helen to the traffic meter slot on Royal Mint Street – the same spot when she met Frankie at the Rendez-View café. After her first mission. Her virgin mission. The Bentley mission. She always intoned *mission* to herself, rather than *kill*. Shouldn't she be well past euphemisms by now?

Hurrying across the Millennium Bridge towards the giant smoke stack, she spotted Frankie. About half way across, he was casually leaning against a railing looking downstream towards Limehouse.

'Something to report? Ain't nothing in the news that I seen.'

A group of a dozen chattering Japanese tourists, walking towards St. Paul's, dawdled to a stop right next to them. Melody nodded her head towards the Tate, then strode off.

They sat on a Thames embankment bench. St. Paul's loomed up proudly on the other side of the river.

Frankie went to speak, but Melody raised her hand forcefully. 'It's done.'

'Really? Because like I said there's no new—'

'Trust me. Mark Higgins rests in pieces. So to speak.'

Frankie laughed loudly, pretending he hadn't heard that gag before. She ran through the Higgins' mission, strike that, the Higgins *kill* with Frankie. He didn't interrupt this time. He sat raptly, nodding, and looking quietly impressed.

'Jesus fucking Christ, girl. Be honest, half-thought that was probably the last I was gonna be seeing you, down in that underground car park. Felt quite sad, matter of fact. Should have known. You're quite resourceful on the sly aincha? Girl Guides, I bet.'

'Girl Scouts, actually.'

'Of course you was.'

'Great. Now that's out of the way. Did you arrange the Aaron thing? I really do need to talk to him, a-sap.'

Frankie handed her another mobile phone to add to her ever growing list of untraceable devices.

'You know the drill. Expect a call after nine tonight. Then make sure the phone is destroyed. Bottom of the Thames, ideal. Sim card best burned.'

CHAPTER

46

'Where the fuck you taking me, lady copper?'

Leia glared dead-eyed at Anthony Gary Millar. She had read the file on the Limehouse murders. Watched the official forensics evidence video shot at the murder scene before anything had been touched. If she lived to be a hundred Leia prayed to never see anything so awful and heartless.

'Shut it, Millar before you accidentally fall down these steps.'

'That'd be against my human rights.'

'Gotta be human first.'

'Oooo, ain't you a right comedian. Hey screws, you heard her threaten me, right? My lawyer be right on that.'

One of the four Ringland prison guards shoved him hard to encourage his forward passage down the steps.

'Did you say something, Detective Sergeant – because we *screws* never heard a thing, did we lads?'

The governor of Ringland heard Leia. He was somewhat

defensive over two linked deaths in his prison in two months. It was the type of statistic that didn't look good on one's record. When she explained the suspicion of a larger conspiracy that might involve another murder, he was more than happy to see Millar removed from his jurisdiction.

The warden of Ridley Youth Detention Centre in Poplar was not so happy. Nigel Spencer was a bulbous, red-faced man in his fifties. He sweated copiously and attempted to mask that fact with liberal amounts of deodorant. It wasn't working.

'I'm not happy at this development DS Jennings. Not happy at all. But it appears I have little say in the matter.'

'I do apologize, warden. But we had no choice. Being just over the river from Ringland makes you the nearest facility with a reasonable level of security—'

'To house a vicious killer. Amongst young offenders. And you know we don't have the exterior security levels of a Category 'A' prison. Or a category anything prison. A ten-foot fence hardly makes us Alcatraz does it?'

Leia had a certain sympathy, but needs must. 'To be fair, warden, not exactly *in amongst.* Millar will be housed in a single cell in your recently completed new wing, constructed specifically for violent youth offenders. Correct?'

Spencer had to nod in reluctant agreement. 'Correct, detective sergeant.'

'Linked to the main facility by a security hub, so it's technically a separate, standalone unit yet to be occupied. I can assure you there will be no interaction at all. Plus I have assigned a rotation of four prison guards on each eight hour shift.'

'Well that's reassuring, isn't it?'

Leia let the sarcasm slide. The man was under pressure. She could hardly argue with his valid point about letting

Millar anywhere near others. It was not introduced at trial, but to Leia's mind Millar was clearly a psychopath. She had seen the video of Hickman doing his final interrogation before Millar was charged.

Millar maintained his sneering smirk through the entire six hours. At first he was convinced that not only was he more intelligent than Hickman, but that he was going to talk his way out of it. It was a delusional stance, of course. His solicitor attempted to stop him talking as Hickman masterfully dismantled him piece by piece. Millar would have none of it. He loved the sound of his own voice. He dismissed his solicitor, insisting that he leave. That's when Millar revealed the heart of darkness.

Hickman:	Then what did you do, Tony?
Millar:	After I shot the bloke right between the jeepers creepers? Fuck did he beg. On and on. Till boom. All over. (*laughs*) Well then I decided to have some fun with his young twat too—
Hickman:	You mean the young girl. That would be Charity Fox, aged thirteen. Her thirteenth birthday being the week before. Her first week as a teenager. Her whole life in front of her.
Millar:	You say so, Mister Hickman.
Hickman:	And by fun, you mean what exactly Tony? What is fun to you?
Millar:	You know. Fuck's sake.
Hickman:	No I don't. You have to tell me, Tony. In your own words.
Millar:	Jesus fucking Christ. I gotta paint you a picture?

Hickman: We know what happened, Tony. We have all the evidence we need. We have captured that picture for the world to see. You know that. I've been through it in great detail with you for, oh, (*looks at his watch*) the past six hours. What I'm trying to elicit, that is – to get you to tell me in your own words, how this was fun. For my own satisfaction, so to speak.

Millar: Bingo. That's it. That's the word, Mister Hickman. Satisfaction. Thank you. It were satisfying. Very satisfying.

Hickman: And how was it satisfying, Tony. To do that to an innocent little girl? I am trying to understand.

Millar: Innocent my arse. And not so little neither. And that was her fault what happened by the way. If she didn't want that to happen, shouldn't have been there in the first place then should she? Shouldn't have done what she did should she? She made it happen.

Hickman: What did the thirteen year old child, Charity Fox, do Tony?

Millar: Well, Billy and Glenn had shagged her twice each already. And the woman was a no-go, like out cold, like she looked near dead anyway, and I'm not a necrowhatsit—

Hickman: That would be Melody Fox. The

	devoted mother to thirteen year old Charity Fox? The lady likely to die soon. That woman?
Millar:	Yeah, yeah, her, what the fuck ever. Who cares?
Hickman:	Let's pretend I care, Tony. What did Charity Fox do?
Millar:	Whatever, Mister Hickman. Like I said, the other two done their dirty deeds with her. And to be honest I didn't fancy sticking my knob in there after them. I mean, fuck's sake. Yieeew. That's fucking dirty horrible. Know what I'm saying? So I sticks it in her mouth like and tells her to suck me off. Perfect. Then the little cunt only goes and bites so fucking hard. It really fucking hurt. So I taught her alright. Dumb bitch.
Hickman:	You taught thirteen year old Charity Fox? How did you do that Tony. How did you teach her?
Millar:	(*laughs*) Easy. Got me gun. Stuck it in her gob and shot her. That taught her alright. Know what I'm saying.

There were conflicting reports on whether Millar was mentally competent to stand trial. Common sense prevailed. There would have been outrage at him getting away with depraved murders – locked up in a cushy psychiatric facility. Many people would have been happy to see Millar hang. Including Leia.

Instead, he was being protected at taxpayers vast expense in the interests of justice.

CHAPTER

47

With Millar safely tucked away at Ridley, Leia decided to follow Hickman's advice and door-knock Melody Fox. If nothing else she wanted to catch her on the hop and look her in the eye. If Leia's theories were remotely adjacent to correct, there had to be balls of steel behind them.

She had been parked for over an hour in the police issue car outside Melody's pleasant house in Golders Green. Leia glanced at her watch. It had progressed by one whole minute since she last looked at 9.05 p.m. A watched door never opened. Leia gave herself another half-hour before calling it a night.

Melody checked the time on the Frankie-supplied mobile phone again. It had clicked up another minute since she last looked, now flashing out 21.06.

After lunch with Chloe, Melody biked back to her south

Kilburn flat. Her plotting pad. She had all but abandoned Golders Green until all debts were paid and events concluded. There was nothing there that linked her to her recent actions. It made sense after Hickman's unexpected visit.

Only one person knew she had rented the top-floor flat – Saul Levin. He would remain resolutely schtum, even under electric cattle prod torture. When this was finally over, she would burn everything related in an industrial incinerator. Clothes. Wigs. Files. Phones. iPads. Laptops. Flash drives. The lot. Except Helen and Monty, of course. They would stay as she tried to start her life again.

She was still bone-tired from her exertions in Dorset. Needing to be sharp to face down Aaron, she slept soundly for a few hours on the sofa. Sharp and ready when the phone finally rang at 21.26.

Melody:	You're late.
Aaron:	Blimey, girl. Don't wake up wiv your knickers on backwards. Ain't an exact bleeding science. Screws are rampaging around at the mo. Can't just start calling till they're more – quiescent.
Melody:	Quiescent? Okay. Sorry.
Aaron:	Hears mucho congrats are in order. The late Mark Higgins sleeps with the fishes. Well done you.

She had to pull the phone away from her ear as Aaron's bellowing laugh almost deafened her.

Melody:	That leaves Millar. Last one.
Aaron:	Yeah. About that.

Melody:	That doesn't sound good.
Aaron:	Hold your horses Lester Piggot. You're gonna like this in the end, if we plays our cards right. Thing is, I can't do Millar no more.
Melody:	You what? What? Why the hell not? You have to, that's the whole bloody agree—
Aaron:	Nah – you don't understand. He's gone girl. Poof, the filth took him this morning. Millar has left the building. They know summit's up I guess.

Melody's grumbling worry (the very reason she needed to talk to Aaron) reared up and bit her like a horse on crack.

Melody:	Think that's because the cops have found a link between the names you gave me, and you personally? Like Samuel. The quid pro quo of the Limehouse gang. Please assure me there's no other links between you and Bentley. You and Borthwick. That it wasn't somehow personal. And therefore obvious if someone would care to investigate?

There was a long pause, before—

Aaron:	Can't do that, girl. Look, half figured this would happen anyway—
Melody:	Fucks sake. You did?

Aaron:	Cops may be slow but they ain't stupid. Was counting on it. Why d'you think Millar's last?
Melody:	Don't follow.
Aaron:	Think about it. Won't speak the words of what that filth done to Charity, blessed be her memory. To my family. You're my family, Melody Fox. Eye for an eye. Tooth for a tooth. What's yours is mine. What's mine is yours.
Melody:	Yeah, but—
Aaron:	But only family. Vengeance means nothing from a stranger. Can't pay for true vengeance, only take it and feel it yourself. Dagger wot takes the eye, knife wot cuts out the heart. Has to be wielded righteously by those so sanctioned. Family. Has to be. Not even Frankie can do that. Proper righteous mensch wot he is.

The scales fell away. Like a blazing revelation from Mount Sinai. Her anger dissipated like a fart in a lift.

Melody:	You left the Grendel for me alone. Manoeuvred events to get him out of an impenetrable Category 'A' prison. Get him somewhere on the outside. Reachable location. Reachable by me. Right?
Aaron:	You got it, girl. Knew you was super- smart like Kevin says.
Melody:	Yeah, but – it's not like he'll be put

	in a local B & B, is it?
Aaron:	Youth detention facility down the road from Ringland. Figured it pretty much had to be there.
Melody:	Oh, okay. Sounds a bit challenging.
Aaron:	Speak to Frankie.
Melody:	I don't know. I wasn't thinking of involving anyone else.
Aaron:	No I mean *speak to Frankie*. He spent two years in Ridley back in the day.

CHAPTER

48

'I think you'll want to see this, sir.'

Gripping a manila folder to her chest, Leia poked her head into Hickman's office. In the seven days since her fruitless attempt to doorknock Melody Fox, she had been juggling the other active murder cases being handled by her team. And she was still overseeing the protection of a degenerate scumbag transferred to a youth facility. Even so, she had found the time to start back-threading on Thomas Bentley and Angus Sebastian Malcolm Ainsworth. While it was true that Ainsworth was not an official case for Scotland Yard, she wasn't investigating from the perspective of the victims to see what popped. She was attacking it from the recently revealed person of interest: Aaron Fuchs.

Bentley and Ainsworth had presented themselves to the world as decent human beings. Bentley was briefly detained at her majesty's pleasure on major fraud allegations. As such, a case file was opened and background investigations undertaken in that one area alone. There was never any whiff of him being a serial rapist. He was never formally charged in the other matter.

Ergo – there was nothing in police records on Ainsworth. However there was a lifetime of files accumulated on Aaron Fuchs, since his first offence at nine years old.

All she needed was a scintilla of evidence that Fuchs had intersected at some point with Ainsworth and Bentley. Then unpick on that thread and see what unravelled. Preferably from both targets, because that would move beyond happenstance, past coincidence, and way into conspiracy.

Hickman ushered her in. He had just finished talking to the Chief Constable of Dorset. That news could wait until Leia gave her updates.

'I'm assuming there's still nothing on the whereabouts of Melody Fox yet?'

'Not a sausage, sir. Though phrasing it like that makes it sound like she's done a runner. We don't know that. Besides, we're not the Stasi. People are still allowed to vanish in Blighty without informing the police.'

'I suppose you could phone her then ping her mobile and see where she is.'

Thing is, if I call her it sort of defeats the object of me catching her off guard. Besides, I already tried tracking her mobile number, the one you gave me. Seems to be turned off. Again that's allowed without necessarily being viewed as suspicious.'

Hickman frowned. 'True. And this is unofficial.' He was hoping Leia's wild, but persuasive conjectures had been proved wrong by now. 'What have you got to show me?'

She pushed the folder across Hickman's desk. 'Top sheet, sir. Has the salient points.'

Hickman scanned the page. Then read it again.

'Interesting. And this is all kosher?'

'Totally, sir. Pretty routine once I realized we should be investigating this from Aaron Fuchs's perspective.'

'You can't beat classic coppering.'

'Bit up from Dixon of Dock Green, but I get your point, sir. Given the two professions of teacher and investment specialist, it struck me that this is where there would be an intersection with Fuchs, if there was one. In their world. Not in Fuchs's world—'

'Good thinking.'

'And bingo, they intersect big time. His son Samuel died of an overdose last year—'

'Ah, I see.'

'Ah, I don't think you do, sir. Thing is, Samuel Fuchs was the good son. Very bright academically, gifted was a word used often. Oxbridge material. Nice, pleasant kid apparently, eager to please. I've seen the school reports. And give Aaron his due, he was determined to keep his youngest son well away from his life. Seems Samuel thrived socially too, despite his dad being who he was. He was on the golden path until Aaron went inside for his first stretch in ninety-nine—'

'I remember that case. I was a uniformed sergeant at Ruislip back then. Heathrow armoured truck heist, one hundred and thirty million in uncut diamonds. Monster robbery bollocksed-up by pure chance. He got eighteen for that. Overturned on appeal in 2003. Though we only ever recovered twenty million worth of stones.'

'Yes, and while he was inside, Aaron decided his son needed to maintain structure and order if he were to fulfil his potential. Had him boarded out to a top private school with an excellent reputation in academics and in sports—'

Hickman almost levitated out of his seat. 'Jesus. The

Bourton school in deepest Cotswolds? Formerly head mastered by the late, unlamented Angus Sebastian Malcolm Ainsworth.'

'Correct, sir. He was only senior master and games master back then. About a year later, Samuel's anti-social behaviour kicked-in big time. Fights, vandalism, shoplifting, petty thefts. The usual litany. Which sort of followed him his entire life after that. Suddenly a normal kid becomes a troubled kid. He was smart enough to get into the LSE, probably on minimal effort from him, but missed out on Oxford and Cambridge. Then the drugs. Then the dealing. Then the dead.'

'You're theorizing the kid was one of Ainsworth's multiple victims? Okay. But why wouldn't Fuchs have killed him back in 2003? When he was out of pokey again? Talk about motive there. Instead, he waits for years, then gets his distant female cousin to do the deed?'

'My guess? Didn't know what his son was enduring back then, sir. You know the stats on child molestation victims. It's all one big secret. Shame and guilt wrapped up in one enormous package pressing down a poor kid. Reinforced by the abuser. A person of authority in the victim's life. Maybe Samuel repressed the whole thing anyway? I checked the Ringland visitor logs. Samuel visited his dad twice last year. Consecutive weeks. First visits since his old man was sent down again.'

Hickman wrapped it around his head. It made sense, unfortunately. 'And intersection number two, with Bentley?'

'World's oldest motive, sir. Money – big money. Scimitar Capital Management. If you remember, Bentley was accused of stock manipulations and insider trading. The case collapsed but in reality investors had lost hundreds of millions in what were alleged to be criminal activities—'

'Let me guess. One of those investors was Aaron Fuchs.'

Leia was comfortable enough to make a joke at her senior commander's expense. 'You should be a detective, sir.'

There was an awkward silence as he let his sergeant hang. It amused him to knock her down a peg or two occasionally.

'Continue.'

'I'm thinking Fuchs wasn't just one of the investors, he was a major player. I think that's where those missing diamonds ended up. I can't actually prove it, but according to the forensic accountant I had look at the original case, it appears one untraceable *foreign* investor based in Israel lost fifty million pounds with Scimitar. A shell company behind a shell company behind another shell company, called Fux United Inc. Fux is Yiddish for Fox.

'Fux U? Subtle.'

'As a Fox. The Scimitar losses were legitimate, or so they appeared. Merely bad investments at the wrong time. Doubt Aaron saw it like that. First rule of thieving, never rob another thief who's bigger and stronger than you.'

Hickman slumped back in the comfortable leather, taking it all in. He couldn't deny that his sergeant had made a compelling direct link between Aaron Fuchs and two recent high profile murders.

'Chief Constable of Dorset called. Five days ago a French trawler came across the floating debris of a speedboat, twenty miles off the Dorset coast. Out from Kimmeridge Bay, if you know the area.

'Not familiar with the locale, sir. Bodies?'

'Oh yes. Five. Burned beyond recognition. They managed to extract DNA from the cadavers, and so far have identified two from our criminal data base. The Dutch are missing an undercover cop, and we've sent the unidentified DNA samples to their lab in Amsterdam.'

'Oh, no. That's bloody awful, sir. Bloody horrible news.'

'It most certainly is. On the bright side, one of the bodies is Mark Higgins.'

Leia perked up immediately. 'Drug empire chappie Mark Higgins?'

'The very one.'

'Okay. Could this be the missing third piece regarding our resident degenerate scumbag Millar?'

'My thought too. According to his chauffeur, Higgins last public appearance was at Sotheby's eight days ago. He paid a world record price for a painting of a boxer, if you can believe it. He was last seen talking to an attractive woman. Red hair. Nicole Kidman red apparently. Not some demented wee Willy MacScotsman ginger painted in woad, screaming about Bannockburn *red*.'

'Bloody hell. Sir.'

CHAPTER

49

'You're positive you were banged up here for two years? Because you don't seem to have a frigging clue what you're doing.'

Melody strained even harder against the door which was refusing to budge. She had been talked into teaming with Frankie for this final endeavour. She had been perfectly content with working solo. And it had worked. It wasn't easy. She had nearly died. Twice. But she was her own boss. Kept her own hours. Now this.

'Crying out loud, Mel. Got us inside didn't I? Looks like they've changed things around a bit since the nineties.'

'No kidding. Didn't you get the memo the Smiths are dead. Genius.'

Speak to Frankie, Aaron had half ordered on yesterday's call from prison. Yeah. Sure. Only this time Melody couldn't be bothered to schlep all over London at his behest, as much as she enjoyed Helen's company. She knocked it about for a bit; but she couldn't see any downside to Frankie knowing where she was living.

'Nice gaff slash crime lair. Who's that hideous, face-punchable creep lurking about downstairs?'

'Naff combover? Bad teeth? Ukrainian accent?'

'That's him.'

'Claims he's *the owner*, but I reckon he's just the hired help for one of the billionaire oligarchs buying up London—'

'Don't get me started, darling.'

'How about getting you started with a cuppa? Just brewed a pot of coffee. But got tea, Earl Grey? Some really smooth Polish vodka. The best I am assured.'

'Coffee's fine, love.'

As they sipped, she could finally run her eyes over this good-looking bloke. Every other occasion they met had been during times of stress. Stress for her, that is. She had him pegged at their first exchange as a deeds not words guy. Her professional opinion based on fifteen years expertise in body language, micro-expressions, verbalization, posture. She didn't even consciously assess people these days. She was like a supercomputer. The data came in, it was processed automatically within her; the human equation answer popped out, just like that.

But now she could relax a tad – and check him out. He reminded her of someone from her past. That chiselled face and great bone structure. She couldn't quite put her finger on it. Then—

Jesus. A traumatic event she had done her best to bury. British Army base Iraq. Major Bell. His personal security detail. Captain Hassan raised his lethal weapon. She was resigned to death and never seeing her beloved Charity again. He was going to finish off Bell, and shoot her in the face. Then boom. Hassan's head exploded. His brains flew all over her.

All clear, sir. He's gone. Let me help you up, miss.

Her mind's eye memory zoomed in on his name tag. Bishop.

Melody grinned manically. 'I don't believe it. Iraq. Major Bell's office. You saved my life in Iraq. I never even thanked you. Shock closed me down for a week.'

A startled Frankie choked a bit on the coffee. 'I did? News to me. But you're welcome.'

'No, I just remembered something weird. I saw your name. Bishop. Tagged on your combat top.'

He twigged now and laughed. 'Weren't me, darling. Has to be my kid brother. Eddie. Some people think we're twins, but we're chalk and cheese. I even mentioned him when we met. Remember? You had the F-S ready to gut me? Told you then, my kid bro Eddie used to be in the Royal Marines. Small world though. Spooky too. Right?'

'That's uh – yes. It's – yes, that does class as rather spooky.'

Frankie half-chuckled. 'Or fate. Looks like the Bishop boys will be saving your arse twice then.'

Melody bristled at the thought. 'I don't need your help Frankie. Certainly don't need saving by anyone.'

'We all need saving, darling. Called being human. No woman is an island and some such. Or you so far gone now you don't get that?'

Melody glowered. That had escalated fast. She considered her answer. 'Sorry, but I can't afford any attachments or weaknesses while I'm doing this—'

'Attachments? Blimey, love. Ain't suggesting we get all lovey-dovey married. But I know that place, Ridley. It's not Cat 'A', but you can't just walk in with a *what-ho Jeeves* neither. There is security in place. Fence. Gate. Barrier.

Cameras. And I know things about it that others don't. Probably not even those who works there today.'

'Know things? What *things* do you know.'

'Well – there's that secret tunnel only I know about. For starters.'

'Secret tunnel? Why didn't you lead with that?'

CHAPTER

50

'No kidding. Didn't you get the memo the Smith's are dead. Genius.'

They had emerged from Frankie's secret tunnel under Ridley. The brick lined, unused mains sewer was still there. It exited into the sub-basement exactly where Frankie discovered it as a sixteen-year-old.

In his *let me help* pitch, Frankie explained that the Victorian building had not always been a youth detention facility. It had been through many iterations – beginning as a purpose-built model school, constructed in 1861 by Quakers for the poor and deserving of Poplar. Being Quakers they had revolutionary ideas regarding the health and physical well-being of children, including open spaces to play. They purchased enough land to accommodate considerable playing fields at the rear; with space for a modest Quaker meeting room. This original footprint comprised the entire detention facility today; and ample room for its soon to be completed new wing.

Beneath the land, under the auspices of the Metropolitan Board of Works, the London Sewage Company was also busy constructing a new network of sewers in response to the Great Stink of 1858. London's raw sewage disaster had finally gotten Parliament involved. After completing a spur section of main sewer tunnel under Ridley, the engineering contemporaries of the recently dead Brunel realized they had made a gross error in the original survey. To save costs they bricked off the spur at its sewer junction, below a main pumping station, half a mile downstream from Ridley.

When Frankie discovered the tunnel, he didn't tell a soul. He had already figured out human nature and keeping secrets. He merely used it to sneak off for the occasional night out after lights out. Always returning before morning rise and shine.

'The door wasn't here back then?'

Melody had been grateful for Frankie's brute strength in levering off the rusted up grill at the pumping station. She had to admit that with fifteen stone of muscle, he was above her strength grade.

'Chill, baby-mama. You got your rucksack. I got mine.'

Frankie's rigid-frame rucksack looked the real deal, with three-times the capacity of her dinky specimen. Apart from that, they were kitted-out in identical black attire. Overalls. Bobble hat that pulled down into a balaclava. Combat boots. The small unplastered brick chamber was lit only by the powerful flashlights they both had strapped to their heads.

He pulled out a cordless drill from said rucksack, unscrewing the hinge bolts. Melody gripped tight on the handle to prevent the possibility of the door tumbling out. Together they slowly levered it from its frame.

They emerged into a dark corridor, also brick lined on

both walls. Frankie ducked because of the low ceiling. At five-eleven in her steel capped boots, Melody had a couple of inches clearance.

'If you studied my fucking ace map professor, which I know you did, being the school swot, then you know this corridor is under the real basement part of the building structure. This way.'

Frankie was on a roll, so Melody didn't respond. She followed him for fifteen feet, stopping under a man-sized thick metal grill. Man-sized as if you were dropping through it at about three-feet square. He pushed up against the grill which obstinately refused to budge. Straining and grunting away, the grill remained implacable, until—

'Okay Hulk, think we can say that's not budging anytime soon.'

'Iron. Been welded in place. Had a feeling that might be the case. Lucky I was a *Blue Peter* kid. Here's one I prepared earlier.'

Frankie pulled out the metal box from his rucksack, eighteen inches high and a foot wide. A coiled hose was attached. He placed it on the ground then removed a heavy plastic unit from the rucksack.

'Nice plasma cutter.'

'Thanks, darling. This battery's got a ten minute cut. That iron's an inch. Four cuts. Should be enough. If not, same time tomorrow?'

'I'll check my diary.'

Ten minutes later Melody took the weight as the iron grill slipped away on Frankie's fourth cut. As she lowered the fifty pounds of iron to the ground, Frankie was clearing the gear away. She had to admit they were making a good team. Although she had no doubt she could have found a way to complete the mission herself, somehow.

Wow. Overconfident much, Melody? Hubris comes before nemesis.

Once she accepted Frankie's assistance, her plan changed. It was probably crazy. But it was already crazy that she could ever be in a position to get to Millar.

Frankie abandoned pushed the gear in the corridor, no attempt to return it to his rucksack.

'I'm up first. Then pass me the rucksacks. I'll pull you up through.'

'Yes. Sir.'

'Don't be a twat about it, love. Okay?'

It was the logical sequence. Why was she being a twat about it?

She cringed. 'Yeah, sorry.'

Frankie hauled her through the grill space into the official basement of Ridley Youth Detention Facility. They flashed their headlights around. It was obviously a dumping ground for detritus from the facility.

'Okay, final check. Got your gear?'

'Certainly have.'

Frankie moved over to the basement door. He turned the handle and pulled it open.

'Okay. This is it. You ready.'

This was it. A flood of images and sounds drowned out the emptiness of her existence for a few seconds. Almost journey's end. An ugly road she would gladly have traded for just one more day with her beautiful daughter. One more hour. To tell her how she had been the most perfect baby ever born; and that nothing Melody ever did in this life could compare to the perfect being she brought into this world.

'Yeah. Let's go.'

Frankie edged into the corridor, she followed two steps behind. Their beams lit the stone-flagged floor. The rough stone steps at the end of the corridor were worn down the middle from over a century of use, before being abandoned in the swinging sixties. Bluish-tinged light was leaking in from the door frame at the top of the steps.

They hurried to the top. Frankie raised his hand to wait. He wasn't taking chances. He slow opened the door.

CREAK—

Even though it was gone midnight (and unlikely anyone would be lurking outside) they flinched as if a bomb had detonated. Frankie switched off his torch and poked his head into the ground floor. The blue night-lights cast a cold, uninviting glow along the corridor.

Frankie ushered Melody into the long corridor, keeping his voice low. 'These are the six ground floor classrooms. Don't look to have changed. We're near the rear of the facility here. We're heading to the front to get access to the other side. That's where the night staff will be. There's a staff recreation room where they tend to hang around. After we clear the front, we both head to the new wing—'

'Look, mate. You don't have to do this for me. Not too late for you to head back. Won't mind, honest.'

Frankie's smile looked grotesque in the blue light. 'It's a two man gig. Like we planned, you watch and wait at the main stairs while I do my thing. Should take sixty seconds. If anything goes wrong and we're separated, we rally back here. Correction, inside this door, in fifteen minutes, come hell or high water. If one of us is missing, like we agreed, the other don't look back. Got it?'

Melody had sussed that Eddie would not be leaving her and would be looking back. As would she. But she played along. 'Got it.'

Frankie squeezed her shoulder. 'I'm all in, love. You know that. Look, we can postpone if there's a problem. Leave now. Mister Fuchs will come up with something else I'm sure. Later date. Millar's in pokey a long time, and he can't escape forever.'

Melody gripped the Star of David on the chain around her neck. Her comfort beads since Aaron had passed his dead young daughter's cherished symbol on to her. She pulled down the bobble hat into full balaclava mode.

'Let's do it.'

CHAPTER

51

It had just gone nine. Leia was watching *The Talented Mr Ripley* again. The Jude Law version, not Alain Delon from the 1960s. She had a thing for the pretty Mr Law, even though he was playing the insufferable rich boy Dickie Greenleaf. Her mobile rang – DC Donald Latimer.

Donny had a thing for her. And Leia wasn't averse to exploiting that. He was happy to be doing her an off-the-books favour. The second time in three days, this would have to be the last time. It wasn't fair on him, as the *thing* wasn't reciprocated. As well as the whole fraternizing with a subordinate *thing*. Not on.

Leia: Donny. Something up?

Donny: Could be, sarge. Been on our man for an hour since he left in the Range Rover. He just stopped outside Euston Station. Waited a few minutes. A woman came across, got in and away they merrily went.

Leia: Description?

Donny: Fit looking. Slim. Tallish. Above average height for a female. Black jeans. Black bomber jacket. Black bobble hat.

Leia: Hair colour?

Donny: Couldn't really see because of the hat, be honest.

Leia: Where are you now?

Donny: Heading east through the city.

Leia: In the direction of Poplar?

Donny: Well, technically, yes, I suppose. But they'd hit Holland if they keep going east. Want me to continue – whoa, shit. Shit.

Leia: Sorry.

Donny: Ah, bollocks, sarge. Total effing bollocks. Can't see the Rover ahead. He was right there as I called you. Might have turned the previous left. A sodding bus did a righty, right in front of me, around another bus on my left. My view of the junction was obscured for like five seconds. Total coincidence, or he spotted me way back, and waited till he could ditch my arse.

Leia: Crap.

Donny: What do you want me to do?

Leia: Shit, shit, shit. Uh – thanks Donny. It's a bust. Might as well call it a night. Go home.

Leia gazed half-heartedly at Jude's frozen face. If her

ramblings were true, then crazy as it sounded, Millar's life was in danger. It was her duty to make sure the bastard was safe, much as it pained her. She had obtained camera footage from Sotheby's showing the auction where Higgins spent a cool two million pounds. The mysterious redhead – with whom he was last seen chatting – avoided exposing her face on any camera. That implied conscious effort. And that had Leia thinking perhaps she had recced Sotheby's on a previous occasion to pinpoint the cameras.

It looked like the woman had finally made a mistake. Back at her office in New Scotland Yard, Leia went through the Sotheby's footage from the day before the auction. There she was. Or at least there she possibly was. A side-on shot of a woman with long, blonde hair who could be the brown-eyed, black-haired Melody Fox. It was frustrating not to have total proof.

Leia looked across at the board which still had the monochrome photograph of Tom Bentley exiting the *Memento Mori* bar. Next to him was the mystery woman with shoulder length blonde hair. The picture was not of the highest quality, and it was impossible to make out the face, above the fact that it was a well dressed, blonde-haired, female, aged between twenty and forty years. And she was wearing what looked like the same outfit as the blonde in Sotheby's.

As she couldn't locate Melody Fox anywhere, Leia back-threaded her reasoning again. She was sure this bloody slippery woman was busy figuring a way of getting to Millar. This had to be the bonus of all bonuses for her. Until now Leia was assuming Fox had a three-for-three *Strangers on a Train* contract with Aaron Fuchs as the second party. By necessity her vengeance was almost voyeuristic. From afar. Maybe Fuchs had videotaped it for her?

It hadn't occurred to Leia that Fuchs had manipulated events to get Millar moved to Ridley. Until now.

Millar would never go back to Ringland with Aaron Fuchs still banged up. And until it could be assessed which prisons would be safe from Fuchs reach, Millar would stay at secure units similar to Ridley. There was no way Fox would (or could) psychologically pass up this opportunity of doing this herself: up close and personal.

Surely she wasn't crazy enough to try to break in. But what else could she do? The woman was nothing if not determined, and probably driven insane by grief. After the first few days it was decided to reduce the number of Ringland prison guards on Millar down to two per shift. The men couldn't be spared on a four guards to one prisoner ratio indefinitely.

Frankie Bishop was Fuchs' long-time, trusted lieutenant on the outside. Bishop had to be the conduit between the two. On a total hunch, Leia decided to do some limited surveillance on Bishop via the doe-eyed Donny.

She had little confidence it would yield anything. She still wasn't sure.

CHAPTER

52

'All set.'

Melody nodded. She was crouched in an alcove under the main stairs leading up to the seventeen dorm rooms housing the fifty incarcerated young men in Ridley. They were watched over by three night warders. In the security hub, near the front entrance, another three night warders were responsible for the ground floor. On the half hour, a warder would walk the floor, check the doors, check the rooms. It took twenty minutes at a leisurely pace. It was 12.10 a.m. They could faintly hear the TV and muffled talking coming from the direction of the security hub.

Frankie had wanted to do it later, around 4 a.m. The time people were at their lowest ebb in their normal sleep cycle. But Melody reasoned differently. With lights out at eleven, it would be around midnight the guards would be most relaxed. They would have completed their routines and probably be gathered for their first break. At 4 a.m.

dawn would be breaking while they were still in, or near the facility. A definite no-no for her.

'Switch?'

Frankie held up the small transmitter for her to see. 'Ready to go.'

Melody checked that the stopwatch on her wrist was set to 00.15.00. 'Okay. Check stopwatches for the countdown. Fifteen minutes from my go.'

Frankie checked. 'Done.'

'Mask time.'

Frankie swung the rucksack down from his shoulders and removed two military helmets. The grey Kevlar helmet had cool additions. A combo night-vision lens and infrared lens was clipped onto the front via a hinged mount. Attached to the side were ear mufflers with a built-in comms receiver. Strapped in front was a full face gas mask with built-in goggles. The circular air filter was screwed into the right side.

He handed one to Melody. 'Can't believe you got this serious kit. And all the other stuff. Still not gonna tell me where?'

'No.'

'Couldn't help notice the Star of David on the back of the helmet.'

Melody smiled as she tightened the straps on the gas mask at the back of her head. Satisfied it was tight, she did the same with the helmet chinstrap. Frankie was ahead, already giving her a thumbs up. She could hear his muffled talking and realized she hadn't clicked on the internal comms.

Frankie burst into her ear. 'Ready, how about you.'

'Yes. I'm good.'

He handed her a packed tactical belt. 'Strap it on. They're your babies.'

Melody did as instructed before giving Frankie the final thumbs up. He did the same. Melody checked the stopwatch. Frankie mirrored her. She took a deep breath through the unpleasant tasting filter. This was it. Even after all she had done in the past few months, it felt surreal.

'Go.'

They pressed their stopwatches simultaneously.

Frankie pulled the pin and rolled a standard L83 British Army smoke grenade towards the security hub. A green swirling cloud of smoke poured out.

The grenade was still rolling as Frankie pressed the switch on his palm-sized transmitter. The three distinct, distant bangs sounded as one. The lights went out instantly. The small incendiary device Frankie had placed inside the building's main electrical fuse box had ignited.

BRRRRRRRRRRRRRRRRRRRRRRRR—

The second tiny incendiary was placed besides the smoke detector at the top of the stairs. The ignition and smoke tripped the building fire alarms instantly.

The third detonation was a remote controlled smoke bomb now pouring out vast volumes upstairs.

Their location was already dark and disorienting. Melody hesitated for a second.

'Pull down your night vision. Now, Mel.'

She sparked into life. That was better. If a bit weird. She could see two versions of Frankie standing next to her in the voluminous smoke. Light green and throbbing red.

'Sorry. I see you.'

'Okay. Hand on my shoulder, I'm leading.'

Melody complied. She was already unsure of her direction. Now she was glad Frankie was here. He started off at a steady pace, with Melody one step behind, left hand on his left shoulder. He knew exactly where he was going. The alarm still blaring as they moved further away from the security hub.

The smoke wasn't as thick at the opposite end of the building from their ingress. The new secure wing was built on the former playing fields at the back. It wasn't strictly a *wing* as it was connected to the old building by a security corridor. Once the facility was open to youthful violent miscreants, these entry points would be manned at the high-capacity security doors on either end, accessed with electronic key cards. Because of the more dangerous nature of Ridley's new clients, a separate emergency generator had been installed in case of a power cut. Such as tonight, when Frankie cut the power by incinerating the main fuse box. Fortunately for them, this option wasn't yet operational.

Frankie stopped at the security doors to the corridor leading to the new wing. Melody stepped from behind, stopwatch was down to 00.13.35 to vacate the building. They had to be out, or at least past the security hub by then, because the local fire brigade would be entering. The smoke was thinner here; but it was still dark.

'Wait one second, gorgeous.'

Frankie pitched another smoke grenade hard back in the direction they had just traversed.

'Okay, let's see if my little idea worked.'

He tried the handle. Apparently his little idea had worked. With the power cut, the three sturdy bolt locks disengaged. The door swung open.

An intense bright light dazzled Melody's right eye through the night vision lens. Half way down the corridor the hotspots of two figures showed via the infrared lens. One had the torch.

Without thinking Melody followed Saul's drilled in instructions to the letter. In one flowing movement she grabbed the device from her tactical belt, pulled the pin and rolled it underarm fast towards the unsuspecting figures.

'Grenade!'

Melody flattened herself against the wall one side of the door, Frankie on the other.

'No need to fucking shou—'

BOOM—

The stun grenade detonated a few feet in front of the two prison guards. Before they could react (being stunned) Melody was on them. Until this point she had only ever hurt bad guys. She didn't hesitate to press the taser into the first guard's neck. He went down instantly. The second must have come to his senses fast. He was big, and struggling to his feet. Melody swept out a leg to take out his standing leg at the ankle. As he fell back again on his back, she tasered him as well. Same effect.

Frankie had already zip tied the first guard's hands and ankles with the plastic restraints. He zip tied those two restraints together to leave the guard hog-tied and helpless.

'Christmas pressie? Box of them stunners do very nicely, love.'

'Aaron confirmed just two guards stationed on site tonight?'

'Yep.'

Melody checked the stopwatch. 00.12.27. 'Then let's get Millar and get out.'

The smoke from Frankie's last grenade was billowing thickly into the corridor.

Melody led the way. She rushed towards the partially open door into the empty facility. Empty except for one. She was anxious to end this journey. Well, almost end it. After tonight.

'Jesus. Hang on.' Frankie was finishing the second guard's hog-tie as Melody hurried through the door.

The sight in her right eye was normalizing. She could make out the details of the main entrance to the facility.

Access looked like it may be problem. Behind the main reception area there was a turnstile-type of device stretching from floor to ceiling. Clearly constructed to restrict entrance and exit to the facility in single file only.

Bollocks, if that's independent of the power supply—

Melody saw the figure on the periphery of her vision as it swung something at her head.

CHAPTER

53

Leia couldn't keep Jude frozen forever. What to do? It had just gone nine. It was lights out in Ridley at 11 p.m. She had a hunch. And she couldn't shake it. A crazy hunch. A hunch sliced so thin it was transparent. But when you eliminate everything else, what is left, et cetera.

She arrived at the main gate just before lights out. Having toyed with phoning the head warden at his home, Leia phoned Bruce McCloud instead. The night warden was an affable Aussie she met a few nights ago. He liked her. Her excuse was a vague something about Millar, and needing to speak to him tonight. If that was at all possible.

'No worries, sarge. I'll tell the main gate to expect you.' He had no reason to doubt her, and it didn't impinge on his routine. George and Dwayne were two of the Ringland guards who had escorted her the day she collected Millar. They were pleased to see Leia. Especially Dwayne.

'So, Sergeant Jennings. Where you from then?'

'London, these days.'

'No. I mean which island your folks from?'

'Ah. I see. Mum's family came from British Guyana via St. Lucia originally—'

'Nice.'

'Dad's from Yorkshire. And we do consider ourselves a separate island, oop North.'

The boredom at being stuck on this shit night duty made the guards happy for any break. It broke their routine, which included a 72-inch TV in the Ringland staff room. All they had at Ridley was Dwayne's radio, and each other. Millar didn't count as human.

They insisted that she joined them on their coffee break first. That suited Leia as she wanted to know about interactions between Fuchs and the *Limehouse Monsters.* They were unaware of anything other than the normal ebb and flow of violent men locked up together It was a tinderbox that only operated as far as the prisoners let it operate. That was understood by all. Head blokes like Fuchs kept the place running smoothly. Every so often there would be a release of pressure, such as the Borthwick murder. It was open and shut to them that Byrnes killed Borthwick – no doubt. It was just a coincidence that the suicide and murder had occurred. They reckoned that moving Millar was a waste of time. Of course, she couldn't share the suspected quid pro quo murders on the outside.

They had Millar packed away in one of the new individual cells. Unlike the unlocked dorms in the old section, this was an individual pod with an electronic lock controlled by them.

'You want to talk to Millar then, sergeant?'

'That is the idea, Dwayne.'

George wasn't as enamoured with Leia, so he laid down the ground rules.

'He ain't normal, sarge, so we can't be having you in his

luxury accommodations. We'll restrain him hand and foot Lecter-style and put him in the infirmary. That way we can stay near.'

She didn't need to speak to Millar. But she was reassured that there was no way anyone uninvited was getting inside to *get* Millar. How could they?

Leia had endured twenty minutes of Millar's grotesquery while Dwayne and George hovered at the far end of the room. Dwayne had the bright idea of restraining him in one of the patient wheelchairs. She was about the wrap up the pointless proceedings and return home to her bed, when the jolt struck.

DARKNESS—

The fire alarm in the old facility started up at the same time.

'Oooo. Any a you afraid of the dark. You should be.'

A flashlight came on and shone over Leia and Millar. Dwayne came charging over. 'Shut it, Millar. Swear to God – you alright, sergeant?'

'No probs. Look guys we need to get out of here, right now.'

All four were congregated together with Dwayne's torch as their only source of light.

'Of course. That is the correct procedure in case of fire.'

'There is no fire George. That's a distraction. Someone is coming for Millar.'

'What the fuck you mean someone's coming for me?'

Dwayne shone the light in Millar's face. 'Ain't telling you again. Shut it. Something you're not telling us, sergeant?'

'You know the reason we moved him from Ringland, Dwayne.'

'Fucking said that old man Fuchs cunt was out to get me

inside. Never said he was coming here—'

Dwayne savagely swung his prison-issue, leather-surfaced baton into Millar's midriff. That knocked the wind out and shut him up.

'I said shut it, arsehole.'

'I'll explain fully once we're out.'

'That be nice. Great – okay sarge, me and George lead the way. You push Millar in the wheelchair. Take the baton. Any more shit, smack him across his ear hard. Hurts like crazy, but no brain damage. Least, minimal.'

Dwayne handed off his baton, then led the way with his flashlight. They exited the infirmary and headed towards the reception area.

Dwayne's flashlight reflected off the first wisps of smoke. 'That's definitely smoke. Let's hurry this, guys.'

Reaching the secure side of reception it was a lot more dense, and unpleasant to breathe.

'How are we going to get the wheelchair through the turnstile, Dwayne?'

'No problem, St. Lucia.'

As George clicked through the turnstile to the front reception, Dwayne dragged Millar up, unlocking the cuffs securing his wrist. Seconds later the wheelchair was folded neatly in half. Dwayne pushed it through to George before manhandling Millar through to his comrade. He was no Jude Law, but Dwayne was an impressively take charge bloke.

He had Millar back in the chair, fully secured as Leia exited the turnstile. The smoke increased massively in volume.

'Come on. Let's go. Let's go.'

Dwayne led again at rapid pace. The locks to the first security door had disengaged. Leia could see Dwayne's torch ahead as he opened the door to the corridor into the old building. More smoke billowed through. The fire alarm was sounding much louder now. Leia wondered if she was utterly wrong. Was this a real raging inferno?

Dwayne and George headed down the corridor. She was about to push through with the wheelchair when she heard a shout from up ahead.

BOOM—

Leia recognized the boom and flash of a stun grenade from training exercises with the hostage and anti-terror boys. Staggering back, she pulled the wheelchair with her. Eyes dazzled. Ears ringing. But far enough away to miss the full impact. She yanked the wheelchair to the side of the door, which had swung almost shut.

It was pitch black. Millar started to babble, so she tapped him with the baton in the spot where she estimated his head to be. Not too hard, but hard enough.

'Shhhh. Shut your gob if you want to live.'

Through the ringing that was definitely a man's muffled voice.

The door crashed open inwards. To her left, Leia clocked the greenish glow, slightly above her head height. Easily recognizable from the same exercises with the Met's crash-bang boys. She swung her baton at the dim light. A shot in the dark alright.

CHAPTER

54

It wasn't a fair fight. The other woman couldn't see. Melody could. Her sightless attacker had the one shot. It was a good shot, considering. But it clattered harmlessly into Melody's Kevlar helmet: the one capable of protecting from high capacity rounds.

It was still a shock though. Melody half leapt sideways turning in the direction of the blow. She processed the woman in the skirt, top and flat shoes. Behind her she saw him. Finally. The monster. Secured to a wheelchair. This was great.

The baton swung again, but Melody had stepped out of range – and pushed up the night-vision lens so it wasn't showing She didn't want to hurt this woman who was obviously on the side of the angels. But Melody was taking Millar, right now. Even better that he was already trussed up and ready to go.

The woman was swinging blindly, grunting with the effort. Using the infrared, Melody manoeuvred herself behind.

'Give it up. I know it's you. Melody Fox, right?'

Fuck. That shook her more than the blow to the helmet.

'I understand. I do. But come on, this is madn—'

From behind, Melody grabbed the woman in a classic choke hold. She didn't stand a chance with Melody having six inches on her petite adversary. The woman slumped unconscious in seconds.

Millar was regaining some of his senses. 'Melody fucking Fox. Are you fucking kidding me. You fucking cunt why ain't you fucking dead? You're supposed to be fucking dead. You's like some fucking unk—'

Frankie punched Millar smack in the nose. Again, unfair fight as he couldn't even see it coming.

'Who's the woman?'

'No idea. Only applied minimal pressure. Should come around pretty fast. Zip tie and gag her.'

Frankie complied while Melody removed a small, aluminium box from her rucksack. Millar was groaning away from the punch. His nose must be broken. She opened the container and removed the prefilled syringe. Stopwatch gave them 00.09.32.

Melody grabbed Millar by the hair and pulled his head back. As roughly as she could she slammed the needle into his neck and pushed in the contents.

He was unconscious before Frankie finished zipping up the mystery woman.

CHAPTER

55

Frankie led the retreat as they raced back to the escape sewer. Melody glanced at the luminous dial of the stopwatch.

00.05.06.

The drugged-up Millar flopped around the wheelchair as Melody careened around a ninety degree corner. The smoke was still thick, but clearing. They still had the advantage; protected in their masks, electronic comms, and night vision.

The fire alarm finally stopped ringing. Only to be replaced by the insistent wail of emergency sirens coming from outside the building. *Shit.* The responders had arrived a couple of minutes ahead of her estimate.

Frankie stopped dead, holding up his arm.

'Wait while I check. Over.'

'Copy.'

They were near the front entrance and the main stairs. She waited while Frankie trotted a few yards ahead.

'Four firemen in breathing gear just ran up the main stairs. When I say go, you go fast. Over.'

'Copy.'

She could hear Frankie breathing hard as they waited. It was forever – as in the cliché – but seconds in reality.

'Go.'

'And here's the other one I prepared earlier.'

Frankie dropped the drugged-up Millar into the foldable wheelchair at the Ridley end of the abandoned main sewer. He hadn't fancied lifting that dead weight the half mile back to the pumping station.

Once they cleared the main entrance, it was plain sailing back the way they came. Her trusty ropes lowered the inert Millar through the drops. But at Frankie's plasma-cut, cast iron grill, she decided *fuck it.* He made a satisfying crack as she dropped him feet first to the flagstones below. Probably an ankle or two broken. Maybe a femur. No matter.

'What did you pump him with? It's very impressive.'

'Five megs Haloperidol. Two megs Lorazepam. Standard instant tranquillizer for psychotic patients. It'll last an hour. Then another one if needs be.'

'Useful to know.'

'Can't get it at Boots, case you were thinking. Don't try this at home, Blue Peter boy.'

'Got it. Shall we go?'

They went, having removed their helmets and reattached their headlights. Frankie pushed the wheelchair-bound Millar this time.

As she couldn't physically throw Millar up through the iron grill into the pumping station, Melody secured him with the rope under his arms. Frankie hauled him up. A few minutes later they loaded him into the back of Frankie's Range Rover. To make sure, Melody refilled the syringe and pumped Millar with another knockout dosage. She could see the bloodied bone protruding from his ankle. Too bad.

Frankie's route took them past the lit-up detention centre. Three fire engines were still in attendance. A large group of youths, mostly in their underwear, were milling around in front of the main gate. They were being corralled by a few policemen. Two ambulances were waiting, headlights still on. She hoped no one was seriously hurt. But that was no longer her problem.

Wow. Did you just rationalize that, Melody? Was it their problem for being in the wrong place at the right time.

Melody turned around to watch the slightly surreal scene recede via the rear window. Frankie was never a look back kind of person. He kept his eyes dead ahead on the road as they headed out of London.

CHAPTER

56

Frankie slammed the shipping container door shut behind him. Melody was finally alone with Millar. Unlike the last time they met, he didn't have his pals to help. The night Millar murdered her family. Killed her.

The illumination came from an array of candles flickering Melody's shadow onto the container walls. They surrounded an easel displaying a large framed photograph of Charity. It was her twelfth birthday party photograph. Her last as the delightful, adorable, mum-centric child about to transition into the moody, rebellious teen.

The idea for the container came from her sojourn into Belgium. Those poor kids locked inside their metal prison. Scared. Chained like animals. No escape. Yes, a container was a perfect solution for what she had in mind for Millar. There would be no escape for him, like there would never be any escape for her. Except the final escape that claims all eventually. Anthony Gary Millar had made sure of that.

Aaron Fuchs had many business interests. Some were

even legitimate. Frankie oversaw all of them while his boss basked at her majesty's pleasure. The *Tommy Owens* transport fleet was one of his most profitable legitimate enterprises. Long before she knew of Aaron's existence, Melody was aware of *Tommy Owens* container lorries thundering up and down the motorways. Charity liked to count them when they travelled anywhere as a family.

Mark Higgins knew all about them too. The reason he wanted an arrangement with Aaron for his drug imports. One of his complaints before Melody shot him twice through the heart.

It was no problem for Frankie to arrange an Owens container to be dropped at the *Big 'A' Metal Yard* on the outskirts of Sevenoaks, Kent. Big 'A' being Aaron's first business front; scrap metal reclamation, car crushing, car parts. All legit. Satisfied customers came and went. It was also the de facto head office for all of Aaron's enterprises. Frankie spent half his time here. He didn't run the business though. That was the site manager, Billy Strange. Frankie had given him the day off, giving Melody the quasi-dungeon to herself. Just her, a chair, a table. And Millar dangling naked from the ceiling.

Using half-inch thick chain links, Frankie had helped shackle and truss the unconscious Millar; hands, feet, arms and torso. The bracelet-block around his broken ankle would be particularly excruciating.

He had gone along with Melody's instructions without comment. She appreciated the effort. They pulled the chains through the four-inch diameter metal eyes attached to the container ceiling. Millar was spreadeagled, dangling in the air, face down. The chains were taut, taking his full weight. His head was six feet off the ground. Toes at five feet, leaving him at an angle of fifteen degrees head to foot. She didn't want him to strain his neck glaring at her.

At the clang of Frankie's departure, she checked the time. 2.52 a.m. He'd been under for two hours. Long enough. Anxious to get on with it. Of course, she took the Hippocratic Oath. Do no harm. But that only covered humans.

The smelling salts had Millar coughing and spluttering his way back to consciousness. She stood back and watched him, as a god may watch an ant.

Don't hurt my daughter. Don't hurt my daughter, don't hurt my daughter. Tell me what you want, please. Just tell—

She felt her cheek, where the brass knuckles had slammed into her as she tried to stop her daughter being violated by brutes.

Millar was confused – naturally. He struggled. The agony of metal on exposed bone tearing through his whole body. He screamed. Not in the way Melody had gone to scream, smashed to the ground before anything came out. This scream was loud. And visceral. And pure. And agony.

And sweet music to her.

The monster stopped struggling and focussed on her. He didn't sound suitably contrite or scared. Yet.

'I recognize you. That cunt we left for—

The effort of talking moved his dangling body in mid-air, which in turn ground his bone against her metal.

—ah, fuck, fuck, fuck. Jesus fuck. That hurts, that fucking hurts, bitch. Let me down. Let me fucking down. Oh, you're dead. You're so fucking dead, lady. You should be dead, that was the fucking plan. Why ain't you dead. Ah fuck that hurts. Stop it hurting, you're a fucking doctor ain't ya? You can't do this.'

Melody continued staring at him. Mute. Unable to speak. She could see the Grendel's lips move. Hear sounds he was making. But her brain had ceased to process the stimuli. Eyes filled. An emotional tsunami hit as she trembled violently. She felt it. How could she do what she meant to do if she was shaking so much? She looked at her hands, which must be twitching uncontrollably like the Parkinson's patients she saw during her residency.

Imperceptible. There was barely any movement. It was in her mind. The raw emotion. The sickness in her guts. The moment passed as she breathed in deeply.

'Lingchi.'

Melody calmed herself. From her bag she removed a dark-brown, leather bundle, tied around by a leather strap.

'Cunnilingfuckinchi. What's the fuck's that supposed to be when it's at home. What's in that?'

She placed the bundle on the table, undid the strap, unspooled it.

A beatific calm had washed over her. 'Back in the day, no one cared about those who the powers-that-be punished. Public humiliation and suffering were important aspects of punishment. And execution. Pour encourager les autres. You know. Ever visit the Tower of London as a kid?'

'What? What? Fucking hated school. And no, I never visited the fucking Tower. You off your bleeding rocker, lady?'

Melody looked at the gleaming array of scalpels, each tucked into its own individual pouch, blade safely ensconced in a transparent plastic cover.

'We Brits loved to hurt along with the best of them. The best of them were the Chinese. They were highly creative and seriously sadistic in their methods. Liked to do things slow and steady. Prolonging death for days. Suitable punishment for a psychopath don't you think?'

Millar finally started to sound a little scared. Still not a scintilla of contrition. 'I'm the psycho here? Lady you got me hanging by fucking chains from the fucking ceiling, you psycho fucking bitch. Come on lady.'

Melody held up a selected scalpel, making sure Millar saw it glint, even in candle light.

'Lingchi is Chinese for *slow slicing*. Better known as the death of a thousand cuts—'

'Lingchink. That's a good one.'

'It served two purposes for the Chinese. The agonizing death thing. Obviously. But that wasn't the most important element to them. You see, to the Chinese, a thousand cuts ensured the victim's soul could never enter the afterlife and be with their ancestors. That terrified and shamed them even more than the hideous death happening in slow motion. Imagine that. Of course, you don't have a soul to worry about the thousand cuts.'

'Fuck you lady. Fuck. You.'

'Only in your case it'll be death by four thousand seven hundred and ninety six cuts. One for each day of my daughter's life. I know. I know. It's not a fair recompense. For the life of an innocent girl. Plus it's got that Shylock-Jewish stereotype vibe. Pound of flesh, and all that. That's her. Charity Fox. The innocent you took from me.'

Melody pointed to the photograph.

The bravado was diminishing. Millar sounded suitably scared. 'Come on lady let me go—'

Melody stepped right up to Millar's face, scalpel at the ready.

'While it's not fair recompense, it's all I have left. That's if I can make you last four thousand seven hundred and ninety six cuts. It won't be easy. Try not to struggle.'

She grabbed his hair with her left hand, jerking his head back.

'One.'

She sliced the first one-inch long cut into his left cheek, not too deep. Despite seeing it coming Millar sounded genuinely surprised. 'Ow. Christ. You cut me. You fucking bitch, you cut me.'

'Something about the concept of death by four thousand, seven-hundred and ninety-six cuts you don't get?'

'Fuck's sake just shoot—'

'Two.' Melody cut his forehead. Again not too deep.

'Please don't do that—'

She grabbed him by the hair again, slicing across his top lip. The blood oozed.

'Three.'

'Fuck, fuck. Stop it.'

Finally, a hint of desperation in his tone. That was more like it. Melody returned to the table and picked up a large tub of salt.

'There's no stopping this Tony. You prefer Tony right? Not Anthony?'

'Fuck you, cunt.'

'Thing about scalpel cuts, they can be imperceptible – at first. So damn sharp. Surgeons slice themselves, don't even notice. However—

Melody poured salt into her open palm.

—-introduce an agent like salt to the wound. Does it hurt like buggery. From just one cut.'

She rubbed the salt into his lip. The effect was instant agony.

'Arrrrrrrrrrrrrrgggggggggggggggggggggghhhhhhhhhhhh hhhh.'

Millar flopped around like a fish on deck, triggering further agony in his ankle. She rubbed salt into the other two cuts.

'Only four thousand seven hundred and ninety three to go.'

'Two hundred and twenty-eight.'

Blood had pooled under Millar. But not too much, considering. The idea was to refrain from bleeding him excessively. Once she tired of his face, she began on the torso and limbs, in a defined sequence. This moved the pain all over his body. Alternating with salt and lemon juice added to the agony.

He wasn't screaming or babbling as much on each new cut. Maybe she should perform complete Lingchi, and start brutally slicing fistfuls of flesh from his limbs and torso. She really didn't like the Shylock connotations. Maybe near the end, depending on the pain he was still feeling.

He had passed out five times. Including from this last cut. She had revived him immediately every time. But now, feeling slightly fatigued, she sat in the chair looking at his inert body. There was little chance she could achieve her target number of cuts before taking out his eyes. The second to last thing she intended to do. The filthy degenerate eyes which had seen her beloved's dying breath.

In her multiple fantasizing of how this scenario played out, she envisaged making him tell her everything of that night. Why the monsters chose them? Was there anything she could have done to prevent being selected for terror? Why did they do it? Why kill us when they had what they wanted?

She remembered working in her room. She remembered reacting to Charity's gut-wrenching scream. But after that, it was mostly a blank, except for Charity's song playing over and over.

Amanda Soresh told her that she may never remember. Or that it might all come flooding back. A random memory triggering a cascade. Another traumatic event could spark her synapses to recall. Maybe *not remembering* was a good thing. The mind protecting the body by burying it so deep that escape was impossible. Soresh wasn't telling Melody something she didn't know. The mind was her speciality. But still—

The TV shouldn't be on.

Melody floated above herself, observing as she heard the second scream. She didn't understand. No mistake. That was her daughter. Melody saw herself leap out of her chair and rush towards the screams. The scene unfolding was one of the vivid horrors Melody could never forget, no matter how hard she tried.

God no.

Her exquisite daughter, her love, her life, was being dragged by her long luxuriant hair across the living room floor. The brute was over six feet, and balaclava masked. To her left was Paul; on his knees in the middle of the room, another beast pressing the barrel of a gun hard into the back of his head.

'Don't hurt my daughter. Don't hurt my daughter. God, don't hurt my daughter. Tell me what you want, please. Just tell—'

The man pulled his gun hand back then lashed Paul across the face with the barrel.

'Where's the safe?'

As Melody went to scream, a gloved fist steamed in from her side—

She watched her head hit the mahogany floor.

Her daughter's attacker had a nondescript flat London accent which crossed the class barriers these days.

'Hey, boss, wot should I do wiv her? Too good to fucking waste is wot I'm saying.'

That was new. Borthwick speaking. She could see him now. She assumed he was speaking to Millar. It fit the crime details as told to her by Hickman.

She was wrong.

'Whatever you like old chap. Do not leave DNA. Anywhere. You got that?'

For the first time, Melody recalled hearing *that* voice. Not the version of Melody lying helpless on the floor. She died that night, alongside Charity and Paul. This Melody was looking down at her long dead body. Still conscious, but no longer cogent.

This Melody tried to see the source of the other voice. She was good with accents. Her work with the military exposed her to a babel of the English speaking world. And this one was surprisingly different. He sounded educated speaking received standard English. But there was also something under, a hint of – Irish? She strained but he remained tantalizingly out of her visual range.

Melody watched as Millar (the other ghoul dressed in human skin) the inhuman, grabbed Charity by the hair, yanking her up.

'On yer feet, bitch.'

'Mummy – mummy – mummy. No. No. No. Argghh. Argghh. You're hurting—'

Charity's raspy words were barely audible.

Melody tried to raise a hand. 'Don't. Please.'

Then her daughter was gone.

She felt herself falling, which was enough to jerk herself awake as her head lolled to one side. Millar still dangled, groaning. The revelation remained, bursting bright in her head.

'There was a fourth man. I remember there was a fourth man.'

Melody leapt from the chair. Grabbing his hair she pulled his face up. She felt nothing looking at the thirty or so, one-inch cuts she had made there. There was still plenty of face time for more.

'There was someone else there. A fourth man. Who was

he?'

She hadn't made any throat cuts yet, so he could still talk.

'No there weren't.'

Melody sliced along his left eye-brow. She had even more of a purpose now. The blood dripped down his pulled up face.

'Don't lie. Whose idea was it to hit our property? You weren't driving round randomly, at night, right?'

'Don't remember.'

An enraged Melody rushed to her doctor's bag to retrieve the trusty Fairburn-Sykes knife.

'Which of you black hearted bastards said, "I got an idea, there's these rich twats in Limehouse, let's show them. Let's teach them a lesson. Fucking one percenters." Who said that? Whose idea was it?'

She grabbed a fistful of flesh on Millar's back. Slicing around and through, she excised a circular piece of Millar, an inch and a half in diameter.

The inchoate screams went on until he passed out. He missed Melody dispassionately explaining as she sliced his flesh: 'Full Lingchi also included slicing small pieces off the victim. Then bigger bits. Then amputations of limbs. They could keep the whole process going for days. You think Hannibal Lecter was original? It's really quite fascinating from a medical point of view. The ancient Chinese knowledge of anatomy was pretty advanced.'

Smelling salts dragged the unconscious Millar back into her pit. She held up his own bloody flesh still oozing in her left hand. No sense of the depravity entered her being. Melody Fox had left the building. Her monster was in control.

'Now you were saying. Whose idea was it?'

His voice had been reduced to a barely audible whisper.

The sneering contempt, even the hatred, had been replaced by broken resignation.

'It were none of us. You're right. It were the other bloke.'

'What other bloke?'

'The one that hired us for the job.'

Melody's whole world split on its axis and disintegrated.

They were hired? Someone hired them?

'Are you fucking with me, Tony?'

'I swears. He was the one what told us what to do and everything when we was there. He bypassed the alarm and all. Opened the gate. It were him, I swears on me sister's life.'

She knew the answer but she still needed him to confirm it. 'This other bloke was there? Inside the property? With you all?'

Hickman told Melody that Paul had complied fully with the orders, presumably in the expectation the gang would take the money and run. Thus leaving his family, scared and shaken, but alive. After he opened the safe, built into the building structure, the gang took the jewellery, gold coins, and cash, about two million pounds worth. That was the motive as far as everyone was concerned. Why wouldn't it be? They found all the stolen goods in the crashed van. No time to divvy it out before the crash.

Melody had to lean in close to his mouth to hear. 'What I'm trying to tell you, yeah.'

'Why keep that to yourself and not tell the police?'

'I ain't no fucking grass. Besides, feller's right fucking not to be messed with. And I got family. All twats really, except me older sister, Siobhán. Brought me up like she was me mum, as our actual mum being a fucking junkie. All I got. Said he'd cut off her fucking head, post it to me at Ringland in a hat box, if I so much as even thought about grassing him up. Know what I mean?'

'Family. Yeah, I know what you mean. What was his name?'

'No idea.'

Melody flashed the knife in front of him, the intent clear. He tried to laugh at the threat, but didn't have the lung capacity. It came out like a strangled, gasping meow.

'Ain't lying. Called himself Michael Caine. And before you ask, you'll never find out where he came from neither.'

'Oh I'll get it out of you, Tony.'

'Caine was Glenn's contact. And you fucking incinerated him. Least, had Fuchs do it, you dumb twat.'

She absorbed this new information for a second or two. 'Yeah, but, if he hired you, how come he let you leave with all our stuff from the safe? What was his cut?'

'Didn't want nothing from the safe, except, some leather briefcase. All he took.'

The shock was too much. She had to sit. The briefcase was way more than nice. It was a gift from Paul after Peach's IPO successfully launched at its offer price of £22.75 per share. The bag was crafted by Bottega Veneta, from Nero crocodile, at a cost of twenty grand. But she could never bring herself to take it to work amongst people who earned less than the cost of a bag in six months. Plus the whole *crocodile skin* thing.

Instead she used the briefcase to store classified military material she worked on at home. This *other* Melody worked on higher than top secret psy-ops scenarios and implementation. Under the Official Secrets Act (she was required to sign) all such knowledge, files, and associated material was classified top secret for one hundred years, on pain of prosecution. She was having second thoughts about the ethics of what she was doing professionally. And she had access to highly sensitive material regarding ops in Iraq and Afghanistan between 2004 and 2012.

Operation Kill Zone, in particular, was a disaster that led to the deaths of over two hundred Iraqis, mainly women and children. The target was a high value leader of the insurgency who kept himself surrounded by civilians at all times. She advised on strategies for drawing him into a narrow kill zone within his normal comfort zone. It was sound in theory, but too risky for collateral damage. She made her opposition known, but was overruled by the brass, who in turn were beholden to their political masters. They needed a big win to show that an increasingly unpopular war was working. No WMD, no appetite.

A year later she was approached by a freelance journalist, Jamie Conté. He was researching the murky *Operation Kill Zone* as told to him by a disillusioned special forces operator. She didn't like Conté. He was more interested in his own advancement than any larger truth. This was his ticket to a bigger job on one of the nationals. However, he pressed her buttons on her own ethical concerns as a doctor. Ludicrous now, of course.

She knew she shouldn't have made copies and taken home the material. Regretted it the second she left the building. It had the names of those involved in overriding her professional recommendations, including big beasts in the cabinet and in the civil service. Names like Sir Menzies Asterion, KCBE. Asterion was head of her section in the MOD when she went to Iraq in 2005. He wasn't a 'K' then, being a mere deputy undersecretary. By the time *Operation Kill Zone* was sanctioned he was a cabinet secretary. His finger-prints were all over the op. After Melody stepped into the shoes of her old boss Dennis Libby, she liaised regularly with Asterion. An obnoxious man with one of those insufferable plummy accents that had escaped from a 1920's Home Counties' tennis match.

If those names got out, all hell would have broken lose. Careers ruined. Ambitions thwarted. The old Melody backed off. Told Conté she had changed her mind. Maybe she should call him now? Find out what he knew back then. And whom he told. Did Conté burn her – how would others know what she had copied? Melody hadn't even told Paul. Conté was the only unauthorized person who knew her role. She has assumed as a journalist he would never reveal his sources.

Is that what this was all about? Retrieving the material and shutting her up. Come on, Melody. Isn't that all a bit conspiracy preposterous. Spy novel shit?

She had presumed the briefcase and its contents had been destroyed in the fire which was started in the *safe* room, after the safe was emptied of valuables. Why would they want files useless to them?

After Soresh discharged Melody from hospital, she was debriefed by the MOD. Asterion made it clear she would never be considered for reappointment. Not that she wanted it. She had other ideas at that point. Melody hadn't thought about those ethical concerns. Until now.

'What did this bloke look like?'

Millar had started to drift off again. The smelling salts were having diminishing returns as his blood loss was greater than she was aiming for. She did get carried away after a hundred cuts, and was not so careful for a while. His screams motivated her. The banality of torture. She plunged the syringe filled with adrenalin into a vein. He shot back to consciousness. She held up his head so he could see the slowly diminishing candles illuminating her daughter's image.

'Am I dead?'

'I said what did he look like?'

Millar was like a new man. He crackled with renewed –

albeit temporary – vigour.

'Average like. White guy. I dunno, maybe six feet tall. Maybe, oh, maybe like fifty? I didn't really look at him. Military type. Met him near the place for the first time that night. That's it really.'

Military type? Oh fuck. It was about her work for the MOD. The stuff she took. The names it contained. Names she had decided not to leak anyway. That's why a break-in was staged. That's why her family was savagely sacrificed. To suppress information.

'Where did Borthwick live?'

'Kentish Town, wiv his bird.'

'Name? Address?'

'Oh, I don't fucking remember. It was years ago. Jesus Christ.'

She sliced his kneecap. The adrenalin helped him feel it to the max.

'Oh Christ. Just fucking kill me. Just fucking kill me, you cunt. You evil fucking cunt.'

'Oh woe is me. Remember harder.'

'Okay, okay. His bird's name's er – er – Julia. Julia Kirk. She was expecting at the time. Named the kid Mia. Yeah that's right. Swear to God I don't know the address no more.'

Melody stood back. She could barely take it in. This was supposed to be the end of her journey. The dead Doctor Melody would have hated her with a vengeance. Which was ironic given her current vengeful activities. But at least there was to have been no more after tonight.

Two roads diverged in a yellow wood, and sorry I could not travel both, and be one traveller, long I stood, and looked down one as far as I could.

She looked down a road in the woods and had taken it. It was dark and deep but not lovely. Maybe she could have returned to the other track. Made a connection back across.

Instead she must head deeper into the heart of darkness.

The pathetic lump of flesh that was left of Millar swayed in his chains. Death by four thousand, four hundred and ninety-six cuts. It was always an unlikely number. He hadn't suffered nearly enough – but she had. Time to put him out of her misery.

Melody picked up her F-S knife. No hesitation as she sliced him from sternum to groin; then watched as his steaming guts spilled out onto the container floor. She felt as empty as he now was.

He tried to thrash, but didn't squeal much. The shock had mostly closed-up his throat and strangled his screams at birth.

She packed everything away before deigning to look back at him one last time, in the flesh. The focus of all her hatred since she came back to life at St. Michael's. The day Hickman had revealed his name; and she begged someone, anyone, to kill them all.

He didn't look so tough now. But he did look so dead. She clanged the door shut, padlocking the container behind her. Frankie had promised to clean up everything when she had finished. What a great guy. Solid, you know. No wonder Aaron treated Frankie like the other good son, the one he hadn't lost.

Her journey continued. Miles to go.

CHAPTER

57

'You sound, oh, different, Mel. Very harsh.'

Melody had texted Frankie from the phone on the seat of the nearly-new Mini Cooper. The car was parked outside the Portacabin on the *Big A* site. It was fun to drive the Mini back to her house in Golders Green. But no Helen. No Monty either, to be honest. She was dog-tired and it was supposed to be over. Yet here we were. One more rabid dog to hunt down.

Worse – that woman at Ridley (who she presumed must have been a policewoman) had named her. To her masked face. Melody had been correct after all. Aaron and his secret games. Someone at Scotland Yard had seen the other pattern based on Aaron's own personal shit list. Clever woman.

She parked the Mini around the corner as Frankie had instructed. No other worries, as he'd send one of his associates to collect it. Just sleep. Which is exactly what she did for nearly twenty-four hours. If she dreamt, she didn't remember.

It felt great to be back in her own bed in Golders Green. Melody brewed a pot of coffee and switched on her personal mobile for the first time in over a week. As expected, it informed her of the many calls she had missed. She had chain emailed her nearest and dearest eight days ago with a short message.

Dear all – Incommunicado for a week or so! Biking up to the Lake District for a quiet break.
Just me and my tent. Phone off, so DON'T WORRY!

That didn't deter Chloe who had left four voicemails. Ruth was always a respecter of her sister's privacy. She had rung once, leaving one voicemail reminding Melody of her promise to celebrate Rosh Hashanah. Kevin was very miffed at the email. Apparently he had always wanted to visit the Lakes. Especially as he been growing some exciting new herb hybrids that would go down well in a tent up north.

First things first. After years of inactivity, Jamie Conté was still reverberating around her brain. She had to see this bloke again. Find out if he had revealed the name of his source. Her name. What if he was the reason her life had been destroyed? What if he gave up her name? That made him complicit in what happened didn't it? Not as guilty as Millar, Borthwick and Smith perhaps. Not as guilty as the fourth monster who orchestrated the house invasion. Nor as guilty as those behind the curtain who ultimately had initiated the clean-up. But no innocent.

Miles to go.

Conté handed her his business card when they met at

Coffee Republic in Soho. That was long gone. She typed his name into google search. There were probably lots of Contés, and he wasn't at all famous, so—

Wow. Google instantly flagged up 913,555 references to Jamie Conté. The top hyperlink was a headline to an article in the Daily Mail:

Freelance journalist dead in Milan trunk,
wearing women's leather bra, panties.

Conté died five weeks after Limehouse. The conspiracy theories in blogs and fringe sites popped up quite early in the listed entries. Italian police concluded that Conté died of asphyxiation after being the sole actor in a sex game that went horribly wrong. They claimed he was unemployed at the time and hadn't been working on any articles.

Her head was swimming. She wasn't sure how to continue. She googled Sir Menzies Asterion. He had his own Wikipedia entry. He retired two weeks after debriefing Melody, departing with a fat juicy pension. The pay rank equivalent of an Admiral of the Fleet. Plum directorships at major companies followed shortly. No doubt his ridiculously plummy accent went down well with the Americans. The juiciest position being at Lemmon Rossiter Partners, the global financial powerhouse based out of New York and London. It's sweet to be in the elite.

Was this her life from now on? Drifting further and further into the dark wood. Melody had phoned her friend as a distraction.

Chloe:	You sound, oh, different, Mel. Very harsh. What did you do up north anyway? Dance naked in the forest?
Melody:	Relaxed. Took in the scenery.

Chloe:	Oh. Okay. Could have gone to our place in St. Kitts for that. With me. On the private beach. Cabana. Not slumming in the mud and rain on your own.
Melody:	The peasants were fine.
Chloe	Oh, very ha ha. I'm not a snob you know. But I do so like my creature comforts. That's all. So shoot me. (*awkward pause*) Look, Mel, darling, you must be, well, I don't know what you must be, feeling. It's all too horrible. Truly appalling. I don't know what to say.
Melody	Sorry?
Chloe:	I've seen the news.
Melody:	I haven't.

She hadn't seen anything since she woke up after her long sleep. No problem guessing what they were blaring. Chloe went through the Millar news. Melody pretended to be surprised. On one aspect she was genuinely surprised. The tabloids uniformly had the Ridley event down as a great escape. *'LIMEHOUSE MONSTER ESCAPES'* being used as the headline on three of them. That was the line, and it was not being contradicted by Scotland Yard.

She grasped that implication immediately. Perfect.

Chloe	Must be devastated, so let's keep you busy. The foundation. Your brilliant mind must have some great ideas on prosaic fundraising by now.
Melody	Yes. My mind says it has. Lots.
Chloe	Fantastic. If you ever answered your

phone or checked your emails, you'd see we're having a small gathering at the house Sunday evening. Tell me then. Your room awaits. Do confirm with an RSVP, darling.

Melody clicked into emails on her laptop. Her usual MacBook Pro, not the one she bought solely used for her dark web investigations. That was tucked away in the rented flat; soon to be incinerated with all other incriminating evidence.

Did she really want to schlep into deepest Oxfordshire to meet the Carrington's top drawer friends again? All they ever talked about was themselves, money, and who's screwing who amongst the great and the not-so-great. Melody's best friends had changed almost as much as she had, maybe not really for the better. And, to be honest, she'd rather kick back and chill with Kevin, whom she hadn't seen in a while. For obvious reasons. Though he would want to puff his new hybrids. Which was great, except for her paranoid wariness about losing self-control and accidentally spilling secrets. Dark secrets.

Melody — Ah, I dunno, love. Okay, I have the email. I sort of promised my cousin Kevin—

She quickly scanned the invite. Yes. There it boringly was: fellow billionaire here, cabinet minister there, scattered A-list entertainers, a not-so-minor royal, and – oh, no way. Bold as brass. Sir Menzies Asterion, KCBE.

Melody: — But you know what, why not? I'm replying right now.

Chloe:	Super-great.
Melody:	And while I'm thinking of other stuff. Tell Ben we should chat about the shares he's been going on about.
Chloe:	Oh thank goodness. He's been driving me nuts. 'Can you call Melody. Can you email Melody. Can you text Melody'. Why he won't do that him—

BRRRRRRRR—BRRRRRRRR—BRRRRRRRR—

Melody:	Bloody doorbell's going. Gotta go. Speak soon okay, or see you next week. Bye.

Melody padded through to the hallway, still in her pyjamas and bare-feet. Peering through the security viewer in the front door, she saw a woman who looked to be in her early thirties. About five-five, business suit with pants instead of skirt, a light brown complexion. Even without the green tinge, she recognized her instantly from Ridley.

Bollocks. Might as well get it over with.

Melody tousled her hair. *Shit. Short blonde.* Racing up stairs, she threw on the expensive black wig that approximated to how the other Melody looked.

Melody confidently opened the door, looking the woman straight in the eye. 'Yes? Can I help you?'

'Melody Fox?'

'Yes.'

'At last we meet officially, Ms Fox. Long sleep? Hope we didn't wake you.' The woman held out her hand, all friendly like. 'Detective Sergeant Leia Jennings.'

Melody gripped Jennings hand, giving her a proper

man's shake. The policewoman reciprocated squeeze for squeeze. Let the mind games begin.

Melody looked sad and troubled. 'I know what this is about, Detective Sergeant.'

'You do? Care to confess?'

'Sorry?'

'Oh nothing. Forget I said that. What is this about, do you think, Ms Fox? Exactly?'

'Please, call me Melody. I assume it's about the escape of Anthony Gary Millar from her majesty's finest. The monster who murdered my family. Left me for dead. You're here to offer me police protection until he's recaptured. Correct?'

Leia had to smile. Melody Fox was good.

CHAPTER

58

Melody had never been in a police station – let alone an interrogation room. She had missed her own case by virtue of a seventeen-month coma. After that, Hickman had always visited her. First at St. Michael's. Later at Ruth's house. Then finally at her own terraced cottage. She knew he felt fatherly towards her, despite their age difference being, what – only fifteen years? She has the magic genes and bone structure for youthful looks. She fully intended to the use those advantages. She had done it before.

The techniques were obvious to her as part of her government role was advising on interrogation strategies for the military. She had agreed to the suggestion that she may care to pop down to the Yard for a chat, including the subject of police protection. The sergeant made it sound as if she was doing Melody a big favour. But Leia Jennings had tipped her hand the night before. She said Melody's name out loud.

No way was she venturing into the lioness's den alone.

Before they left Golders Green, Melody insisted on calling the number Frankie had scribbled on a scrap of paper.

The room was sterile and bright. She sat at a metal table bolted to the floor. The plastic chair was uncomfortable. Cameras in all four corners observed her from every angle. Jennings had left her with a surly uniformed constable for company. She had no choice given the phone call Melody had insisted on making. Melody had invoked her rights and the police had no right to question her without legal representation. After the Conté revelation she felt clearer. It was over. Then it wasn't. She had to suck it up and carry on. What more did she have to do?

No doubt Hickman was observing from some remote hub. And he would be greatly conflicted over what was happening. This Leia Jennings character was an ambitious little firebrand. Cunning too. She had but one goal. To nail her. Why else was she waiting at Ridley?

Melody mused on whether Scotland Yard was using the *FFACE* micro-expression analysis system she helped develop for MI6. Did they even know of her involv—

The door opened. Jennings breezed in, not quite as smug-looking as at the door knock. She was followed by an elegant black woman, dressed in expensive, business-Armani. Frankie had told Melody that she was involved with his younger brother Eddie, the property tycoon. Top drawer.

Melody stood up. The woman was slightly taller than her own above average five-ten.

Leia was not so sanguine. 'Okay Ms Fox. Your lawyer has arrived. In case you wondered who she was.'

The woman extended her hand. 'Hello Melody. Sarah Olongo-Hitchens. Let's get you out of here right now, shall we?'

'Oh hang on, Ms Olongo-Hitchens. Ms Fox came down

here voluntarily to talk about—'

'You advised Ms Fox of her rights?'

Melody stood by mute as the two other alpha females glowered at each other in some sort of death match. First Eddie – now Sarah. It was nice to have someone else defending you.

'Well yes – no. Not really. She's not being questioned in that sense. Ms Fox expressed concern about police protection which is why we—'

'Not really? Really? Detective Sergeant?'

The whirlwind woman turned from Jennings, smiling sweetly at her new client. 'Melody, a mutual associate has assured me there's no need to call upon the stretched resources of the Metropolitan police.'

'Really?'

'Yes. He offers guaranteed safe accommodation for the duration of the manhunt for this despicable criminal, Millar.'

'That's very kind. I accept.'

'So there we have it Detective Sergeant. The pretext for luring my client for a cosy chat has been removed.'

'Luring? Now hang on a second. It was Ms Fox herself who mentioned the possibility of police protection—'

'And why wouldn't she? According to our esteemed news media—'

Leia bristled. 'Tabloid news media.'

'Tabloid. Broadsheet. Whatever. By their own public utterances, Scotland Yard is investigating an elaborate escape plot; possibly involving the murder of fellow gang members; in order to trigger Millar's removal from an impregnable Category 'A' prison to an insecure location. As his life was in danger—'

'From himself, as it turns out.'

'Thank you, Melody. Yes, from himself Detective

Sergeant Jennings. Let's not forget who is the ultimate victim in all this. My client, Ms Fox. Now, it's all being dredged up again in the most lurid detail. It's simply too horrendous and inhuman.'

'No one is denying Ms Fox's status here. It's just that there have been some unexplained, uh – events that may indicate some sort of larger pattern—'

'May indicate? Unexplained events? What does that even mean. Can you be more specific?'

'At this time I cannot go into any detail. I simply wanted to ask Ms Fox if—'

'Then at this time I am taking my client – right now – to an undisclosed location for her own protection. Come on, Melody.'

'Can you confirm if this is you, Ms Fox?'

Jennings dropped two large photographs on the table. Melody recognized herself immediately, of course. The blurred shot of her as long-blonde haired Mrs Dalloway, exiting *Memento Mori* with Tom Bentley. The sharper shot of her, from the back, in Nicole Kidman-esque fine red hair at Sotheby's.

'Don't answer that, Melody. We're leaving, Detective Sergeant Jennings.'

Melody ignored legal advice, running fingers from both hands through her fake hair. 'Clearly not me. As you can see.'

Sarah took hold of Melody's elbow and propelled her towards the door.'

'Wigs, Ms Fox. Still could be you. Same tall-girl height, five feet ten. We worked it out.'

Melody was almost out of the door when she allowed herself a smirk. She had won this round. This Jennings character had a bee in her bonnet about her alright. A huge buzzing bumble of a bee. That fact had been confirmed.

The photos were legally a whole solar system away from being evidence or facts. Luckily the policewoman had tipped her hand and knocked out of turn.

They had no evidence of any greater conspiracy. Only suspicions. Now Melody also had a stated, plausible reason why she was disappearing for a while. It could not have worked out any better.

'If you wish to contact my client, please do so through me first, Detective Sergeant. Are we understood?'

Melody smirked again. Only this time, Leia Jennings saw it.

CHAPTER

59

'Julia Kirk?'

'Er – yeah. Who wants to know?'

The disembodied, tinny voice of Julia Kirk squeaked into the morning air. The large Kentish Town house must have been grand in its Victorian heyday. Today, it was just another of the seedier properties profitably divided into the multiple bedsits and flats of North London. Exactly like Melody's current rental. Except more downmarket.

It was surprisingly easy to track down Julia. Melody had assumed it would prove harder than going to Kentish Town public library and checking the electoral rolls. Surely anyone associated with an evil sociopath like Glenn Borthwick wouldn't register to vote? *Stereotyping, Mel.*

'Glad he's dead, be honest. Used to beat me something rotten. And the stuff he done, y'know? I ain't never telling little Mia. Ever. Poor mite having that for a dad.'

Julia glanced anxiously towards the bedroom to make sure her four-year-old daughter was still collecting her dollies to show the friendly lady.

'I'm so sorry.'

'Yeah, me too, Virginia. So will I be able to read any of your stuff then? I'm going to night school. I never really was big on reading like, y'know at school. But little Mia's asking me all these questions all the fu – all the flipping time. And I was – am sort of right ashamed like, y'know, that I can't answer, being I wasn't that good at the reading lark. But now my night school tutor Imran says he reckons I could do me, I mean do *my* GCSE in English next year at this rate. We ain't, we haven't got much, but you at least want your kid to be proud of her own mum right? For who she is. Teach her to read even. So other kids don't call her spazzy-mum, your mum's a moron, or suchlike.'

Melody's eyes welled up. This woman wasn't who she assumed she would be. They didn't have much, including a dad. But every penny went on her child. That was obvious.

'That's wonderful Julia. You're a terrific mother. Anyone can see that.'

She blew her nose on a tissue from her two thousand pounds worth of Bottega Veneta intrecciato leather shoulder bag. Worth double the contents of the entire flat. Melody suddenly felt very small.

'Anyway, this true crime book I'm writing about the Limehouse murders—'

'I won't be in it, right?'

'Absolutely not. You have my word, there will be no reference to you or Mia. The name Kirk will never be mentioned. Beside it's not really that sort of boo—'

'Look. Look. Lady. Look. This is Mrs Mouse. And she's Angela. And this one here, she's Dora the Explorer. She's visiting us from, from – from Wales. Where she's been exploring. Are you going to play with me? Can the lady play with me, mummy? Please? Please? Please?'

The excited Mia had bounced in from the bedroom she shared with her mum, clutching her prized possessions. That stopped all serious talk for the next twenty minutes. Melody happily played with the delightful Mia. The sins of the father were not visited upon the daughter. It was her unexpected pleasure.

Finally it was time for Mia's nap. Melody took out her notepad and pen (like a real writer) and asked about Borthwick. After the horrible personal stuff, Melody swung around to his acquaintances outside the gang of three. Julia reeled off several of the scumbags she had the misfortune to meet in the two years she hung around with him.

'Any military types? Posh accents? That sort of thing.'

Julia laughed hard. 'Only military thing he ever followed were the Arsenal. See I never knew what an arsenal was till Imran told me. Means place to store weapons.'

'I know.'

'Course you do, Virginia. You're like a dead-brainy, I mean a really clever woman. Educated and whatnot. I can tell that. You look familiar though. We ever met?'

Melody was in her normal, cropped, bottle-blonde hair. Not her natural, long, thick, black mane that appeared in all the photos broadcast at the time. 'I don't think so.'

'Just can't place – hey, hang on. There was something. Imran says I have a very good memory, I just need to use it. You asked did he have any posh pals from the military?'

'He did?'

'No. But I remember this one time, not long after we started going out, when I was still living at me – at my grandmother's house. He had this huge fight with Millar over some bet. Tony refused to pay up, so Glenn got the right hump. They never talked for a month. Anyway, one morning Glenn turns up at grannies with two black eyes, she was out thank God. Broken nose. Arm in a plaster.

God forgive me, I knew he was a bad-un then, but not what he did to that poor family. I should have walked away, but it's not that easy. Anyway he tells me he was in a rumble at a club. But I got it out of him in the end. Turns out he decided to do some thieving at a big house up near Hampstead. Breaks in, only the bloke was home. Caught Glenn and beat the living daylights out of him. I laughed, poetic justice they call that, Imran said. That's the first time Glenn punched me. Knocked a tooth clean out.'

A horrified Melody gripped Julia's hand. 'What a bastard. I'm so sorry. But how's that related to the military?'

'Turns out the bloke was an ex-Colonel or something high up. Had his own security company. Was actually fitting himself a new alarm system when my moronic *fella* broke in. See, Glenn reckoned he was a real hard nut. Could take care of anyone. But this Irish guy—'

'Irish? He was Irish?'

'That's what Glenn said. Posh Irish. Anyway, this bloke beat the living tar out of him. All that kung fu type of thing Glenn said. But the bloke never called the cops on him. Took his wallet with his driving licence, credit cards and the like. Told Glenn that the beating was sufficient punishment. Broke his arm, then gave him a whisky. Weird.'

Melody slumped back into the chair. Weird indeed. But starting to make a twisted sense if you go looking for it. Security bloke accidentally makes contact with a feral scumbag who's in a gang of fellow scumbags. He sees an opportunity. Instead of pressing charges, he pockets that info for a rainy day. That rainy day was the Limehouse job. Maybe there were previous rainy days. Many other scumbags. The powers-that-be don't want their fingerprints on what is colloquially known as black ops. Those things are contracted out to sinister ex-military types skilled at making problems disappear. Suicide. Car accidents. Heart attacks. House invasions gone wrong. Melody had never bought the conspiracy theory nuts whose whole existence revolves around the government being out to get them. Until now.

'Did *Glenn*, happen to tell you the address?

'Nah. Only that it was up in Hampstead. Expensive.'

'Don't suppose he kept records?'

'Nah. He weren't – he wasn't that type. All he ever did when he wasn't thieving or down the boozer, was play his stupid video games, really loud. All that violent war and gang stuff. Sniper. Grand Theft Auto. Sleeper Cell. They was, were, his favourites. Never forget those. Should sell them really, maybe earn a few bob.'

'You still have them?'

'Oh yeah, two boxes full of his rubbish. The police never asked, so I kept them. Top of the wardrobe in the bedroom. Want to see?'

Melody rooted around in her bag. 'I do. And before I forget, I want to recompense you for your time and invaluable assistance.' She retrieved a bundle of twenty pound notes, handing the thousand pounds to a surprised Julia.

'Blimey, that's – you don't have to do—'

'Nonsense. Buy something for Mia. Something nice. And yourself.'

Now it was Julia's time to tear-up.

Julia was right. The boxes were full of rubbish. Old packs of playing cards. DVDs of imported hard core porn. Knives. Lots of knives. Knuckle dusters. Old mobiles phones. The detritus of an uncurious mind. There were also thirty video games for either Playstation or X-Box. Sleeper Cell and its many variants did seem to be a favoured title in this collection.

Charity was an X-Box kid. She loved her games too. Not just benign examples, such as FIFA. Grand Theft Auto was a favourite, even though Melody was uneasy about the levels of simulated violence. Borthwick had three variants of GTA in the boxes. She recognized two titles from her daughter's collection. But the third was new to her. *Grand Theft Auto: Home Invasion.* The connection was painfully obvious. She opened that display box. And there it was. A business card. Deposited inside, waiting to be uncovered in the light of day by Melody Fox, of all people.

Mia had woken up and was helping her mum make lunch in their tiny kitchen. Melody declined their offer to join them. She had to be off. But only after promising the distraught Mia that she'd be back soon to play with her and Mrs Mouse again.

Melody let herself out. Before she departed, she checked her bag again. It still contained the remaining nine-thousand pounds in crisp new notes. She had been prepared to pay the then unknown Julia that much for information. Dropping the bundles on the sofa, she closed the door behind her.

CHAPTER

60

'Bloody hell, Saul. Can you get the gear or not?'

'Alte makhsheyfe, this girl. She goes too far. Then a long mile morer.'

'Oh, so now I'm an old witch, not a princess? And morer isn't a word in English.'

'Oh, oh, vey is mir. Now she speaks Yiddish. Since when does the proper girl speak Yiddish.'

'There's this thing called the internet. Heard of it old man?'

Saul knocked back his third shot of Belvedere unfiltered Polish vodka. They had returned to his favourite haunt: the Polish dive in Vauxhall imaginatively called the Polska Bar.

'Yi, yi, I have no escape.'

Melody laughed. Having held her own on the Krav Maga mat with Saul (for a few minutes at least) she had become more feisty in their verbal fights.

'You should know by now that there's no escape from me, old man.'

'Vy you out and about anyvays? Not scared that Millar shtunk track you down? He escape, papers say.'

'Don't believe everything you read in the papers. Or see on TV. He's not coming back Freddy Kreuger style.'

Saul laughed. But his serious eyes told a different story. 'I bet.' He gripped her shoulder with his hairy, bear-like mitt. Then pulled her in, curling his arm gently around her head. He planted a proud fatherly kiss on her forehead.

'Proud.'

Melody let him hold her there for a while. Then pulled away.

'Are you crying?'

'Yi, yi, yi. No escape.'

'Back to my original question. Can you source what I need?'

'You think this is vey to go? Peoples like this. I knows peoples like this. I am peoples like this—'

'No you're not. You're nothing like this. Like them.'

'Exactly. Vorse than me. You think you take me? You good. Very, very good. Best voman I train outside military, maybe. Natural. Committed. And maybe tventy years, fifteen years back, ven young girl, you start then. Maybe. But, basm – no vey you take me. Or him. Not in this real life.'

CHAPTER

61

'You saw the interview, sir?'

Hickman was sitting upright in his office, drumming fingers on the desk, getting on Leia's nerves. He had watched Melody's interactions in the *FFACE* unit in the basement-complex at New Scotland Yard. The new Forensic Facial Analysis & Capture Equipment was an excellent tool. Unfortunately, they had been *legally* unable to deploy the three ultra high definition cameras to capture Melody's smallest micro-expressions. Her veracity could not be tested and used against her.

This Melody Fox was not the woman he first met at St. Michael's. He didn't mean her physical and mental recovery. That was obvious, and to be expected given time. It wasn't that. It was her whole demeanour. She was in control. She knew they had nothing. And not because of any fault by them. Because she had designed it that way. Hickman had seen this before in the most successful criminals. She had him fooled when he visited the Golders

Green house to inform her of Smith's so-called suicide. It was a brilliant, glib performance given on the fly.

Hence, he was convinced that his Detective Sergeant was on to something; and that the body of Anthony Gary Millar would never be found. One way of getting closure.

'I think – I think, you have plenty of conjecture, supposition, theories. What you don't seem to have is any damn evidence that can possibly tie Melody Fox to three known murder victims. Bentley, Ainsworth and Higgins—'

'But sir, what about the—'

'Let alone the official suicide of Smith. Murder of Borthwick, which, may I remind you, has been resolved with a confession. And last but not least, the recent so-called escape of Millar.'

The deflating Leia saw where this was going. Six deaths. Nothing on Fox. The sheer bloody chutzpah of the woman was starting to get to her too. How was any of this even possible? She was – is – a doctor for crying put loud. Mind you, so was Crippen. And Shipman. And Mengele.

'One bit of good news on the Bentley investigation, sir. From his victims' perspective that is. Just heard the team have found the remains of Poppy Andrews.'

Hickman sadly perked up. 'That's a relief. You met the parents last month, didn't you?'

'Yes. Me and DC Latimer. Poppy's mum has dementia now. Naturally, Poppy's dad had been relieved to finally know her likely fate, but distraught they would never get to bury their daughter. This didn't sit well with Donny – Latimer, sir. His gran has dementia, so took it personally. Last month he started going back in his own time through every piece of physical evidence we collected on Bentley—'

'Can't beat classic coppering. Send me a detailed report, but give me a top line now.'

'Right, well, about two weeks ago Latimer starts on the

receipts. Bentley seems to have kept every receipt for everything he ever bought since he was eighteen.'

'Bit obsessional.'

'By kept, I mean threw into bin liners, in no particular order. Ten of them. Donny went through each one. Not looking for anything in particular, just anything in the nineties and early two-thousands, to eliminate it. Most of them are for the London area. Then Donny finds one from July tenth, two thousand. The Flying Fish restaurant in St. Ives, Cornwall. We have no link between Bentley and Cornwall. The restaurant went bust in 2003. Ploughing on, Donny finds another receipt for the same place, from 1997. Only this one has a St. Ives phone number scribbled on it in biro.'

Hickman had resumed drumming his fingers again. 'Top line, sergeant.'

'Right, sir. The number belonged to a local solicitors. In 1997 they handled the estate of one Sally Georgina Seton, née Bentley, who had left her secluded cottage on the outskirts of St. Ives to her beloved grandson, Thomas. We didn't pick it up sooner because he kept the property totally off the public records radar. Still working out how. The important thing is, and very discreetly, yesterday the Cornwall constabulary started excavating the small back garden. The first body they hit was Poppy. Same clothes as the video. Then three more bodies, as yet unidentified.'

Hickman stopped drumming and leaned back in chair. This was one victory, small in the scheme of things, but huge for the Andrews family and three others. Closure of a sort.

'Brilliant work, Leia. Tell Latimer.'

'Will do. He's a good bloke. Diligent. Hard charger. Definite promotion-track material, sir.'

'As are you, sergeant. As are you. Strictly between us,

I've spoken to the Commissioner about your Inspector level trajectory. He's keen to see you make that next step in the foreseeable future. Which means within the year. You should face the media on the Andrews news. Alongside Latimer of course.'

Leia smiled modestly at the kudos.

'So, what next, sir? On Melody Fox?'

'Beats me.'

CHAPTER

62

The private lane had no street lighting and the darkness of the night matched her soul. Melody scrunched down in the driver's seat. Switching on Monty's AC would have been great with the oppressive humidity fuelled by the thick cloud covering London. Thunderstorms had been forecast after a hellishly hot few days in the capital.

She checked the house again through her binoculars. The interior lights had been on for over an hour, but she knew they were being controlled by the sophisticated alarm system. Melody was well up on the Sabretooth 5000: the ultimate house security system according to the website.

'Recommend it? I have the Sabretooth 5000 protecting my very own properties Mrs Dalloway. Both, as a matter of fact. In the UK, and over in Ireland. Not cheap of course. Not that this will be a problem for you, I'm sure. But the 5000 is definitely the one I would recommend. The package includes everything. Impact proofed windows against high velocity rounds and bomb fragments. Armour plated, fully ventilated panic room. Motion sensors. Thermal sensors for body temp. Dedicated phone line to our own rapid response teams. It's really a snip at two-fifty kay installation. Fifty kay per annum security fee, set for three years, reviewed thereafter. But can one really put a price on one's own personal protection. And the protection of your precious family. You know I'm right.'

Melody smiled sweetly at the founder and head of GSN: the term Quint preferred for Global Security Network. She knew he was incorrect. The Sabretooth 5000 was the system installed in her Limehouse home when she and Paul purchased the place.

She was redeploying her *quietly radiating money and class ensemble*; first tested at the Terra Turris to gain access to Tom Bentley's apartment. The Stella McCartney dress was complemented with the Bottega Veneta bag; the Jimmy Choo's; and the Ermenegildo Zegna Honey Horn Couture sunglasses. Her shoulder length blonde wig and exquisite, blue contact lenses completed the deception.

It was mid-morning when she strolled confidently into GSN's swish first floor offices at 24 Golden Square, Soho. Having staked out the building, from her table outside the Portuguese coffee shop, *Vida e Caffe*, she knew Bernard Quint was definitely inside.

Quint was out of his office and in reception before Melody had received her coffee from the receptionist. No doubt he kept an eye on his monitors for prospective, ripe walk-ins.

The man was charm itself, ushering her into his large office. The wall behind his desk held a plaque displaying ersatz regimental colours. Below the gaudy GSN logo, in place of the usual Latin motto, were the words *Secure.*

Protect. Serve.

Melody was well into her prepared spiel as a concerned homeowner as she tapped her midriff in a protective maternal gesture.

'All you ever seem to read about is violent attacks. Burglaries. Home invasions. And now that I'm expecting, I need to feel safe in my own home. If you can't feel safe in your own home where can you feel safe – Mr Quint? Sorry, do you prefer Colonel Quint?'

She pierced straight through his eyes to the back of his skull. Not a flicker. She knew *how* the Limehouse Monsters had gained access. Obvious now. She knew the *why* thanks to Jamie Conté clearly burning his source, *her*. All she needed to confirm was the *cui bono*.

It had to be Asterion. He had so much to lose. Mind you, so did many others. She knew some of their names, but not their faces. What level of influence could sanction the murder of its own citizens in their own home to cover up the real motive? Before she killed him, Quint would confirm that Asterion and other bigwigs had contracted and paid him. Before she killed them all.

Miles to go.

He grinned, amused. 'Oh, I was Lieutenant-Colonel Quint actually. For my sins, to be sure. Only my men use that soubriquet these days. But please, Bernard is fine.'

It was important to visit him in his lair. Not only to fully confirm her theories but for her own sanity. She had no recollection of him that night, until Millar sparked a vivid voice memory. He was exactly as described by Millar, and confirmed second-hand by Julia Kirk. Posh Irish.

Her plan was simple. Reconnoitre Quint's house. Access Quint's house. Search Quint's house. Wait for Quint to appear. Make Quint talk. Kill Quint.

She exited Monty and headed for the property. He had

upgraded from Hampstead, which in itself was exclusive. Whetstone being an oasis of small lanes, dense woodland, and expensive houses in the north-west corner of north London. Up from Finchley, next to Totteridge, not far from Golders Green. The plebeian Northern Line underground bordered it to the east. People who can afford to live in Whetstone do not use the Tube.

She was parked on a two-mile long lane that eventually sidled discretely into the A1. At this end, the super-exclusive houses had varying degrees of access and security. Quint's large 1950s four-storey detached had a substantial wall, and large gate blocking the well-lit drive. The house next door was not so Fort Knoxy. Small unsecured iron gate. Rather dark.

Melody crept along the twenty-feet high hedge between the two houses. On reconnaissance yesterday, she had noticed the scaffolding on the side of the house next door. How thoughtful of the owners to have scheduled roof repairs. The roofers had handily left a couple of extendable aluminium ladders flat on the ground.

She found the best spot in the hedge to place the extended ladder. Her new high grade rucksack was heavy. The separate large kit bag didn't help. After lugging herself to the top of the wide hedge, she lowered the bag onto Quint's garage roof which butted up to the side of his house.

She pulled up the ladder, manoeuvring it against the house wall. It peaked just above the guttering below the pitched tile roof.

Ten minutes later, Melody had prised out eight slate tiles to leave a four-feet square hole in the roof. Lugging up the bag, then the rucksack, she lowered them into the loft space below her new, un-alarmed entrance.

The loft was empty. And hot. She stripped naked and

removed *the suit* from the kit bag. Saul had explained the technology behind the device. Stealth ingress. The skintight suit was embedded with tens of thousands of pinhead diodes, linked together by smaller than a hair-width's fibre. She strapped the small battery pack (in the same material) to her back and pulled on the full face mask.

Ever think you'd look like the bloody gimp from Pulp Fiction, Mel?

First thing first. Disable the alarm and the rest will follow. Leaving the rucksack and kitbag in the loft, Melody dropped silently onto the carpeted fourth-floor corridor. Various sensors dotted across both walls. No alarm rang out. Good start. But it could be a silent alarm straight to the security response, informing Quint by text that his fortress had been breached.

Possible. But Saul knew the system usually triggered a hideous wail to alert all residents and encourage criminals to flee, thereby adding to the safety factor.

The house was silent, barring a grandfather clock tocking away. She knew Quint's current location and all was going to plan. Stealth gimp made her way undetected downstairs to the main hallway entrance. The Sabretooth 5000 alarm panel was on the wall next to the door. The red digital readout confirmed that it was fully armed. Yet here she was. One zero to the crazy gimp.

Connecting the cable from her phone into the unit's USB slot, she hit speed dial. The call was expected and the alarm was linked instantly to another of Saul's associates. He had associates all over the globe who owed him favours. In Shanghai, Bert Kwang held the Sabretooth franchise for the Peoples' Republic. For Saul, he was only too happy to set up the transmission of an authentic factory reset code direct into Quint's system. The digital display changed from red to green with the message *System Disarmed/Please Reset*

Entry Code flashing.

Great. Phase one complete. Melody peeled off the face mask, sweat pouring down her head. She raced back to the loft to ditch the gimp suit, and grab the gear needed to complete phase two. Such as her clothes.

After a quick recce of the house, she went to Quint's main study on the ground floor. Unlike his work office in Golden Square, it was filled with military memorabilia. Regimental sword on one wall. Framed photos of muddied men in combat gear toting high powered weaponry. A selection of expensive bottles of Scotch on a small table. It wasn't a hub of operations; it was a reflective room to toast past glories. The laptop on the solid oak desk was password protected, therefore nothing doing without hacktavist expertise. But she had neglected to bring her Gunter along. The desk drawers held no secrets either.

Time to work. The best spot was a couple of feet in, across the door entrance into the room. From the rucksack, she removed the Claymore mine and the rest of the gear. The Claymore's three and a half pounds of blow-you-in-half lethality was perfectly safe at the moment. Safe till armed, that is.

Working at speed, Melody screwed together the tubular parts to construct a two-feet high metal tripod frame. She positioned it on the highly polished wooden floor, against the wall to the right of the person entering the room. The compact Claymore slid neatly down into the vertical frame. The directional charge would send the blast horizontally across the room. Seven hundred tiny steel balls taking out Quint's legs. And his balls, of course.

Now for the self-arming and triggering laser. She had preassembled the second tripod with a small battery power laser already attached. The two tripod heights were synchronized for the laser beam and the receiver pad on the

Claymore. The first leg break of the laser armed the explosives. Next was the sneaky, evil part. The second-leg break of the laser did not detonate the Claymore. The big boom only occurred once the leg carried on and the beam restored. Even if the victim sussed what had happened, he is stuck in a no-win.

Melody squatted down to position the laser tripod directly opposite the Claymore's receiver pad. The laser beeped three times as it synchronized precisely with the pad.

She rose to arm the Claymore—

COLD—

The oh-so recognizable barrel of a gun pressed hard into Melody's neck.

CHAPTER

63

Melody Fox had been in Bernard Quint's head for quite some time. He was surprised she survived the fire at Limehouse. That wasn't the plan. But that's what you get employing scumbags one-level-above amateur. Borthwick and his crew had been a mistake. Some might say that the van crashing was bad luck. Quint knew you made your own luck in this game.

Yes, it was his error that she lived. But there was no way he could finish the job in St. Michael's. That would negate the elaborate home invasion false-flag. The boys received their messages about never grassing unless they wanted any nearest and dearest to be nearest and deadest. His employers were a bit miffed, but she hadn't seen him. Only Paul McCrae had seen Quint when he made him open the safe. Two .22s to the noggin removed that problem, no problemo. Then she recovered, but so what? Everyone had what they wanted, well, except her of course. But then—

The first *Limehouse Monsters* death was an interesting

happenstance. The second was a fire alarm ringing in his head. But he was stymied by being in Argentina on a lucrative merc contract. Then Millar happened.

Borthwick knew Quint. Worse – he had a business card which Quint acknowledged was foolish of him to supply. Not good. Millar knew Borthwick of course. So there was a direct link back to him that someone could uncover. What he couldn't yet figure was how the pathetic woman he failed to kill could possibly be involved.

That's why Melody Fox was on his mind when an expensively attired, cracking blonde walked in two days ago. She looked worth his time. His routine was to run facial recognition on everyone who passed the hi-def camera focussed on the front door. Just to be sure.

Thanks to his government contracts with MI5, MI6 and GCHQ, he had inveigled semi-permanent access to all government data bases. The normally cool Quint was ruffled when GCHQ and MI6 popped within sixty seconds. His throat tightened. They both gave a ninety-seven per cent probability of this woman (claiming to be Virginia Dalloway) was Melody Fox. The balls on her. In one way he was quietly admiring. Of course, he would have to kill Melody Fox properly this time.

'I need to feel safe in my own home. If you can't feel safe in you own home where can you feel safe – Mr Quint? Sorry, do you prefer Colonel Quint?'

'Oh, I was Lieutenant-Colonel Quint, actually. For my sins. Only my men use that soubriquet. But please, Bernard is fine.'

She was good. Without the facial recognition software he would never have guessed. To be fair, he had only seen her in photographs prior to the job. He did see her that night, half-dead in a crumpled heap on the floor, but he was rather busy getting the documents from the safe.

Quint did his fake spiel to the fake client as he tried to figure out her angle. Had to want to kill him. But how did she know – Millar? And why come here? His home turf. To confirm it was him? She had ethics and didn't want to make a mistake? Accent. She must have heard him barking out orders to his amateur crew. Tracked him down somehow. Must have been Millar.

Ah, not just to kill him. She wanted to know who hired him. That meant coercion on her part. She would be coming for him. At his house most likely. The place he felt most comfortable and unsuspecting. Tit for Tat. Her house. His house. Only he would be waiting for her. On his real home turf. Where she could answer a few questions from him instead; starting with who else knew about Bernard Quint.

COLD—

The barrel of the gun pressed hard into her neck.

'Claymore. Laser trigger. Where did a nice lady head doctor like you get kit like this?'

Quint circled around, keeping the gun on her. It was a .22 Ruger with a suppressor. He was dressed in standard British Army battledress camo, his face blackened. He looked weird, and it felt creepy. Though that was the least of her problems.

'I have my sources.'

Keeping the gun pointed at her head, Quint circled back behind.

'I bet you do. And that stealth suit? Impressive. I've only just heard about that myself.'

'How. How did—'

'Oh, been observing you the whole time from my ops room in the basement. Bad move coming to my office first.

Revealed your position. Never a good military strategy.'

Quint pushed Melody towards the leather chair behind the desk. No doubt he would shoot her on the spot if she even looked at him the wrong way.

'Never thought you'd recognize me. And I wanted to be sure it was you. That night.'

Quint produced a pair of metal handcuffs. 'Secure your right hand first. Then both hands behind your back.'

Melody complied.

CLICK—

Quint pushed her into the chair, then put the desk between them. The gun still steady on her face. He wasn't smug or superior at his triumph – rather, she sensed a weary resignation.

'This is all so unnecessary. What's done is done. Why couldn't you let sleeping dogs lie?'

'Why did you destroy my life?'

Quint laughed. Was she was being obtuse on purpose?

'My job. Nothing personal. Money of course. And let me guess, you came to kill me. But first you were going to make me talk, tell you who hired me and why? Hence – the Claymore and the laser trigger? I trip it, you leave me dangling until I gave up my client. Promise you'll disarm the little bugger, let me live. That about it?'

'Seemed a good plan at the time.'

'Darling, I've been tortured by the very best. Pro psychopaths. All I gave up was my tailor in Savile Row. Poor bugger. I still miss Gianluca. And his suits.'

'All heart, eh?'

Quint sneered at her naivety. 'All a state of mind see. That was never a good plan for a professional, more in the gifted amateur league. Wonder what you'll give up to me?'

'I don't know anything. You're the one with the secrets.'

Quint backed away a few paces, still keeping his weapon

on her.

'Promise I won't mark your face if you tell me everything I want to know. I love beauty, believe it not. So I'll make it quick. Semi-professional courtesy in your case.'

Quint turned for a second to pick up the aluminium briefcase rom the rear wall shelf. He placed it on the desk in front of her. Unopened. An unspoken menacing horror of something painful to come? Classic psychological warfare to induce fear and dread.

'Look, Quint. No need for that. I'll tell you what you want to know. Just tell me who it was. I have to know.'

Quint smiled again, offering her a pitying look of magnanimity. 'Not knowing is the absolute worst, right? Kills you. There are more things in heaven and earth, Horatio, than are dreamt of in your philosophy.

Fuck's sake, this evil arsehole really thinks he's a philosopher king.

Quint studied her for several seconds before shrugging to himself. 'Fair enough. I accept your terms, hardly breaches client confidentiality now. But you first. Who knows about me? Be specific.'

Melody took a deep breath. This was it. She had to know, even though it put her closest comrades in the gravest danger from a psycho who had no compunction about murdering a child.

'Two, which means probably three people. Saul Levin. Frankie Bishop. And therefore most likely his boss, Aaron Fuchs. My cousin.'

Quint's smile disappeared momentarily as he digested the last name. 'Jesus Christ. Well that's not good. Not fucking good at all. Anyone else? Your sister?'

'No, no, no, no. That's it. I swear my sister has no idea. About anything. No need to go there. Please.'

'And your poncey rich friends, like Chloe Carrington?

I'll know if you're lying.'

Melody took deep breaths. 'Like I said, those three I mentioned are it. No more.'

Quint stared hard at her, as if he too was a human lie detector machine, like Melody. 'Jesus. This is already a right cluster-fuck. However – y'know what? I believe you about the rest. Okay, agreed. They stay out of our little imbroglio. Where is Millar by the way?'

'Cut up about his bad life choices.'

Quint chuckled. 'I like you. I really do. Under diff—'

Your turn. Be specific.'

Lowering the gun, he pushed the power button on the laptop before entering his 26-digit password from memory.

'I have honour, believe it or not. I could tell you. But why not show you instead.'

'Show me?'

'I record all my clients. They don't know of course. All stored on my personal server secured deep inside a former military nuclear bunker in Latvia—'

Quint typed in his second password, the one that accessed the nuclear-hardened server. Melody counted at least thirty characters this time. Quint had long since crossed the thick line between caution and paranoia.

'Impressive.'

'It's my ultimate failsafe. You'll be surprised at how untrustworthy people are. Everyone. Especially when what they perceive as their way of life comes under the slightest threat. I blame our diseased class system. Who wants a fucking bogus knighthood anyway?'

'Tell me about it.'

Quint had placed the gun on the furthest reaches of the desk as he typed away with both hands. Melody calculated her odds of launching herself at him, headbutting his nose. Then what? He stopped typing and swivelled the laptop around so that she could see the screen.

'Okay, fair's fair. You told me what I wanted. You're Jewish, right? Old testament. Not sure what that means. Church of Ireland myself. Baptized and all, for what it's worth. Maybe there's a great beyond we all go to.'

'We don't believe in hell. Jews that is. Pity really, for you.'

'Hell's on earth, missy.'

Quint pressed the play button. The four-year old video file fired into life. It was darkish, but clearly the video came from a vehicle's dashboard camera. Quint was in the driver's seat. He turned to face the person in the back. His soft Dublin accent boomed.

'Okay, cash is all here. Job's a go. Sure you want to pull the trigger on this? Home invasion gone wrong. No survivors. Clear the safe. Not too late to pull out. Course, I keep the two million, but you get to keep your humanity. Lesson learned.'

Melody leaned in closer to the screen, straining to see past Quint to the figure in the back. She couldn't make out a person, just a black void. She didn't need to. The voice projected unseen from the laptop's tinny speakers.

'Wheels in motion. Too much riding on this now. Do it.'

Melody would have recognized that effortlessly superior, plummy Home Counties' accent anywhere.

'Was it all worth it, Doctor Melody Fox? Knowing? Will you die happy now?'

Melody leaned back in the chair and shrugged. 'You think many people die happy?'

'Touché. But I am a man of my word. I won't hurt you. Though I have hurt many others, for far less inconvenience than this cluster fuck you've left me to sort.'

Quint raised his .22 and levelled it at her forehead.

'Wait. I lied.'

Quint smirked. 'Nah. I don't think so. But I did, darling. This is going to mark your face. Just a bit. Sorry.'

PHUT—

The .22 pistol has long been the assassin's close quarters weapon of choice. There is rarely any exit wound as the slug rattles around the brain, massively destroying grey matter. That means very little visible blood and mess.

PHUT—

Just to make sure though, the double tap is invariably applied. Maybe even a third to the heart.

Saul was right. She couldn't take Quint on her own. Oh, she could get the drop on him and maybe finish him off. Of that she was convinced. But she wanted more. Needed more.

In the week prior, Melody used all her considerable psy-ops powers to create a detailed profile of Lt. Colonel Bernard Quint. She soon realized a direct attack wouldn't yield the right results. He wouldn't give up information. It wasn't in his DNA. In the 1990's, Quint was kidnapped by Hezbollah the Lebanon. Brutally tortured of course; routine for them and their Iranian masters. Some people claim torture is not reliable as a means of gathering information. Unfortunately, it is. Ask William Buckley, Beruit CIA station chief. A case study in MI6. She had seen the videos the Iranians made as they tortured Buckley in Tehran – then posted the videos to his family in the US. He gave up everything and every asset.

One caveat, psychological and physical torture are generally reliable against most people, but not all. That's why it's used. That and the powerful sadistic pleasure of maiming your enemy. Melody knew all about that, having strayed into the territory recently.

Quint was one of the few who resisted giving up anything important. Except, as he was to later quip, his tailor; to buy him time to escape. The only way he would volunteer what she needed was for Melody to psy-ops him into the illusion of having control. Every action he took, he had to imagine came from his mind, when the reality was Melody pushing and pulling him. The fruit of the poisoned tree.

Once Saul learned that Quint had privileged access to UK intel databases to run facial recognition software, her path became clear. Make him believe he had cleverly unmasked her poking around his business. A reverso scenario to Bentley when he did have the drop on her.

Virginia Dalloway was just the person to jolt him into action. The deaths of Borthwick and Smith would have alerted him to a job long left behind in his past. The so-called *escape* of Millar would have unsettled him and put him on edge. No doubt she was the last person he expected facial recognition to turn up. But he would be expecting something. Melody was counting on that predator instinct. He was thinking he had lured her into his bear trap, when in fact—

PHUT—

Quint's face bounced hard into the desk before he slid down onto the floor.

PHUT—

'Vell done, Princess. It vorked.'

Melody could now fully see the black-clad figure who had been partially obscured behind Quint for the past minute or so. 'Cutting it fine old man.'

'Meh. Vos vaiting you slip handcuffs like I teach you.'

Melody stood up and waved the handcuffs in his face. 'Taa-daa.'

They stood over Quint. Saul still holding his .22 pistol.

His Mossad favoured Beretta Model 70. Melody picked up Quint's Ruger.

He was staring up, flat on his back, trying no doubt to compute what had just happened. Tried to speak but nothing came out. Tried to move but all motor functions had ceased. A small flow of blood was pooling around his back.

Saul bent down to look Quint in the eye. 'Lign in drerd un bakn beygl. Put two in seventh vertebrae ya meshugenah twat. Yeah, me that good.' That off his chest, he spat in Quint's face.

'Told you it'd work. Surprised you didn't fall off the roof, old man.'

'Funny girl. Ve go now, princess.'

Melody stared down at another monster dressed in human skin. He had no more answers for her. It was all for money, power and prestige. It was just a job. What a world.

Quint stared back. Part of him, the pro part, probably had a grudging respect. Melody knew from her detailed research that Quint had outmanoeuvred major league terrorists. But here he was, flat on his back, unable to move, staring up at a shrink. A lousy fucking shrink, for God's sake, who had outmanoeuvred the mighty Quint. Was that the faintest – a smile? She smiled back at him.

PHUT—

She put one in his right eye.

PHUT—

Another in his left.

CHAPTER

64

The imposing gates of Cordingay House loomed up in front of Melody. Monty was looking particularly down at heel and dirt-caked on this humid, cloudy Sunday. The short spell of hot temperatures in the south was forecast to be ending tonight with violent thunderstorms. That should give Monty a welcome, cleansing drench of good, honest rainwater.

A couple of recalcitrant peacocks ambled in front of her on the half mile schlep along the treelined drive. The stunning 18th century Cordingay House loomed up. She parked déclassée Monty amongst the Bentleys, and the Park Lane showroom of expensive motors.

'You made it. Late as usual.' Chloe buzzed around Melody like an excited puppy who had misplaced her mum for a hour, then sniffed her out again.

'I swear to God you're harder to see than the Queen these days. What on earth are you doing? Slumming around the Lake District. Up to I don't know what. You look fabbo, by the way. And I simply adore the hair. It's terribly Jean Seberg and Jean-Paul Belmondo. You know my adoration of French new wave.'

Melody had been greeted at the magnificent front door, by a faux 18th century bewigged footman slash flunky. He insisted on leading her through the Italian-marbled grand hallway, then through the huge drawing room to the rear of the house. He was an actor who really wanted to direct, and this was just a role. It was a long walk. Most of the forty guests were already mingling on the elevated terrace, accessed from the huge floor to ceiling windows in the drawing room.

The view still took Melody's breath away. An Italianate terrace garden stretching out a hundred yards; planted with hundreds of thousands of annuals; laid out in intricate designs between towering bushes shaped into geometric ovals, circles, oblongs and squares. The stunning manmade view was framed by the natural lush green of the Oxfordshire hills in the distance. The gardens ended with a large maze. To the left was an enormous lake; behind which was a secluded Doric temple, surrounded by ash trees and a huge weeping willow bowing down in deference to the glittering lake. The temple was supposedly a *folly* erected in 1715 by the house's original owner. But this slice of paradise was no folly.

Melody would have preferred jeans and a T-shirt, but the invite did say *formal*. Dinner jackets and bowties for the men. Expensive frocks for the ladies. That meant rolling out another simple, elegant McCartney and high heels. Though her bag, safely ensconced in her room, had all sorts of goodies, depending on how the evening turned out. She had no real idea about her next move. Around her neck she wore Sophia's Star of David.

'You look fabbo yourself, as per usual.'

Chloe looked around semi-dramatically searching for a particular face. The way dramatic people do when they think they're being inconspicuous. 'Look, don't kill me, but I invited that simply scrumptious new author I'm shaping, think I mentioned—'

'Okay. And?'

'And – you'll like him. Maybe. Anyway, Donald's nice. He read English at – okay, it was Oxford. I never said he was perfect. Ergo, you're a couple for the evening. Had to be done.'

Melody was half-distracted as she was also scanning her fellow guests, only far more subtly than her friend. She hadn't seen her target as yet. The biggest monster of them all.

'That's fine, Chloe. I have to sit next to someo—'

The unexpected hand on her shoulder made her jump. 'Mel, there you are.'

She span around. There he was. Large as life, bold as brass. The final monster tracked down in its natural habitat of the great and the good. Totally unaware that his diabolical secret was now revealed – to her. The very richly retired Sir Menzies Asterion, KCBE, OBE, was standing next to Ben. In her high heels, she had a couple of inches on Asterion.

Melody's head buzzed, her gaze zooming in and out of focus. 'God, Ben! You made me jump.'

'Gosh I'm so sorry, Mel. I was going to formally introduce you to Sir Menzies Asterion. Newest member of Peach's operating board. Then I literally just found out you know each other. We're lucky to have someone of his sterling reputation on board.'

Board member? Asterion? You've got to be fucking kidding me.

'When did that happen?'

'Ten days ago. Don't you ever read your company

emails? You were invited to attend, or allocate your proxy. Though the vote was unanimous, so your 8.7% would have made no difference on this occasion.'

Ten days ago? About the time Millar was being gutted.

'Yes. Sorry, Ben. Been a bit busy on a couple of projects. But I'm totally focused now.'

'Gallivanting up north on your motorbike doesn't count as a project, Mel.'

Thanks, Chloe, love. Give away all my secrets why don't you?

A distant roll of thunder disturbed the animated chatter from the guests. The sky had darkened in the past few minutes. Asterion was looking uncomfortable – maybe guilt had finally eaten into his desiccated soul. He cleared his throat and thrust out a limp-wristed hand.

'Doctor Fox. Terribly good to see you again. A great deal has – changed since our time at the Ministry of Defence.'

The effortlessly superior plummy accent certainly hadn't changed. Melody scowled and nodded.

'Sir Menzies has been so invaluable over in New York, smoothing through the latest share offerings at Lemmon Rossiter. We all felt he would make a fine addition to our board too.'

'I simply do my best, Ben. It's an honour for me to offer what little talents I have to the global success of Peach. After all, as the ads say, "Life's a peach. Take a big bite".'

Wonder how the board would react if they knew about all the deaths you're responsible for, you two-faced lying fucker.

'Talking shares, Mel, Chloe said you had some news.'

Melody was happy to let Ben know she had decided to retain her small stake of voting shares, but Chloe had other ideas. 'That's enough Peach biz you lot, until after supper.'

Before either could object, the first drops of rain fell. Within a minute, the down was in full pour. By then, Chloe and Ben had ushered all the guests into the drawing room to be seated at the forty-head table.

The meal was served by staff dressed-up in the same 18th century kitsch uniforms as the doorman. A moody Melody could only pick at the five superb courses.

Donald was just about tolerable, if somewhat full of himself. He thought he was imbuing his debut novel (provisionally entitled *Ashanti*) with the secrets of life. Melody was unconvinced. He was an adolescent thirty-one. From leafy Devonshire. A contributing opinion editor for the Guardian.

What the fuck did he know about anything to have an opinion worth expressing to the world?

Given the circumstances, her mood could not have been more murderous as they chomped and chatted. The Vienna Quintet playing away in the far corner. She hadn't realized, until now, how much she loathed these smug, self satisfied, Tuscany-villa people en masse. Not just the monster. Not loathing them as individuals, of course. Chloe was her friend. It was a dichotomy.

Was she was ever like them? She thought of Aunt Sharon. The grateful warmth of the Shabbat meals, greatly missed while on her journey for the past six months. These people here weren't grateful for anything. They should be. It could all be ripped away in an instant. Without second thought. By monsters.

The rain had drizzled to a lull by the time the lavish meal wound down. Thunder rumbled over Cordingay a few seconds after the distant flash of lightning. Donald had disappeared, last seen chatting to a young British actress making it big in Hollywood. The wench was raptly impressed by the Devonshire lad. Some guests lingered around the table whilst others dispersed to various rooms for cigars, coffee, brandy. Chloe and Ben were judiciously spreading themselves amongst all the movers and shakers. They were good at that. Asterion was nowhere to be seen.

It was dark when Melody escaped Chloe's clutches. Feigning feeling unwell, and needing to lie down, she slipped away to her room on the second-floor. Time to retrieve the vital tools from her overnight bag. The F-S and taser were de rigueur, of course. No girl should leave home without them. No room for the baton or a bundle of nylon rope. She had held onto Quint's handcuffs for sentimental reasons, two pair being better than one. What the heck, there was still room in her handbag. In went Saul's night vision/infrared goggles. You never know.

Even tooled up, she didn't *have* to do anything tonight. He wasn't going anywhere. Well, maybe New York. If needs must, make like the Boy Scouts.

Always anticipate vorld's full of vicked bastards, Princess. Be prepared.

Her bedroom overlooked the terrace, well lit by ersatz Venetian lamps. As she was gazing at the flashes above the distant hills Asterion wandered out, cigar and brandy glass in hand. He strolled over to a small group of chatting guests at a table, including Ben. After a brief chat, he left for the Italianate garden. Mozart drifted out from the drawing room. All so civilized. She weighed up her options.

Hurrying down to the terrace, fellow guests were too engrossed to spot that Melody had switched from Jimmy Choo's, into something far more sensible. There was no bumping into Chloe. Melody knew her friend would be loudly holding forth, in one of the many smaller rooms.

Asterion was nowhere to be seen. It was unlikely he had returned from his evening sojourn without passing her.

Ah, bugger, where's Ben disappeared to? Not in the house. What if he followed Asterion? So much for that little scenario. Looks like tonight's not the night after all.

The electrically charged air was deliciously refreshing and much cooler than the muggy oppression of recent days. A brilliant flash lit up the sky. The rolling thunder took less time to envelop them than earlier. A violent storm was closing in on Cordingay.

She exited the marble-floored terrace and hurried along the garden towards the maze, a hundred yards further on. About twenty yards down, away on her right she heard the unmistakable sounds of two people having a very good time together. Something she hadn't seriously thought about since she awoke from her dreamless sleep. It was off the path and away from the lights. That can't be Asterion. Can it? Dirty old man amongst his other crimes?

Melody crept a few yards to her right, past the twenty-feet tall manicured oval topiary. She could make out the two figures by the 16th century statue of Athena. She didn't need the night vision goggles to see it wasn't Asterion. The young British starlet was leaning forward, hands gripping Athena's ample breasts for support. Thrusting and grunting behind her was the Devonshire lad.

Oh, really classy dinner companion choice, Chloe. Cheers, love.

They were oblivious to her presence. Creeping back to the true path a flash lit up the night sky again to the west. The low rumble arrived even faster this time.

The air was rich with the coppery tang of the imminent downpour. Melody spotted Asterion sitting on the wrought iron bench next to the maze entrance. Still puffing on his cigar, sipping something expensive from his glass. His attention was aimed to his right where the lightning show was increasing in frequency by the minute – totally unaware of her presence.

Melody had stepped off the well-lit path into the semi-shadows, about thirty feet away. She was musing on what to do next, and finally decided to move, when—

Ben stepped out from the maze entrance, zipping up his trouser fly. Asterion stood up at his hosts re-entrance.

'And the righteous fury of Zeus was unleashed upon the ungrateful mortals, who were sore afraid of his jealous wrath. In his fury Zeus, laid waste to the many temples the mortals had built to worship their false idols.'

'Very good, Menzies. Homer or some such?'

'Benefits of a classics education, old boy. I'm heading back to your fine house before Zeus unleashes a fiery bolt on both of us, coming?'

'I love this air just before the storm. Invigorates the lungs. You trot off. Be right behind you.'

Melody stepped back another few paces to stand besides one of the square shaped topiaries. Her hand went into her bag, gripping her killing knife. Asterion hurried past, oblivious. Now what? Wait for Ben to also escape Zeus's wrath? Or move her arse now?

Best scarper off, right behind Asterion, Mel, love. Been nearly four years. Que sera sera. The monster will keep a day, a week, or whatever.

Melody turned to follow—

A hand touched her shoulder. This time she swivelled around in one smooth movement, grabbed and twisted the offending wrist with her left hand, while locking the arm with her own right arm. Pressing down into a break position.

'Owww, owww. Jesus Christ, Mel. It's me – Ben. Lemme go. You're breaking my fucking arm.'

She released him as quickly as she'd pinned him.

'Bloody hell Ben, don't sneak up like that.'

'Last time, I promise. Where on earth did you learn to do that?'

Her heart had spiked to double her normal rate. Adrenalin rush will do that. 'Self-defence classes. Where did you learn to sneak up like that?'

'Spotted you lurking when I came out after, you know. Got to say it looked a tad creepy. Then I figured you'd had previous with Asterion and weren't too anxious to be all lovey-dovey. Thought I'd surprise you. Foolishly.'

'Well, you did.'

Ben laughed loudly as he rubbed his arm, as if that would help. 'Yeah. I can still feel that. Okay, all better now.'

The sky lit up again. This time it was close enough to illuminate their faces in jagged etched relief. Did she look as creepy as Ben did in the Hammer Horror lighting? Melody glanced past Ben to receding Asterion, lengthening his stride through the gardens.

'Sorry, Ben.'

'Okay, as you're here. I know you've been a bit on the fence over the shares. I get it—'

'Yes. About them.'

'How about this? To sweeten the deal, taking into account the emotional attachment involved, with Paul, and all, how about we up the fair and set price per share by, say, twenty per cent? Which is more than generous.'

That caught her by surprise. 'More than generous. How about thirty per cent? That's even more than generous.'

Ben smiled. It looked forced. He hesitated for a second. 'Okay, thirty per cent.'

'How about fifty per cent? Sixty per cent? Double?'

Ben wasn't smiling so much now. 'Melody. Come on. Be serious.'

'Add my eight point seven, Chloe's percentage, and yours, including the forced sale of Paul's shares, you would have an outright voting majority, right?'

'Fifty point five per cent. Yes. It's just business, Mel. My fiduciary duty. Honest to God, nothing personal.'

'Nothing personal. Funny – that's what another guy said

to me recently too.'

'I know. It's a cliché.'

FLASH—

The clouds lit up with massive, hyper-bright jolt. Melody counted the gap.

One. Two. Three.

CRACK—

'Actually, now that I think about it, you know him.'

'Uh – okay, so I know—'

'Bernard Quint. Global Security Network.'

CHAPTER

65

Melody leaned in closer to the screen, straining to see past Quint to the figure in the back seat. When the voice boomed out unseen, from the laptop's tinny speakers, that was no longer necessary.

'Wheels in motion. Too much riding on this now. Do it.'

Melody would have recognized that effortlessly superior, plummy Home Counties accent anywhere. Even if Ben Carrington hadn't shuffled forward to show his face on camera.

Despair rolled over her. A giant surfer's wave at Big Sur crashing into her. The video continued to drive the knife into her dead heart.

'Cold, Mister Carrington. Bit of a psycho on the side aren't you? And you're sure you want to kill them all?'

Ben did not hesitate. 'Sure. Why not. Just make sure you personally retrieve everything from the safe. Especially the crocodile skin briefcase. You do that personally. Not those goons you use.'

'Crocodile?'

'Yeah, it's called a Bottega Veneta. Twenty grand can you believe.'

Quint licked his lips. 'I guess that's some very important shit in there. Important to you, that is.'

'You don't need to know.'

'Actually, I do. Why is it worth all this? Right now, or the contract's voided.'

'Okay. Jesus. Let's just say, my partner and I have totally different visions of the future of our little venture. I have more of a Steve Jobs, Bill Gates, multi-billionaire vibe. Sad to say Paul's turned into a bleeding-brain Gandhi open source commie loser.'

'So?'

'So – he has me over a barrel with some morals clause bullshit. I need to destroy that information. And anyone he may have told.'

'The kid too?'

'If it was a real home invasion gone wrong, would they hesitate? Especially after doing the woman and her live-in-lover in horrible fashion?'

'Actually, now that I think about it, you know him.'

'Uh – okay, so I know—'

'Bernard Quint. Global Security Network. The now very dead Bernar—'

He was faster than she expected after the ease with which she had him bent double in an painful arm lock. Without any hesitation, middleweight boxing Cambridge Blue Ben left-hooked her on the side of the head. As she staggered sideways and backwards, Ben bounced forward on his toes, arms up in boxing pose for a combination follow up. Her best strategy was to go down.

Hitting the deck, she rolled out of range before pulling herself up onto one knee, head swimming from the blow. Ben charged at her, wildly swinging punches down trying to pummel her head again. Melody had already grabbed the F-S from her bag. She slashed out wildly at his legs.

'Ahhhhhhhhh, fuck.'

The blade sliced his calf, hitting bone with a sickening judder. That had to hurt. Badly.

Ben's momentum took him flying past her towards the path. It took a few seconds to clear her head. Scrambling to her feet she raced after Ben as he disappeared into the maze. That made no sense. Her dress was hardly ideal gear for the task at hand. Which was what? Ever since Quint's study she'd been blinded by an incandescent rage leaving her unable to reason clearly. Events were controlling her, and she was out of control. She could have bided her time, then struck as Saul had taught her. All alone somewhere, not at a glitzy affair.

Too late now. Melody raced into the maze as another flash of lightning boomed even closer. Most people act irrationally under stress and duress. Now he was the wounded animal. Still – it was a maze. A dead end by definition. Did he think he could hide? His dead end now, no matter what.

The maze was well-lit by the same Venetian lamps. She could clearly see the trail of blood-crumbs he was leaving. She took her time. Mazes were built for ambushes behind every turn.

Approaching the final turn, the blood drips continued. Melody gripped her knife and took a breath. Nothing else mattered – this is how it ends for both of them.

She rushed in, ready to overwhelm. Nothing. The maze's centre was empty except for the large bronze statue, and two iron benches. Impossible. The blood led here. He couldn't have doubled back, she would have seen him. There was no second trail, and only one route out. But if he had slipped past her, that was it. All over for both of them. She had Ben of the Quint video. He was finished. But she'd killed Quint to get it. She couldn't make this one disappear like Millar and Quint.

Think, Mel. Think, think, think, think, think. Why would anyone rush into a maze to escape?

She walked over to the statue.

Because there's a hidden exit, stupid.

When the Carringtons bought Cordingay House in the summer of 2012, Chloe told her the old pile had been built by the obsessed Graecophile, Lord Cordingay. He was much influenced by his pal Alexander Pope. The ten-feet tall bronze statue was a 1715 contemporary rendering of King Minos of Crete, most infamous for constructing the original Labyrinth to imprison the monstrous Minotaur.

King Minos was cast in one piece with an integral large, oblong, bronze plinth. This rested on a raised stone dais. The King was very imposing. She looped around the dais. There it was – a small drop of blood. He was here. This didn't make sense. Unless—

Crazy idea. Melody felt around the bronze plinth. It was solid. Minos was depicted cradling a lyre in one arm, and gripping a long spear vertically in his right hand. She checked the hand holding the spear. Odd. Unlike the rest of the statue, the spear was not cast as part of the whole. It ran through the hand to rest on the plinth. She strained to pull up on the spear. Nothing. She pushed down—

CLICK—

The spear ratcheted an inch down into the plinth. The plinth itself slid a fraction to the left revealing the faintest sliver of light from below. She pushed the plinth sideways. It slid easily across the dais to expose a shaft dropping down a good twenty feet. Melody clambered onto the iron ladder bolted to a wall. No sign of Ben lurking below. To her right was a metal flywheel with a protruding handle. She rotated it anticlockwise. As the plinth slowly ground its way back, the heavens opened with huge gobs of rain. The clean water washed over her face until the plinth clicked back into place, and the world above ceased to exist in sound or vision.

Melody warily slid down the ladder towards the faint light at the bottom. She dropped into a stone built corridor with a semicircular barrel vault roof. Not rough stone, nor the utilitarian bricks she encountered in the Poplar sewer tunnels. This was the same white Portland stone used in the construction of Cordingay, laid out in a classical Greek or maybe Roman construction. It was bone-cold down here. At least fifteen degrees lower than above ground.

The cast iron lamp holder attached to the wall looked authentically Victorian, except it was electric and not gas. The dim incandescent bulb was more modern. An insulated electric cable ran along the wall from the small junction box with a lever. There was a small pool of blood on the stone floor. He had waited here, presumably thinking he was hidden from her. Then what? When the plinth rolled back he scuttled away, shocked like a wounded rat?

The stone was not uniformly smooth, being punctuated by ancient Greek letters engraved into the walls. Not her subject. King Minos was the end of the line, so there was only one direction to go. Ahead was a T-junction. Any telltale blood-crumbs? No such luck. Left or right? She went right. The dim lights were spaced every twenty feet or so. Not all the bulbs were working. Again with the carved ancient Greek.

Another T-junction loomed up. She looked back at her first turning before rooting around her handbag. With the red lipstick Melody drew a small arrow on the stone, pointing back to the first junction. She turned left this time along a corridor which curved in both directions. That took her quite a distance to a left only turn. Then left again. Then – the dead end of a small antechamber. Carved into the wall was more ancient Greek. Above which, a master craftsman had exquisitely carved, in relief, a bull's head. Obvious now.

It's a labyrinth. This Lord Cordingay character built an actual secret bloody labyrinth. Under the estate. How nuts was that? How far could this thing stretch? To the house?

Was Chloe aware of this buried folly of all follies? Unlikely. Knowledge of an actual working labyrinth would be shouted from the rooftops. Mazes were a penny a pound, but who has a real underground labyrinth in England? In the world? One more thing Ben had kept from Chloe, Melody guessed.

She checked her watch. It was thirty minutes since she slipped away from her room. Retracing her steps back, Melody smudged her lipstick arrows to show they were now redundant.

Back to her first misstep. Standing stock still, straining to hear. Not a thing. She banged the handle of the F-S against the wall. The place was acoustically dead.

Right turn this time. Then a slice of luck at the next near identical junction. To the left, a few yards on, the first splat of blood showed. She'd cut him to the bone. Ben must have self-tourniqueted back at the entrance, probably with his bow tie. Most likely she had severed his leg tendons.

She followed the blood-crumb along the gently curving corridor. Then another, and another. His physical effort would have triggered a fight or flight adrenalin rush, which would be pumping his heart faster, causing the blood to flow faster.

The twists and turns were making her head spin. The lighting was getting iffy, with a growing frequency in the number of dead bulbs, leaving dark pools of danger around every turn. It was slow and laborious, especially having to lipstick mark her way. Where was her monster heading? In the tale of the Minotaur, the beast had a lair deep in the furthest corner of the labyrinth. There he devoured the helpless Athenian tributes who could not find their way out. Maybe she should find her way out? Retrace her steps back and rethink, instead of rambling around semi-blindly. Then—

Shit. Lights out. This was not good. Her heart rate spiked up again. She wasn't particularly claustrophobic, but down here, in the pitch black? Obviously Ben had access to another junction box. Or had he doubled back along the labyrinth's true path, while she was hitting dead ends? He had let her wander around for a while before cutting the light. No doubt assuming she would be hopelessly lost by now.

She grabbed the night vision goggles from her bag. Only one problem. Night vision works on amplifying available light. And despite being incredibly sensitive, there was zero available light down here to amplify. Melody strapped the goggles to her head and adjusted the infrared lens.

The nearest incandescent bulb still glowed yellowy red and hot. That wasn't all. On the wall were unmistakable heat spots in the rough, blobby shape of two hands. Ben had leaned here, transferring his body warmth to the cool stone. Feeling weak from blood loss? Not long ago either. She looked down at the floor. Two tiny heat spots also glowed. Blood drips.

Ben's telltale heart was betraying him. Melody gleefully followed, making faster progress than before. He had used the walls for support. How apt that Ben's flesh and blood map was taking her to wherever he was dragging himself.

The residual heat spots glowed redder and hotter. Melody was catching up. Her current corridor was curving slightly, the blood-heat blobs were showing every yard or so now. She sped up, anxious, then—

The merest hint of light amplified in the night vision lens. There was a gap in the wall to her left, a few yards ahead. Melody slowed down.

She stood stock still in the entrance. It was a chamber of some sort. She could only discern that through the night vision lens. The tiniest sliver of light, which had leaked into the corridor, was coming from above, at the far end of the chamber. Ahead was another huge bronze statue. The Minotaur: a bull's head on a man's body. So this was the monster's lair.

The sound of rain drumming was unmistakable. There must be a second entrance to the labyrinth, or exit in Ben's case. Somewhere back onto the estate. And it was open.

Bollocks.

Ben couldn't be that far ahead with his injury. She had to hunt and put down her wounded animal before he made it back to the house. If that happened, her fanatical monomaniacal quest for vengeance was all over. Without considering, Melody scampered towards the rear of the chamber—

SMASH—

From the dark, Ben came hurtling at her from behind, as best he could on one leg. The force smashing Melody into the unforgiving bronze. The Minotaur's hanging arm catching her like a heavyweight's savage uppercut to the gut. Wind knocked out, she smacked hard into the ground, gasping for breath, praying a lung hadn't been punctured. Her bag and goggles flew from her. Now she was blind and unarmed, like him. For a second.

The light came on in the room. But not yet in her head, which was still swimming in pain and still trying to compute what had happened.

No time to recover. He was on top of her, throttling away. The monster's leg was damaged, but his large hands worked perfectly.

Melody struggled to breathe. This was killing her. The monster was killing her. Black spots were racing across her eyes as her brain was fast being starved of oxygen. Death would follow soon. Sweet death beyond all pain and guilt. Tempting. Would she meet Charity and Paul again? The eternal mystery about to be revealed.

This felt familiar. Oh yeah: Saul's graduation exercise. The first and only time she had ever bested him in hand to hand Krav Maga. How did she handle this same problem that time?

'Fuck, Mel. Never saw this one coming. Gotta admit. Well fucking played by the way. But I win again. No one knows about my little labyrinth. Someone may find your bones next century I suppose.'

Ven push come to shove it in, ya gotta be vicked to ya bones. Then you live, Princess, and the meshugenah creep dies. Better that vay, right?

Yeah, much better that vay. In one supreme effort, Melody stiff-armed her right palm and slammed it under his chin. Ben's head snapped back as blood and teeth flew from his mouth. The shock forced his hands to loosen their death-grip from around her throat.

Before he could react, she straight-punched him in his balls twice, then rolled him off her chest. As he lay writhing Melody scrambled to her feet, stomping him in the face. Once. Twice. Thrice. Then another few times for good measure, until he was a bloody heap on the stone slabs.

He was beyond talking for a while after that damage.

Just in case, she found the taser in her bag and hit him with 50,000 volts, keeping him quiescent while she got her breath back.

Damn. Probably two ribs broken. But nothing punctured. She checked his sliced leg. Nothing too life-threatening. She grunted in pain, hauling Ben's still comatose body to the Minotaur. She hadn't the time to linger as she did with Millar.

In this space, no one can hear you scream.

That was it. She removed his clothes leaving him naked. After spreadeagling Ben on his stomach, Melody double handcuffed the monster who had devoured her family. Each wrist secured to an ankle of the bronze Minotaur, leaving him unable to move, let alone to stand.

Ben came around, spluttering out a mouthful of blood and shattered teeth. His babbling was hard to understand through his swollen mouth and face; but he thought Melody would be calling the police.

She had nothing to say. What did it matter now? It took all her strength not to gut him on the spot.

What was about to happen dawned on Ben when Melody switched off the lighting at the second junction box.

'Don't you fucking leave me here. Fuck. Fuck. Don't leave me in the dark. Please, Mel. I'm begging. Kill me first. Don't fucking leave me down here like this.'

He was still bellowing as she slowly ascended the ladder into the Doric temple on the far side of the lake.

This second opening was secreted similarly under a statue. Artemis this time. The huntress. Even with the entrance open, Ben's frantic screams and shouts were only a dim, distant echo. When Artemis rolled back over the plinth, the sound and fury dwindled to less than nothing.

The violent storm had moved on east. The rain had

ceased falling. The rumbles of thunder were growing distant. The flashes of light vanishing over the horizon

All was quiet again. Except for the pitiful moans and sobs welling up from Melody as she lay curled on the ground, heard only by the creatures of the night.

CHAPTER

66

'Six? Still can't believe you just scoffed down all six, one after another.'

'Woman of my word, Frankie. Tis the best profiteroles place in Paris. And they were all different. Though if I had to chose a fave, it would be *Ma Cherie Fleur d'Orange*.'

That place was *Profiterole Cherie*, on la rue Debelleyme, in the 3rd arrondissement. Melody had demolished six of the most fabulous confections this side of heaven.

'May wee, I liked that orange one too. Preferred the one with the ice cream, Mont Blanc. Have to admit, beats Dunkin' Donuts. Take it you've been here before and we didn't just stumble on it?'

Melody smiled. A good memory bringing pleasure to dull the pain. 'Paul brought me. We'd just started going out. Spur of the moment. Decided on a mad weekend in Paris. You know how it is.'

Frankie laughed the melodious deep-rolling rumble he had for a laugh. 'Wish I did, love.'

'Became our thing whenever in Paris.'

'Honoured then. Thanks for bringing me. Here. And gay Paree.'

She looked at Frankie. He wasn't a *good man*, like Paul. Most likely he was a bad man. A very bad man. He did things considered bad, on the bidding of Aaron Fuchs. Outside the law. But who was she to judge? He was a man she could certainly trust. He'd stepped up for her. And he was pretty damn attractive now that she had time to think about it.

'My pleasure. How's your room?'

'Er, it's the George Cinq. How d'ya think? Must be costing you a pretty packet.'

'More than afford it. Besides, you earned it.'

A momentary flash of anger radiated at her. 'I didn't help you to *earn* anything.'

Melody gripped Frankie's arm resting on the table. 'Sorry. That didn't come out right. I know that. I appreciate that.'

'Right. Good. Okay then. Glad we cleared that up.'

He was a tad embarrassed now. Especially as he fancied her. Who wouldn't?

'What I'm trying to say – this – this is all new for me Frankie. Well, new again. You know what I mean. I like you, mate. A lot.'

She moved her hand from his arm, and squeezed his hand. Let it hang.

'But?'

'No but. But if there was a *but*. But – let's just enjoy Paris. Take it from there.'

'Sounds like a plan, doll.'

Frankie picked up the French newspaper from the table. The main story was about thousands of French farmers burning effigies of bigwig politicos. Below that, below the fold, a photograph of Ben Carrington stared out at him. He handed the paper to her.

'What's it say then?'

'The headline is, "English billionaire Ben Carrington still missing. Police baffled". Words to that effect.'

Melody quickly scanned the text. 'In the three weeks since famed tech wizard Mr Benjamin Carrington mysteriously disappeared from his – exclusive chateau, the police remain disconcerted as to the motive, not ruling out anything from suicide to kidnapping, blah, blah. Then it mentions Lord Lucan.'

'Look. Don't need to tell me anything. In fact, don't tell me anything. Guessing the cops gonna be disconcerted for a while yet?'

She laughed out loud at the thought. Her ribs were a lot better now. Though they still twinged a bit when she laughed.

'Maybe even discombobulated.'

Melody had finally dragged herself from the paved floor of the Doric temple and headed to the house. Over an hour since she left her room, perfectly attired. Now – what a mess. Yet it could be explained to Chloe. She felt unwell. Went for a stroll. Got caught in the downpour. Slipped in a mud pile. Fell in the lake. Took shelter.

What couldn't be explained was the large coincidence of Chloe's husband also being discovered slightly missing. She headed back by a circuitous route to the one place where she could sneak back in. All she needed was a little luck; and a huge effort.

The large basement kitchen had a tradesman's entrance around the side of the house. Fingers crossed, Melody tried the door. It opened. The meal had been prepared here by a world-class chef and his hired help. Melody glanced inside. The lights were on, but silence reigned.

A large basket near the door was filled with the food-soiled apparel worn by the kitchen staff. Melody grabbed a pile of the white tops before rushing over to the dumb waiter in the far corner. She opened the door. No way could she squeeze into that tight space, apart from her weight. She pressed one of the well-worn brass buttons on the wall next to the door. The dumb waiter trundled up, on its way to the third floor.

She climbed into the now empty shaft and looked up. At the sound of voices entering the kitchen, she quietly closed the door. As fast as she could, Melody prepared. First, pulling on two of the tops. Wrapping the other two around each knee, knotting them in place with the arms.

In the Dolomites adventure, Saul cajoled her through that first tough climb of a 100-feet high chimney. Over two gruelling hours she learned how to use the opposing pressures of hands, knees, feet, and back on the sidewalls of a tight vertical space. Driven on by Saul, six feet below her all the way.

Wedging herself on both sides of this chimney, she slowly levered herself up in the semi-darkness. The pain from her ribs was unbearable. But Melody bore it. It took twenty minutes of agonizing effort to reach the dumb waiter's entrance into her bedroom corridor.

Hauling herself through the gap, Melody was near to passing out. Her arms and legs were black from the dirt inside the shaft.

Lurching back into her room, she ripped off what was left of her dress and the tops. After washing the dirt from her hands and face, she staggered to the bed, pulling the sheet up to her chin. Every muscle in her body was on fire.

Almost immediately there was a tap on her door. It was

Chloe.

'Jesus. You look bloody awful, Mel.'

'Don't feel too clever either. Must be a bug.'

Chloe placed her hand on Melody's forehead. 'You're roasting up.'

Melody studied her friend. Chloe was smart. Much smarter than Ben, who really lucked out when he fell in with Paul at Cambridge. Paul was the true original thinker. Ben was more a follower than leader. Even with his wife.

Yet Chloe's husband had managed to fool her smart friend for a long time. Was that really possible?

Melody could never keep anything back from Paul. It was difficult to keep secrets in a truly intimate relationship. Now that the thought had popped, it was hard to unpop.

'Sorry. How's the little soirée going?'

'Winding down. Though I have no bloody clue where Ben is.'

'What do you mean?'

'Last time anyone saw my better half, he was down near the maze with that Menzies character. Who's a total creep, by the way. I have no idea why Ben invited him onto the board. Then this bloody inconvenient thunderstorm really hit. Now I can't find him.'

Melody half-smiled as her mind churned over. Chloe no doubt assumed it was for moral encouragement.

'Well, logic dictates he can't have gone too far, can he?'

'Of course. You're right, Mel. I'm being silly.'

Chloe padded to the window overlooking the terrace. She didn't see Melody continue to study her intensely. Was her great pal Chloe really innocent? Unaware of the monster to whom she was married for fifteen years? The ghoul she slept next to every night?

'Has to be around somewhere. He'll turn up. Always does. My Ben.'

Chloe turned to look at her best of friends. She smiled, instantly back to being contented with her greater than great life of purpose – and pleasure.

Melody half smiled in return.

'If he doesn't show, we'll both go dig him up. Together. Right Chlo-me-me-me?'

Miles to go before she sleeps.

ABOUT THE AUTHOR

Liverpool born DJSmith is a former copywriter and creative director now living in North Wales.

DJ also writes movie screenplays and television scripts – not always in the crime genre.

His next novel – *The Dead of Egypt* – is a crime thriller set in 1910, which asks:

What if –
Before Agatha Christie sold her first murder novel, young Aggi solved her first murder case.

The Dead of Egypt was shortlisted for the Crime Writers' Association *Debut Dagger Award 2022.*

EMAIL the author: davidjacksmith3@gmail.com